KEN FOLLETT

THE MAN FROM ST PETERSBURG

PAN BOOKS

First published 1982 in Great Britain by Hamish Hamilton

This edition published 1998 by Pan Books
an imprint of Pan Macmillan, a division of Macmillan Publishers Limited
Pan Macmillan, 20 New Wharf Road, London N1 9RR
Basingstoke and Oxford
Associated companies throughout the world
www.panmacmillan.com

ISBN 978-1-4472-2834-9

1 3 5 7 9 8 6 4 2

A CIP catalogue record for this book is available from
the British Library.

Typeset by CentraCet, Cambridge
Printed in the UK by
CPI Group (UK) Ltd, Croydon CR0 4YY

THE MAN FROM ST PETERSBURG

Ken Follett was only twenty-seven when he wrote the award-winning novel *Eye of the Needle*, which became an international bestseller. He has since written several equally successful novels including, most recently, *Fall of Giants*. He is also the author of the non-fiction bestseller *On Wings of Eagles*. Ken Follett lives with his family in London and Hertfordshire.

Visit the Ken Follett website at
www.ken-follett.com

Also by Ken Follett

THE MODIGLIANI SCANDAL
PAPER MONEY
EYE OF THE NEEDLE
TRIPLE
THE KEY TO REBECCA
ON WINGS OF EAGLES
LIE DOWN WITH LIONS
THE PILLARS OF THE EARTH
NIGHT OVER WATER
A DANGEROUS FORTUNE
A PLACE CALLED FREEDOM
THE THIRD TWIN
THE HAMMER OF EDEN
CODE TO ZERO
JACKDAWS
HORNET FLIGHT
WHITEOUT
WORLD WITHOUT END
FALL OF GIANTS

‘One can’t love humanity. One can only love people’

Graham Greene

ACKNOWLEDGEMENTS

In writing this book I was helped by many friends. My grateful thanks to Alan Earney, Pat Golbitz, M. E. Hirsh, Elaine Koster, Diana Levine, Caren Meyer and her moles, Sue Rapp, Pamela Robinson and the staff of Bertram Rota Ltd, Hilary Ross, Christopher Sinclair-Stevenson, Daniel Starer, Colin Tennant, and – alphabetically last but in every other way first – Al Zuckerman.

The quotation on pages 71–2 is taken from *The Times* of 4 June 1914.

The quotation on pages 317–18 is taken from *The Times* of 29 June 1914.

'After the Ball' on page 288 was written by Chad K. Harris and published in the UK by Francis Day and Hunter.

'Her Dilemma' on pages 417–18 is taken from *The Complete Poems* by Thomas Hardy, published by Papermac.

CHAPTER ONE

It was a slow Sunday afternoon, the kind Walden loved. He stood at an open window and looked across the park. The broad, level lawn was dotted with mature trees: a Scots pine, a pair of mighty oaks, several chestnuts, and a willow like a head of girlish curls. The sun was high and the trees cast dark, cool shadows. The birds were silent, but a hum of contented bees came from the flowering creeper beside the window. The house was still, too. Most of the servants had the afternoon off. The only weekend guests were Walden's brother George, George's wife Clarissa, and their children. George had gone for a walk, Clarissa was lying down, and the children were out of sight. Walden was comfortable: he had worn a frock coat to church, of course, and in an hour or two he would put on his white tie and tails for dinner, but in the meantime he was at ease in a tweed suit and a soft-collared shirt. Now, he thought, if only Lydia will play the piano tonight, it will have been a perfect day.

He turned to his wife. 'Will you play, after dinner?'

Lydia smiled. 'If you like.'

Walden heard a noise and turned back to the window. At the far end of the drive, a quarter of a mile away, a motor car appeared. Walden felt a twinge of irritation, like the sly stab of pain in his right leg before a rainstorm. Why should a car annoy me? he thought. He was not against motor cars – he owned a Lanchester and used it regularly to travel to and from London – although in the summer they were a terrible nuisance to the village, sending up clouds of dust from the unpaved road as they roared through. He was thinking of putting down a couple of hundred yards of tarmacadam along the street. Ordinarily he would not have hesitated, but roads had not been his responsibility since 1909 when Lloyd George had set up the Roads Boards – and that, he realized, was the source of his irritation. It had been a characteristic piece of Liberal legislation: they took money from Walden in order to do themselves what he would have done anyway, then they failed to do it. I suppose I'll pave the road myself in the end, he thought; it's just annoying to pay for it twice.

The motor car turned into the gravel forecourt and came to a noisy, shuddering halt opposite the south door. Exhaust fumes drifted in at the window, and Walden held his breath. The driver got out, wearing helmet, goggles and a heavy motoring coat, and opened the door for the passenger. A short man in a black coat and a black felt hat stepped down from the car. Walden recognized the man, and his heart sank: the peaceful summer afternoon was over.

'It's Winston Churchill,' he said.

Lydia said: 'How embarrassing.'

The man just refused to be snubbed. On Thursday

he had sent a note which Walden had ignored. On Friday he had called on Walden at his London house, and had been told that the Earl was not at home. Now he had driven all the way to Norfolk on a Sunday. He would be turned away again. Does he think his stubbornness is impressive? Walden wondered.

He hated to be rude to people but Churchill deserved it. The Liberal government in which Churchill was a Minister was engaged in a vicious attack on the very foundations of English society – taxing landed property, undermining the House of Lords, trying to give Ireland away to the Catholics, emasculating the Royal Navy, and yielding to the blackmail of trade unions and damned socialists. Walden and his friends would not shake hands with such people.

The door opened and Pritchard came into the room. He was a tall Cockney with brilliantined black hair and an air of gravity which was transparently fake. He had run away to sea as a boy, and had jumped ship in East Africa. Walden, there on safari, had hired him to supervise the native porters, and they had been together ever since. Now Pritchard was Walden's major-domo, travelling with him from one house to another, and as much of a friend as a servant could be.

'The First Lord of the Admiralty is here, my lord,' Pritchard said.

'I'm not at home,' Walden said.

Pritchard looked uncomfortable. He was not used to throwing out Cabinet Ministers. My father's butler would have done it without turning a hair, Walden thought; but old Thomson is graciously retired, growing roses in the garden of that little cottage in the village, and somehow Pritchard has never acquired that unassailable dignity.

Pritchard began to drop his aitches, a sign that he was either very relaxed or very tense. 'Mr Churchill said you'd say not at 'ome, my lord, and 'e said to give you this letter.' He proffered an envelope on a tray.

Walden did *not* like to be pushed. He said crossly: 'Give it back to him—' Then he stopped, and looked again at the handwriting on the envelope. There was something familiar about the large, clear, sloping letters.

'Oh, dear,' said Walden.

He took the envelope, opened it, and drew out a single sheet of heavy white paper, folded once. At the top was the royal crest, printed in red. Walden read:

Buckingham Palace
May 1st. 1914.

My dear Walden

You will see young Winston.

George R. I

'It's from the King,' Walden said to Lydia.

He was so embarrassed that he flushed. It was *frightfully* bad form to drag the King into something like this. Walden felt like a schoolboy who is told to stop quarrelling and get on with his prep. For a moment he was tempted to defy the King. But the consequences . . . Lydia would no longer be received by the Queen, people would be unable to invite the Waldens to parties at which a member of the Royal Family would be present, and – worst of all – Walden's daughter Charlotte could not be presented at court as a debutante. The family's social life would be wrecked. They might as well go and live in another country. No, there was no question of disobeying the King.

Walden sighed. Churchill had defeated him. In a way it was a relief, for now he could break ranks and no one could blame him. *Letter from the King, old boy,* he would say in explanation; *nothing to be done, you know.*

'Ask Mr Churchill to come in,' he said to Pritchard.

He handed the letter to Lydia. The Liberals really did not understand how the monarchy was supposed to work, he reflected. He murmured: 'The King is just not firm enough with these people.'

Lydia said: 'This is becoming awfully boring.'

She was not bored at all, Walden thought, in fact she probably found it all quite exciting; but she said that because it was the kind of thing an English countess would say, and since she was not English but Russian she liked to say typically English things, the way a man speaking French would say *alors* and *hein?* a lot.

Walden went to the window. Churchill's motor car was still rattling and smoking in the forecourt. The driver stood beside it, with one hand on the door, as if he had to hold it like a horse to stop it wandering away. A few servants were gazing at it from a safe distance.

Pritchard came in and said: 'Mr Winston Churchill.'

Churchill was forty, exactly ten years younger than Walden. He was a short, slender man who dressed in a way Walden thought was a shade too elegant to be quite gentlemanly. His hair was receding rapidly, leaving a peak at the forehead and two curls at the temples which, together with his short nose and the permanent sardonic twinkle in his eye, gave him a mischievous look. It was easy to see why the cartoonists regularly portrayed him as a malign cherub.

Churchill shook hands and said cheerfully: 'Good afternoon, Lord Walden.' He bowed to Lydia. 'Lady Walden, how do you do.' Walden thought: What is it about him that grates so on my nerves?

Lydia offered him tea and Walden told him to sit down. Walden would not make small talk: he was impatient to know what all the fuss was about.

Churchill began: 'First of all my apologies, together with the King's, for imposing myself on you.'

Walden nodded. He was not going to say it was perfectly all right.

Churchill said: 'I might add that I should not have done so, other than for the most compelling reasons.'

'You'd better tell me what they are.'

'Do you know what has been happening in the money market?'

'Yes. The discount rate has gone up.'

'From one-and-three-quarters to just under three per cent. It's an enormous rise, and it has come about in a few weeks.'

'I presume you know why.'

Churchill nodded. 'German companies have been factoring debts on a vast scale, collecting cash and buying gold. A few more weeks of this, and Germany will have got in everything owing to her from other countries, while leaving her debts to them outstanding – and her gold reserves will be higher than they have ever been before.'

'They are preparing for war.'

'In this and other ways. They have raised a levy of one billion marks, over and above normal taxation, to improve an army which is already the strongest in Europe. You will remember that in 1909, when Lloyd George increased British taxation by fifteen million pounds sterling, there was almost a revolution. Well, a billion marks is equivalent to *fifty* million pounds. It's the biggest levy in European history—'

'Yes, indeed,' Walden interrupted. Churchill was threatening to become histrionic: Walden did not want him making speeches. 'We Conservatives have been worried about German militarism for some time. Now, at the eleventh hour, you're telling me that we were right.'

Churchill was unperturbed. 'Germany will attack France, almost certainly. The question is, will we come to the aid of France?'

'No,' Walden said in surprise. 'The Foreign Secretary has assured us that we have no obligations to France—'

'Sir Edward is sincere, of course,' Churchill said. 'But he is mistaken. Our understanding with France is such that we could not possibly stand aside and watch her defeated by Germany.'

Walden was shocked. The Liberals had convinced everyone, him included, that they would not lead England into war; and now one of their leading Ministers was saying the opposite. The duplicity of the politicians was infuriating, but Walden forgot that as he began to contemplate the consequences of war. He thought of the young men he knew who would have to fight: the patient gardeners in his park, the cheeky footmen, the brown-faced farm-boys, the hell-raising undergraduates, the languid idlers in the clubs of St James's . . . then that thought was overtaken by another, much more chilling, and he said: 'But can we win?'

Churchill looked grave. 'I think not.'

Walden stared at him. 'Dear God, what have you people done?'

Churchill became defensive. 'Our policy has been to avoid war; and you can't do that and arm yourself to the teeth at the same time.'

'But you have failed to avoid war.'

'We're still trying.'

'But you think you will fail.'

Churchill looked belligerent for a moment, then swallowed his pride. 'Yes.'

'So what will happen?'

'If England and France together cannot defeat Germany, then we must have another ally, a third country on our side: Russia. If Germany is divided, fighting on two fronts, we can win. The Russian army is incompetent and corrupt, of course – like everything else in that country – but it doesn't matter so long as they draw off part of Germany's strength.'

Churchill knew perfectly well that Lydia was Russian, and it was characteristically tactless of him to disparage her country in her presence, but Walden let it pass, for he was highly intrigued by what Churchill was saying. 'Russia already has an alliance with France,' he said.

'It's not enough,' Churchill said. 'Russia is obliged to fight if France is the victim of aggression. It is left to Russia to decide whether France is the victim or the aggressor in a particular case. When war breaks out both sides always claim to be the victim. Therefore the alliance obliges Russia to do no more than fight if she wants to. We need Russia to be freshly and firmly committed to our side.'

'I can't imagine you chaps joining hands with the Czar.'

'Then you misjudge us. To save England, we'll deal with the devil.'

'Your supporters won't like it.'

'They won't know.'

Walden could see where all this was leading, and the prospect was exciting. 'What have you in mind? A secret treaty? Or an unwritten understanding?'

'Both.'

Walden looked at Churchill through narrowed eyes. This young demagogue might have a brain, he thought; and that brain might not be working in my interest. So the Liberals want to do a secret deal with the Czar, despite the hatred which the English people have for the brutal Russian regime – but why tell me? They want to rope me in somehow, that much is clear. For what purpose? So that if it all goes wrong they will have a Conservative on whom to put the blame? It will take a plotter more subtle than Churchill to lead me into such a trap.

Walden said: 'Go on.'

'I have initiated naval talks with the Russians, along the lines of our military talks with the French. They've been going on for a while at a rather low level, and now they are about to get serious. A young Russian admiral is coming to London. His name is Prince Aleksei Andreivitch Orlov.'

Lydia said: 'Aleks!'

Churchill looked at her. 'I believe he is related to you, Lady Walden.'

'Yes,' Lydia said, and for some reason Walden could not even guess at she looked uneasy. 'He is the son of my elder sister, which makes him my . . . cousin?'

'Nephew,' Walden said.

'I didn't know he had become admiral,' Lydia added. 'It must be a recent promotion.' She was her usual, perfectly composed self, and Walden decided he had imagined that moment of unease. He was pleased that Aleks would be coming to London: he was very fond of the lad. Lydia said: 'He is young to have so much authority.'

'He's thirty,' Churchill said to Lydia, and Walden recalled that Churchill, at forty, was very young to be in charge of the entire Royal Navy. Churchill's expression seemed to say: The world belongs to brilliant young men like me and Orlov.

But you need me for something, Walden thought.

'In addition,' Churchill went on, 'Orlov is nephew to the Czar, through his father the late Prince, and – more importantly – he is one of the few people other than Rasputin whom the Czar likes and trusts. If anyone in the Russian naval establishment can swing the Czar on to our side, Orlov can.'

Walden asked the question that was on his mind. 'And my part in all this?'

'I want you to represent England in these talks – and I want you to bring me Russia on a plate.'

The fellow could never resist the temptation to be melodramatic, Walden thought. 'You want Aleks and me to negotiate an Anglo-Russian military alliance?'

'Yes.'

Walden saw immediately how difficult, challenging and rewarding the task would be. He concealed his excitement, and resisted the temptation to get up and pace about.

Churchill was saying: 'You know the Czar personally. You know Russia and speak Russian fluently. You're Orlov's uncle by marriage. Once before you have persuaded the Czar to side with England rather than with Germany – in 1906, when you intervened to prevent the ratification of the Treaty of Bjorko.' Churchill paused. 'Nevertheless, you were not our first choice to represent Britain at these negotiations. The way things are at Westminster . . .'

'Yes, yes.' Walden did not want to start discussing *that.* 'However, something changed your mind.'

'In a nutshell, you were the Czar's choice. It seems you are the only Englishman in whom he has any faith. Anyway, he sent a telegram to his cousin the King, insisting that Orlov deal with you.'

Walden could imagine the consternation among the Radicals when they learned they would have to involve a reactionary old Tory peer in such a clandestine scheme. 'I should think you were horrified,' he said.

'Not at all. In foreign affairs our policies are not so much at odds with yours. And I have always felt that domestic political disagreements were no reason why your talents should be lost to His Majesty's Government.'

Flattery now, Walden thought. They want me badly. Aloud he said: 'How would all this be kept secret?'

'It will seem like a social visit. If you agree, Orlov will stay with you for the London season. You will introduce him to society. Am I right in thinking that your daughter is due to come out this year?' He looked at Lydia.

'That's right,' she said.

'So you'll be going about a good deal anyway. Orlov is a bachelor, as you know, and obviously very eligible, so we can noise it abroad that he's looking for an English wife. He may even find one.'

'Excellent idea.' Suddenly Walden realized that he was enjoying himself. He had once been a kind of semi-official diplomat under the Conservative governments of Salisbury and Balfour, but for the last eight years he had taken no part in international politics. Now he had a chance to go back on stage, and he began to remember how absorbing and fascinating the whole business was: the secrecy; the gambler's art of negotiation; the conflicts of personalities; the cautious use of persuasion, bullying or the threat of war. The Russians were not easy to deal with, he recalled; they tended to be capricious, obstinate and arrogant. But Aleks would be manageable. When Walden married

Lydia, Aleks had been at the wedding, a ten-year-old in a sailor suit. Later Aleks had spent a couple of years at Oxford University, and had visited Walden Hall in the vacations. The boy's father was dead, so Walden gave him rather more time than he might normally have spent with an adolescent, and was delightfully rewarded by a friendship with a lively young mind.

It was a splendid foundation for a negotiation. I believe I might be able to bring it off, he thought. What a triumph that would be!

Churchill said: 'May I take it, then, that you'll do it?'

'Of course,' said Walden.

Lydia stood up. 'No, don't get up,' she said as the men stood with her. 'I'll leave you to talk politics. Will you stay for dinner, Mr Churchill?'

'I've an engagement in Town, unfortunately.'

'Then I shall say goodbye.' She shook his hand.

She went out of the Octagon, which was where they always had tea, and walked across the great hall, through the small hall, and into the flower-room. At the same time one of the under-gardeners – she did not know his name – came in through the garden door with an armful of tulips, pink and yellow, for the dinner table. One of the things Lydia loved about England in general and Walden Hall in particular was the wealth of flowers, and she always had fresh ones cut morning and evening, even in winter when they had to be grown in the hothouses.

The gardener touched his cap – he did not have to

take it off unless he was spoken to, for the flower room was notionally part of the garden – and laid the flowers on a marble table, then went out. Lydia sat down and breathed the cool, scented air. This was a good room in which to recover from shocks, and the talk of St Petersburg had unnerved her. She remembered Aleksei Andreivitch as a shy, pretty little boy at her wedding; and she remembered *that* as the most unhappy day of her life.

It was perverse of her, she thought, to make the flower room her sanctuary. This house had rooms for almost every purpose: different rooms for breakfast, lunch, tea and dinner, a room for billiards and another in which to keep guns, special rooms for washing clothes, ironing, making jam, cleaning silver, hanging game, keeping wine, brushing suits . . . Her own suite had a bedroom, a dressing-room and a sitting-room. And yet, when she wanted to be at peace, she would come here and sit on a hard chair and look at the crude stone sink and the cast-iron legs of the marble table. Her husband also had an unofficial sanctuary, she had noticed: when Stephen was disturbed about something he would go to the gun-room and read the game book.

So Aleks would be her guest in London for the season. They would talk of home, and the snow and the ballet and the bombs; and seeing Aleks would make her think of another young Russian, the man she had not married.

It was nineteen years since she had seen that man, but still the mere mention of St Petersburg could bring him to mind, and make her skin crawl beneath the watered silk of her tea-gown. He had been nineteen, the same age as she, a hungry student with long black hair, the face of a wolf and the eyes of a spaniel. He was as thin as a rail. His skin was white, the hair of his body soft, dark and adolescent; and he had clever, clever hands. She blushed now, not at the thought of his body but at the thought of her own, betraying her, maddening her with pleasure, making her cry out shamefully. I was wicked, she thought; and I am wicked still, for I should like to do it again.

She thought guiltily of her husband. She hardly ever thought of him without feeling guilty. She had not loved him when they married, but she loved him now. He was strong-willed and warm-hearted, and he adored her. His affection was constant and gentle and entirely lacking in the desperate passion which she had once known. He was happy, she thought, only because he had never known that love could be wild and hungry.

I no longer crave that kind of love, she told herself. I have learned to live without it, and over the years it has become easier. So it should – I'm almost forty!

Some of her friends were still tempted, and they yielded, too. They did not speak to her of their affairs, for they sensed she did not approve; but they gossiped about others, and Lydia knew that at some country-house parties there was a lot of . . . well, adultery. Once Lady Girard had said to Lydia, with the condescending air of an older woman who gives sound advice to a young hostess: 'My dear, if you have the Viscountess and Charlie Stott at the same time you simply *must* put them in adjoining bedrooms.' Lydia had put them at opposite ends of the house, and the Viscountess had never come to Walden Hall again.

People said all this immorality was the fault of the late King, but Lydia did not believe them. It was true that he had befriended Jews and singers, but that did not make him a rake. Anyway, he had stayed at Walden Hall twice – once as Prince of Wales and once as King Edward the Seventh – and he had behaved impeccably both times.

She wondered whether the new King would ever come. It was a great strain, to have a monarch to stay, but such a thrill to make the house look its very best and have the most lavish meals imaginable and buy twelve new dresses just for one weekend. And if this King were to come, he might grant the Waldens the coveted *entrée* – the right to go into Buckingham Palace by the garden entrance on big occasions, instead of queuing up in The Mall along with two hundred other carriages.

She thought about her guests this weekend. George was Stephen's younger brother: he had Stephen's charm but none of Stephen's seriousness. George's daughter Belinda was eighteen, the same age as Charlotte. Both girls would be coming out this season. Belinda's mother had died some years ago and George had married again, rather quickly. His second wife, Clarissa, was much younger than he, and quite vivacious. She had given him twin sons. One of the twins would inherit Walden Hall when Stephen died, unless Lydia gave birth to a boy late in life. I could, she thought; I feel as if I could, but it just doesn't happen.

It was almost time to be getting ready for dinner. She sighed. She felt comfortable and natural in her tea-gown, with her fair hair dressed loosely; but now she would have to be laced into a corset and have her hair piled high on her head by a maid. It was said that some of the young women were giving up corsets altogether. That was all right, Lydia supposed, if you were naturally shaped like the figure 8; but she was small in all the wrong places.

She got up and went outside. That under-gardener was standing by a rose tree, talking to one of the maids. Lydia recognized the maid: she was Annie, a pretty, voluptuous, empty-headed girl with a wide, generous smile. She stood with her hands in the pockets of her apron, turning her round face up to the sun and laughing at something the gardener had said. Now *there* is a girl who doesn't need a corset, Lydia thought. Annie was supposed to be supervising Charlotte and Belinda, for the governess had the afternoon off. Lydia said sharply: 'Annie! Where are the young ladies?'

Annie's smile disappeared and she dropped a curtsey. 'I can't find them, m'lady.'

The gardener moved off sheepishly.

'You don't appear to be looking for them,' Lydia said. 'Off you go.'

'Very good, m'lady.' Annie ran toward the back of the house. Lydia sighed: the girls would not be there, but she could not be bothered to call Annie back and reprimand her again.

She strolled across the lawn, thinking of familiar and pleasant things, pushing St Petersburg to the back of her mind. Stephen's father, the seventh Earl of Walden, had planted the west side of the park with rhododendrons and azaleas. Lydia had never met the old man, for he had died before she knew Stephen, but by all accounts he had been one of the great larger-than-life Victorians. His bushes were now in full glorious bloom, and made a rather un-Victorian blaze of assorted colours. We must have somebody paint a picture of the house, she thought; the last one was done before the park was mature.

She looked back at Walden Hall. The grey stone of the south front looked beautiful and dignified in the afternoon sunshine. In the centre was the south door. The farther, east wing contained the drawing-room and various dining-rooms, and behind them a straggle of kitchens, pantries and laundries running higgledy-piggledy to the distant stables. Nearer to her, on the west side, were the morning-room, the Octagon, and at the corner the library; then, around the corner along the west front, the billiard-room, the gun-room, her flower-room, a smoking-room and the estate office. On the first floor, the family bedrooms were mostly on the south side, the main guest-rooms on the west side, and the servants' rooms over the kitchens to the north-east, out of sight. Above the first floor was an irrational collection of towers, turrets and attics. The whole facade was a riot of ornamental stonework in the best Victorian rococo manner, with flowers and chevrons and sculpted coils of rope, dragons and lions and cherubim, balconies and battlements, flagpoles and sundials and gargoyles. Lydia loved the place, and she was grateful that Stephen – unlike many of the old aristocracy – could afford to keep it up.

She saw Charlotte and Belinda emerge from the shrubbery across the lawn. Annie had not found them, of course. They both wore wide-brimmed hats and summer frocks with schoolgirls' black stockings and low black shoes. Because Charlotte was coming out this season, she was occasionally permitted to put up her hair and dress for dinner, but most of the time Lydia treated her like the child she was, for it was bad for children to grow up too fast. The two cousins were deep in conversation, and Lydia wondered idly what they were talking about. What was on my mind when I was eighteen? she asked herself; and then she remembered a young man with soft hair and clever hands, and she thought: Please, God, let me keep my secrets.

'Do you think we'll *feel* different after we've come out?' Belinda said.

Charlotte had thought about this before. 'I shan't.'

'But we'll be grown up.'

'I don't see how a lot of parties and balls and picnics can make a person grow up.'

'We'll have to have corsets.'

Charlotte giggled. 'Have you ever worn one?'

'No, have you?'

'I tried mine on last week.'

'What's it like?'

'Awful. You can't walk upright.'

'How did you look?'

Charlotte gestured with her hands to indicate an enormous bust. They both collapsed laughing. Charlotte caught sight of her mother, and put on a contrite face in anticipation of a reprimand; but Mama seemed preoccupied, and merely smiled vaguely as she turned away.

'It will be fun, though,' said Belinda.

'The season? Yes,' Charlotte said doubtfully. 'But what's the point of it all?'

'To meet the right sort of young man, of course.'

'To look for husbands, you mean.'

They reached the great oak in the middle of the lawn, and Belinda threw herself down on the seat beneath the tree, looking faintly sulky. 'You think coming out is all very silly, don't you?' she said.

Charlotte sat beside her and looked across the carpet of turf to the long south front of Walden Hall. The tall Gothic windows glinted in the afternoon sun. From here the house looked as if it might be rationally and regularly planned, but behind that facade it was really an enchanting muddle. She said: 'What's silly is being made to wait so long. I'm not in a hurry to go to balls and leave cards on people in the afternoon and meet young men – I shouldn't mind if I never did those things – but it makes me so angry to be treated like a child still. I hate having supper with Marya, she's quite ignorant, or pretends to be. At least in the dining-room you get some conversation. Papa talks about interesting things. When I get bored Marya suggests we play cards.

I don't want to *play* anything, I've been playing all my life.' She sighed. Talking about it had made her angrier. She looked at Belinda's calm, freckled face with its halo of red curls. Charlotte's own face was oval, with a rather distinctive straight nose and a strong chin, and her hair was thick and dark. Happy-go-lucky Belinda, she thought; these things really don't bother her, *she* never gets intense about anything.

Charlotte touched Belinda's arm. 'Sorry. I didn't mean to carry on so.'

'It's all right.' Belinda smiled indulgently. 'You always get cross about things you can't possibly change. Do you remember that time you decided you wanted to go to Eton?'

'Never!'

'You most certainly did. You made a terrible fuss. Papa had gone to school at Eton, you said, so why shouldn't you?'

Charlotte had no memory of that, but she could not deny that it sounded just like her at ten years old. She said: 'But do you really think these things can't possibly be different? Coming out, and going to London for the season, and getting engaged, and then marriage . . .'

'You could have a scandal and be forced to emigrate to Rhodesia.'

'I'm not quite sure how one goes about having a scandal.'

'Nor am I.'

They were silent for a while. Sometimes Charlotte wished she were passive like Belinda. Life would be simpler – but then again, it would be awfully dull. She said: 'I asked Marya what I'm supposed to *do* after I get married. Do you know what she said?' She imitated her governess's throaty Russian accent. 'Do? Why, my child, you will do *nothing*.'

'Oh, that's silly,' Belinda said.

'Is it? What do my mother and yours do?'

'They're Good Society. They have parties and stay about at country houses and go to the opera and . . .'

'That's what I mean. Nothing.'

'They have babies—'

'Now that's another thing. They make such a *secret* about having babies.'

'That's because it's . . . vulgar.'

'Why? What's vulgar about it?' Charlotte saw herself becoming *enthusiastic* again. Marya was always telling her not to be *enthusiastic*. She took a deep breath and lowered her voice. 'You and I have got to have these babies. Don't you think they might tell us something about how it happens? They're very keen for us to know all about Mozart and Shakespeare and Leonardo da Vinci.'

Belinda looked uncomfortable but very interested. She feels the same way about it as I do, Charlotte thought; I wonder how much she knows?

Charlotte said: 'Do you realize they grow inside you?'

Belinda nodded, then blurted out: 'But how does it start?'

'Oh, it just happens, I think, when you get to about twenty-one. That's really why you have to be a debutante and come out – to make sure you get a husband before you start having babies.' Charlotte hesitated. 'I think,' she added.

Belinda said: 'Then how do they get out?'

'I don't know. How big are they?'

Belinda held her hands about two feet apart. 'The twins were this big when they were a day old. She thought again, and narrowed the distance. 'Well, perhaps this big.'

Charlotte said: 'When a hen lays an egg, it comes out . . . behind.' She avoided Belinda's eyes. She had never had such an intimate conversation with anyone, ever. 'The egg seems too big, but it does come out.'

Belinda leaned closer and spoke quietly. 'I saw Daisy drop a calf once. She's the Jersey cow on the Home Farm. The men didn't know I was watching. That's what they call it, "dropping" a calf.'

Charlotte was fascinated. 'What happened?'

'It was horrible. It looked as if her tummy opened up, and there was a lot of blood and things.' She shuddered.

'It makes me scared,' Charlotte said. 'I'm afraid it will happen to me before I find out all about it. Why won't they *tell* us?'

'We shouldn't be talking about such things.'

'We've damn well got a right to talk about them!'

Belinda gasped. 'Swearing makes it worse!'

'I don't care.' It maddened Charlotte that there was no way to find out these things, no one to ask, no book to consult . . . She was struck by an idea. 'There's a locked cupboard in the library – I bet there are books about all this sort of thing in there. Let's look!'

'But if it's locked . . .'

'Oh, I know where the key is, I've known for years.'

'We'll be in terrible trouble if we're caught.'

'They're all changing for dinner now. This is our chance.' Charlotte stood up.

Belinda hesitated. 'There'll be a row.'

'I don't care if there is. Anyway, I'm going to look in the cupboard, and you can come if you want.' Charlotte turned and walked toward the house. After a moment Belinda ran up beside her, as Charlotte had known she would.

They went through the pillared portico and into the cool, lofty great hall. Turning left, they passed the morning-room and the Octagon, then entered the library. Charlotte told herself she was a woman and entitled to know, but all the same she felt like a naughty little girl.

The library was her favourite room. Being on a corner of the house it was very bright, lit by three big windows. The leather-upholstered chairs were old and surprisingly comfortable. In winter there was a fire all day, and there were games and jigsaw puzzles as well as two or three thousand books. Some of the books were ancient, having been here since the house was built, but many were new, for Mama read novels and Papa was interested in lots of different things – chemistry, agriculture, travel, astronomy and history. Charlotte liked particularly to come here on Marya's day off, when the governess was not able to snatch away *Far from the Madding Crowd* and replace it with *The Water Babies.* Sometimes Papa would be here with her, sitting at the

Victorian pedestal desk and reading a catalogue of agricultural machinery or the balance sheet of an American railroad, but he never interfered with her choice of books.

The room was empty now. Charlotte went straight to the desk, opened a small, square drawer in one of the pedestals, and took out a key.

There were three cupboards against the wall beside the desk. One contained games in boxes and another had cartons of writing-paper and envelopes embossed with the Walden crest. The third was locked. Charlotte opened it with the key.

Inside were twenty or thirty books and a pile of old magazines. Charlotte glanced at one of the magazines. It was called *The Pearl*. It did not seem promising. Hastily, she picked out two books at random, without looking at the titles. She closed and locked the cupboard and replaced the key in the desk drawer.

'There!' she said triumphantly.

'Where can we go to look at them?' Belinda hissed.

'Remember the hideaway?'

'Oh! Yes!'

'Why are we whispering?'

They both giggled.

Charlotte went to the door. Suddenly she heard a voice in the hall, calling: 'Lady Charlotte . . . Lady Charlotte . . .'

'It's Annie, she's looking for us,' Charlotte said. 'She's nice, but so dim-witted. We'll go out the other way, quickly.' She crossed the library and went through the far door into the billiard-room, which led in turn to the gun-room; but there was someone in the gun-room. She listened for a moment.

'It's my Papa,' Belinda whispered, looking scared. 'He's been out with the dogs.'

Fortunately there was a pair of French doors from the billiard-room on to the west terrace. Charlotte and Belinda crept out and closed the doors quietly behind them. The sun was low and red, casting long shadows across the lawns.

'Now how do we get back in?' Belinda said.

'Over the roofs. Follow me!'

Charlotte ran around the back of the house and through the kitchen garden to the stables. She stuffed the two books into the bodice of her dress and tightened her belt so that they should not fall out.

From a corner of the stable yard she could climb, by a series of easy steps, to the roof over the servants' quarters. First she stood on the lid of a low iron bunker which was used to store logs. From there she hauled herself on to the corrugated tin roof of a lean-to shed where tools were kept. The shed leaned against the wash-house. She stood upright on the corrugated tin and lifted herself on to the slate roof of the wash-house. She turned to look behind: Belinda was following.

Lying face down on the sloping slates, Charlotte edged along crabwise, holding on with the palms of her hands and the sides of her shoes, until the roof ended up against a wall. Then she crawled up the roof and straddled the ridge.

Belinda caught up with her and said: 'Isn't this dangerous?'

'I've been doing it since I was nine years old.'

Above them was the window of an attic bedroom shared by two parlourmaids. The window was high in the gable, its top corners almost reaching the roof which sloped down on either side. Charlotte stood upright and peeped into the room. No one was there. She pulled herself on to the window-ledge and stood up.

She leaned to the left, got an arm and a leg over the edge of the roof, and hauled herself on to the slates. She turned back and helped Belinda up.

They lay there for a moment, catching their breath. Charlotte remembered being told that Walden Hall had four acres of roof. It was hard to believe until you came up here and realized you could get lost among the ridges and valleys. From here it was possible to reach any part of the roofs by using the footways, ladders and tunnels provided for the maintenance men who came every spring to clean gutters, paint drain-pipes and replace broken tiles.

Charlotte got up. 'Come on, the rest is easy,' she said.

There was a ladder to the next roof, then a board footway, then a short flight of wooden steps leading to a small, square door set in a wall. Charlotte unlatched the door and crawled through, and she was in the hideaway.

It was a low, windowless room with a sloping ceiling and a plank floor which would give you splinters if you were not careful. She imagined it had once been used as a storeroom: anyway, it was now quite forgotten. A door at one end led into a closet off the nursery, which had not been used for many years. Charlotte had discovered the hideaway when she was eight or nine, and had used it occasionally in the game – which she seemed to have been playing all her life – of escaping from supervision. There were cushions on the floor, candles in jars, and a box of matches. On one of the cushions lay a battered and floppy toy dog which had been hidden here eight years ago after Marya, the governess, had threatened to throw him away. A tiny occasional table bore a cracked vase full of coloured pencils, and a red leather writing-case. Walden Hall was inventoried every few years, and Charlotte could recall Mrs Braithwaite, the housekeeper, saying that the oddest things went missing.

Belinda crawled in and Charlotte lit the candles. She took the two books from her bodice and looked at the titles. One was called *Household Medicine* and the other *The Romance of Lust.* The medical book seemed more promising. She sat on a cushion and opened it. Belinda sat beside her, looking guilty. Charlotte felt as if she were about to discover the secret of life.

She leafed through the pages. The book seemed explicit and detailed on rheumatism, broken bones and measles, but when it arrived at childbirth it suddenly became impenetrably vague. There was some mysterious stuff about cramps, waters breaking, and a cord which had to be tied in two places then cut with scissors which had been dipped in boiling water. This chapter was evidently written for people who already knew a lot about the subject. There was a drawing of a naked woman. Charlotte noticed, but was too embarrassed to tell Belinda, that the woman in the drawing had no hair in a certain place where Charlotte had a great deal. Then there was a diagram of a baby inside a woman's tummy, but no indication of a passage by which the baby might emerge.

Belinda said: 'It must be that the doctor cuts you open.'

'Then what did they do in history, before there were doctors?' Charlotte said. 'Anyway, this book's no good.' She opened the other at random and read aloud the first sentence that came to her eye. 'She lowered herself with lascivious slowness until she was completely impaled upon my rigid shaft, whereupon she commenced her delicious rocking movements to and fro.' Charlotte frowned, and looked at Belinda.

'I wonder what it means?' said Belinda.

Feliks Kschessinsky sat in a railway carriage waiting for the train to pull out of Dover Station. The carriage was cold. He was quite still. It was dark outside, and he could see his own reflection in the window: a tall man with a neat moustache, wearing a black coat and a bowler hat. There was a small suitcase on the rack above his head. He might have been the travelling representative of a Swiss watch manufacturer, except that anyone who looked closely would have seen that the coat was cheap, the suitcase was cardboard, and the face was not the face of a man who sold watches.

He was thinking about England. He could remember

when, in his youth, he had upheld England's constitutional monarchy as the ideal form of government. The thought amused him, and the flat white face reflected in the window gave him the ghost of a smile. He had since changed his mind about the ideal form of government.

The train moved off, and a few minutes later Feliks was watching the sun rise over the orchards and hop fields of Kent. He never ceased to be astonished at how *pretty* Europe was. When he first saw it he had suffered a profound shock, for like any Russian peasant he had been incapable of imagining that the world could look this way. He had been on a train then, he recalled. He had crossed hundreds of miles of Russia's thinly populated north-western provinces, with their stunted trees, their miserable villages buried in snow, and their winding mud roads; then, one morning, he had woken up to find himself in Germany. Looking at the neat green fields, the paved roads, the dainty houses in the clean villages, and the flower beds on the sunny station platform, he had thought he was in Paradise. Later, in Switzerland, he had sat on the verandah of a small hotel, warmed by the sun yet within sight of snow-covered mountains, drinking coffee and eating a fresh, crusty roll, and he had thought: People here must be so happy.

Now, watching the English farms come to life in the early morning, he recalled dawn in his home village: a grey, boiling sky and a bitter wind; a frozen swampy field with puddles of ice and tufts of coarse grass rimed with frost; himself in a worn canvas smock, his feet already numb in felt shoes and clogs; his father striding along beside him, wearing the threadbare robes of an impoverished country priest, arguing that God was good. His father had loved the Russian people because God loved them. It had always been perfectly obvious to Feliks that God hated the people, for He treated them so cruelly.

That discussion had been the start of a long journey, a journey which had taken Feliks from Christianity through socialism to anarchist terror, from Tambov province through St Petersburg and Siberia to Geneva. And in Geneva he had made the decision which brought him to England. He recalled the meeting. He had almost missed it . . .

He almost missed the meeting. He had been to Cracow, to negotiate with the Polish Jews who smuggled the magazine, *Mutiny*, across the border into Russia. He arrived in Geneva after dark, and went straight to Ulrich's tiny back-street printing shop. The editorial committee was in session: four men and two girls, gathered around a candle, in the rear of the shop behind the gleaming press, breathing the smells of newsprint and oiled machinery, planning the Russian revolution.

Ulrich brought Feliks up to date on the discussion. He had seen Josef, a spy for the Ochrana, the Russian secret police. Josef secretly sympathized with the revolutionaries, and gave the Ochrana false information for their money. Sometimes the anarchists would give him true but harmless tidbits, and in return Josef warned them of Ochrana activities.

This time Josef's news had been sensational. 'The Czar wants a military alliance with England,' Ulrich told Feliks. 'He is sending Prince Orlov to London to negotiate. The Ochrana know about it because they have to guard the Prince on the journey through Europe.'

Feliks took off his hat and sat down, wondering whether this was true. One of the girls, a sad, shabby Russian, brought him tea in a glass. Feliks took a half-eaten lump of sugar from his pocket, placed it between his teeth, and sipped the tea through the sugar in the peasant manner.

'The point being,' Ulrich went on, 'that England could then have a war with Germany and make the Russians fight it.'

Feliks nodded.

The shabby girl said: 'And it won't be the princes and counts who get killed – it will be the ordinary Russian people.'

She was right, Feliks thought. The war would be fought by the peasants. He had spent most of his life among those people. They were hard, surly and narrow-minded, but their foolish generosity and their occasional spontaneous outbursts of sheer fun gave a hint of how they might be in a decent society. Their concerns were the weather, animals, disease, childbirth and outwitting the landlord. For a few years, in their late teens, they were sturdy and straight, and could smile and run fast and flirt; but soon they became bowed and grey and slow and sullen. Now Prince Orlov would take those young men in the springtime of their lives and march them in front of cannon to be shot to pieces or maimed for ever, no doubt for the very best reasons of international diplomacy.

It was things like this that made Feliks an anarchist.

'What is to be done?' said Ulrich.

'We must blaze the news across the front page of *Mutiny*!' said the shabby girl.

They began to discuss how the story should be handled. Feliks listened. Editorial matters interested him little. He distributed the magazine and wrote articles about how to make bombs, and he was deeply discontented. He had become terribly civilized in Geneva. He drank beer instead of vodka, wore a collar and a tie, and went to concerts of orchestral music. He had a job in a bookshop. Meanwhile Russia was in turmoil. The oil workers were at war with the Cossacks, the parliament was impotent, and a million workers were on strike. Czar Nicolas II was the most incompetent and asinine ruler a degenerate aristocracy could produce. The country was a powder barrel waiting for a spark, and Feliks wanted to be that spark. But it was fatal to go back. Joe Stalin had gone back, and no sooner had he set foot on Russian soil than he had been sent to Siberia. The secret police knew the exiled revolutionaries better than they knew those still at home. Feliks was chafed by his stiff collar, his leather shoes and his circumstances.

He looked around at the little group of anarchists: Ulrich, the printer, with white hair and an inky apron, an intellectual who loaned Feliks books by Proudhon and Kropotkin but also a man of action who had once helped Feliks rob a bank; Olga, the shabby girl, who had seemed to be falling in love with Feliks until, one day, she saw him break a policeman's arm and became frightened of him; Vera, the promiscuous poetess; Yevno, the philosophy student who talked a lot about a cleansing wave of blood and fire; Hans, the watchmaker, who saw into people's souls as if he had them under his magnifying glass; and Piotr, the dispossessed Count, writer of brilliant economic tracts and inspirational revolutionary editorials. They were sincere and hardworking people, and all very clever. Feliks knew their importance, for he had been inside Russia among the desperate people who waited impatiently for smuggled newspapers and pamphlets and passed them from hand to hand until they fell to pieces. Yet it was not enough, for economic tracts were no protection against police bullets, and fiery articles would not burn palaces.

Ulrich was saying: 'This news deserves wider circulation than it will get in *Mutiny*. I want every peasant in Russia to know that Orlov would lead him into a useless and bloody war over something that concerns him not at all.'

Olga said: 'The first problem is whether we will be believed.'

Feliks said: 'The first problem is whether the story is true.'

'We can check,' Ulrich said. 'The London comrades could find out whether Orlov arrives when he is supposed to arrive, and whether he meets the people he needs to meet.'

'It's not enough to spread the news,' Yevno said excitedly. 'We must put a stop to this!'

'How?' said Ulrich, looking at young Yevno over the top of his wire-rimmed spectacles.

'We should call for the assassination of Orlov – he is a traitor, betraying the people, and he should be executed.'

'Would that stop the talks?'

'It probably would,' said Count Piotr. 'Especially if the assassin were an anarchist. Remember, England gives political asylum to anarchists, and this infuriates the Czar. Now, if one of his princes were killed in England by one of our comrades, the Czar might well be angry enough to call off the whole negotiation.'

Yevno said: 'What a story we would have then! We could say that Orlov had been assassinated by one of us for treason against the Russian people.'

'Every newspaper in the world would carry *that* report,' Ulrich mused.

'Think of the effect it would have at home. You know how Russian peasants feel about conscription – it's a death sentence. They hold a funeral when a boy goes into the army. If they learned that the Czar was planning to make them fight a major European war, the rivers would run red with blood . . .'

He was right, Feliks thought. Yevno always talked like that, but this time he was right.

Ulrich said: 'I think you're in dreamland, Yevno.

Orlov is on a secret mission – he won't ride through London in an open carriage waving to the crowds. Besides, I know the London comrades – they've never assassinated anyone. I don't see how it can be done.'

'I do,' Feliks said. They all looked at him. The shadows on their faces shifted in the flickering candlelight. 'I know how it can be done.' His voice sounded strange to him, as if his throat was constricted. 'I'll go to London. I'll kill Orlov.'

The room was suddenly quiet, as all the talk of death and destruction suddenly became real and concrete in their midst. They stared at him in surprise, all except Ulrich, who smiled knowingly, almost as if he had planned, all along, that it would turn out this way.

CHAPTER TWO

LONDON WAS unbelievably rich. Feliks had seen extravagant wealth in Russia, and much prosperity in Europe, but not on this scale. Here *nobody* was in rags. In fact, although the weather was warm, everyone was wearing several layers of heavy clothing. Feliks saw carters, street vendors, sweepers, labourers and delivery boys – all sporting fine factory-made coats without holes or patches. All the children wore boots. Every woman had a hat, and such hats! They were mostly enormous things, as broad across as the wheel of a dog-cart, and decorated with ribbons, feathers, flowers and fruit. The streets were teeming. He saw more motor cars in the first five minutes than he had in all his life. There seemed to be as many cars as there were horse-drawn vehicles. On wheels or on foot, everyone was rushing.

In Piccadilly Circus all the vehicles were at a standstill, and the cause was one familiar in any city: a horse had fallen and its cart had overturned. A crowd of men struggled to get beast and wagon upright, while from the pavement flower-girls and ladies with painted faces shouted encouragement and made jokes.

As he went farther east his initial impression of great

wealth was somewhat modified. He passed a domed cathedral which was called St Paul's, according to the map he had bought at Victoria Station, and thereafter he was in poorer districts. Abruptly, the magnificent facades of banks and office buildings gave place to small row houses in varying states of disrepair. There were fewer cars and more horses, and the horses were thinner. Most of the shops were street stalls. There were no more delivery boys. Now he saw plenty of barefoot children – not that it mattered, for in this climate, it seemed to him, they had no need of boots anyway.

Things got worse as he penetrated deeper into the East End. Here were crumbling tenements, squalid courtyards and stinking alleys, where human wrecks dressed in rags picked over piles of garbage, looking for food. Then Feliks entered Whitechapel High Street, and saw the familiar beards, long hair and traditional robes of assorted Orthodox Jews, and tiny shops selling smoked fish and kosher meat: it was like being in the Russian Pale, except that the Jews did not look frightened.

He made his way to No. 165 Jubilee Street, the address Ulrich had given him. It was a two-storey building that looked like a Lutheran chapel. A notice outside said the Worker's Friend Club and Institute was open to all working men regardless of politics, but another notice betrayed the nature of the place by announcing that it had been opened in 1906 by Peter Kropotkin. Feliks wondered whether he would meet the legendary Kropotkin here in London.

He went in. He saw in the lobby a pile of newspapers,

also called *The Worker's Friend* but in Yiddish: *Der Arbeter Fraint.* Notices on the walls advertised lessons in English, a Sunday school, a trip to Epping Forest, and a lecture on *Hamlet.* Feliks stepped into the hall. The architecture confirmed his earlier instincts: this had definitely been the nave of a nonconformist church once upon a time. However, it had been transformed by the addition of a stage at one end and a bar at the other. On the stage a group of men and women appeared to be rehearsing a play. Perhaps this was what anarchists did in England, Feliks thought; that would explain why they were allowed to have clubs. He went over to the bar. There was no sign of alcoholic drink, but on the counter he saw gefilte fish, pickled herring, and – joy! – a samovar.

The girl behind the counter looked at him and said: 'Nu?'

Feliks smiled.

A week later, on the day that Prince Orlov was due to arrive in London, Feliks had lunch at a French restaurant in Soho. He arrived early and picked a table near the door. He ate onion soup, fillet steak and goat's cheese, and drank half a bottle of red wine. He ordered in French. The waiters were deferential. When he finished, it was the height of the lunch-hour rush. At a moment when three of the waiters were in the kitchen and the other two had their backs to him he calmly got up, went to the door, took his coat and hat, and left without paying.

He smiled as he walked down the street. He enjoyed stealing.

He had quickly learned how to live in this town on almost no money. For breakfast he would buy sweet tea and a slab of bread from a street stall for twopence, but that was the only food he would pay for. At lunchtime he stole fruit or vegetables from street stalls. In the evening he would go to a charity soup kitchen and get a bowl of broth and unlimited bread in return for listening to an incomprehensible sermon and singing a hymn. He had five pounds in cash but it was for emergencies.

He was living at Dunstan Houses in Stepney Green, in a five-storey tenement building where lived half the leading anarchists in London. He had a mattress on the floor in the apartment of Rudolf Rocker, the charismatic blond German who edited *Der Arbeter Fraint*. Rocker's charisma did not work on Feliks, who was immune to charm, but Feliks respected the man's total dedication. Rocker and his wife Milly kept open house for anarchists, and all day – and half the night – there were visitors, messengers, debates, committee meetings, and endless tea and cigarettes. Feliks paid no rent, but each day he brought home something – a pound of sausages, a packet of tea, a pocketful of oranges – for the communal larder. They thought he bought these things, but of course he stole them.

He told the other anarchists he was here to study at the British Museum and finish his book about natural anarchism in primitive communities. They believed him. They were friendly, dedicated and harmless: they sincerely believed the revolution could be brought about by education and trade unionism, by pamphlets and lectures and trips to Epping Forest. Feliks knew that most anarchists outside Russia were like this. He did not hate them, but secretly he despised them, for in the end they were just frightened.

Nevertheless, among such groups there were generally a few violent men. When he needed them he would seek them out.

Meanwhile he worried about whether Orlov would come and about how he would kill him. Such worries were useless, and he tried to distract his mind by working on his English. He had learned a little of the language in cosmopolitan Switzerland. During the long train journey across Europe he had studied a school textbook for Russian children and an English translation of his favourite novel, *The Captain's Daughter*, by Pushkin, which he knew almost by heart in Russian. Now he read *The Times* every morning in the reading-room of the Jubilee Street club, and in the afternoons he walked the streets, striking up conversations with drunks, vagrants and prostitutes – the people he liked best, the people who broke the rules. The printed words in books soon meshed with the sounds all around him, and already he could say anything he needed to. Before long he would be able to talk politics in English.

After leaving the restaurant he walked north, across Oxford Street, and entered the German quarter west of Tottenham Court Road. There were a lot of revolutionists among the Germans, but they tended to be communists rather than anarchists. Feliks admired the discipline of the communists but he was suspicious of their authoritarianism; and besides, he was temperamentally unsuited to party work.

He walked all the way across Regents Park and entered the middle-class suburb to its north. He wandered around the tree-lined streets, looking into the small gardens of the neat brick villas, searching for a bicycle to steal. He had learned to ride a bicycle in Switzerland, and had discovered that it was the perfect vehicle for shadowing someone, for it was manoeuvrable and inconspicuous, and in city traffic it was fast enough to keep up with a motor car or a carriage. Sadly, the bourgeois citizens of this part of London seemed to keep their bicycles locked away. He saw one cycle being ridden along the street, and was tempted to knock the rider off the machine, but at that moment there were three pedestrians and a baker's van in the road, and Feliks did not want to create a scene. A little later he saw a boy delivering groceries, but the boy's cycle was too conspicuous, with a large basket on the front and a metal plate, hanging from the crossbar, bearing the name of the grocer. Feliks was beginning to toy with alternative strategies when at last he saw what he needed.

A man of about thirty came out of one of the gardens wheeling a bicycle. The man wore a straw boater and a striped blazer which bulged over his paunch. He leaned his cycle against the garden wall and bent down to put on his trouser-clips.

Feliks approached him rapidly.

The man saw his shadow, looked up, and muttered: 'Good afternoon.'

Feliks knocked him down.

The man rolled on to his back and looked up at Feliks with a stupid expression of surprise.

Feliks fell on him, dropping one knee into the middle button of the striped blazer. The man's breath left his body in a whoosh, and he was winded, helpless, gasping for air.

Feliks stood up and glanced toward the house. A young woman stood at a window watching, her hand raised to her open mouth, her eyes wide with fright.

He looked again at the man on the ground: it would be a minute or so before he even thought about getting up.

Feliks climbed on the bicycle and rode away rapidly.

A man who has no fear can do anything he wants, Feliks thought. He had learned that lesson eleven years ago, in a railway siding outside Omsk. It had been snowing . . .

It was snowing. Feliks sat in an open railway truck, on a pile of coal, freezing to death.

He had been cold for a year, ever since he escaped from the chain gang in the gold mine. In that year he had crossed Siberia, from the frozen north almost to the Urals. Now he was a mere thousand miles from civilization and warm weather. Most of the way he had walked, although sometimes he rode in railcars or on wagons full of pelts. He preferred to ride with cattle, for they kept him warm and he could share their feed. He was vaguely aware that he was little more than an animal himself. He never washed, his coat was a blanket stolen from a horse, his ragged clothes were full of lice and there were fleas in his hair. His favourite food was raw birds' eggs. Once he had stolen a pony, ridden it to death, then eaten its liver. He had lost his sense of time. He knew it was autumn, by the weather, but he did not know what month he was in. Often he found himself unable to remember what he had done the day before. In his saner moments he realized he was half mad. He never spoke to people. When he came to a town or village he skirted it, pausing merely to rob the garbage tip. He knew only that he had to keep going west, for it would be warmer there.

But the coal train had been shunted into a siding, and Feliks thought he might be dying. There was a guard, a burly policeman in a fur coat, who was there to stop peasants taking coal for their fires . . . As that thought occurred to him Feliks realized he was having a lucid moment, and that it might be his last. He wondered what had brought it on, then he smelled the policeman's dinner. But the policeman was big and healthy and had a gun.

I don't care, Feliks thought; I'm dying anyway.

So he stood up, and picked up the biggest lump of coal he could carry, and staggered over to the policeman's hut, and went in, and hit the startled policeman over the head with the lump of coal.

There was a pot on the fire and stew in the pot, too

hot to eat. Feliks carried the pot outside and emptied it out into the snow, then he fell on his knees and ate the food mixed with cooling snow. There were lumps of potato and turnip, and fat carrots, and chunks of meat. He swallowed them whole. The policeman came out of the hut and hit Feliks with his club, a heavy blow across the back. Feliks was wild with rage that the man should try to stop him eating. He got up from the ground and flew at the man, kicking and scratching. The policeman fought back with his club but Feliks could not feel the blows. He got his fingers to the man's throat and squeezed. He would not let go. After a while the man's eyes closed, then his face went blue, then his tongue came out, then Feliks finished the stew.

He ate all the food in the hut, and warmed himself by the fire, and slept in the policeman's bed. When he woke up he was sane. He took the boots and the coat off the corpse and walked to Omsk. On the way he made a remarkable discovery about himself: he had lost the ability to feel fear. Something had happened in his mind, as if a switch had closed. He could think of nothing that could possibly frighten him. If hungry, he would steal; if chased, he would hide; if threatened, he would kill. There was nothing he wanted. Nothing could hurt him any more. Love, pride, desire and compassion were forgotten emotions.

They all came back, eventually, except the fear.

When he reached Omsk he sold the policeman's fur coat and bought trousers and a shirt, a waistcoat and a topcoat. He burned his rags and paid one rouble for a hot bath and a shave in a cheap hotel. He ate in a restaurant, using a knife instead of his fingers. He saw the front page of a newspaper, and remembered how to read; and then he knew he had come back from the grave.

He sat on a bench in Liverpool Street Station, his bicycle leaning against the wall beside him. He wondered what Orlov was like. He knew nothing about the man other than his rank and mission. The Prince might be a dull, plodding, loyal servant of the Czar, or a sadist and a lecher, or a kindly white-haired old man who liked nothing better than to bounce his grandchildren on his knee. It did not matter: Feliks would kill him anyway.

He was confident he would recognize Orlov, for Russians of that type had not the faintest conception of travelling unobtrusively, secret mission or no.

Would Orlov come? If he did come, and arrived on the very train Josef had specified, and if he subsequently met with the Earl of Walden as Josef had said he would, then there could hardly be any further doubt that Josef's information had been accurate.

A few minutes before the train was due a closed coach drawn by four magnificent horses clattered by and drove straight on to the platform. There was a coachman in front and a liveried footman hanging on behind. A railwayman in a military-style coat with shiny buttons strode after the coach. The railwayman spoke to the coachman and directed him to the far end of the platform. Then a stationmaster in a frock coat and top hat arrived, looking important, consulting his fob watch and comparing it critically with the station clocks. He opened the carriage door for the passenger to step down.

The railwayman walked past Feliks' bench, and Feliks grabbed his sleeve. 'Please, sir,' he said, putting on the wide-eyed expression of a naive foreign tourist. 'Is that the King of England?'

The railwayman grinned. 'No, mate, it's only the Earl of Walden.' He walked on.

So Josef had been right.

Feliks studied Walden with an assassin's eye. He was tall, about Feliks' height, and beefy – easier to shoot than a small man. He was about fifty. Except for a slight limp he seemed fit: he could run away, but not very fast. He wore a highly visible light-grey morning coat and a top hat of the same colour. His hair under the hat was short and straight, and he had a spade-shaped beard patterned after that of the late King Edward VII. He stood on the platform, leaning on a cane – potential weapon – and favouring his left leg. The coachman, the footman and the stationmaster bustled about him like bees around the queen. His stance was relaxed. He did not look at his watch. He paid no attention to the flunkies around him. He is used to this, Feliks thought; all his life he has been the important man in the crowd.

The train appeared, smoke billowing from the funnel of the engine. I could kill Orlov now, Feliks thought, and he felt momentarily the thrill of the hunter as he closes with his prey; but he had already decided not to do the deed today. He was here to observe, not to act. Most anarchist assassinations were bungled because of haste or spontaneity, in his view. He believed in planning and organisation, which were anathema to many anarchists; but they did not realize that a man could plan his own actions – it was when he began to organize the lives of others that he became a tyrant.

The train halted with a great sigh of steam. Feliks stood up and moved a little closer to the platform. Toward the far end of the train was what appeared to be a private car, differentiated from the rest by the colours of its bright new paintwork. It came to a stop precisely opposite Walden's coach. The stationmaster stepped forward eagerly and opened a door.

Feliks tensed, peering along the platform, watching the shadowed space in which his quarry would appear.

For a moment everyone waited; then Orlov was there. He paused in the doorway for a second, and in that time Feliks' eye photographed him. He was a small man wearing an expensive-looking heavy Russian coat with a fur collar, and a black top hat. His face was pink and youthful, almost boyish, with a small moustache and no beard. He smiled hesitantly. He looked vulnerable. Feliks thought: So much evil is done by people with innocent faces.

Orlov stepped off the train. He and Walden embraced, Russian fashion, but quickly; then they got into the coach.

That was rather hasty, Feliks thought.

The footman and two porters began to load luggage on to the carriage. It rapidly became clear that they could not get everything on, and Feliks smiled to think of his own cardboard suitcase, half empty.

The coach was turned around. It seemed the footman was being left behind to take care of the rest of the luggage. The porters came to the carriage window, and a grey-sleeved arm emerged and dropped coins into their hands. The coach pulled away. Feliks mounted his bicycle and followed.

In the tumult of the London traffic it was not difficult for him to keep pace. He trailed them through the city, along the Strand, and across St James's Park. On the far side of the park the coach followed the boundary road for a few yards then turned abruptly into a walled forecourt.

Feliks jumped off his bicycle and wheeled it along the grass at the edge of the park until he stood across the road from the gateway. He could see the coach drawn up at the imposing entrance to a large house. Over the roof of the coach he saw two top hats, one black and one grey, disappear into the building. Then the door closed, and he could see no more.

Lydia studied her daughter critically. Charlotte stood in front of a large pier glass, trying on the debutante's gown she would wear to be presented at court. Madame Bourdon, the thin, elegant dressmaker, fussed about her with pins, tucking a flounce here and fastening a ruffle there.

Charlotte looked both beautiful and innocent – just the effect that was called for in a debutante. The dress, of white tulle embroidered with crystals, went down almost to the floor and partly covered the tiny pointed shoes. Its neckline, plunging to waist level, was filled in with a crystal corsage. The train was four yards of cloth-of-silver lined with pale pink chiffon and caught at the end by a huge white-and-silver bow. Charlotte's dark hair was piled high and fastened with a tiara which had belonged to the previous Lady Walden, Stephen's mother. In her hair she wore the regulation two white plumes.

My baby has almost grown up, Lydia thought.

She said: 'It's very lovely, Madame Bourdon.'

'Thank you, my lady.'

Charlotte said: 'It's terribly uncomfortable.'

Lydia sighed. It was just the kind of thing Charlotte *would* say. Lydia said: 'I wish you wouldn't be so frivolous.'

Charlotte knelt down to pick up her train. Lydia said: 'You don't have to kneel. Look, copy me and I'll show you how it's done. Turn to the left.' Charlotte did so, and the train draped down her left side. 'Gather it with your left arm, then make another quarter turn to the left.' Now the train stretched out along the floor in front of Charlotte. 'Walk forward, using your right hand to loop the train over your left arm as you go.'

'It works.' Charlotte smiled. When she smiled, you could feel the glow. She used to be like this all the time, Lydia thought. When she was little, I always knew what was going on in her mind. Growing up is learning to deceive.

Charlotte said: 'Who taught *you* all these things, Mama?'

'Your Uncle George's first wife, Belinda's mother, coached me before I was presented.' She wanted to say: These things are easy to teach, but the hard lessons you must learn on your own.

Charlotte's governess Marya came into the room. She was an efficient, unsentimental woman in an iron-grey dress, the only servant Lydia had brought from St Petersburg. Her appearance had not changed in nineteen years. Lydia had no idea how old she was: fifty? Sixty?

Marya said: 'Prince Orlov has arrived, my lady. Why, Charlotte, you look magnificent!'

It was almost time for Marya to begin calling her 'Lady Charlotte', Lydia thought. She said: 'Come down as soon as you've changed, Charlotte.' Charlotte immediately began to unfasten the shoulder-straps which held her train. Lydia went out.

She found Stephen in the drawing-room, sipping sherry. He touched her bare arm and said: 'I love to see you in summer dresses.'

She smiled. 'Thank you.' He looked rather fine himself, she thought, in his grey coat and silver tie. There was more grey and silver in his beard. *We might have been so happy, you and I . . .* Suddenly she wanted to kiss his cheek. She glanced around the room: there was a footman at the sideboard pouring sherry. She had to restrain the impulse. She sat down and accepted a glass from the footman. 'How is Aleks?'

'Much the same as always,' Stephen replied. 'You'll see, he'll be down in a minute. What about Charlotte's dress?'

'The gown is lovely. It's her attitude that disturbs me. She's unwilling to take anything at face value these days. I should hate her to become *cynical*.'

Stephen refused to worry about that. 'You wait until some handsome Guards officer starts paying attention to her – she'll soon change her mind.'

The remark irritated Lydia, implying as it did that all girls were the slaves of their romantic natures. It was the kind of thing Stephen said when he did not want to think about a subject. It made him sound like a hearty, empty-headed country squire, which he was not. But he was convinced that Charlotte was no different from any other eighteen-year-old girl, and he would not hear otherwise. Lydia knew that Charlotte had in her make-up a streak of something wild and un-English which had to be suppressed.

Irrationally, Lydia felt hostile toward Aleks on account of Charlotte. It was not his fault, but he represented the St Petersburg factor, the danger of the past. She shifted restlessly in her chair, and caught Stephen observing her with a shrewd eye. He said: 'You can't possibly be nervous about meeting little Aleks.'

She shrugged. 'Russians are so unpredictable.'

'He's not very Russian.'

She smiled at her husband, but their moment of intimacy had passed, and now there was just the usual qualified affection in her heart.

The door opened. Be calm, Lydia told herself.

Aleks came in. 'Aunt Lydia!' he said, and bowed over her hand.

'How do you do, Aleksei Andreivitch,' she said formally. Then she softened her tone and added: 'Why, you still look eighteen.'

'I wish I were,' he said, and his eyes twinkled.

She asked him about his trip. As he replied, she found herself wondering why he was still unmarried. He had a title which on its own was enough to knock many girls – not to mention their mothers – off their feet; and on top of that he was strikingly good-looking and enormously rich. I'm sure he's broken a few hearts, she thought.

'Your brother and your sisters send their love,' Aleks was saying, 'and ask for your prayers.' He frowned. 'St Petersburg is very unsettled now – it's not the town you knew.'

Stephen said: 'We've heard about this monk.'

'Rasputin. The Czarina believes that God speaks through him, and she has great influence over the Czar. But Rasputin is only a symptom. All the time there are strikes, and sometimes riots. The people no longer believe that the Czar is holy.'

'What is to be done?' Stephen asked.

Aleks sighed. 'Everything. We need efficient farms, more factories, a proper parliament like England's, land reform, trade unions, freedom of speech . . .'

'I shouldn't be in too much of a hurry to have trade unions, if I were you,' Stephen said.

'Perhaps. Still, somehow Russia must join the twentieth century. Either we, the nobility, must do it, or the people will destroy us and do it themselves.'

Lydia thought he sounded more radical than the Radicals. How things must have changed at home, that a prince could talk like this! Her sister Tatyana, Aleks' mother, referred in her letters to 'the troubles' but gave no hint that the nobility was in real danger. But then, Aleks was more like his father, the old Prince Orlov, a political animal. If he were alive today he would talk like this.

Stephen said: 'There is a third possibility, you know; a way in which the aristocracy and the people might yet be united.'

Aleks smiled, as if he knew what was coming. 'And that is?'

'A war.'

Aleks nodded gravely. They think alike, Lydia reflected; Aleks always looked up to Stephen; Stephen was the nearest thing to a father that the boy had, after the old Prince died.

Charlotte came in, and Lydia stared at her in surprise. She was wearing a frock Lydia had never seen, of cream lace lined with chocolate-brown silk. Lydia would never have chosen it – it was rather *striking* – but there was no denying that Charlotte looked ravishing. Where did she buy it? Lydia wondered. When did she start buying clothes without taking me along? Who told her that those colours flatter her dark hair and brown eyes? Does she have a trace of make-up on? And why isn't she wearing a corset?

Stephen was also staring. Lydia noticed that he had stood up, and she almost laughed. It was a dramatic acknowledgement of his daughter's grown-up status, and what was funny was that it was clearly involuntary. In a moment he would feel foolish, and he would realize that standing up every time his daughter walked into a room was a courtesy he could hardly sustain in his own house.

The effect on Aleks was even greater. He sprang to his feet, spilled his sherry, and blushed crimson. Lydia thought: Why, he's shy! He transferred his dripping glass from his right hand to his left, so that he was unable to shake with either, and he stood there looking helpless. It was an awkward moment, for he needed to compose himself before he could greet Charlotte, but he was clearly waiting to greet her before he would compose himself. Lydia was about to make some inane remark just to fill the silence when Charlotte took over.

She pulled the silk handkerchief from Aleks' breast pocket and wiped his right hand with it, saying: 'How do you do, Aleksei Andreivitch,' in Russian. She shook his now-dry right hand, took the glass from his left hand, wiped the glass, wiped the left hand, gave him back the glass, stuffed the handkerchief back into his pocket, and made him sit down. She sat beside him and said: 'Now that you've finished throwing the sherry around, tell me about Diaghilev. He's supposed to be a strange man. Have you met him?'

Aleks smiled. 'Yes, I've met him.'

As Aleks talked, Lydia marvelled. Charlotte had dealt with the awkward moment without hesitation, and had gone on to ask a question – one which she had presumably prepared in advance – which succeeded in taking Orlov's mind off himself and making him feel at ease. And she had done all that as smoothly as if she had had twenty years' practice. Where had she learned such poise?

Lydia caught her husband's eye. He too had noted Charlotte's graciousness, and he was smiling from ear to ear in a glow of fatherly pride.

Feliks paced up and down in St James's Park, pondering what he had seen. From time to time he glanced across the road at the graceful white facade of Walden's house, rising over the high forecourt wall like a noble head above a starched collar. He thought: They believe they are safe in there.

He sat on a bench, in a position from which he could still see the house. Middle-class London swarmed about him, the girls in their outrageous headgear, the clerks and shopkeepers walking homeward in their dark suits and bowler hats. There were gossiping nannies with babies in perambulators or overdressed toddlers; there were top-hatted gentlemen on their way to and from the clubs of St James's; there were liveried footmen walking tiny ugly dogs. A fat woman with a big bag of shopping plumped herself down on the bench beside him and said: 'Hot enough for you?' He was not sure what would be the appropriate reply, so he smiled and looked away.

It seemed that Orlov had realized his life might be

in danger in England. He had shown himself for only a few seconds at the station, and not at all at the house. Feliks guessed that he had requested, in advance, that he be met by a closed coach, for the weather was fine and most people were driving in open landaus.

Until today this killing had been planned in the abstract, Feliks reflected. It had been a matter of international politics, diplomatic quarrels, alliances and ententes, military possibilities, the hypothetical reactions of far-away Kaisers and Czars. Now, suddenly, it was flesh and blood; it was a real man, of a certain size and shape; it was a youthful face with a small moustache, a face which must be smashed by a bullet; it was a short body in a heavy coat, which must be turned into blood and rags by a bomb; it was a clean-shaven throat above a spotted tie, a throat which must be sliced open to gush blood.

Feliks felt completely capable of doing it. More than that, he was eager. There were questions – they would be answered; there were problems – they would be solved; it would take nerve – he had plenty.

He visualized Orlov and Walden inside that beautiful house, in their fine soft clothes, surrounded by quiet servants. Soon they would have dinner at a long table whose polished surface reflected like a mirror the crisp linen and silver cutlery. They would eat with perfectly clean hands, even the fingernails white, and the women wearing gloves. They would consume a tenth of the food provided and send the rest back to the kitchen. They might talk of racehorses or the new ladies' fashions or a king they all knew. Meanwhile the people who were to fight the war shivered in hovels in the cruel Russian climate – yet could still find an extra bowl of potato soup for an itinerant anarchist.

What a joy it will be to kill Orlov, he thought; what sweet revenge. When I have done that I can die satisfied.

He shivered.

'You're catching a cold,' said the fat woman.

Feliks shrugged.

'I've got him a nice lamb chop for his dinner, and I've made an apple pie,' she said.

'Ah,' said Feliks. What on earth was she talking about? He got up from the bench and walked across the grass toward the house. He sat on the ground with his back to a tree. He would have to observe this house for a day or two and find out what kind of life Orlov would lead in London: when he would go out and to where; how he would travel – coach, landau, motor car or cab; how much time he would spend with Walden. Ideally he wanted to be able to predict Orlov's movements and so lie in wait for him. He might achieve that simply by learning his habits. Otherwise he would have to find a way of discovering the Prince's plans in advance – perhaps by bribing a servant in the house.

Then there was the question of what weapon to use and how to get it. The choice would depend upon the detailed circumstances of the killing. Getting it would depend on the Jubilee Street anarchists. For this purpose the amateur-dramatics group could be ignored, as could the Dunstan Houses intellectuals and indeed all those with visible means of support. But there were four or five angry young men who always had money for drinks and, on the rare occasions when they talked politics, spoke of anarchism in terms of expropriating the expropriators, which was jargon for financing the revolution by theft. They would have weapons or know where to get them.

Two young girls who looked like shop assistants strolled by his tree, and he heard one of them say: '. . . told him, if you think just because you take a girl to the Bioscope and buy her a glass of brown ale you can . . .' Then they were past.

A peculiar feeling came over Feliks. He wondered whether the girls had caused it – but no, they meant nothing to him. Am I apprehensive? he thought. No. Fulfilled? No, that comes later. Excited? Hardly.

He finally figured out that he was happy.

It was very odd indeed.

That night Walden went to Lydia's room. After they had made love she slept, and he lay in the dark with her head on his shoulder, remembering St Petersburg in 1895.

He was always travelling in those days – America, Africa, Arabia – mainly because England was not big enough for him and his father both. He found St Petersburg society gay but prim. He liked the Russian landscape and the vodka. Languages came easily to him but Russian was the most difficult he had ever encountered and he enjoyed the challenge.

As the heir to an earldom, Stephen was obliged to

pay a courtesy call on the British Ambassador; and the Ambassador, in his turn, was expected to invite Stephen to parties and introduce him around. Stephen went to the parties because he liked talking politics with diplomats almost as much as he liked gambling with officers and getting drunk with actresses. It was at a reception in the British Embassy that he first met Lydia.

He had heard of her previously. She was spoken of as a paragon of virtue and a great beauty. She *was* beautiful, in a frail, colourless sort of way, with pale skin, pale blond hair, and a white gown. She was also modest, respectable, and scrupulously polite. There seemed to be nothing to her, and Walden detached himself from her company quite quickly.

But later he found himself seated next to her at dinner, and he was obliged to converse with her. The Russians all spoke French, and if they learned a third language it was German, so Lydia had very little English. Fortunately Stephen's French was good. Finding something to talk about was a bigger problem. He said something about the government of Russia, and she replied with the reactionary platitudes that were two-a-penny at the time. He spoke about his enthusiasm, big-game hunting in Africa, and she was interested for a while, until he mentioned the naked black pygmies, at which point she blushed and turned away to talk with the man on her other side. Stephen told himself he was not very interested in her, for she was the kind of girl one married, and he was not planning to marry. Still she left him with the nagging feeling that there was more to her than met the eye.

Lying in bed with her nineteen years later, Walden thought: She still gives me that nagging feeling; and he smiled ruefully in the dark.

He had seen her once more that evening in St Petersburg. After dinner he had lost his way in the labyrinthine embassy building, and had wandered into the music-room. She was there alone, sitting at the piano, filling the room with wild, passionate music. The tune was unfamiliar and almost discordant; but it was Lydia that fascinated Stephen. The pale, untouchable beauty was gone: her eyes flashed, her head tossed, her body trembled with emotion, and she seemed altogether a different woman.

He never forgot that music. Later he discovered that it had been Tchaikovsky's piano concerto in B flat minor, and since then he went to hear it played at every opportunity, although he never told Lydia why.

When he left the embassy he went back to his hotel to change his clothes, for he had an appointment to play cards at midnight. He was a keen gambler but not a self-destructive one: he knew how much he could afford to lose, and when he had lost it he stopped playing. Had he run up enormous debts he would have been obliged to ask his father to pay them, and that he could not bear to do. Sometimes he won quite large sums. However, that was not the appeal of gambling for him: he liked the masculine companionship, the drinking, and the late hours.

He did not keep that midnight rendezvous. Pritchard, his valet, was tying Stephen's tie when the British Ambassador knocked on the door of the hotel suite.

His Excellency looked as if he had got out of bed and dressed hastily. Stephen's first thought was that some kind of revolution was going on and all the British would have to take refuge in the embassy.

'Bad news, I'm afraid,' said the Ambassador. 'You'd better sit down. Cable from England. It's your father.'

The old tyrant was dead of a heart attack at sixty-five.

'Well, I'm damned,' Stephen said. 'So soon.'

'My deepest sympathy,' the Ambassador said.

'It was very good of you to come personally.'

'Not at all. Anything I can do.'

'You're very kind.'

The Ambassador shook his hand and left.

Stephen stared into space, thinking about the old man. He had been immensely tall, with a will of iron and a sour disposition. His sarcasm could bring tears to your eyes. There were three ways to deal with him: you could become like him, you could go under, or you could go away. Stephen's mother, a sweet, helpless Victorian girl, had gone under, and died young. Stephen had gone away.

He pictured his father lying in a coffin, and thought: You're helpless at last. Now you can't make housemaids cry, or footmen tremble, or children run and hide. You're powerless to arrange marriages, evict tenants, or defeat parliamentary bills. You'll send no more thieves to jail, transport no more agitators to Australia. Ashes to ashes, dust to dust.

In later years he revised his opinion of his father. Now, in 1914, at the age of fifty, Walden could admit to himself that he had inherited some of his father's values: love of knowledge, a belief in rationalism, a commitment to good work as the justification of a man's existence. But back in 1895 there had been only bitterness.

Pritchard had brought a bottle of whisky on a tray and said: 'This is a sad day, my lord.'

That *my lord* startled Stephen. He and his brother had courtesy titles – Stephen's was Lord Highcombe – but they were always called 'sir' by the servants, and 'my lord' was reserved for their father. Now, of course, Stephen was the Earl of Walden. Along with the title, he now possessed several thousands of acres in the south of England, a big chunk of Scotland, six race-horses, Walden Hall, a villa in Monte Carlo, a shooting-box in Scotland and a seat in the House of Lords.

He would have to live at Walden Hall. It was the family seat, and the Earl always lived there. He would put in electric light, he decided. He would sell some of the farms and invest in London property and North American railroads. He would make his maiden speech in the House of Lords – what would he speak on? Foreign policy, probably. There were tenants to be looked after, several households to be managed. He would have to appear in court in the season, and give shooting parties and hunt balls—

He needed a wife.

The role of Earl of Walden could not be played by a bachelor. Someone must be hostess at all those parties, someone must reply to invitations, discuss menus with cooks, allocate bedrooms to guests, and sit at the foot of the long table in the dining-room of Walden Hall. There must be a Countess of Walden.

There must be an heir.

'I need a wife, Pritchard.'

'Yes, my lord. Our bachelor days are over.'

The next day Walden saw Lydia's father and formally asked permission to call on her.

Twenty years later he found it difficult to imagine how he could have been so wickedly irresponsible, even in his youth. He had never asked himself whether she was the right wife for him, only whether she was suited to be a countess. He had never wondered whether he could make her happy. He had assumed that the hidden passion released when she played the piano would be released for him, and he had been wrong.

He called on her every day for two weeks – there was no possibility of getting home in time for his father's funeral – and then he proposed, not to her but to her father. Her father saw the match in the same practical terms as Walden. Walden explained that he wanted to marry immediately, although he was in mourning, because he had to get home and manage the estate. Lydia's father understood perfectly. They were married six weeks later.

What an arrogant young fool I was, he thought. I imagined that England would always rule the world and I would always rule my own heart.

The moon came out from behind a cloud and illuminated the bedroom. He looked down at Lydia's sleeping face. I didn't foresee this, he thought; I didn't know that I would fall helplessly, hopelessly in love with you. I asked only that we should like each other, and in the end that was enough for you but not for me. I never thought that I would *need* your smile, yearn for your kisses, long for you to come to *my* room at night; I never thought that I would be frightened, *terrified* of losing you.

She murmured in her sleep and turned over. He pulled his arm from under her neck, then sat up on the edge of the bed. If he stayed any longer he would nod off, and it would not do to have Lydia's maid find them in bed together when she came in with the morning cup of tea. He put on his dressing-gown and his carpet slippers and walked softly out of the room, through the twin dressing-rooms, and into his own bedroom. I'm such a lucky man, he thought as he lay down to sleep.

Walden surveyed the breakfast table. There were pots of coffee, China tea and Indian tea; jugs of cream, milk and cordial; a big bowl of hot porridge; plates of scones and toast; and little pots of marmalade, honey and jam. On the sideboard was a row of silver dishes, each warmed by its own spirit lamp, containing scrambled eggs, sausages, bacon, kidneys and haddock. On the cold table were pressed beef, ham and tongue. The fruit bowl, on a table of its own, was piled with nectarines, oranges, melons and strawberries.

This ought to put Aleks in a good mood, he thought.

He helped himself to eggs and kidneys and sat down.

The Russians would have their price, he thought; they would want something in return for their promise of military help. He was worried about what the price might be. If they were to ask for something England could not possibly grant, the whole deal would collapse immediately, and then . . .

It was his job to make sure it did not collapse.

He would have to manipulate Aleks. The thought made him uncomfortable. Having known the boy for so long should have been a help, but in fact it might have been easier to negotiate in a tough way with someone about whom one did not care personally.

I must put my feelings aside, he thought; we must have Russia.

He poured coffee and took some scones and honey. A minute later Aleks came in, looking bright-eyed and well-scrubbed. 'Sleep well?' Walden asked him.

'Wonderfully well.' Aleks took a nectarine and began to eat it with a knife and fork.

'Is that all you're having?' Walden said. 'You used to love English breakfast – I remember you eating porridge, cream, eggs, beef and strawberries and then asking cook for more toast.'

'I'm not a growing boy any more, Uncle Stephen.'

I might do well to remember that, Walden thought.

After breakfast they went into the morning-room. 'Our new five-year plan for the army and navy is about to be announced,' Aleks said.

That's what he does, Walden thought; he tells you something before he asks you for something. He remembered Aleks saying: I'm planning to read Clausewitz this summer, Uncle. By the way, may I bring a guest to Scotland for the shooting?

'The budget for the next five years is seven-and-a-half billion roubles,' Aleks went on.

At ten roubles to the pound sterling, Walden calculated, that made £750 million. 'It's a massive programme,' he said, 'but I wish you had begun it five years ago.'

'So do I,' said Aleks.

'The chances are that the programme will hardly have started before we're at war.'

Aleks shrugged.

Walden thought: He won't commit himself to a forecast of how soon Russia might be at war, of course. 'The first thing you should do is increase the size of the guns on your Dreadnoughts.'

Aleks shook his head. 'Our third Dreadnought is about to be launched. The fourth is being built now. Both will have 12-inch guns.'

'It's not enough, Aleks. Churchill has gone over to 15-inch guns for ours.'

'And he's right. Our commanders know that, but our politicians don't. You know Russia, Uncle: new ideas are viewed with the utmost distrust. Innovation takes for ever.'

We're fencing, Walden thought. 'What *is* your priority?'

'A hundred million roubles will be spent immediately on the Black Sea fleet.'

'I should have thought the North Sea was more important.' For England, anyway.

'We have a more Asian viewpoint than you – our bullying neighbour is Turkey, not Germany.'

'They might be allies.'

'They might indeed.' Aleks hesitated. 'The great weakness of the Russian Navy,' he went on, 'is that we have no warm-water port.'

It sounded like the beginning of a prepared speech. This is it, Walden thought; we're getting to the heart of the matter now. But he continued to fence. 'What about Odessa?'

'On the Black Sea coast. While the Turks hold Constantinople and Gallipoli, they control the passage between the Black Sea and the Mediterranean; so for strategic purposes the Black Sea might as well be an inland lake.'

'Which is why the Russian Empire has been trying to push southward for hundreds of years.'

'Why not? We're Slavs, and many of the Balkan peoples are Slavs. If they want national freedom, of course we sympathize.'

'Indeed. Still, if they get it, they will probably let your navy pass freely into the Mediterranean.'

'Slav control of the Balkans would help us. Russian control would help even more.'

'No doubt – although it's not on the cards, as far as I can see.'

'Would you like to give the matter some thought?'

Walden opened his mouth to speak then closed it abruptly. This is it, he thought; this is what they want, this is the price. We can't give Russia the Balkans, for

God's sake! If the deal depends on that, there will be no deal . . .

Aleks was saying: 'If we are to fight alongside you, we must be strong. The area we are talking about is the area in which we need strengthening, so naturally we look to you for help there.'

That was putting it as plainly as could be: Give us the Balkans and we'll fight with you.

Pulling himself together, Walden frowned as if puzzled and said: 'If Britain had control of the Balkans, we could – at least in theory – give the area to you. But we can't give you what we haven't got, so I'm not sure how we can strengthen you – as you put it – in that area.'

Aleks' reply was so quick that it must have been rehearsed. 'But you might acknowledge the Balkans as a Russian sphere of influence.'

Aah, that's not so bad, Walden thought. That we *might* be able to manage.

He was enormously relieved. He decided to test Aleks' determination before winding up the discussion. He said: 'We could certainly agree to favour you over Austria or Turkey in that part of the world.'

Aleks shook his head. 'We want more than that,' he said firmly.

It had been worth a try. Aleks was young and shy, but he could not be pushed around. Worse luck.

Walden needed time to reflect, now. For Britain to do as Russia wanted would mean a significant shift in international alignments, and such shifts, like movements of the earth's crust, caused earthquakes in unexpected places.

'You may like to talk with Churchill before we go any farther,' Aleks said with a little smile.

You know damn well I will, Walden thought. He realized suddenly how well Aleks had handled the whole thing. First he had scared Walden with a completely outrageous demand; then, when he put forward his real demand, Walden had been so relieved that he welcomed it.

I thought I was going to manipulate Aleks, but in the event he manipulated me.

Walden smiled. 'I'm proud of you, my boy,' he said.

That morning Feliks figured out when, where and how he was going to kill Prince Orlov.

The plan began to take shape in his mind while he read *The Times* in the library of the Jubilee Street club. His imagination was sparked by a paragraph in the 'Court Circular' column:

> Prince Aleksei Andreivitch Orlov arrived from St Petersburg yesterday. He is to be the guest of the Earl and Countess of Walden for the London Season. Prince Orlov will be presented to their Majesties the King and Queen at the Court on Thursday, June 4th.

Now he knew for certain that Orlov would be at a certain place, on a certain date, at a certain time.

Information of this kind was essential to a carefully planned assassination. Feliks had anticipated that he would get the information either by speaking to one of Walden's servants or by observing Orlov and identifying some habitual rendezvous. Now he had no need to take the risks involved in interviewing servants or trailing people. He wondered whether Orlov knew that his movements were being advertised by the newspapers, as if for the benefit of assassins. It was typically English, he thought.

The next problem was how to get sufficiently close to Orlov to kill him. Even Feliks would have difficulty getting into a royal palace. But this question also was answered by *The Times*. On the same page as the Court Circular, sandwiched between a report of a dance given by Lady Bailey and the details of the latest wills, he read:

THE KING'S COURT
Arrangements for Carriages

> In order to facilitate the arrangements for calling the carriages of the company at their Majesties' Courts at Buckingham Palace, we are requested to state that in the case of the company having the privilege of the entrée at the Pimlico entrance the coachman of each carriage returning to take up is required to leave with the constable stationed on the left of the gateway a card distinctly written with the name of the lady or gentleman to whom the carriage belongs, and in the case of the carriages of the

general company returning to take up at the grand entrance a similar card should be handed to the constable stationed on the left of the archway leading to the Quadrangle of the Palace.

To enable the company to receive the advantage of the above arrangements, it is necessary that a footman should accompany each carriage, as no provision can be made for calling the carriages beyond giving the names to the footmen waiting at the door, with whom it rests to bring the carriage. The doors will be open for the reception of the company at 8.30 o'clock.

Feliks read it several times: there was something about the prose style of *The Times* that made it extremely difficult to comprehend. It seemed at least to mean that as people left the palace their footmen were sent running to fetch their carriages, which would be parked somewhere else.

There must be a way, he thought, that I can contrive to be in or on the Walden carriage when it returns to the palace to pick them up.

One major difficulty remained. He had no gun.

He could have got one easily enough in Geneva, but then to have carried it across international frontiers would have been risky: he might have been refused entry into England if his baggage had been searched.

It was surely just as easy to get a gun in London, but he did not know how, and he was most reluctant to make open inquiries. He had observed gun shops in the West End of London and noted that all the customers who went in and out looked thoroughly upper-class: Feliks would not get served in there even if he had the money to buy their beautifully made precision firearms. He had spent time in low-class pubs, where guns were surely bought and sold among criminals, but he had not seen it happen, which was hardly surprising. His only hope was the anarchists. He had got into conversation with those of them whom he thought 'serious', but they never talked of weapons, doubtless because of Feliks' presence. The trouble was that he had not been around long enough to be trusted. There were always police spies in anarchist groups, and while this did not prevent the anarchists welcoming newcomers, it made them wary.

Now the time for surreptitious investigation had run out. He would have to ask directly how guns were to be obtained. It would require careful handling. And immediately afterwards he would have to sever his ties with Jubilee Street and move to another part of London, to avoid the risk of being traced.

He considered the young Jewish tearaways of Jubilee Street. They were angry and violent boys. Unlike their parents, they refused to work like slaves in the sweat-shops of the East End, sewing the suits that the aristocracy ordered from Savile Row tailors. Unlike their parents, they paid no attention to the conservative sermonizing of the rabbis. But as yet they had not decided whether the solutions to their problems lay in politics or in crime.

His best prospect, he decided, was Nathan Sabelinsky. A man of about twenty, he had rather Slavic good looks, and wore very high stiff collars and a yellow waistcoat. Feliks had seen him around the spielers off the Commercial Road: he must have had money to spend on gambling as well as clothes.

He looked around the library. The other occupants were an old man asleep, a woman in a heavy coat reading *Das Kapital* in German and making notes, and a Lithuanian Jew bent over a Russian newspaper, reading with the aid of a magnifying glass. Feliks left the room and went downstairs. There was no sign of Nathan or any of his friends. It was a little early for him: if he worked at all, Feliks thought, he worked at night.

Feliks went back to Dunstan Houses. He packed his razor, his clean underwear and his spare shirt in his cardboard suitcase. He told Milly, Rudolf Rocker's wife: 'I've found a room. I'll come back this evening to say thank you to Rudolf.' He strapped the suitcase to the back seat of the bicycle and rode west, to central London, then north to Camden Town. Here he found a street of high, once-grand houses which had been built for pretentious middle-class families who had now moved to the suburbs at the ends of the new railway lines. In one of them Feliks rented a dingy room from an Irish woman called Bridget. He paid her ten shillings in advance of two weeks' rent.

By midday he was back in Stepney, outside Nathan's home in Sidney Street. It was a small row house of the two-rooms-up-and-two-down type. The front door was wide open. Feliks walked in.

The noise and the smell hit him like a blow. There, in a room about twelve feet square, some fifteen or twenty people were working at tailoring. Men were using machines, women were sewing by hand, and children were pressing finished garments. Steam rose from the ironing-boards to mingle with the smell of sweat. The machines clattered, the irons hissed, and the workers jabbered incessantly in Yiddish. Pieces of cloth cut ready for stitching were piled on every available patch of floor space. Nobody looked up at Feliks: they were all working furiously fast.

He spoke to the nearest person, a girl with a baby at her breast. She was hand-sewing buttons on to the sleeve of a jacket. 'Is Nathan here?' he said.

'Upstairs,' she said without pausing in her work.

Feliks went out of the room and up the narrow staircase. Each of the two small bedrooms had four beds. Most of them were occupied, presumably by people who worked at night. He found Nathan in the back room, sitting on the edge of a bed, buttoning his shirt.

Nathan saw him and said: 'Feliks, *wie gehts*?'

'I need to talk to you,' Feliks said in Yiddish.

'So talk.'

'Come outside.'

Nathan put on his coat and they went out into Sidney Street. They stood in the sunshine, close to the open window of the sweat-shop, their conversation masked by the noise from inside.

'My father's trade,' said Nathan. 'He'll pay a girl fivepence for machining a pair of trousers – an hour's work for her. He'll pay another threepence to the girls who cut, press, and sew on buttons. Then he will take the trousers to a West End tailor and get paid ninepence. Profit, one penny – enough to buy one slice of bread. If he asks the West End tailor for tenpence he'll be thrown out of the shop, and the work will be given to one of the dozens of Jewish tailors out in the street with their machines under their arms. I won't live like that.'

'Is this why you're an anarchist?'

'Those people make the most beautiful clothes in the world – but did you see how *they* are dressed?'

'And how will things be changed – by violence?'

'I think so.'

'I was sure you would feel this way. Nathan, I need a gun.'

Nathan laughed nervously. 'What for?'

'Why do anarchists usually want guns?'

'You tell me, Feliks.'

'To steal from thieves, to oppress tyrants, and to kill murderers.'

'Which are you going to do?'

'I'll tell you – if you *really* want to know . . .'

Nathan thought for a moment, then said: 'Go to the Frying Pan pub on the corner of Brick Lane and Thrawl Street. See Garfield the Dwarf.'

'Thank you!' said Feliks, unable to keep the note of triumph out of his voice. 'How much will I have to pay?'

'Five shillings for a pinfire.'

'I'd rather have something more reliable.'

'Good guns are expensive.'

'I'll just have to haggle.' Feliks shook Nathan's hand. 'Thank you.'

Nathan watched him climb on his bicycle. 'Maybe you'll tell me about it, afterwards.'

Feliks smiled. 'You'll read about it in the papers.' He waved a hand and rode off.

He cycled along Whitechapel Road and Whitechapel High Street, then turned right into Osborn Street. Immediately, the character of the streets changed. This was the most run-down part of London he had yet seen. The streets were narrow and very dirty, the air smoky and noisome, the people mostly wretched. The gutters were choked with filth. But despite all that the place was as busy as a beehive. Men ran up and down with handcarts, crowds gathered around street stalls, prostitutes worked every corner, and the workshops of carpenters and bootmakers spilled out on to the pavements.

Feliks left his bicycle outside the door of the Frying Pan: if it was taken he would just have to steal another one. To enter the pub he had to step over what looked like a dead cat. Inside was a single room, low and bare, with a bar at the far end. Older men and women sat on benches around the walls, while younger people stood in the middle of the room. Feliks went to the bar and asked for a glass of ale and a cold sausage.

He looked around and spotted Garfield the Dwarf. He had not seen him before because the man was standing on a chair. He was about four feet tall, with a large head and a middle-aged face. A very big black dog sat on the floor beside his chair. He was talking to two large, tough-looking men dressed in leather waistcoats and collarless shirts. Perhaps they were bodyguards. Feliks noted their large bellies and grinned to himself, thinking: I'll eat them up alive. The two men held quart pots of ale, but the dwarf was drinking what looked like gin. The barman handed Feliks his drink and his sausage. 'And a glass of the best gin,' Feliks said.

A young woman at the bar looked at him and said: 'Is that for me?' She smiled coquettishly, showing rotten teeth. Feliks looked away.

When the gin came he paid and walked over to the group, who were standing near a small window which looked on to the street. Feliks stood between them and the door. He addressed the dwarf. 'Mr Garfield?'

'Who wants him?' said Garfield in a squeaky voice.

Feliks offered the glass of gin. 'May I speak to you about business?'

Garfield took the glass, drained it, and said: 'No.'

Feliks sipped his ale. It was sweeter and less fizzy than Swiss beer. He said: 'I wish to buy a gun.'

'I don't know what you've come here for, then.'

'I heard about you at the Jubilee Street club.'

'Anarchist, are you?'

Feliks said nothing.

Garfield looked him up and down. 'What kind of gun would you want, if I had any?'

'A revolver. A good one.'

'Something like a Browning seven-shot?'

'That would be perfect.'

'I haven't got one. If I had I wouldn't sell it. And if I sold it I'd have to ask five pounds.'

'I was told a pound at the most.'

'You was told wrong.'

Feliks reflected. The dwarf had decided that, as a foreigner and an anarchist, Feliks could be rooked. All right, Feliks thought, we'll play it your way. 'I can't afford more than two pounds.'

'I couldn't come down below four.'

'Would that include a box of ammunition?'

'All right, four pounds including a box of ammunition.'

'Agreed,' Feliks said. He noticed one of the bodyguards smothering a grin. After paying for the drinks and the sausage, Feliks had three pounds fifteen shillings and a penny.

Garfield nodded at one of his companions. The man went behind the bar and out through the back door. Feliks ate his sausage. A minute or two later the man came back carrying what looked like a bundle of rags. He glanced at Garfield, who nodded. The man handed the bundle to Feliks.

Feliks unfolded the rags and found a revolver and a small box. He took the gun from its wrappings and examined it.

Garfield said: 'Keep it down, no need to show it to the whole bleeding world.'

The gun was clean and oiled, and the action worked smoothly. Feliks said: 'If I do not look at it, how do I know it is good?'

'Where do you think you are, Harrods?'

Feliks opened the box of cartridges and loaded the chambers with swift, practised movements.

'Put the fucking thing away,' the dwarf hissed. 'Give me the money quick and fuck off out of it. You're fucking mad.'

A bubble of tension rose in Feliks' throat, and he swallowed dryly. He took a step back and pointed the gun at the dwarf.

Garfield said: 'Jesus, Mary and Joseph.'

'Shall I test the gun?' Feliks said.

The two bodyguards stepped sideways in opposite directions so that Feliks could not cover them both with the one gun. Feliks' heart sank: he had not expected them to be that smart. Their next move would be to jump him. The pub was suddenly silent. Feliks realized he could not get to the door before one of the bodyguards reached him. The big dog growled, sensing the tension in the air.

Feliks smiled and shot the dog.

The bang of the gun was deafening in the little room. Nobody moved. The dog slumped to the floor, bleeding. The dwarf's bodyguards were frozen where they stood.

Feliks took another step back, reached behind him, and found the door. He opened it, still pointing the gun at Garfield, and stepped out.

He slammed the door, stuffed the gun in his coat pocket, and jumped on his bicycle.

He heard the pub door open. He pushed himself off and began to pedal. Somebody grabbed his coat sleeve. He pedalled harder and broke free. He heard a shot, and ducked reflexively. Someone screamed. He dodged around an ice-cream vendor and turned a corner. In the distance he heard a police whistle. He looked behind. Nobody was following him.

Half a minute later he was lost in the warrens of Whitechapel.

He thought: Six bullets left.

CHAPTER THREE

Charlotte was ready. The gown, agonized over for so long, was perfect. To complete it she wore a single blush rose in her corsage and carried a spray of the same flowers, covered in chiffon. Her diamond tiara was fixed firmly to her upswept hair, and the two white plumes were securely fastened. Everything was fine.

She was terrified.

'As I enter the Throne Room,' she said to Marya, 'my train will drop off, my tiara will fall over my eyes, my hair will come loose, my feathers will lean sideways, and I shall trip over the hem of my gown and go flat on the floor. The assembled company will burst out laughing, and no one will laugh louder than Her Majesty the Queen. I shall run out of the palace and into the park and throw myself into the lake.'

'You ought not to talk like that,' said Marya. Then, more gently, she added: 'You'll be the loveliest of them all.'

Charlotte's mother came into the bedroom. She held Charlotte at arm's length and looked at her. 'My dear, you're beautiful,' she said, and kissed her.

Charlotte put her arms around Mama's neck and

pressed her cheek against her mother's, the way she had used to as a child, when she had been fascinated by the velvet smoothness of Mama's complexion. When she drew away, she was surprised to see a hint of tears in her mother's eyes.

'You're beautiful too, Mama,' she said.

Lydia's gown was of ivory charmeuse, with a train of old ivory brocade lined in purple chiffon. Being a married lady she wore three feathers in her hair as opposed to Charlotte's two. Her bouquet was sweet-peas and petunia roses.

'Are you ready?' she said.

'I've been ready for ages,' Charlotte said.

'Pick up your train.'

Charlotte picked up her train the way she had been taught.

Mama nodded approvingly. 'Shall we go?'

Marya opened the door. Charlotte stood aside to let her mother go first, but Mama said: 'No, dear – it's your night.'

They walked in procession, Marya bringing up the rear, along the corridor and down to the landing. When Charlotte reached the top of the grand staircase she heard a burst of applause.

The whole household was gathered at the foot of the stairs: housekeeper, cook, footmen, maids, skivvies, grooms and boys. A sea of faces looked up at her with pride and delight. Charlotte was touched by their affection: it was a big night for them, too, she realized.

In the centre of the throng was Papa, looking magnificent in a black velvet tail-coat, knee breeches, and silk stockings, with a sword at his hip and a cocked hat in his hand.

Charlotte walked slowly down the stairs.

Papa kissed her and said: 'My little girl.'

The cook, who had known her long enough to take liberties, plucked at her sleeve and whispered: 'You look wonderful, m'lady.'

Charlotte squeezed her hand and said: 'Thank you, Mrs Harding.'

Aleks bowed to her. He was resplendent in the uniform of an admiral in the Russian Navy. What a handsome man he is, Charlotte thought; I wonder whether someone will fall in love with him tonight.

Two footmen opened the front door. Papa took Charlotte's elbow and gently steered her out. Mama followed on Aleks' arm. Charlotte thought: If I can just keep my mind blank all evening, and go automatically wherever people lead me, I shall be all right.

The coach was waiting outside. William the coachman and Charles the footman stood, wearing the Walden livery, at attention on either side of the door. William, stout and greying, was calm; but Charles looked excited. Papa handed Charlotte into the coach, and she sat down gratefully. I haven't fallen over yet, she thought.

The other three got in. Pritchard brought a hamper and put it on the floor of the coach before closing the door.

The coach pulled away.

Charlotte looked at the hamper. 'A picnic?' she said. 'But we're only going half a mile!'

'Wait till you see the queue,' Papa said. 'It will take us almost an hour to get there.'

It occurred to Charlotte that she might be more bored than nervous this evening.

Sure enough, the carriage stopped at the Admiralty end of The Mall, half a mile from Buckingham Palace. Papa opened the hamper and took out a bottle of champagne. The basket also contained chicken sandwiches, hothouse peaches, and a cake.

Charlotte sipped a glass of champagne but she could not eat anything. She looked out of the window. The pavements were thronged with idlers watching the procession of the mighty. She saw a tall man with a thin, handsome face leaning on a bicycle and staring intently at their coach. Something about his look made Charlotte shiver and turn away.

After such a grand exit from the house, she found that the anticlimax of sitting in the queue was calming. By the time the coach passed through the palace gates and approached the grand entrance she was beginning to feel more her normal self – sceptical, irreverent and impatient.

The coach stopped and the door was opened. Charlotte gathered her train in her left arm, picked up her skirts with her right hand, stepped down from the coach and walked into the palace.

The great red-carpeted hall was a blaze of light and colour. Despite her scepticism she felt a thrill of excitement when she saw the crowd of white-gowned women and men in glittering uniforms. The diamonds flashed, the swords clanked and the plumes bobbed.

Red-coated Beefeaters stood at attention on either side.

Charlotte and Mama left their wraps in the cloakroom then, escorted by Papa and Aleks, walked slowly through the hall and up the grand staircase, between the Yeomen of the Guard with their halberds and the massed red and white roses. From there they went through the picture gallery and into the first of three state drawing-rooms with enormous chandeliers and mirror-bright parquet floors. Here the procession ended and people stood around in groups, chatting and admiring one another's clothes. Charlotte saw her cousin Belinda with Uncle George and Aunt Clarissa. The two families greeted each other.

Uncle George was wearing the same clothes as Papa, but because he was so fat and red-faced he looked awful in them. Charlotte wondered how Aunt Clarissa, who was young and pretty, felt about being married to such a lump.

Papa was surveying the room as if looking for someone. 'Have you seen Churchill?' he said to Uncle George.

'Good Lord, what do you want him for?'

Papa took out his watch. 'We must take our places in the Throne Room – we'll leave you to look after Charlotte, if we may, Clarissa.' Papa, Mama and Aleks left.

Belinda said to Charlotte: 'Your dress is gorgeous.'

'It's awfully uncomfortable.'

'I *knew* you were going to say that!'

'You're ever so pretty.'

'Thank you.' Belinda lowered her voice. 'I say, Prince Orlov is rather dashing.'

'He's very sweet.'

'I think he's more than *sweet*.'

'What's that funny look in your eye?'

Belinda lowered her voice even more. 'You and I must have a long talk very soon.'

'About what?'

'Remember what we discussed in the hideaway? When we took those books from the library at Walden Hall?'

Charlotte looked at her uncle and aunt, but they had turned away to talk to a dark-skinned man in a pink satin turban. 'Of course I remember.'

'About that.'

Silence descended suddenly. The crowd fell back toward the sides of the room to make a gangway in the middle. Charlotte looked around and saw the King and Queen enter the drawing-room, followed by their pages, several members of the Royal Family, and the Indian bodyguard.

There was a great sigh of rustling silk as every woman in the room sank to the floor in a curtsey.

In the Throne Room, the orchestra concealed in the Minstrels' Gallery struck up 'God Save the King'. Lydia looked toward the huge doorway guarded by gilt giants. Two attendants walked in backwards, one carrying a gold stick and one a silver. The King and Queen entered at a stately pace, smiling faintly. They mounted the dais and stood in front of the twin thrones. The rest of their entourage took their places near by, remaining standing.

Queen Mary wore a gown of gold brocade and a crown of emeralds. She's no beauty, Lydia thought, but they say he adores her. She had once been engaged to her husband's elder brother, who had died of pneumonia; and the switch to the new heir to the throne had seemed coldly political at the time. However, everyone now agreed that she was a good queen and a good wife. Lydia would have liked to know her personally.

The presentations began. One by one the wives of ambassadors came forward, curtsied to the King, curtsied to the Queen, then backed away. The ambassadors followed, dressed in a great variety of gaudy comic-opera uniforms, all but the United States Ambassador who wore ordinary black evening clothes, as if to remind everyone that Americans did not really believe in this sort of nonsense.

As the ritual went on, Lydia looked around the room, at the crimson satin on the walls, the heroic frieze below the ceiling, the enormous candelabra, and the thousands of flowers. She loved pomp and ritual, beautiful clothes and elaborate ceremonies; they moved and soothed her at the same time. She caught the eye of the Duchess of Devonshire, the Mistress of the Robes, and they exchanged a discreet smile. She spotted John Burns, the socialist President of the Board of Trade, and was amused to see the extravagant gilt embroidery on his court dress.

When the diplomatic presentations ended, the King and Queen sat down. The Royal Family, the diplomats, and the most senior nobility followed suit. Lydia and Walden, along with the lesser nobility, had to remain standing.

At last the presentation of the debutantes began. Each girl paused just outside the Throne Room while an attendant took her train from her arm and spread it behind her. Then she began the endless walk along the red carpet to the thrones, with all eyes on her. If a girl could look graceful and unselfconscious there, she could do it anywhere.

As the debutante approached the dais she handed her invitation card to the Lord Chamberlain, who read out her name. She curtsied to the King, then to the Queen. Few girls curtsied elegantly, Lydia thought. She had had a great deal of trouble getting Charlotte to practise at all: perhaps other mothers had the same problem. After the curtsies the debutante walked on, careful not to turn her back on the thrones until she was safely hidden in the watching crowd.

The girls followed one another so closely that each was in danger of treading on the train of the one in front. The ceremony seemed to Lydia to be less personal, more perfunctory than it had used to be. She herself had been presented to Queen Victoria in the season of 1896, the year after she married Walden. The old Queen had not sat on a throne, but on a high stool which gave the impression that she was standing. Lydia had been surprised at how little Victoria was. She had had to kiss the Queen's hand. That part of the ceremony had now been dispensed with, presumably to save time. It made the court seem like a factory for turning out the maximum number of debutantes in the shortest possible time. Still, the girls of today did not know the difference and probably would not care if they did.

Suddenly Charlotte was at the entrance, and the attendant was laying down her train, then giving her a gentle push, and she was walking along the red carpet, head held high, looking perfectly serene and confident. Lydia thought: This is the moment I have lived for.

The girl ahead of Charlotte curtsied – and then the unthinkable happened.

Instead of getting up from her curtsey, the debutante looked at the King, stretched out her arms in a gesture of supplication, and cried in a loud voice:

'*Your Majesty, for God's sake stop torturing women!*'

Lydia thought: A suffragette!

Her eyes flashed to her daughter. Charlotte was standing dead still, halfway to the dais, staring at the tableau with an expression of horror on her ashen face.

The shocked silence in the Throne Room lasted only for a split second. Two gentlemen-in-waiting were the fastest to react. They sprang forward, took the girl firmly by either arm, and marched her unceremoniously away.

The Queen was blushing crimson. The King managed to appear as if nothing had happened. Lydia looked again at Charlotte, thinking: Why did my daughter have to be next in line?

Now all eyes were on Charlotte. Lydia wanted to call out to her: Pretend it never happened! Just carry on!

Charlotte stood still. A little colour came back into her cheeks. Lydia could see that she was taking a deep breath.

Then she walked forward. Lydia could not breathe. Charlotte handed her card to the Lord Chamberlain, who said: 'Presentation of Lady Charlotte Walden.' Charlotte stood before the King.

Lydia thought: Careful!

Charlotte curtsied perfectly.

She curtsied again to the Queen.

She half-turned, and walked away.

Lydia let out her breath in a long sigh.

The woman standing next to Lydia – a baroness whom she vaguely recognized but did not really know – whispered: 'She handled that very well.'

'She's my daughter,' Lydia said with a smile.

Walden was secretly amused by the suffragette. Spirited girl! he thought. Of course, if *Charlotte* had done such a thing at the court he would have been horrified, but as it was someone else's daughter he regarded the incident as a welcome break in the interminable ceremony. He had noticed how Charlotte had carried on, unruffled: he would have expected no less of her. She was a highly self-assured young lady, and in his opinion Lydia should congratulate herself on the girl's upbringing instead of worrying all the time.

He had used to enjoy these occasions, years ago. As a young man he had quite liked to put on court dress and cut a dash. In those days he had had the legs for it, too. Now he felt foolish in knee-breeches and silk stockings, not to mention a damn great steel sword. And he had attended so many courts that the colourful ritual no longer fascinated him.

He wondered how King George felt about it. Walden liked the King. Of course, by comparison with his father Edward VII, George was a rather colourless, mild fellow. The crowds would never shout 'Good old Georgie!' the way they had shouted 'Good old Teddy!' But in the end they would like George for his quiet charm and his modest way of life. He knew how to be firm, although as yet he did it too rarely; and Walden liked a man who could shoot straight. Walden thought he would turn out very well indeed.

Finally the last debutante curtsied and passed on, and the King and Queen stood up. The orchestra played the national anthem again, the King bowed, and the Queen curtsied, first to the ambassadors, then to the ambassadors' wives, then the Duchesses, and lastly the Ministers. The King took the Queen by the hand. The pages picked up her train. The attendants went out backwards. The royal couple left, followed by the rest of the company in order of precedence.

They divided to go into three supper-rooms: one for the Royal Family and their close friends, one for the diplomatic corps, and one for the rest. Walden was a friend, but not an intimate friend, of the King: he went with the general assembly. Aleks went with the diplomats.

In the supper-room Walden met up with his family again. Lydia was glowing. Walden said: 'Congratulations, Charlotte.'

Lydia said: 'Who was that awful girl?'

'I heard someone say she's the daughter of an architect,' Walden replied.

'That explains it,' said Lydia.

Charlotte looked mystified. 'Why does that explain it?'

Walden smiled. 'Your Mama means that the girl is not quite out of the top drawer.'

'But why does she think the King tortures women?'

'She was talking about the suffragettes. But let's not go into all that tonight; this is a great occasion for us. Let's have supper. It looks marvellous.'

There was a long buffet table loaded with flowers and hot and cold food. Servants in the scarlet-and-gold royal livery waited to offer the guests lobster, filleted trout, quail, York ham, plovers' eggs, and a host of pastries and desserts. Walden got a loaded plate and sat down to eat. After standing about in the Throne Room for more than two hours he was hungry.

Sooner or later Charlotte would have to learn about the suffragettes, their hunger strikes, and the consequent force-feeding; but the subject was indelicate, to say the least, and the longer she remained in blissful ignorance the better, Walden thought. At her age life should be all parties and picnics, frocks and hats, gossip and flirtation.

But everyone was talking about 'the incident' and 'that girl'. Walden's brother George sat beside him and said without preamble: 'She's a Miss Mary Blomfield, daughter of the late Sir Arthur Blomfield. Her mother was in the drawing-room at the time. When she was told what her daughter had done she fainted right off.' He seemed to relish the scandal.

'Only thing she could do, I suppose,' Walden replied.

'Damn shame for the family,' George said. 'You won't see Blomfields at court again for two or three generations.'

'We shan't miss them.'

'No.'

Walden saw Churchill pushing through the crowd toward where they sat. He had written to Churchill about his talk with Aleks, and he was impatient to discuss the next step – but not *here.* He looked away, hoping Churchill would get the hint. He should have known better than to hope that such a subtle message would get through.

Churchill bent over Walden's chair. 'Can we have a few words together?'

Walden looked at his brother. George wore an expression of horror. Walden threw him a resigned look and got up.

'Let's walk in the picture gallery,' Churchill said.

Walden followed him out.

Churchill said: 'I suppose you, too, will tell me that this suffragette protest is all the fault of the Liberal Party.'

'I expect it is,' Walden said. 'But that isn't what you want to talk about.'

'No indeed.'

The two men walked side by side through the long gallery. Churchill said: 'We can't acknowledge the Balkans as a Russian sphere of influence.'

'I was afraid you'd say that.'

'What do they want the Balkans *for*? I mean, forgetting all this nonsense about sympathy with Slav nationalism.'

'They want passage through to the Mediterranean.'

'That would be to our advantage, if they were our allies.'

'Exactly.'

They reached the end of the gallery and stopped. Churchill said: 'Is there some way we can give them that passage without redrawing the map of the Balkan Peninsula?'

'I've been thinking about that.'

Churchill smiled. 'And you've got a counter-proposal.'

'Yes.'

'Let's hear it.'

Walden said: 'What we're talking about here are three stretches of water: the Bosphorus, the Sea of Marmara, and the Dardanelles. If we can give them those waterways, they won't need the Balkans. Now, suppose that whole passage between the Black Sea and the Mediterranean could be declared an international waterway, with free passage to ships of all nations guaranteed jointly by Russia and England.'

Churchill started walking again, slow and thoughtful. Walden walked beside him, waiting for his answer.

Eventually Churchill said: 'That passage *ought* to be an international waterway, in any event. What you're suggesting is that we offer, as if it were a concession, something which we want anyway.'

'Yes.'

Churchill looked up and grinned suddenly. 'When it comes to Machiavellian manoeuvring, there's no one to beat the English aristocracy. All right. Go ahead and propose it to Orlov.'

'You don't want to put it to the Cabinet?'

'No.'

'Not even to the Foreign Secretary?'

'Not at this stage. The Russians are certain to want to modify the proposal – they'll want details of how the guarantee is to be enforced, at least – so I'll go to the Cabinet when the deal is fully elaborated.'

'Very well.' Walden wondered just how much the Cabinet knew about what Churchill and he were up to. Churchill, too, could be Machiavellian. Were there wheels within wheels?

Churchill said: 'Where is Orlov now?'

'In the diplomatic supper-room.'

'Let's go and put it to him right away.'

Walden shook his head, thinking that people were correct when they accused Churchill of being impulsive. 'This is not the moment.'

'We can't wait for the moment, Walden. Every day counts.'

It will take a bigger man than you to bully me, Walden thought. He said: 'You're going to have to leave that to my judgement, Churchill. I'll put this to Orlov tomorrow morning.'

Churchill seemed disposed to argue, but he restrained himself visibly and said: 'I don't suppose Germany will declare war tonight. Very well.' He looked at his watch. 'I'm going to leave. Keep me fully informed.'

'Of course. Goodbye.'

Churchill went down the staircase and Walden returned to the supper-room. The party was breaking up. Now that the King and Queen had disappeared and everyone had been fed there was nothing to stay for. Walden rounded up his family and took them downstairs. They found Aleks in the great hall.

While the ladies went into the cloakroom Walden asked one of the attendants to summon his carriage.

All in all, he thought as he waited, it had been a rather successful evening.

The Mall reminded Feliks of the streets in the Old Equerries Quarter of Moscow. It was a wide, straight avenue that ran from Trafalgar Square to Buckingham Palace. On one side was a series of grand houses including St James's Palace. On the other side was St James's Park. The carriages and motor cars of the great were lined up on both sides of The Mall for half its length. Chauffeurs and coachmen leaned against their vehicles, yawning and fidgeting, waiting to be summoned to the palace to collect their masters and mistresses.

The Walden carriage waited on the park side of The Mall. Their coachman, in the blue-and-pink Walden livery, stood beside the horses, reading a newspaper by the light of a carriage lamp. A few yards away, in the darkness of the park, Feliks stood watching him.

Feliks was desperate. His plan was in ruins.

He had not understood the difference between the English words 'coachman' and 'footman' and consequently he had misunderstood the notice in *The Times* about summoning carriages. He had thought that the driver of the coach would wait at the palace gate until his master emerged, then would come running to fetch the coach. At that point, Feliks had planned, he would have overpowered the coachman, taken his livery, and driven the coach to the palace himself.

What happened in fact was that the coachman stayed with the vehicle and the footman waited at the palace gate. When the coach was wanted, the footman would come running; then he and the coachman would go with the carriage to pick up the passengers. That meant Feliks had to overpower two people, not one; and the difficulty was that it had to be done surreptitiously, so that none of the hundreds of other servants in The Mall would know anything was wrong.

Since realizing his mistake a couple of hours ago he had worried at the problem, while he watched the coachman chatting with his colleagues, examining a nearby Rolls-Royce car, playing some kind of game with halfpennies, and polishing the carriage windows. It might have been sensible to abandon the plan, and kill Orlov another day.

But Feliks hated that idea. For one thing, there was no certainty that another good opportunity would arise. For another, Feliks wanted to kill him now. He had been anticipating the bang of the gun, the way the Prince would fall; he had composed the coded cable which would go to Ulrich in Geneva; he had pictured the excitement in the little printing shop, and then the headlines in the world's newspapers, and then the final wave of revolution sweeping through Russia. I can't postpone this any longer, he thought; I want it now.

As he watched, a young man in green livery approached the Walden coachman and said: 'What ho, William.'

So the coachman's name is William, Feliks thought.

William said: 'Mustn't grumble, John.'

Feliks did not understand that.

'Anything in the news?' said John.

'Yeah, revolution. The King says that next year all the coachmen can go in the palace for supper and the toffs will wait in The Mall.'

'A likely tale.'

'You're telling me.'

John moved on.

I can get rid of William, Feliks thought, but what about the footman?

In his mind he ran over the probable sequence of events. Walden and Orlov would come to the palace door. The doorman would alert Walden's footman, who would run from the palace to the carriage – a distance of about a quarter of a mile. The footman would see Feliks dressed in the coachman's clothes, and would sound the alarm.

Suppose the footman arrived at the parking-place to find that the carriage was no longer there?

That was a thought!

The footman would wonder whether he had misremembered the spot. He would look up and down. In something of a panic he would search for the coach. Finally he would admit defeat and return to the palace to tell his master that he could not find the coach. By which time Feliks would be driving the coach and its owner through the park.

It could still be done!

It was more risky than before, but it could still be done.

There was no more time for reflection. The first two or three footmen were already running down The Mall. The Rolls-Royce car in front of the Walden coach was summoned. William put on his top hat in readiness.

Feliks emerged from the bushes and walked a little way toward him, calling: 'Hey! Hey, William!'

The coachman looked toward him, frowning.

Feliks beckoned urgently. 'Come here, quick!'

William folded his newspaper, hesitated, then walked slowly toward Feliks.

Feliks allowed his own tension to put a note of panic into his voice. 'Look at this!' he said, pointing to the bushes. 'Do you know anything about this?'

'What?' William said, mystified. He drew level and peered the way Feliks was pointing.

'This.' Feliks showed him the gun. 'If you make a noise I'll shoot you.'

William was terrified. Feliks could see the whites of his eyes in the half-dark. He was a heavily built man, but he was older than Feliks. If he does something foolish and messes this up I'll kill him, Feliks thought savagely.

'Walk on,' Feliks said.

The man hesitated.

I've got to get him out of the *light.* 'Walk, you bastard!'

William walked into the bushes.

Feliks followed him. When they were about fifty yards away from The Mall Feliks said: 'Stop.'

William stopped and turned around.

Feliks thought: If he's going to fight, this is where he will do it. He said: 'Take off your clothes.'

'What?'

'Undress.'

'You're mad,' William whispered.

'You're right – I'm mad! Take off your clothes!'

William hesitated.

If I shoot him, will people come running? Will the bushes muffle the sound? Could I kill him without making a hole in his uniform? Could I take his coat off and run away before anyone arrives?

Feliks cocked the gun.

William began to undress.

Feliks could hear the increasing activity in The Mall: motor cars started, harness jingled, hooves clattered and men shouted to one another and to their horses. Any minute now the footman might come running for the Walden coach. 'Faster!' Feliks said.

William got down to his underwear.

'The rest also,' Feliks said.

William hesitated. Feliks lifted the gun.

William pulled off his undershirt, dropped his underpants, and stood naked, shivering with fear, covering his genitals with his hands.

'Turn around,' said Feliks.

William turned his back.

'Lie on the ground, face down.'

He did so.

Feliks put down the gun. Hurriedly, he took off his coat and hat and put on the livery coat and the top hat which William had dropped on the ground. He contemplated the knee-breeches and white stockings, but decided to leave them: when he was sitting up on the coach no one would notice his trousers and boots, especially in the uncertain light of the street lamps.

He put the gun into the pocket of his own coat and folded the coat over his arm. He picked up William's clothes in a bundle.

William tried to look around.

'Don't move!' Feliks said sharply.

Softly, he walked away.

William would stay there for a while then, naked as he was, he would try to get back to the Walden house unobserved. It was highly unlikely that he would report that he had been robbed of his clothes before he had a chance to get some more, unless he was an extraordinarily immodest man. Of course if he had known Feliks was going to kill Prince Orlov he might have thrown modesty to the winds – but how could he possibly guess that?

Feliks pushed William's clothes under a bush, then walked out into the lights of The Mall.

This was where things might go wrong. Until now he had been merely a suspicious person lurking in the bushes. From this moment on he was plainly an imposter. If one of William's friends – John, for instance – should look closely at his face, the game would be up.

He climbed rapidly on to the coach, put his own coat on the seat beside him, adjusted his top hat, released the brake, and flicked the reins. The coach pulled out into the road.

He sighed with relief. I've got this far, he thought; I'll get Orlov!

As he drove down The Mall he watched the pavements, looking for a running footman in the blue-and-pink livery. The worst possible mischance would be for the Walden footman to see him now, and recognize the colours, and jump on to the back of the coach. Feliks cursed as a motor car pulled out in front of him, forcing him to slow the horses to a halt. He looked around anxiously. There was no sign of the footman. After a moment the road was clear and he went on.

At the palace end of the avenue he spotted an empty space on the right, the side of the road farther from the park. The footman would come along the opposite pavement and would not see the coach. He pulled into the space and set the brake.

He climbed down from the seat and stood behind the horses, watching the opposite pavement. He wondered whether he would get out of this alive.

In his original plan there had been a good chance that Walden would get into the carriage without so much as a glance at the coachman, but now he would surely notice that his footman was missing. The palace doorman would have to open the coach door and pull down the steps. Would Walden stop and speak to the coachman, or would he postpone inquiries until he got home? If he were to speak to Feliks then Feliks would have to reply and his voice would give the game away. What will I do then? Feliks thought.

I'll shoot Orlov at the palace door, and take the consequences.

He saw the footman in blue-and-pink running along the far side of The Mall.

Feliks jumped on to the coach, released the brake, and drove into the courtyard of Buckingham Palace.

There was a queue. Ahead of him, the beautiful women and the well-fed men climbed into their carriages and cars. Behind him, somewhere in The Mall, the Walden footman was running up and down, hunting for his coach. How long before he returned?

The palace servants had a fast and efficient system for loading guests into vehicles. While the passengers were getting into the carriage at the door, a servant was calling the owners of the second in line, and another servant was inquiring the name of the people for the third.

The line moved, and a servant approached Feliks. 'The Earl of Walden,' Feliks said. The servant went inside.

They mustn't come out too soon, Feliks thought.

The line moved forward, and now there was only a motor car in front of him. Pray God it doesn't stall, he thought. The chauffeur held the doors for an elderly couple. The car pulled away.

Feliks moved the coach to the porch, halting it a little too far forward, so that he was beyond the wash of light from inside, and his back was to the palace doors.

He waited, not daring to look around.

He heard the voice of a young girl say, in Russian: 'And how many ladies proposed marriage to you this evening, Cousin Aleks?'

A drop of sweat ran down into Feliks' eye and he wiped it away with the back of his hand.

A man said: 'Where the devil is my footman?'

Feliks reached into the pocket of the coat beside him and got his hand on the butt of the revolver. Six shots left, he thought.

Out of the corner of his eye he saw a palace servant spring forward, and a moment later he heard the door of the coach being opened. The vehicle rocked slightly as someone got in.

'I say, William, where's Charles?'

Feliks tensed. He imagined he could feel Walden's

eyes boring into the back of his head. The girl's voice said: 'Come on, Papa,' from inside the carriage.

'William's getting deaf in his old age . . .' Walden's words were muffled as he got into the coach. The door slammed.

'Right away, coachman!' said the palace servant.

Feliks breathed out, and drove away.

The release of tension made him feel weak for a moment. Then, as he guided the carriage out of the courtyard, he felt a surge of elation. Orlov was in his power, shut in a box behind him, caught like an animal in a trap. Nothing could stop Feliks now.

He drove into the park.

Holding the reins in his right hand, he struggled to get his left arm into his topcoat. That done, he switched the reins to his left hand and got his right arm in. He stood up and shrugged the coat up over his shoulders. He felt in the pocket and touched the gun.

He sat down again and wound a scarf around his neck.

He was ready.

Now he had to choose his moment.

He had only a few minutes. The Walden house was less than a mile from the palace. He had bicycled along this road the night before, to reconnoitre. He had found two suitable places, where a street lamp would illuminate his victim and there was thick shrubbery near by into which he could disappear afterwards.

The first spot loomed up fifty yards ahead. As he approached it he saw a man in evening dress pause beneath the lamp to light his cigar. He drove past the spot.

The second place was a bend in the road. If there was someone there, Feliks would just have to take a chance, and shoot the intruder if necessary.

Six bullets.

He saw the bend. He made the horses trot a little faster. From inside the coach he heard the young girl laugh.

He came to the bend. His nerves were as taut as piano-wire.

Now.

He dropped the reins and heaved on the brake. The horses staggered and the carriage shuddered and jerked to a halt.

From inside the coach he heard a woman cry and a man shout. Something about the woman's voice bothered him, but there was no time to wonder why. He jumped down to the ground, pulled the scarf up over his mouth and nose, took the gun from his pocket and cocked it.

Full of strength and rage, he flung open the coach door.

CHAPTER FOUR

A WOMAN CRIED out, and time stood still.

Feliks knew the voice. The sound hit him like a mighty blow. The shock paralysed him.

He was supposed to locate Orlov, point the gun at him, pull the trigger, make sure he was dead with another bullet, then turn and run into the bushes . . .

Instead he looked for the source of the cry, and saw her face. It was startlingly familiar, as if he had last seen it only yesterday, instead of nineteen years ago. Her eyes were wide with panic, and her small red mouth was open.

Lydia.

He stood at the door of the coach with his mouth open under the scarf, the gun pointing nowhere, and he thought: My Lydia – here in *this carriage* . . .

As he stared at her he was dimly aware that Walden was moving, with uncanny slowness, close by him on his left; but all Feliks could think was: This is how she used to look, wide-eyed and open-mouthed, when she lay naked beneath me, her legs wrapped around my waist, and she stared at me and began to cry out with delight . . .

Then he saw that Walden had drawn a sword –

For God's sake, *a sword*?

– and the blade was glinting in the lamplight as it swept down, and Feliks moved too slowly and too late, and the sword bit into his right hand, and he dropped the gun and it went off with a bang as it hit the road.

The explosion broke the spell.

Walden drew back the sword and thrust at Feliks' heart. Feliks moved sideways. The point of the sword went through his coat and jacket and stuck into his shoulder. He jumped back reflexively and the sword came out. He felt a rush of warm blood inside his shirt.

He stared down at the road, looking for the gun, but he could not see it. He looked up again, and saw that Walden and Orlov had collided as they tried simultaneously to get out through the narrow carriage door. Feliks' right arm hung limply at his side. He realized he was unarmed and helpless. He could not even strangle Orlov, for his right arm was useless. He had failed utterly, and all because of the voice of a woman from the past.

After all that, he thought bitterly; after all that.

Full of despair, he turned and ran away.

Walden roared: 'Damned villain!'

Feliks' wound hurt every step. He heard someone running behind him. The footsteps were too light to be Walden's: Orlov was chasing him. He teetered on the edge of hysteria as he thought: Orlov is chasing *me* – and I am running away!

He darted off the road and into the bushes. He

heard Walden shout: 'Aleks, come back, he's got a gun!' They don't know I dropped it, Feliks thought. If only I still had it I could shoot Orlov now.

He ran a little way farther then stopped, listening. He could hear nothing. Orlov had given up.

He leaned against a tree. He was exhausted by his short sprint. When he had caught his breath he took off his topcoat and the stolen livery coat and gingerly touched his wounds. They hurt like the devil, which he thought was probably a good sign, for if they had been very grave they would have been numb. His shoulder bled slowly, and throbbed. His hand had been sliced in the fleshy part between thumb and forefinger, and it bled fast.

He had to get out of the park before Walden had a chance to raise the hue and cry.

With difficulty he drew on the topcoat. He left the livery coat on the ground where it lay. He squeezed his right hand under his left armpit, to relieve the pain and slow the flow of blood. Wearily, he headed toward The Mall.

Lydia.

It was the second time in his life that she had caused a catastrophe. The first time, in 1895, in St Petersburg—

No. He would not allow himself to think about her, not yet. He needed his wits about him now.

He saw with relief that his bicycle was where he had left it, under the overhanging branches of a big tree. He wheeled it across the grass to the edge of the park. Had Walden alerted the police yet? Were they looking for a tall man in a dark coat? He stared at the scene in

The Mall. The footmen were still running, the car engines roaring, the carriages manoeuvring. How long had it been since Feliks had climbed up on to the Walden coach – twenty minutes? In that time the world had turned over.

He took a deep breath and wheeled the bicycle into the road. Everyone was busy, nobody looked at him. Keeping his right hand in his coat pocket, he mounted the machine. He pushed off and began to pedal, steering with his left hand.

There were bobbies all around the palace. If Walden mobilized them quickly they could cordon off the park and the roads around it. Feliks looked ahead, toward Admiralty Arch. There was no sign of a roadblock.

Once past the arch he would be in the West End and they would have lost him.

He began to get the knack of cycling one-handed, and increased his speed.

As he approached the arch a motor car drew alongside him and, at the same time, a policeman stepped into the road ahead. Feliks stopped the bicycle and prepared to run – but the policeman was merely holding up the traffic to permit another car, belonging presumably to some kind of dignitary, to emerge from a gateway. When the car came out the policeman saluted then waved the traffic on.

Feliks cycled through the arch and into Trafalgar Square.

Too slow, Walden, he thought with satisfaction.

It was midnight, but the West End was bright with street lights and crowded with people and traffic. There were policemen everywhere and no other cyclists: Feliks was conspicuous. He considered abandoning the bicycle and walking back to Camden Town, but he was not sure he could make the journey on foot: he seemed to be tiring.

From Trafalgar Square he rode up St Martin's Lane, then left the main streets for the back alleys of Theatreland. A dark lane was suddenly illuminated as a stage door opened and a bunch of actors came out, talking loudly and laughing. Farther on he heard groans and sighs, and passed a couple making love standing up in a doorway.

He crossed into Bloomsbury. Here it was quieter and darker. He cycled north up Gower Street, past the classical facade of the deserted university. Pushing the pedals became an enormous effort, and he ached all over. Just a mile or two more, he thought.

He dismounted to cross the busy Euston Road. The lights of the traffic dazzled him. He seemed to be having difficulty focusing his eyes.

Outside Euston Station he got on the bicycle again and pedalled off. Suddenly he felt dizzy. A street light blinded him. The front wheel wobbled and hit the kerb. Feliks fell.

He lay on the ground, dazed and weak. He opened his eyes and saw a policeman approaching. He struggled to his knees.

'Have you been drinkin'?' the policeman said.

'Feel faint,' Feliks managed.

The policeman took his right arm and hauled him to his feet. The pain in his wounded shoulder brought

Feliks to his senses. He managed to keep his bleeding right hand in his pocket.

The policeman sniffed audibly and said: 'Hmm.' His attitude became more genial when he discovered that Feliks did not smell of drink. 'Will you be all right?'

'In a minute.'

'Foreigner, are you?'

The policeman had noticed his accent. 'French,' Feliks said. 'I work at the Embassy.'

The policeman became more polite. 'Would you like a cab?'

'No, thank you. I have only a little way to go.'

The policeman picked up the bicycle. 'I should wheel it home if I were you.'

Feliks took the bicycle from him. 'I will do that.'

'Very good, sir. Bong noo-wee.'

'Bonne nuit, officer.' With an effort Feliks produced a smile. Pushing the bicycle with his left hand, he walked away. I'll turn into the next alley and sit down for a rest, he resolved. He looked back over his shoulder: the policeman was still watching him. He made himself keep on walking, although he desperately needed to lie down. The next alley, he thought. But when he came to an alley he passed it, thinking: Not this one, but the next.

And in that way he got home.

It seemed hours later that he stood outside the high terraced house in Camden Town. He peered through a fog at the number on the door to make sure this was the right place.

To get to his room he had to go down a flight of

stone steps to the basement area. He leaned the bicycle against the wrought-iron railings while he opened the little gate. He then made the mistake of trying to wheel the bicycle down the steps. It slid out of his grasp and fell into the area with a loud clatter. A moment later his landlady, Bridget, appeared at the street door in a shawl.

'What the divil is it?' she called.

Feliks sat on the steps and made no reply. He decided he would not move for a while, until he felt stronger.

Bridget came down and helped him to his feet. 'You've had a few too many drinks,' she said. She made him walk down the steps to the basement door.

'Give us your key,' she said.

Feliks had to use his left hand to take the key from his right trouser pocket. He gave it to her and she opened the door. They went in. Feliks stood in the middle of the little room while she lit the lamp.

'Let's have your coat off,' she said.

He let her remove his coat, and she saw the bloodstains. 'Have you been fightin'?'

Feliks went and lay on the mattress.

Bridget said: 'You look as if you lost!'

'I did,' said Feliks, and he passed out.

An agonizing pain brought him around. He opened his eyes to see Bridget bathing his wounds with something that stung like fire. 'This hand should be stitched,' she said.

'Tomorrow,' Feliks breathed.

She made him drink from a cup. It was warm water with gin in it. She said: 'I haven't any brandy.'

He lay back and let her bandage him.

'I could fetch the doctor but I couldn't be payin' him.'

'Tomorrow.'

She stood up. 'I'll look at you first thing in the morning.'

'Thank you.'

She went out, and at last Feliks allowed himself to remember.

> It has happened in the long run of ages that everything which permits men to increase their production, or even to continue it, has been appropriated by the few. The land belongs to the few, who may prevent the community from cultivating it. The coal-pits, which represent the labour of generations, belong again to the few. The lace-weaving machine, which represents, in its present state of perfection, the work of three generations of Lancashire weavers, belongs also to the few; and if the grandsons of the very same weaver who invented the first lace-weaving machine claim their right to bring one of these machines into motion, they will be told: 'Hands off! This machine does not belong to you!' The railroads belong to a few shareholders, who may not even know where is situated the railway which brings them a yearly income larger than that of a medieval king. And if the children of those

people who died by the thousands in digging the tunnels should gather and go – a ragged and starving crowd – to ask bread or work from the shareholders, they would be met with bayonets and bullets.

Feliks looked up from Kropotkin's pamphlet. The bookshop was empty. The bookseller was an old revolutionist who made his money selling novels to wealthy women, and kept a hoard of subversive literature in the back of the shop. Feliks spent a lot of time in here.

He was nineteen. He was about to be thrown out of the prestigious Spiritual Academy for truancy, indiscipline, long hair and associating with Nihilists. He was hungry and broke, and soon he would be homeless, and life was wonderful. He cared about nothing other than ideas, and he was learning every day new things about poetry, history, psychology, and – most of all – politics.

Laws on property are not made to guarantee either to the individual or to society the enjoyment of the produce of their own labour. On the contrary, they are made to rob the producer of a part of what he has created. When, for example, the law establishes Mr So-and-so's right to a house, it is not establishing his right to a cottage he has built for himself, or to a house he has erected with the help of some of his friends. In that case no one would have disputed his right! On the contrary, the law is establishing his right to a house which is not the product of his labour.

The anarchist slogans had sounded ridiculous when he had first heard them: Property is theft, Government is tyranny, Anarchy is justice. It was astonishing how, when he had really thought about them, they came to seem not only true but crashingly obvious. Kropotkin's point about laws was undeniable. No laws were required to prevent theft in Feliks' home village: if one peasant stole another's horse, or his chair, or the coat his wife had embroidered, then the whole village would see the culprit in possession of the goods and make him give them back. The only stealing that went on was when the landlord demanded rent; and the policeman was there to enforce that theft. It was the same with government. The peasants needed no one to tell them how the plough and the oxen were to be shared between their fields: they decided among themselves. It was only the ploughing of the landlord's fields that had to be enforced.

> We are continually told of the benefits conferred by laws and penalties, but have the speakers ever attempted to balance the benefits attributed to laws and penalties against the degrading effects of these penalties upon humanity? Only calculate all the evil passions awakened in mankind by the atrocious punishments inflicted in our streets! Man is the cruellest animal on earth. And who has pampered and developed the cruel instincts if it is not the king, the judge and the priests, armed with law, who caused flesh to be torn off in strips, boiling pitch to be poured into wounds, limbs to be dislocated, bones

to be crushed, men to be sawn asunder to maintain their authority? Only estimate the torrent of depravity let loose in human society by the 'informing' which is countenanced by judges, and paid in hard cash by governments, under pretext of assisting in the discovery of 'crime'. Only go into the jails and study what man becomes when he is steeped in the vice and corruption which oozes from the very walls of our prisons. Finally, consider what corruption, what depravity of mind is kept up among men by the idea of obedience, the very essence of law; of chastisement; of authority having the right to punish; of the necessity for executioners, jailers, and informers – in a word, by all the attributes of law and authority. Consider this, and you will assuredly agree that a law inflicting penalties is an abomination which should cease to exist.

Peoples without political organization, and therefore less depraved than ourselves, have perfectly understood that the man who is called 'criminal' is simply unfortunate; and that the remedy is not to flog him, to chain him up, or to kill him, but to help him by the most brotherly care, by treatment based on equality, by the usages of life among honest men.

Feliks was vaguely aware that a customer had come into the shop and was standing close to him, but he was concentrating on Kropotkin.

No more laws! No more judges! Liberty, equality and practical human sympathy are the only effective barriers we can oppose to the anti-social instincts of certain among us.

The customer dropped a book and he lost his train of thought. He glanced away from his pamphlet, saw the book lying on the floor beside the customer's long skirt, and automatically bent down to pick it up for her. As he handed it to her he saw her face.

He gasped. 'Why, you're an angel!' he said with perfect honesty.

She was blonde and petite, and she wore a pale grey fur the colour of her eyes, and everything about her was pale and light and fair. He thought he would never see a more beautiful woman, and he was right.

She stared back at him and blushed, but she did not turn away. It seemed, incredibly, that she found something fascinating in him, too.

After a moment he looked at her book. It was *Anna Karenina*. 'Sentimental rubbish,' he said. He wished he had not spoken, for his words broke the spell. She took the book and turned away. He saw then that there was a maid with her, for she gave the book to the maid and left the shop. The maid paid for the book. Looking through the window, Feliks saw the woman get into a carriage.

He asked the bookseller who she was. Her name was Lydia, he learned, and she was the daughter of Count Shatov.

He found out where the Count lived, and the next day he hung around outside the house in the hope of seeing her. She went in and out twice, in her carriage, before a groom came out and chased Feliks off. He did not mind, for the last time her carriage passed she had looked directly at him.

The next day he went to the bookshop. For hours he read Bakunin's *Federalism, Socialism and Anti-Theologism* without understanding a single word. Every time a carriage passed he looked out of the window. Whenever a customer came into the shop his heart missed a beat.

She came in at the end of the afternoon.

This time she left the maid outside. She murmured a greeting to the bookseller and came to the back of the shop, where Feliks stood. They stared at each other. Feliks thought: She loves me, why else would she come?

He meant to speak to her, but instead he threw his arms around her and kissed her. She kissed him back, hungrily, opening her mouth, hugging him, digging her fingers into his back.

It was always like that with them: when they met they threw themselves at each other like animals about to fight.

They met twice more in the bookshop and once, after dark, in the garden of the Shatov house. That time in the garden she was in her nightclothes. Feliks put his hands under the woollen nightgown and touched her body all over, as boldly as if she were a street girl, feeling and exploring and rubbing; and all she did was moan.

She gave him money so that he could rent a room of his own, and thereafter she came to see him almost every day for six astonishing weeks.

The last time was in the early evening. He was sitting at the table, wrapped in a blanket against the cold, reading Proudhon's *What is Property?* by candlelight. When he heard her footstep on the stairs he took his trousers off.

She rushed in, wearing an old brown cloak with a hood. She kissed him, sucked his lips, bit his chin, and pinched his sides.

She turned and threw off the cloak. Underneath it she was wearing a white evening gown that must have cost hundreds of roubles. 'Unfasten me, quickly,' she said.

Feliks began to undo the hooks at the back of the dress.

'I'm on my way to a reception at the British Embassy, I only have an hour,' she said breathlessly. 'Hurry, please.'

In his haste he ripped one of the hooks out of the material. 'Damn, I've torn it.'

'Never mind!'

She stepped out of the dress, then pulled off her petticoats, her chemise and her drawers, leaving on her corset, hose and shoes. She flung herself into his arms. As she was kissing him she pulled down his underpants.

She said: 'Oh, God, I love the smell of your thing.'

When she talked like that it drove him wild.

She pulled her breasts out of the top of her corset and said: 'Bite them. Bite them hard. I want to feel them all evening.'

A moment later she pulled away from him. She lay

on her back on the bed. Where the corset ended, moisture glistened in the sparse blonde hair between her thighs.

She spread her legs and lifted them into the air, opening herself to him. He gazed at her for a moment, then fell on her.

She grabbed his penis with her hands and pushed it inside her greedily.

The heels of her shoes tore the skin of his back and he did not care.

'Look at me,' she said. 'Look at me!'

He looked at her with adoration in his eyes.

An expression of panic came over her face.

She said: 'Look at me, I'm coming!'

Then, still staring into his eyes, she opened her mouth and screamed.

'Do you think other people are like us?' she said.

'In what way?'

'Filthy.'

He lifted his head from her lap and grinned. 'Only the lucky ones.'

She looked at his body, curled up between her legs. 'You're so compact and strong, you're perfect,' she said. 'Look how your belly is flat, and how neat your bottom is, and how lean and hard your thighs are.' She ran a finger along the line of his nose. 'You have the face of a prince.'

'I'm a peasant.'

'Not when you're naked.' She was in a reflective

mood. 'Before I met you, I *was* interested in men's bodies, and all that; but I used to pretend I wasn't, even to myself. Then you came along and I just couldn't pretend any more.'

He licked the inside of her thigh.

She shuddered. 'Have you ever done this to another girl?'

'No.'

'Did you used to pretend, as well?'

'No.'

'I think I knew that, somehow. There's a look about you, wild and free like an animal, you never obey anyone, you just do what you want.'

'I never before met a girl who would let me.'

'They all wanted to, really. Any girl would.'

'Why?' he said egotistically.

'Because your face is so cruel and your eyes are so kind.'

'Is that why you let me kiss you in the bookshop?'

'I didn't *let* you – I had no choice.'

'You could have yelled for help, afterwards.'

'By then all I wanted was for you to do it again.'

'I must have guessed what you were really like.'

It was her turn to be egotistical. 'What am I really like?'

'Cold as ice on the surface, hot as hell below.'

She giggled. 'I'm such an actor. Everyone in St Petersburg thinks I'm so *good.* I'm held up as an example to younger girls, just like Anna Karenina. Now that I know how bad I really am, I have to pretend to be twice as virginal as before.'

'You can't be twice as virginal as anything.'

'I wonder if they're all pretending,' she resumed. 'Take my father. If he knew I was here, like this, he'd die of rage. But he must have had the same feelings when he was young – don't you think?'

'I think it's an imponderable,' Feliks said. 'But what *would* he do, really, if he found out?'

'Horsewhip you.'

'He'd have to catch me first.' Feliks was struck by a thought. 'How old are you?'

'Almost eighteen.'

'My God, I could go to jail for seducing you.'

'I'd make Father get you out.'

He rolled over on to his front and looked at her. 'What are we going to do, Lydia?'

'When?'

'In the long term.'

'We're going to be lovers until I come of age, and then we'll get married.'

He stared at her. 'Do you mean that?'

'Of *course.*' She seemed genuinely surprised that he had not made the same assumption. 'What else could we do?'

'You want to marry me?'

'Yes! Isn't that what you want?'

'Oh, *yes,*' he breathed. 'That's what I want.'

She sat up, with her legs spread either side of his face, and stroked his hair. 'Then that's what we'll do.'

Feliks said: 'You never tell me how you manage to get away to come here.'

'It's not very interesting,' she said. 'I tell lies, I bribe servants, and I take risks. Tonight, for example. The reception at the embassy starts at half past six. I left home at six o'clock and I'll get there at a quarter past seven. The carriage is in the park – the coachman thinks I'm taking a walk with my maid. The maid is outside this house, dreaming about how she will spend the ten roubles I will give her for keeping her mouth shut.'

'It's ten to seven,' Feliks said.

'Oh, God. Quick, do it to me with your tongue before I have to go.'

That night Feliks was asleep, dreaming about Lydia's father – whom he had never seen – when they burst into his room carrying lamps. He woke instantly and jumped out of bed. At first he thought students from the university were playing a prank on him. Then one of them punched his face and kicked him in the stomach, and he knew they were the secret police.

He assumed they were arresting him on account of Lydia, and he was terrified for her. Would she be publicly disgraced? Was her father crazy enough to make her give evidence in court against her lover?

He watched the police put all his books and a bundle of letters in a sack. The books were all borrowed, but none of the owners was foolish enough to put his name inside. The letters were from his father and his sister Natasha – he had never had any letters from Lydia, and now he was thankful for that.

He was marched out of the building and thrown into a four-wheel cab.

They drove across the Chain Bridge and then followed the canals, as if avoiding the main streets. Feliks asked: 'Am I going to the Litovsky prison?' Nobody replied, but when they went over the Palace Bridge he realized he was being taken to the notorious Fortress of St Peter and St Paul, and his heart sank.

On the other side of the bridge the carriage turned left and entered a dark arched passage. It stopped at a gate. Feliks was taken into a reception hall, where an army officer looked at him and wrote something in a book. He was put in the cab again and driven deeper into the fortress. They stopped at another gate, and waited several minutes until it was opened from the inside by a soldier. From there Feliks had to walk through a series of narrow passages to a third iron gate which led to a large damp room.

The prison governor sat at a table. He said: 'You are charged with being an anarchist. Do you admit it?'

Feliks was elated. So this was nothing to do with Lydia! 'Admit it?' he said. 'I boast of it.'

One of the policemen produced a book which was signed by the governor. Feliks was stripped naked, then given a green flannel dressing-gown, a pair of thick woollen stockings, and two yellow felt slippers much too big.

From there an armed soldier took him through more gloomy corridors to a cell. A heavy oak door closed behind him, and he heard a key turn in the lock.

The cell contained a bed, a table, a stool and a washstand. The window was an embrasure in an enormously thick wall. The floor was covered with painted felt, and the walls were cushioned with some kind of yellow upholstery.

Feliks sat on the bed.

This was where Peter I had tortured and killed his own son. This was where Princess Tarakanova had been kept in a cell which flooded so that the rats climbed all over her to save themselves from drowning. This was where Catherine II buried her enemies alive.

Dostoevsky had been imprisoned here, Feliks thought proudly; so had Bakunin, who had been chained to a wall for two years. Nechayev had died here.

Feliks was at once elated to be in such heroic company and terrified at the thought that he might be here for ever.

The key turned in the lock. A little bald man with spectacles came in, carrying a pen, a bottle of ink, and some paper. He set them down on the table and said: 'Write the names of all the subversives you know.'

Feliks sat down and wrote: Karl Marx, Frederick Engels, Peter Kropotkin, Jesus Christ—

The bald man snatched away the paper. He went to the door of the cell and knocked. Two hefty guards came in. They strapped Feliks to the table and took off his slippers and stockings. They began to lash the soles of his feet with whips.

The torture went on all night.

When they pulled out his fingernails, he began to give them made-up names and addresses, but they told him they knew they were false.

When they burned the skin of his testicles with a candle flame he named all his student friends, but still they said he was lying.

Each time he passed out they revived him. Sometimes they would stop for a while, and allow him to think it was all over at last; then they would begin again and he would beg them to kill him so that the pain would stop. They carried on long after he had told them everything he knew.

It must have been around dawn that he passed out for the last time.

When he came round he was lying on the bed. There were bandages on his feet and hands. He was in agony. He wanted to kill himself but he was too weak to move.

The bald man came into the cell in the evening. When he saw him, Feliks began to sob with terror. The man just smiled and went away.

He never came back.

A doctor came to see Feliks each day. Feliks tried without success to pump him for information: Did anyone outside know that Feliks was here? Had there been any messages? Had anyone tried to visit? The doctor just changed the dressings and went away.

Feliks speculated. Lydia would have gone to his room and found the place in disarray. Someone in the house would have told her that the secret police had taken him away. What would she have done then? Would she make frantic inquiries, careless of her reputation?

Would she have been discreet, and gone quietly to see the Minister of the Interior with some story about the boyfriend of her maid having been jailed in error?

Every day he hoped for word from her, but it never came.

Eight weeks later he could walk almost normally, and they released him without explanation.

He went to his lodging. He expected to find a message from her there, but there was nothing, and his room had been let to someone else. He wondered why Lydia had not continued to pay the rent.

He went to her house and knocked at the front door. A servant answered. Feliks said: 'Feliks Davidovitch Kschessinsky presents his compliments to Lydia Shatova—'

The servant slammed the door.

Finally he went to the bookshop. The old bookseller said: 'Hello! I've got a message for you. It was brought yesterday by *her* maid.'

Feliks tore open the envelope with trembling fingers. It was written, not by Lydia, but by the maid. It read:

> *I have been Let Go and have no job it is all your fault She is wed and gone to England yesterday now you know the wages of Sin.*

He looked up at the bookseller with tears of anguish in his eyes. 'Is that all?' he cried.

He learned no more for nineteen years.

*

Normal regulations had been temporarily suspended in the Walden house, and Charlotte sat in the kitchen with the servants.

The kitchen was spotless, for of course the family had dined out. The fire had gone out in the great range, and the high windows were wide open, letting in the cool night air. The crockery used for servants' meals was racked neatly in the dresser; the cook's knives and spoons hung from a row of hooks; her innumerable bowls and pans were out of sight in the massive oak cupboards.

Charlotte had had no time to be frightened. At first, when the coach stopped so abruptly in the park, she had been merely puzzled; and after that her concern had been to stop Mama screaming. When they got home she had found herself a little shaky, but now, looking back, she found the whole thing rather exciting.

The servants felt the same way. It was very reassuring to sit around the massive bleached wooden table and talk things over with these people who were so much a part of her life: the cook, who had always been motherly; Pritchard, whom Charlotte respected because Papa respected him; the efficient and capable Mrs Mitchell, who as housekeeper always had a solution to any problem.

William the coachman was the hero of the hour. He described several times the wild look in his assailant's eyes as the man menaced him with the gun. Basking in the awestruck gaze of the under-house-parlourmaid, he recovered rapidly from the indignity of having walked into the kitchen stark naked.

'Of course,' Pritchard explained, 'I naturally presumed the thief just wanted William's clothes. I knew Charles was at the palace, so he could drive the coach. I thought, I wouldn't inform the police until after speaking to his lordship.'

Charles the footman said: 'Imagine how I felt when I found the carriage gone! I said to myself, I'm sure it was left here. Oh, well, I thinks, William's moved it. I run up and down The Mall, I look everywhere. In the end I go back to the palace. "Here's trouble," I says to the doorman, "the Earl of Walden's carriage has gone missing." He says to me: "Walden?" he says – not very respectful—'

Mrs Mitchell interrupted: 'Palace servants, they think they're better than the nobility—'

'He says to me: "Walden's gone, mate." I thought Gorblimey, I'm for it! I come running through the park, and halfway home I find the carriage, and my lady having hysterics, and my lord with blood on his sword!'

Mrs Mitchell said: 'And, after all that, nothing stolen.'

'A lewnatic,' said Charles. 'An ingenious lewnatic.'

There was general agreement.

The cook poured the tea and served Charlotte first. 'How is my lady now?' she said.

'Oh, she's all right,' Charlotte said. 'She went to bed and took a dose of laudanum. She must be asleep by now.'

'And the gentlemen?'

'Papa and Prince Orlov are in the drawing-room, having a brandy.'

The cook sighed heavily. 'Robbers in the park and suffragettes at the court – I don't know what we're coming to.'

'There'll be a socialist revolution,' said Charles. 'You mark my words.'

'We'll all be murdered in our beds,' the cook said lugubriously.

Charlotte said: 'What did the suffragette mean about the King torturing women?' As she spoke she looked at Pritchard, who was sometimes willing to explain to her things she was not supposed to know about.

'She was talking about force-feeding,' Pritchard said. 'Apparently it's painful.'

'Force-feeding?'

'When they won't eat, they're fed by force.'

Charlotte was mystified. 'How on earth is that done?'

'Several ways,' said Pritchard with a look which indicated he would not go into detail about all of them. 'A tube through the nostrils is one.'

The under-house-parlourmaid said: 'I wonder what they feed them.'

Charles said: 'Probably 'ot soup.'

'I can't believe this,' Charlotte said. 'Why should they refuse to eat?'

'It's a protest,' said Pritchard. 'Makes difficulties for the prison authorities.'

'Prison?' Charlotte was astonished. 'Why are they in prison?'

'For breaking windows, making bombs, disturbing the peace . . .'

'But what do they want?'

There was a silence as the servants realized that Charlotte had no idea what a suffragette was.

Finally Pritchard said: 'They want votes for women.'

'Oh.' Charlotte thought: Did I know that women couldn't vote? She was not sure. She had never thought about that sort of thing.

'I think this discussion has gone quite far enough,' said Mrs Mitchell firmly. 'You'll be in trouble, Mr Pritchard, for putting wrong ideas into my lady's head.'

Charlotte knew that Pritchard never got into trouble, because he was practically Papa's friend. She said: 'I wonder why they care so much about something like voting?'

There was a ring, and they all looked instinctively at the bellboard.

'Front door!' said Pritchard. 'At this time of night!' He went out, pulling on his coat.

Charlotte drank her tea. She felt tired. The suffragettes were puzzling and rather frightening, she decided; but all the same she wanted to know more.

Pritchard came back. 'Plate of sandwiches, please, Cook,' he said. 'Charles, take a fresh soda-siphon to the drawing-room.' He began to arrange plates and napkins on a tray.

'Well, come on,' Charlotte said. 'Who is it?'

'A gentleman from Scotland Yard,' said Pritchard.

*

Basil Thomson was a bullet-headed man with light-coloured receding hair, a heavy moustache, and a penetrating gaze. Walden had heard of him. His father had been Archbishop of York. Thomson had been educated at Eton and Oxford, and had done service in the Colonies as a Native Commissioner and as Prime Minister of Tonga. He had come home to qualify as a barrister and then had worked in the Prison Service, ending up as Governor of Dartmoor Prison with a reputation as a riot-breaker. From prisons he had gravitated toward police work, and had become an expert on the mixed criminal–anarchist milieu of London's East End. This expertise had got him the top job in the Special Branch, the political police force.

Walden sat him down and began to recount the evening's events. As he spoke he kept an eye on Aleks. The boy was superficially calm, but his face was pale, he sipped steadily at a glass of brandy-and-soda, and his left hand clutched rhythmically at the arm of his chair.

At one point Thomson interrupted Walden, saying: 'Did you notice when the carriage picked you up that the footman was missing?'

'Yes, I did,' Walden said. 'I asked the coachman where he was, but the coachman seemed not to hear. Then, because there was such a crush at the palace door, and my daughter was telling me to hurry up, I decided not to press the matter until we got home.'

'Our villain was relying on that, of course. He must have a cool nerve. Go on.'

'The carriage stopped suddenly in the park, and the door was thrown open by the man.'

'What did he look like?'

'Tall. He had a scarf or something over his face. Dark hair. Staring eyes.'

'All criminals have staring eyes,' Thomson said. 'Earlier on, had the coachman got a better look at him?'

'Not much. At that time the man wore a hat, and of course it was dark.'

'Hm. And then?'

Walden took a deep breath. At the time he had been not so much frightened as angry, but now, when he looked back on it, he was full of fear for what might have happened to Aleks, or Lydia, or Charlotte. He said: 'Lady Walden screamed, and that seemed to disconcert the fellow. Perhaps he had not expected to find any women in the coach. Anyway, he hesitated.' And thank God he did, he thought. 'I poked him with my sword, and he dropped the gun.'

'Did you do him much damage?'

'I doubt it. I couldn't get a swing in that confined space, and of course the sword isn't particularly sharp. I blooded him, though. I wish I had chopped off his damned head.'

The butler came in, and conversation stopped. Walden realized he had been talking rather loudly. He tried to calm himself. Pritchard served sandwiches and brandy-and-soda to the three men. Walden said: 'You'd better stay up, Pritchard, but you can send everyone else to bed.'

'Very good, my lord.'

When he had gone Walden said: 'It is possible that

this was just a robbery. I have let the servants think that, and Lady Walden and Charlotte too. However, a robber would hardly have needed such an elaborate plan, to my mind. I am perfectly certain that it was an attempt on Aleks' life.'

Thomson looked at Aleks. 'I'm afraid I agree. Have you any idea how he knew where to find you?'

Aleks crossed his legs. 'My movements haven't been secret.'

'That must change. Tell me, sir, has your life ever been threatened?'

'I live with threats,' Aleks said tightly. 'There has never been an attempt before.'

'Is there any reason why you in particular should be the target of Nihilists or revolutionists?'

'For them, it is enough that I am a p-prince.'

Walden realized that the problems of the English establishment, with suffragettes and Liberals and trade unions, were trivial by comparison with what the Russians had to cope with, and he felt a surge of sympathy for Aleks.

Aleks went on in a quiet, controlled voice: 'However, I am known to be something of a reformer, by Russian standards. They could pick a more appropriate victim.'

'Even in London,' Thomson agreed. 'There's always a Russian aristocrat or two in London for the season.'

Walden said: 'What are you getting at?'

Thomson said: 'I'm wondering whether the villain knew what Prince Orlov is doing here, and whether his motive for tonight's attack was to sabotage your talks.'

Walden was dubious. 'How would the revolutionists have found that out?'

'I'm just speculating,' Thomson replied. '*Would* this be an effective way to sabotage your talks?'

'Very effective indeed,' Walden said. The thought made him go cold. 'If the Czar were to be told that his nephew had been assassinated in London by a revolutionist – especially if it were an expatriate Russian revolutionist – he would go through the roof. You know, Thomson, how the Russians feel about our having their subversives here – our open-door policy has always caused friction at the diplomatic level. Something like this could destroy Anglo-Russian relations for twenty years. There would be no question of an alliance then.'

Thomson nodded. 'I was afraid of that. Well, there's no more we can do tonight. I'll set my department to work at dawn. We'll search the park for clues, and interview your servants, and I expect we'll round up a few anarchists in the East End.'

Aleks said: 'Do you think you will catch the man?'

Walden longed for Thomson to give a reassuring answer, but it was not forthcoming. 'It won't be easy,' Thomson said. 'He's obviously a planner, so he'll have a bolt-hole somewhere. We've no proper description of him. Unless his wounds take him to hospital, our chances are slim.'

'He may try to kill me again,' Aleks said.

'So we must take evasive action. I propose you should move out of this house tomorrow. We'll take the top floor of one of the hotels for you, in a false name, and give you a bodyguard. Lord Walden will have to meet with you secretly, and you'll have to cut out social engagements, of course.'

'Of course.'

Thomson stood up. 'It's very late. I'll set all this in motion.'

Walden rang for Pritchard. 'You've got a carriage waiting, Thomson?'

'Yes. Let us speak on the telephone tomorrow morning.'

Pritchard saw Thomson out, and Aleks went off to bed. Walden told Pritchard to lock up, then went upstairs.

He was not sleepy. As he undressed he let himself relax, and feel all the conflicting emotions which he had so far held at bay. He felt proud of himself, at first – after all, he thought, I drew a sword and fought off an assailant: not bad for a man of fifty with a gouty leg! Then he became depressed when he recalled how coolly they had all discussed the diplomatic consequences of the death of Aleks – bright, cheerful, shy, handsome, clever Aleks, whom Walden had seen grow into a man.

He got into bed and lay awake, reliving the moment when the carriage door flew open and the man stood there with the gun; and now he was frightened, not for himself or Aleks, but for Lydia and Charlotte. The thought that they might have been killed made him tremble in his bed. He remembered holding Charlotte in his arms, eighteen years ago, when she had blonde hair and no teeth; he remembered her learning to walk and forever falling on her bottom; he remembered giving her a pony of her own, and thinking that her joy when she saw it gave him the biggest thrill of his life; he remembered her just a few hours ago, walking into the royal presence with her head held high, a grown woman and a beautiful one. If she died, he thought, I don't know that I could bear it.

And Lydia: if Lydia were dead I would be alone. The thought made him get up and go through to her room. There was a nightlight beside her bed. She was in a deep sleep, lying on her back, her mouth a little open, her hair a blonde skein across the pillow. She looked soft and vulnerable. I have never been able to make you understand how much I love you, he thought. Suddenly he needed to touch her, to feel that she was warm and alive. He got into bed with her and kissed her. Her lips responded but she did not wake up. Lydia, he thought, I could not live without you.

Lydia had lain awake for a long time, thinking about the man with the gun. It had been a brutal shock, and she had screamed in sheer terror – but there was more to it than that. There had been something about the man, something about his stance, or his shape, or his clothes, that had seemed dreadfully sinister in an almost supernatural way, as if he were a ghost. She wished she could have seen his eyes.

After a while she had taken another dose of laudanum, and then she slept. She dreamed that the man with the gun came to her room and got into bed with her. It was her own bed, but in the dream she was eighteen years old again. The man put his gun down on the white pillow beside her head. He still had the scarf around his face. She realized that she loved him. She kissed his lips through the scarf.

He made love to her beautifully. She began to think that she might be dreaming. She wanted to see his face. She said *Who are you?* and a voice said *Stephen.* She knew this was not so, but the gun on the pillow had somehow turned into Stephen's sword, with blood on its point; and she began to have doubts. She clung to the man on top of her, afraid that the dream would end before she was satisfied. Then, dimly, she began to suspect that she was doing in reality what she was doing in the dream; yet the dream persisted. Strong physical pleasure possessed her. She began to lose control. Just as her climax began the man in the dream took the scarf from his face, and in that moment Lydia opened her eyes, and saw Stephen's face above her; and then she was overcome by ecstasy, and for the first time in nineteen years she cried for joy.

CHAPTER FIVE

Charlotte looked forward with mixed feelings to Belinda's coming-out ball. She had never been to a town ball, although she had been to lots of country balls, many of them at Walden Hall. She liked to dance and she knew she did it well, but she hated the cattle-market business of sitting out with the wallflowers and waiting for a boy to pick you out and ask you to dance. She wondered whether this might be handled in a more civilized way among the 'Smart Set'.

They got to Uncle George and Aunt Clarissa's Mayfair house half an hour before midnight, which Mama said was the earliest time one could decently arrive at a London ball. A striped canopy and a red carpet led from the kerb to the garden gate, which had somehow been transformed into a Roman triumphal arch.

But even that did not prepare Charlotte for what she saw when she passed through the arch. The whole side-garden had been turned into a Roman atrium. She gazed about her in wonderment. The lawns and the flower beds had been covered over with a hardwood dance floor stained in black and white squares to look like marble tiles. A colonnade of white pillars, linked with chains of laurel, bordered the floor. Beyond the pillars, in a kind of cloister, there were raised benches for the sitters-out. In the middle of the floor a fountain in the form of a boy with a dolphin splashed in a marble basin, the streams of water lit by coloured spotlights. On the balcony of an upstairs bedroom a band played ragtime. Garlands of smilax and roses decorated the walls, and baskets of begonias hung from the balcony. A huge canvas roof, painted sky-blue, covered the whole area from the eaves of the house to the garden wall.

'It's a miracle!' Charlotte said.

Papa said to his brother: 'Quite a crowd, George.'

'We invited eight hundred. What the devil happened to you in the park?'

'Oh, it wasn't as bad as it sounded,' Papa said with a forced smile. He took George by the arm, and they moved to one side to talk.

Charlotte studied the guests. All the men wore full evening dress – white tie, white waistcoat and tails. It particularly suited the young men, or at least the slim men, Charlotte thought: it made them look quite dashing as they danced. Observing the dresses, she decided that hers and her mother's, though rather tasteful, were a trifle old-fashioned, with their wasp waists and ruffles and sweepers: Aunt Clarissa wore a long, straight, slender gown with a skirt almost too tight to dance in, and Belinda had harem pants.

Charlotte realized she knew nobody. Who will dance with me, she wondered, after Papa and Uncle George? However, Aunt Clarissa's younger brother Jonathan waltzed with her then introduced her to three men who were at Oxford with him, each of whom danced with her. She found their conversation monotonous: they said the floor was good, and the band – Gottlieb's – was good, then they ran out of steam. Charlotte tried: 'Do you believe that women should have the vote?' The replies she got were: 'Certainly not,' 'No opinion,' and 'You're not one of *them*, are you?'

The last of her partners, whose name was Freddie, took her into the house for supper. He was a rather sleek young man, with regular features – handsome, I suppose, Charlotte thought – and fair hair. He was at the end of his first year at Oxford. Oxford was rather jolly, he said, but he confessed he was not much of a one for reading books, and he rather thought he would not go back in October.

The inside of the house was festooned with flowers and bright with electric light. For supper there was hot and cold soup, lobster, quail, strawberries, ice-cream, and hothouse peaches. 'Always the same old food for supper,' Freddie said. 'They all use the same caterer.'

'Do you go to a lot of balls?' Charlotte asked.

''Fraid so. All the time, really, in the season.'

Charlotte drank a glass of champagne-cup in the hope that it would make her feel more gay, then she left Freddie and wandered through a series of reception-rooms. In one of them several games of bridge were under way. Two elderly duchesses held court in another. In a third, older men played billiards while younger men smoked. Charlotte found Belinda there with a cigarette in her hand. Charlotte had never seen the point of tobacco, unless one wanted to look sophisticated. Belinda certainly looked sophisticated.

'I adore your dress,' Belinda said.

'No, you don't. But *you* look sensational. How did you persuade your stepmother to let you dress like that?'

'She'd like to wear one herself!'

'She seems so much younger than my Mama. Which she is, of course.'

'And being a stepmother makes a difference. Whatever happened to you after the court?'

'Oh, it was extraordinary! A madman pointed a gun at us!'

'Your Mama was telling me. Weren't you simply terrified?'

'I was too busy calming Mama. Afterwards I was scared to death. Why did you say, at the palace, that you wanted to have a long talk with me?'

'Ah! Listen.' She took Charlotte aside, away from the young men. 'I've discovered how they come out.'

'What?'

'Babies.'

'Oh!' Charlotte was all ears. 'Do tell.'

Belinda lowered her voice. 'They come out between your legs, where you make water.'

'It's too small!'

'It stretches.'

How awful, Charlotte thought.

'But that's not all,' Belinda said. 'I've found out how they start.'

'How?'

Belinda took Charlotte's elbow and they walked to the far side of the room. They stood in front of a mirror garlanded with roses. Belinda's voice fell almost to a whisper. 'When you get married, you know you have to go to bed with your husband.'

'Do you?'

'Yes.'

'Papa and Mama have separate bedrooms.'

'Don't they adjoin?'

'Yes.'

'That's so that they can get into the same bed.'

'Why?'

'Because, to start a baby, the husband has to put his pego into that place – where the babies come out.'

'What's a pego?'

'Hush! It's a thing men have between their legs – haven't you ever seen a picture of Michelangelo's *David*?'

'No.'

'Well, it's a thing they make water with. Looks like a finger.'

'And you have to do *that* to start babies?'

'Yes.'

'And all married people have to do it?'

'Yes.'

'How dreadful. Who told you all this?'

'Viola Pontadarvy. She swore it was true.'

And somehow Charlotte knew it *was* true. Hearing it was like being reminded of something she had forgotten. It seemed, unaccountably, to make sense. Yet she felt physically shocked. It was the slightly queasy feeling she sometimes got in dreams, when a terrible suspicion turned out to be correct, or when she was afraid of falling and suddenly found she *was* falling.

'I'm jolly glad you found out,' she said. 'If one got married without knowing . . . how embarrassing it would be!'

'That happens to some girls, apparently,' Belinda said. 'Your mother is supposed to explain it all to you the night before your wedding, but if your mother is too shy you just . . . find out when it happens.'

'Thank Heaven for Viola Pontadarvy.' Charlotte was struck by a thought. 'Has all this got something to do with . . . bleeding, you know, every month?'

'I don't know.'

'I expect it has. It's all connected – all the things people don't talk about. Well, now we know why they don't talk about it – it's so disgusting.'

'The thing you have to do in bed is called sexual intercourse, but Viola says the common people call it swiving.'

'She knows a lot.'

'She's got brothers. They told her years ago.'

'How did they find out?'

'From older boys at school. Boys are ever so interested in that sort of thing.'

'Well,' Charlotte said, 'it does have a sort of horrid fascination.'

Suddenly she saw in the mirror the reflection of Aunt Clarissa. 'What are you two doing huddled in a corner?' she said. Charlotte flushed, but apparently Aunt Clarissa did not want an answer, for she went on: 'Do please move around and talk to people, Belinda – it is your party.'

She went away, and the two girls moved on through the reception-rooms. The rooms were arranged on a circular plan so that you could walk through them all and end up where you had started, at the top of the staircase. Charlotte said: 'I don't think I could ever bring myself to do it.'

'Couldn't you?' Belinda said with a funny look.

'What do you mean?'

'I don't know. I've been thinking about it. It might be quite nice.'

Charlotte stared at her.

Belinda looked embarrassed. 'I must go and dance,' she said. 'See you later on!'

She went down the stairs. Charlotte watched her go, and wondered how many more shocking secrets life had to reveal.

She went back into the supper-room and got another glass of champagne-cup. What a peculiar way for the human race to perpetuate itself, she thought. She supposed animals did something similar. What about birds? No, birds had eggs. And such words! *Pego* and *swiving*. All these hundreds of elegant and refined people around her knew those words, but never mentioned them. Because they were never mentioned, they were embarrassing. Because they were embarrassing, they were never mentioned. There was something very *silly* about the whole thing. If the Creator had ordained that people should swive, why pretend that they did not?

She finished her drink and went outside to the dance floor. Papa and Mama were dancing a polka, and doing it rather well. Mama had got over the incident in the park, but it still preyed on Papa's mind. He looked very fine in white tie and tails. When his leg was bad he would not dance, but obviously it was giving him no trouble tonight. He was surprisingly light on his feet for a big man. Mama seemed to be having a wonderful time. She was able to let herself go a bit when she danced. Her usual studied reserve fell away, and she smiled radiantly and let her ankles show.

When the polka was over Papa caught Charlotte's eye and came over. 'May I have this dance, Lady Charlotte?'

'Certainly, my lord.'

It was a waltz. Papa seemed distracted, but he whirled her around the floor expertly. She wondered whether she looked radiant, like Mama. Probably not. Suddenly she thought of Papa and Mama swiving, and found the idea terribly embarrassing.

Papa said: 'Are you enjoying your first big ball?'

'Yes, thank you,' she said dutifully.

'You seem thoughtful.'

'I'm on my best behaviour.' The lights and the bright colours blurred slightly, and suddenly she had to concentrate on staying upright. She was afraid she might fall over and look foolish. Papa sensed her unsteadiness and held her a little more firmly. A moment later the dance ended.

Papa took her off the floor. He said: 'Are you feeling quite well?'

'Yes, but I was dizzy for a moment.'

'Have you been smoking?'

Charlotte laughed. 'Certainly not.'

'That's the usual reason young ladies feel dizzy at balls. Take my advice: when you want to try tobacco, do it in private.'

'I don't think I want to try it.'

She sat out the next dance, and then Freddie turned up again. As she danced with him, it occurred to her that all the young men and girls, including Freddie and herself, were supposed to be looking for husbands or wives during the season, especially at balls like this. For the first time she considered Freddie as a possible husband for herself. It was unthinkable.

Then what kind of husband do I want? she wondered. She really had no idea.

Freddie said: 'Jonathan just said "Freddie, meet Charlotte," but I gather you're called Lady Charlotte Walden.'

'Yes. Who are you?'

'Marquis of Chalfont, actually.'

So, Charlotte thought, we're socially compatible.

A little later she and Freddie got into conversation with Belinda and Freddie's friends. They talked about a new play, called *Pygmalion,* which was said to be absolutely hilarious but quite vulgar. The boys spoke of going to a boxing match, and Belinda said she wanted to go too, but they all said it was out of the question. They discussed jazz music. One of the boys was something of a connoisseur, having lived for a while in the United States; but Freddie disliked it, and talked rather pompously about 'the negrification of society'. They all drank coffee and Belinda smoked another cigarette. Charlotte began to enjoy herself.

It was Charlotte's Mama who came along and broke up the party. 'Your father and I are leaving,' she said. 'Shall we send the coach back for you?'

Charlotte realized she was tired. 'No, I'll come,' she said. 'What time is it?'

'Four o'clock.'

They went to get their wraps. Mama said: 'Did you have a lovely evening?'

'Yes, thank you, Mama.'

'So did I. Who were those young men?'

'They know Jonathan.'

'Were they nice?'

'The conversation got quite interesting, in the end.'

Papa had called the carriage already. As they drove away from the bright lights of the party, Charlotte remembered what had happened last time they rode in a carriage, and she felt scared.

Papa held Mama's hand. They seemed happy. Charlotte felt excluded. She looked out of the window. In the dawn light she could see four men in silk hats walking up Park Lane, going home from some night club perhaps. As the carriage rounded Hyde Park

Corner Charlotte saw something odd. 'What's that?' she said.

Mama looked out. 'What's what, dear?'

'On the pavement. Looks like people.'

'That's right.'

'What are they doing?'

'Sleeping.'

Charlotte was horrified. There were eight or ten of them, up against a wall, bundled in coats, blankets and newspapers. She could not tell whether they were men or women, but some of the bundles were small enough to be children.

She said: 'Why do they sleep there?'

'I don't know, dear,' Mama said.

Papa said: 'Because they've nowhere else to sleep, of course.'

'They have no homes?'

'No.'

'I didn't know there was anyone that poor,' Charlotte said. 'How dreadful.' She thought of all the rooms in Uncle George's house, the food that had been laid out to be picked at by eight hundred people all of whom had had dinner, and the elaborate gowns they wore new each season while people slept under newspapers. She said: 'We should do something for them.'

'We?' Papa said. 'What should *we* do?'

'Build houses for them.'

'All of them?'

'How many are there?'

Papa shrugged. 'Thousands.'

'Thousands! I thought it was just those few.' Charlotte was devastated. 'Couldn't you build small houses?'

'There's no profit in house property, especially at that end of the market.'

'Perhaps you should do it anyway.'

'Why?'

'Because the strong should take care of the weak. I've heard you say that to Mr Samson.' Samson was the bailiff at Walden Hall, and he was always trying to save money on repairs to tenanted cottages.

'We already take care of rather a lot of people,' Papa said. 'All the servants whose wages we pay, all the tenants who farm our land and live in our cottages, all the workers in the companies we invest in, all the government employees who are paid out of our taxes—'

'I don't think that's much of an excuse,' Charlotte interrupted. 'Those poor people are sleeping on the *street*. What will they do in winter?'

Mama said sharply: 'Your Papa doesn't need excuses. He was born an aristocrat and he has managed his estate carefully. He is entitled to his wealth. Those people on the pavement are idlers, criminals, drunkards and ne'er-do-wells.'

'Even the children?'

'Don't be impertinent. Remember you still have a great deal to learn.'

'I'm just beginning to realize how much,' Charlotte said.

As the carriage turned into the courtyard of their

house, Charlotte glimpsed one of the street sleepers beside the gate. She decided she would take a closer look.

The coach stopped beside the front door. Charles handed Mama down, then Charlotte. Charlotte ran across the courtyard. William was closing the gates. 'Just a minute,' Charlotte called.

She heard Papa say: 'What the devil . . . ?'

She ran out into the street.

The sleeper was a woman. She lay slumped on the pavement with her shoulders against the courtyard wall. She wore a man's boots, woollen stockings, a dirty blue coat, and a very large once-fashionable hat with a bunch of grubby artificial flowers in its brim. Her head was slumped sideways and her face was turned toward Charlotte.

There was something familiar about the round face and the wide mouth. The woman was young . . .

Charlotte cried: 'Annie!'

The sleeper opened her eyes.

Charlotte stared at her in horror. Two months ago Annie had been a housemaid at Walden Hall in a crisp clean uniform with a little white hat on her head, a pretty girl with a large bosom and an irrepressible laugh. 'Annie, what happened to you?'

Annie scrambled to her feet and bobbed a pathetic curtsey. 'Oh, Lady Charlotte, I was hoping I would see you, you was always good to me, I've nowhere to turn—'

'But how did you get like this?'

'I was let go, m'lady, without a character, when they found out I was expecting the baby, I know I done wrong—'

'But you're not married!'

'But I was courting Jimmy, the under-gardener . . .'

Charlotte recalled Belinda's revelations, and realized that if all that was true it would indeed be possible for girls to have babies without being married. 'Where is the baby?'

'I lost it.'

'You *lost* it?'

'I mean, it came too early, m'lady, it was born dead.'

'How horrible,' Charlotte whispered. That was something else she had not known to be possible. 'And why isn't Jimmy with you?'

'He run away to sea. He *did* love me, I know, but he was frightened to wed, he was only seventeen . . .' Annie began to cry.

Charlotte heard Papa's voice. 'Charlotte, come in this instant.'

She turned to him. He stood at the gate in his evening clothes, with his silk hat in his hand, and suddenly she saw him as a big, smug, cruel old man. She said: 'This is one of the servants you care for so well.'

Papa looked at the girl. 'Annie! What is the meaning of this?'

Annie said: 'Jimmy run away, m'lord, so I couldn't wed, and I couldn't get another position because you never gave me a character, and I was ashamed to go home, so I come to London . . .'

'You came to London to beg,' Papa said harshly.

'Papa!' Charlotte cried.

'You don't understand, Charlotte—'

'I understand perfectly well—'

Mama appeared and said: 'Charlotte, get away from that creature!'

'She's not a creature, she's Annie.'

'Annie!' Mama shrilled. 'She's a fallen woman!'

'That's enough,' Papa said. 'This family does not hold discussions in the street. Let us go in immediately.'

Charlotte put her arm around Annie. 'She needs a bath, new clothes and a hot breakfast.'

'Don't be ridiculous!' Mama said. The sight of Annie seemed to have made her almost hysterical.

'All right,' Papa said. 'Take her into the kitchen. The parlourmaids will be up by now. Tell them to take care of her. Then come and see me in the drawing-room.'

Mama said: 'Stephen, this is insane—'

'Let us go *in*,' said Papa.

They went in.

Charlotte took Annie downstairs to the kitchen. A skivvy was cleaning the range and a kitchenmaid was slicing bacon for breakfast. It was just past five o'clock: Charlotte had not realized they started work so early. They both looked at her in astonishment when she walked in, in her ball gown, with Annie at her side.

Charlotte said: 'This is Annie. She used to work at

Walden Hall. She's had some bad luck but she's a good girl. She must have a bath. Find new clothes for her and burn her old ones. Then give her breakfast.'

For a moment they were both dumbstruck, then the kitchenmaid said: 'Very good, m'lady.'

'I'll see you later, Annie,' Charlotte said.

Annie seized Charlotte's arm. 'Oh, thank you, m'lady.'

Charlotte went out.

Now there will be trouble, she thought as she went upstairs. She did not care as much as she might have. She almost felt that her parents had betrayed her. What had her years of education been for, when in one night she could find out that the most important things had never been taught her? No doubt they talked of protecting young girls, but Charlotte thought deceit might be the appropriate term. When she thought of how ignorant she had been until tonight, she felt so foolish, and that made her angry.

She marched into the drawing-room.

Papa stood beside the fireplace holding a glass. Mama sat at the piano, playing double-minor chords with a pained expression on her face. They had drawn back the curtains. The room looked odd in the morning, with yesterday's cigar butts in the ashtrays and the cold early light on the edges of things. It was an evening room, and wanted lamps and warmth, drinks and footmen, and a crowd of people in formal clothes.

Everything looked different today.

'Now, then, Charlotte,' Papa began. 'You don't

understand what kind of woman Annie is. We let her go for a reason, you know. She did something very wrong which I cannot explain to you—'

'I know what she did,' Charlotte said, sitting down. 'And I know who she did it with. A gardener called Jimmy.'

Mama gasped.

Papa said: 'I don't believe you have any idea what you're talking about.'

'And if I haven't, whose fault is it?' Charlotte burst out. 'How did I manage to reach the age of eighteen without learning that some people are so poor they sleep in the street, that maids who are expecting babies get dismissed, and that – that – men are not made the same as women? Don't stand there telling me I don't understand these things and I have a lot to learn! I've spent all my life learning and now I discover most of it was lies! How dare you! How dare you!' She burst into tears, and hated herself for losing control.

She heard Mama say: 'Oh, this is too foolish.'

Papa sat beside her and took her hand. 'I'm sorry you feel that way,' he said. 'All young girls are kept in ignorance of certain things. It is done for their own good. We have never lied to you. If we did not tell you just how cruel and coarse the world is, that was only because we wanted you to enjoy your childhood for as long as possible. Perhaps we made a mistake.'

Mama snapped: 'We wanted to keep you out of the trouble that Annie got into!'

'I wouldn't put it quite like that,' Papa said mildly.

Charlotte's rage evaporated. She felt like a child again. She wanted to put her head on Papa's shoulder, but her pride would not let her.

'Shall we all forgive each other, and be pals again?' Papa said.

An idea which had been quietly budding in Charlotte's mind now blossomed, and she spoke without thinking. 'Would you let me take Annie as my personal maid?'

Papa said: 'Well . . .'

'We won't even think of it!' Mama said hysterically. 'It is quite out of the question! That an eighteen-year-old girl who is the daughter of an earl should have a scarlet woman as a maid! No, absolutely and finally, no!'

'Then what will she do?' Charlotte asked calmly.

'She should have thought of that when— She should have thought of that before.'

Papa said: 'Charlotte, we cannot possibly have a woman of bad character to live in this house. Even if I would allow it, the servants would be scandalized. Half of them would give notice. We shall hear mutterings even now, just because the girl has been allowed into the kitchen. You see, it is not just Mama and I who shun such people – it is the whole of society.'

'Then I shall buy her a house,' Charlotte said, 'and give her an allowance and be her friend.'

'You've no money,' Mama said.

'My Russian grandfather left me something.'

Papa said: 'But the money is in my care until you

reach the age of twenty-one, and I will not allow it to be used for that purpose.'

'Then what is to be done with her?' Charlotte said desperately.

'I'll make a bargain with you,' Papa said. 'I will give her money to get decent lodgings, and I'll see that she gets a job in a factory.'

'What would be my part of the bargain?'

'You must promise not to try to make contact with her, ever.'

Charlotte felt very tired. Papa had all the answers. She could no longer argue with him, and she did not have the power to insist. She sighed.

'All right,' she said.

'Good girl. Now, then, I suggest you go and find her and tell her the arrangement, then say goodbye.'

'I'm not sure I can look her in the eye.'

Papa patted her hand. 'She will be very grateful, you'll see. When you've spoken to her, you go to bed. I'll see to all the details.'

Charlotte did not know whether she had won or lost, whether Papa was being cruel or kind, whether Annie should feel saved or spurned. 'Very well,' she said wearily. She wanted to tell Papa that she loved him, but the words would not come. After a moment she got up and left the room.

On the day after the fiasco Feliks was awakened at noon by Bridget. He felt very weak. Bridget stood beside his bed with a large cup in her hand. Feliks sat up and took the cup. The drink was wonderful. It seemed to consist of hot milk, sugar, melted butter and lumps of bread. While he drank it Bridget moved around his room, tidying up, singing a sentimental song about boys who gave their lives for Ireland.

She went away and came back again with another Irishwoman of her own age who was a nurse. The woman stitched his hand and put a dressing on the puncture wound in his shoulder. Feliks gathered from the conversation that she was the local abortionist. Bridget told her that Feliks had been in a fight in a pub. The nurse charged a shilling for the visit and said: 'You won't die. If you'd had yourself seen to straight away you wouldn't have bled so much. As it is you'll feel weak for days.'

When she had gone Bridget talked to him. She was a heavy, good-natured woman in her late fifties. Her husband had got into some kind of trouble in Ireland and they had fled to the anonymity of London, where he died of the booze, she said. She had two sons who were policemen in New York and a daughter who was in service in Belfast. There was a vein of bitterness in her which showed in an occasional sarcastically humorous remark, usually at the expense of the English.

While she was explaining why Ireland should have Home Rule Feliks went to sleep. She woke him again in the evening to give him hot soup.

On the following day his physical wounds began visibly to heal, and he started to feel the pain of his emotional wounds. All the despair and self-reproach which he had felt in the park as he ran away now came back to him. Running away! How could it happen?

Lydia.

She was now Lady Walden.

He felt nauseous.

He made himself think clearly and coolly. He had known that she married and went to England. Obviously the Englishman she married was likely to be both an aristocrat and a man with a strong interest in Russia. Equally obviously, the person who negotiated with Orlov had to be a member of the establishment and an expert on Russian affairs. I couldn't have guessed it would turn out to be the same man, Feliks thought, but I should have realized the possibility.

The coincidence was not as remarkable as it had seemed, but it was no less shattering. Twice in his life Feliks had been utterly, blindly, deliriously happy. The first time was when, at the age of four – before his mother died – he had been given a red ball. The second was when Lydia fell in love with him. But the red ball had never been taken from him.

He could not imagine a greater happiness than that which he had had with Lydia – nor a disappointment more appalling than the one that followed. There had certainly been no such highs and lows in Feliks' emotional life since then. After she left he began to tramp the Russian countryside, dressed as a monk, preaching the anarchist gospel. He told the peasants that the land was theirs because they tilled it; that the wood in the forest belonged to anyone who felled a tree; that nobody had a right to govern them except themselves, and because self-government was no government it was called anarchy. He was a wonderful preacher and he made many friends, but he never fell in love again, and he hoped he never would.

His preaching phase had ended in 1899, during the national student strike, when he was arrested as an agitator and sent to Siberia. The years of wandering had already inured him to cold, hunger and pain; but now, working in a chain gang, using wooden tools to dig out gold in a mine, labouring on when the man chained to his side had fallen dead, seeing boys and women flogged, he came to know darkness, bitterness, despair, and finally hatred. In Siberia he had learned the facts of life: steal or starve, hide or be beaten, fight or die. There he had acquired cunning and ruthlessness. There he had learned the ultimate truth about oppression: that it works by turning its victims against each other instead of against their oppressors.

He escaped, and began the long journey into madness which ended when he killed the policeman outside Omsk, and realized that he had no fear.

He returned to civilization as a full-blooded revolutionist. It seemed incredible to him that he had once scrupled to throw bombs at the noblemen who maintained those Siberian convict mines. He was enraged by the government-inspired pogroms against the Jews in the west and south of Russia. He was sickened by the wrangling between Bolsheviks and Mensheviks at the second congress of the Social Democratic Party. He was inspired by the magazine that came from Geneva, called *Bread and Liberty*, with the quote from Bakunin on its masthead: 'The urge to destroy is also a creative urge.' Finally, hating the government, disenchanted with the socialists, and convinced by the anarchists, he went to a mill town called Bialystock and founded a group called Struggle.

Those had been the glory years. He would never forget young Nisan Farber, who had knifed the mill owner outside the synagogue on the Day of Atonement. Feliks himself had shot the chief of police. Then he took the fight to St Petersburg, where he founded another anarchist group, The Unauthorized, and planned the successful assassination of the Grand Duke Sergei. That year – 1905 – in St Petersburg there were killings, bank robberies, strikes and riots: the revolution seemed only days away. Then came the repression – more fierce, more efficient, and a great deal more bloodthirsty than anything the revolutionists had ever done. The secret police came in the middle of the night to the homes of The Unauthorized, and they were all arrested, except Feliks, who killed one policeman and maimed another and escaped to Switzerland, for by then nobody could stop him, he was so determined and powerful and angry and ruthless.

In all those years, and even in the quiet years in Switzerland which followed, he had never loved anyone. There had been people of whom he had grown mildly fond – a pig-keeper in Georgia, an old Jewish bomb-maker in Bialystock, Ulrich in Geneva – but they tended to pass into and then out of his life. There had been women, too. Many women sensed his violent nature and shied away from him, but those of them who found him attractive found him extremely so. Occasionally he had yielded to the temptation, and he had always been more or less disappointed. His parents were both dead and he had not seen his sister for twenty years. Looking back, he could see his life since Lydia as a slow slide into anaesthesia. He had survived by becoming less and less sensitive, through the experiences of imprisonment, torture, the chain gang, and the long, brutal escape from Siberia. He no longer cared even for himself: this, he had decided, was the meaning of his lack of fear, for one could only be afraid on account of something for which one cared.

He liked it this way.

His love was not for people, it was for *the* people. His compassion was for starving peasants in general, and sick children and frightened soldiers and crippled miners in general. He hated nobody in particular: just all princes, all landlords, all capitalists and all generals.

In giving his personality over to a higher cause he knew he was like a priest, and indeed like one priest in particular: his father. He no longer felt diminished by this comparison. He respected his father's high-mindedness and despised the cause it served. He, Feliks, had chosen the right cause. His life would not be wasted.

This was the Feliks that had formed over the years, as his mature personality emerged from the fluidity of youth. What had been so devastating about Lydia's scream, he thought, was that it had reminded him that there might have been a different Feliks, a warm and loving man, a sexual man, a man capable of jealousy, greed, vanity and fear. Would I rather be that man? he asked himself. That man would long to stare into her wide grey eyes and stroke her fine blonde hair, to see her collapse into helpless giggles as she tried to learn how to whistle, to argue with her about Tolstoy, to eat black bread and smoked herrings with her and to watch her screw up her pretty face at her first taste of vodka. That man would be *playful.*

He would also be *concerned.* He would wonder whether Lydia was happy. He would hesitate to pull the trigger for fear she might be hit by a ricochet. He might be reluctant to kill her nephew in case she were fond of the boy. That man would make a poor revolutionist.

No, he thought as he went to sleep that night; I would not want to be that man. He is not even dangerous.

In the night he dreamed that he shot Lydia, but when he woke up he could not remember whether it had made him sad.

On the third day he went out. Bridget gave him a shirt and a coat which had belonged to her husband. They fitted badly, for he had been shorter and wider than Feliks. Feliks' own trousers and boots were still wearable, and Bridget had washed the blood off.

He mended the bicycle, which had been damaged when he dropped it down the steps. He straightened a buckled wheel, patched a punctured tyre, and taped the split leather of the saddle. He climbed on and rode a short distance, but he realized immediately that he was not yet strong enough to go far on it. He walked instead.

It was a glorious sunny day. At a second-hand clothes

stall in Mornington Crescent he gave a halfpenny and Bridget's husband's coat for a lighter coat that fitted him. He felt peculiarly happy, walking through the streets of London in the summer weather. I've nothing to be happy about, he thought; my clever, well-organized, daring assassination plan fell to pieces because a woman cried out and a middle-aged man drew a sword. What a fiasco!

It was Bridget who had cheered him up, he decided. She had seen that he was in trouble and she had given help without thinking twice. It reminded him of the great-heartedness of the people in whose cause he fired guns and threw bombs and got himself sliced up with a sword. It gave him strength.

He made his way to St James's Park and took up his familiar station opposite the Walden house. He looked at the pristine white stonework and the high, elegant windows. You can knock me down, he thought, but you can't knock me out; if you knew I was back here again, you'd tremble in your patent-leather shoes.

He settled down to watch. The trouble with a fiasco was that it put the intended victim on his guard. It would now be very difficult indeed to kill Orlov because he would be taking precautions. But Feliks would find out what those precautions were, and he would evade them.

At eleven a.m. the carriage went out, and Feliks thought he saw behind the glass a spade-shaped beard and a top hat: Walden. It came back at one. It went out again at three, this time with a feminine hat inside, belonging presumably to Lydia, or perhaps to the daughter of the family; whoever it was returned at five. In the evening several guests came and the family apparently dined at home. There was no sign of Orlov. It rather looked as if he had moved out.

I'll find him, then, he thought.

On his way back to Camden Town he bought a newspaper. When he arrived home Bridget offered him tea, so he read the paper in her parlour. There was nothing about Orlov either in the Court Circular or the Social Notes.

Bridget saw what he was reading. 'Interesting material, for a fellow such as yourself,' she said sarcastically. 'You'll be making up your mind which of the balls to attend tonight, no doubt.'

Feliks smiled and said nothing.

Bridget said: 'I know what you are, you know. You're an anarchist.'

Feliks was very still.

'Who are you going to kill?' she said. 'I hope it's the bloody King.' She drank tea noisily. 'Well, don't stare at me like that. You look as if you're about to slit me throat. You needn't worry, I won't tell on you. My husband did for a few of the English in his time.'

Feliks was nonplussed. She had guessed – and she approved! He did not know what to say. He stood up and folded his newspaper. 'You're a good woman,' he said.

'If I was twenty years younger I'd kiss you. Get away before I forget myself.'

'Thank you for the tea,' Feliks said. He went out.

He spent the rest of the evening sitting in the drab

basement room, staring at the wall, thinking. Of course Orlov was lying low, but where? If he was not at the Walden house, he might be at the Russian Embassy, or at the home of one of the embassy staff, or at an hotel, or at the home of one of Walden's friends. He might even be out of London, at a house in the country. There was no way to check all the possibilities.

It was not going to be so easy. He began to worry.

He considered following Walden around. It might be the best he could do, but it was unsatisfactory. Although it was possible for a bicycle to keep pace with a carriage in London, it could be exhausting for the cyclist, and Feliks knew that he could not contemplate it for several days. Suppose then that, over a period of three days, Walden visited several private houses, two or three offices, an hotel or two and an embassy – how would Feliks find out which of those buildings Orlov was in? It was possible, but it would take time.

Meanwhile the negotiations would be progressing and war was drawing nearer.

And suppose that, after all that, Orlov was still living in Walden's house and had decided simply not to go out?

Feliks went to sleep gnawing at the problem and woke up in the morning with the solution.

He would ask Lydia.

He polished his boots, washed his hair, and shaved. He borrowed from Bridget a white cotton scarf which, worn around his throat, concealed the fact that he had neither collar nor tie. At the second-hand clothes stall in Mornington Crescent he found a bowler hat which fitted him. He looked at himself in the stallholder's cracked, frosted mirror. He looked dangerously respectable. He walked on.

He had no idea how Lydia would react to him. He was quite sure that she had not recognized him on the night of the fiasco: his face had been covered and her scream had been a reaction to the sight of an anonymous man with a gun. Assuming he could get in to see her, what would she do? Would she throw him out? Would she immediately begin to tear off her clothes, the way she had used to? Would she be merely indifferent, thinking of him as someone she knew in her youth and no longer cared for?

He wanted her to be shocked and dazed and still in love with him, so that he would be able to make her tell him a secret.

Suddenly he could not remember what she looked like. It was very odd. He knew she was a certain height, neither fat nor thin, with pale hair and grey eyes; but he could not bring to mind a picture of her. If he concentrated on her nose he could see that, or he could visualize her vaguely, without definite form, in the bleak light of a St Petersburg evening; but when he tried to focus on her she faded away.

He arrived at the park and hesitated outside the house. It was ten o'clock. Would they have got up yet? In any event, he thought he should probably wait until Walden left the house. It occurred to him that he might even see Orlov in the hall – at a time when he had no weapon.

If I do I'll strangle him with my hands, he thought savagely.

He wondered what Lydia was doing right now. She might be dressing. Ah, yes, he thought, I can picture her in a corset, brushing her hair before a mirror. Or she might be eating breakfast. There would be eggs and meat and fish, but she would eat a small piece of a soft roll and a slice of apple.

The carriage appeared at the entrance. A minute or two later someone got in and it drove to the gate. Feliks stood on the opposite side of the road as it emerged. Suddenly he was looking straight at Walden, behind the window of the coach, and Walden was looking; at him. Feliks had an urge to shout: 'Hey, Walden, I fucked her first!' Instead he grinned and doffed his hat. Walden inclined his head in acknowledgement, and the carriage passed on.

Feliks wondered why he felt so elated.

He walked through the gateway and across the courtyard. He saw that there were flowers in every window of the house, and he thought: Ah, yes, she always loved flowers. He climbed the steps to the porch and pulled the bell at the front door.

Perhaps she will call the police, he thought.

A moment later a servant opened the door. Feliks stepped inside. 'Good morning,' he said.

'Good morning, sir,' the servant said.

So I *do* look respectable. 'I should like to see the Countess of Walden. It is a matter of great urgency. My name is Constantine Dmitrich Levin. I am sure she will remember me from St Petersburg.'

'Yes, sir. Constantine . . . ?'

'Constantine Dmitrich Levin. Let me give you my

card.' Feliks fumbled inside his coat. 'Ach! I brought none.'

'That's all right, sir. Constantine Dmitrich Levin.'

'Yes.'

'If you will be so good as to wait here, I'll see if the Countess is in.'

Feliks nodded, and the servant went away.

CHAPTER SIX

THE QUEEN ANNE bureau-bookcase was one of Lydia's favourite pieces of furniture in the London house. Two hundred years old, it was of black lacquer decorated in gold with vaguely Chinese scenes of pagodas, willow trees, islands and flowers. The flap front folded down to form a writing-table and to reveal red-velvet-lined pigeonholes for letters and tiny drawers for paper and pens. There were large drawers in the bombé base, and the top, above her eye-level as she sat at the table, was a bookcase with a mirrored door. The ancient mirror showed a cloudy, distorted reflection of the morning-room behind her.

On the writing-table was an unfinished letter to her sister, Aleks' mother, in St Petersburg. Lydia's handwriting was small and untidy. She had written, in Russian: *I don't know what to think about Charlotte* and then she had stopped. She sat, looking into the cloudy mirror, musing.

It was turning out to be a very eventful season in the worst possible way. After the suffragette protest at the court and the madman in the park she had thought there could be no more catastrophes. And for a few days life had been calm. Charlotte was successfully launched. Aleks was no longer around to disturb Lydia's equanimity, for he had fled to the Savoy Hotel and did not appear at society functions. Belinda's ball had been a huge success. That night Lydia had forgotten her troubles and had a wonderful time. She had danced the waltz, the polka, the two-step, the tango and even the Turkey Trot. She had partnered half the House of Lords, several dashing young men, and – most of all – her husband. It was not really chic to dance with one's own husband quite as much as she had. But Stephen looked so fine in his white tie and tails, and he danced so well, that she had given herself up to pleasure. Her marriage was definitely in one of its happier phases. Looking back over the years, she had the feeling that it was often like this in the season. And then Annie had turned up to spoil it all.

Lydia had only the vaguest recollection of Annie as a housemaid at Walden Hall. One could not possibly know all the servants at an establishment as large as that: there were some fifty indoor staff, and then the gardeners and grooms. Nor was one known to all the servants: on one famous occasion, Lydia had stopped a passing maid in the hall and asked her whether Lord Walden was in his room, and had received the reply: 'I'll go and see, madam – what name shall I say?'

However, Lydia remembered the day Mrs Braithwaite, the housekeeper at Walden Hall, had come to her with the news that Annie would have to go because she was pregnant. Mrs Braithwaite did not say 'pregnant', she said 'overtaken in moral transgression'. Both Lydia and Mrs Braithwaite were embarrassed, but neither was shocked: it had happened to housemaids before and it would happen again. They had to be let go – it was the only way to run a respectable house – and naturally they could not be given references in those circumstances. Without a 'character' a maid could not get another job in service, of course; but normally she did not need a job, for she either married the father of the child or went home to mother. Indeed, years later, when she had brought up her children, such a girl might even find her way back into the house, as a laundrymaid or kitchenmaid, or in some other capacity which would not bring her into contact with her employers.

Lydia had assumed that Annie's life would follow that course. She remembered that a young under-gardener had left without giving notice and run away to sea – that piece of news had come to her attention because of the difficulty of finding boys to work as gardeners for a sensible wage these days – but of course no one ever told her the connection between Annie and the boy.

We're not harsh, Lydia thought; as employers we're relatively generous. Yet Charlotte reacted as if Annie's plight were my fault. I don't know where she gets her ideas. What was it she said? 'I know what Annie did and I know who she did it with.' In Heaven's name, where did the child learn to speak like that? I dedicated my whole life to bringing her up to be pure and clean and decent, not like me *don't even think that*—

She dipped her pen in the inkwell. She would have liked to share her worries with her sister, but it was so hard in a letter. It was hard enough in person, she thought. Charlotte was the one with whom she really wanted to share her thoughts. Why is it that when I try I become shrill and tyrannical?

Pritchard came in. 'A Mr Constantine Dmitrich Levin to see you, my lady.'

Lydia frowned. 'I don't think I know him.'

'The gentleman said it was a matter of urgency, m'lady, and seemed to think you would remember him from St Petersburg.' Pritchard looked dubious.

Lydia hesitated. The name was distinctly familiar. From time to time Russians whom she hardly knew would call on her in London. They usually began by offering to take back messages, and ended by asking to borrow the passage money. Lydia did not mind helping them. 'All right,' she said. 'Show him in.'

Pritchard went out. Lydia inked her pen again, and wrote: *What can one do when the child is eighteen years old and has a will of her own? Stephen says I worry too much. I wish—*

I can't even talk to Stephen properly, she thought. He just makes soothing noises.

The door opened, and Pritchard said: 'Mr Constantine Dmitrich Levin.'

Lydia spoke over her shoulder in English. 'I'll be with you in a moment, Mr Levin.' She heard the butler close the door as she wrote: – *that I could believe him.* She put down her pen and turned around.

He spoke to her in Russian. 'How are you, Lydia?'

Lydia whispered: 'Oh, my *God.*'

It was as if something cold and heavy had descended

over her heart, and she could not breathe. Feliks stood in front of her: tall, and thin as ever, in a shabby coat with a scarf, holding a foolish English hat in his left hand. He was as familiar as if she had seen him yesterday. His hair was still long and black, without a hint of grey. There was that white skin, the nose like a curved blade, the wide, mobile mouth, and the sad soft eyes.

He said: 'I'm sorry to shock you.'

Lydia could not speak. She struggled with a storm of mixed emotions: shock, fear, delight, horror, affection and dread. She stared at him. He was *older*. His face was lined: there were two sharp creases in his cheeks, and downturning wrinkles at the corners of his lovely mouth. They seemed like lines of pain and hardship. In his expression there was a hint of something which had not been there before – perhaps ruthlessness, or cruelty, or just inflexibility. He looked tired.

He was studying her, too. 'You look like a girl,' he said wonderingly.

She tore her eyes away from him. Her heart pounded like a drum. Dread became her dominant feeling. If Stephen should come back early, she thought, and walk in here now, and give me that look that says Who is this man? and I were to blush, and mumble, and—

'I wish you'd say something,' Feliks said.

Her eyes returned to him. With an effort, she said: 'Go away.'

'No.'

Suddenly she knew she did not have the strength of will to make him leave. She looked over to the bell which would summon Pritchard. Feliks smiled as if he knew what was in her mind.

'It's been nineteen years,' he said.

'You've aged,' she said abruptly.

'You've changed.'

'What did you expect?'

'I expected this,' he said. 'That you would be afraid to admit to yourself that you are happy to see me.'

He had always been able to see into her soul with those soft eyes. What was the use of pretending? He knew all about pretending, she recalled. He had understood her from the moment he first set eyes on her.

'Well?' he said. 'Aren't you happy?'

'I'm frightened, too,' she said, and then she realized she had admitted to being happy. 'And you?' she added hastily. 'How do you feel?'

'I don't feel much at all, any more,' he said. His face twisted into an odd, pained smile. It was a look she had never seen on him in the old days. She felt intuitively that he was telling the truth at that moment.

He drew up a chair and sat close to her. She jerked back convulsively. He said: 'I won't hurt you—'

'Hurt me?' Lydia gave a laugh that sounded unexpectedly brittle. 'You'll ruin my life!'

'You ruined mine,' he replied; then he frowned as if he had surprised himself.

'Oh, Feliks, I didn't mean to.'

He was suddenly tense. There was a heavy silence. He gave that hurt smile again, and said: 'What happened?'

She hesitated. She realized that all these years she

had been longing to explain it to him. She began: 'That night you tore my gown . . .'

'What are you going to do about this tear in your gown?' Feliks asked.

'The maid will put a stitch in it before I arrive at the embassy,' Lydia replied.

'Your maid carries needles and thread around with her?'

'Why else would one take one's maid when one goes out to dinner?'

'Why indeed?' He was lying on the bed watching her dress. She knew that he loved to see her put her clothes on. He had once done an imitation of her pulling up her drawers which had made her laugh until it hurt.

She took the gown from him and put it on. 'Everybody takes an hour to dress for the evening,' she said. 'Until I met you I had no idea it could be done in five minutes. Button me up.'

She looked in the mirror and tidied her hair while he fastened the hooks at the back of her gown. When he had finished he kissed her shoulder. She arched her neck. 'Don't start again,' she said. She picked up the old brown cloak and handed it to him.

He helped her on with it. He said: 'The lights go out when you leave.'

She was touched. He was not often sentimental. She said: 'I know how you feel.'

'Will you come tomorrow?'

'Yes.'

At the door she kissed him and said: 'Thank you.'

'I love you dearly,' he said.

She left him. As she went down the stairs she heard a noise behind her and looked back. Feliks' neighbour was watching her from the door of the next apartment. He looked embarrassed when he caught her eye. She nodded politely to him, and he withdrew. It occurred to her that he could probably hear them making love through the wall. She did not care. She knew that what she was doing was wicked and shameful but she refused to think about it.

She went out into the street. Her maid was waiting on the corner. Together they walked to the park where the carriage was waiting. It was a cold evening, but Lydia felt as if she were glowing with her own warmth. She often wondered whether people could tell, just by looking at her, that she had been making love.

The coachman put down the step of the carriage for her and avoided her eyes. He knows, she thought with surprise; then she decided that that was fanciful.

In the coach the maid hastily repaired the back of Lydia's gown. Lydia changed the brown cloak for a fur wrap. The maid fussed with Lydia's hair. Lydia gave her ten roubles for her silence. Then they were at the British Embassy.

Lydia composed herself and went in.

It was not difficult, she found, to assume her other personality and become the modest, virginal Lydia whom polite society knew. As soon as she entered the real world she was terrified by the brute power of her passion for Feliks and she became quite genuinely a trembling lily. It was no act. Indeed, for most of the hours in the day she felt that this well-behaved maiden was her real self, and she thought she must be somehow possessed while she was with Feliks. But when he was there, and also when she was alone in bed in the middle of the night, she knew that it was her official persona that was evil, for it would have denied her the greatest joy she had ever known.

So she entered the hall, dressed in becoming white, looking young and a little nervous.

She met her cousin Kiril, who was nominally her escort. He was a widower of thirty-something years, an irritable man who worked for the Foreign Minister. He and Lydia did not much like each other, but because his wife was dead, and because Lydia's parents did not enjoy going out, Kiril and Lydia had let it be known that they should be invited together. Lydia always told him not to trouble to call for her. This was how she managed to meet Feliks clandestinely.

'You're late,' Kiril said.

'I'm sorry,' she replied insincerely.

Kiril took her into the salon. They were greeted by the Ambassador and his wife, and then introduced to Lord Highcombe, elder son of the Earl of Walden. He was a tall, handsome man of about thirty, in well-cut but rather sober clothes. He looked very English, with his short, light-brown hair and blue eyes. He had a smiling, open face which Lydia found mildly attractive. He spoke good French. They made polite conversation for a few moments, then he was introduced to someone else.

'He seems rather pleasant,' Lydia said to Kiril.

'Don't be fooled,' Kiril told her. 'Rumour has it that he's a tearaway.'

'You surprise me.'

'He plays cards with some officers I know, and they were telling me that he drinks them under the table some nights.'

'You know so much about people, and it's always bad.'

Kiril's thin lips twisted in a smile. 'Is that my fault or theirs?'

Lydia said: 'Why is he here?'

'In St Petersburg? Well, the story is that he has a very rich and domineering father, with whom he doesn't see eye to eye; so he's drinking and gambling his way around the world while he waits for the old man to die.'

Lydia did not expect to speak to Lord Highcombe again, but the Ambassador's wife, seeing them both as eligible, seated them side by side at dinner. During the second course he tried to make conversation. 'I wonder whether you know the Minister of Finance?' he said.

'I'm afraid not,' Lydia said coldly. She knew all about the man, of course, and he was a great favourite of the Czar; but he had married a woman who was not only divorced but also Jewish, which made it rather awkward for people to invite him. She suddenly thought how scathing Feliks would be about such prejudices; then the Englishman was speaking again.

'I should be most interested to meet him. I understand

he's terribly energetic and forward-looking. His Trans-Siberian Railway project is marvellous. But people say he's not very refined.'

'I'm sure Sergei Yulevitch Witte is a loyal servant of our adored sovereign,' Lydia said politely.

'No doubt,' Highcombe said, and turned back to the lady on his other side.

He thinks I'm boring, Lydia thought.

A little later she asked him: 'Do you travel a great deal?'

'Most of the time,' he replied. 'I go to Africa almost every year, for the big game.'

'How fascinating! What do you shoot?'

'Lion, elephant . . . a rhinoceros, once.'

'In the jungle?'

'The hunting is in the grasslands to the east, but I did once go as far south as the rain forest, just to see it.'

'And is it how it is pictured in books?'

'Yes, even to the naked black pygmies.'

Lydia felt herself flush, and she turned away. Now why did he have to say that? she thought. She did not speak to him again. They had conversed enough to satisfy the dictates of etiquette, and clearly neither of them was keen to go farther.

After dinner she played at the Ambassador's wonderful grand piano for a while, then Kiril took her home. She went straight to bed to dream of Feliks.

The next morning after breakfast a servant summoned her to her father's study.

The Count was a small, thin, exasperated man of

fifty-five. Lydia was the youngest of his four children – the others were a sister and two brothers, all married. Their mother was alive but in continual bad health. The Count saw little of his family. He seemed to spend most of his time reading. He had one old friend who came to play chess. Lydia had vague memories of a time when things were different, and they were a jolly family around a big dinner-table; but it was a long time ago. Nowadays a summons to the study meant only one thing: trouble.

When Lydia went in he was standing in front of the writing-table, his hands behind his back, his face twisted with fury. Lydia's maid stood near the door with tears on her cheeks. Lydia knew then what the trouble was, and she felt herself tremble.

There was no preamble. Her father began by shouting: 'You have been seeing a boy secretly!'

Lydia folded her arms to stop herself shaking. 'How did you find out?' she said with an accusing look at the maid.

Her father made a disgusted noise. 'Don't look at *her*,' he said. 'The coachman told me of your extraordinarily long walks in the park. Yesterday I had you followed.' His voice rose again. 'How could you act like that – like a peasant girl?'

How much did he know? Not everything, surely! 'I'm in love,' Lydia said.

'In love?' he roared. 'You mean you're in heat!'

Lydia thought he was about to strike her. She took several paces backward and prepared to run. He knew everything. It was total catastrophe. What would he do?

He said: 'The worst of it is, you can't possibly marry him.'

Lydia was aghast. She was prepared to be thrown out of the house, cut off without a penny, and humiliated; but he had in mind worse punishment than that. 'Why can't I marry him?' she cried.

'Because he's practically a serf and an anarchist to boot. Don't you understand – you're ruined!'

'Then let me marry him and live in ruin!'

'No!' he yelled.

There was a heavy silence. The maid, still in tears, sniffed monotonously. Lydia heard a ringing in her ears.

'This will kill your mother,' the Count said.

Lydia whispered: 'What are you going to do?'

'You'll be confined to your room for now. As soon as I can arrange it, you'll enter a convent.'

Lydia stared at him in horror. It was a sentence of death.

She ran from the room.

Never to see Feliks again – the thought was utterly unbearable. Tears rolled down her face. She ran to her bedroom. She could not possibly suffer this punishment. I shall die, she thought; I shall die.

Rather than leave Feliks for ever she would leave her family for ever. As soon as this idea occurred to her she knew it was the only thing to do – and the time to do it was now, before her father sent someone to lock her into the room.

She looked in her purse: she had only a few roubles.

She opened her jewellery case. She took out a diamond bracelet, a gold chain, and some rings, and stuffed them into her purse. She put on her coat and ran down the back stairs. She left the house by the servants' door.

She hurried through the streets. People stared at her, running in her fine clothes, with tears on her face. She did not care. She had left society for good. She was going to elope with Feliks.

She quickly became exhausted and slowed to a walk. Suddenly the whole affair did not seem so disastrous. She and Feliks could go to Moscow, or to a country town, or even abroad, perhaps Germany. Feliks would have to find work. He was educated, so he could at least be a clerk, possibly better. She might take in sewing. They would rent a small house and furnish it cheaply. They would have children, strong boys and pretty girls. The things she would lose seemed worthless: silk dresses, society gossip, ubiquitous servants, huge houses and delicate foods.

What would it be like, living with him? They would get into bed and actually go to sleep together – how romantic! They would take walks, holding hands, not caring who saw that they were in love. They would sit by the fireside in the evenings, playing cards or reading or just talking. Any time she wanted, she could touch him, or kiss him, or take off her clothes for him.

She reached his house and climbed the stairs. What would his reaction be? He would be shocked, then elated; then he would become practical. They would have to leave immediately, he would say, for her father could send people after them to bring her back. He would be decisive. 'We'll go to X,' he would say, and he would talk about tickets and a suitcase and disguises.

She took out her key, but the door to his apartment hung open and askew on its hinges. She went in, calling: 'Feliks, it's me – oh!'

She stopped in the doorway. The whole place was in a mess, as if it had been robbed, or there had been a fight. Feliks was not there.

Suddenly she was terribly afraid.

She walked around the small apartment, feeling dazed, stupidly looking behind the curtains and under the bed. All his books were gone. The mattress had been slashed. The mirror was broken, the one in which they watched themselves making love one afternoon when it had been snowing outside.

Lydia wandered aimlessly into the hallway. The occupant of the next apartment stood in his doorway. Lydia looked at him. 'What happened?' she said.

'He was arrested last night,' the man replied.

And the sky fell in.

She felt faint. She leaned against the wall for support. Arrested! Why? Where was he? Who had arrested him? How could she elope with him if he was in jail?

'It seems he was an anarchist.' The neighbour grinned suggestively and added: 'Whatever else he might have been.'

It was too much to bear, that this should have happened on the very day that Father had—

'Father,' Lydia whispered. 'Father did this.'

'You look ill,' the neighbour said. 'Would you like to come in and sit down for a moment?'

Lydia did not like the look on his face. She could not cope with this leering man on top of everything else. She pulled herself together and, without answering him, made her way slowly down the stairs and went out into the street.

She walked slowly, going nowhere, wondering what to do. Somehow she had to get Feliks out of jail. She had no idea how to go about it. Should she appeal to the Minister of the Interior? To the Czar? She did not know how to reach them except by going to the right receptions. She could write – but she needed Feliks *today*. Could she visit him in jail? At least then she would know how he was, and he would know she was fighting for him. Maybe, if she arrived in a coach, dressed in fine clothes, she could overawe the jailer . . . But she did not know where the jail was – there might be more than one – and she did not have her carriage; and if she went home her father would lock her up and she would never see Feliks—

She fought back the tears. She was so ignorant of the world of police and jails and criminals. Whom could she ask? Feliks' anarchist friends would know all about that sort of thing, but she had never met them and did not know where to find them.

She thought of her brothers. Maks was managing the family estate in the country, and he would see Feliks from Father's point of view and would completely approve of what Father had done. Dmitri – empty-headed, effeminate Dmitri – would sympathize with Lydia but be helpless.

There was only one thing to do. She must go and plead with her father for Feliks' release.

Wearily, she turned around and headed for home.

Her anger toward her father grew with every step she took. He was supposed to love her, care for her, and ensure her happiness – and what did he do? Tried to ruin her life. She knew what she wanted, she knew what would make her happy. Whose life was it? Who had the right to decide?

She arrived home in a rage.

She went straight to the study and walked in without knocking. 'You've had him arrested,' she accused.

'Yes,' her father said. His mood had altered. His mask of fury had gone, to be replaced by a thoughtful, calculating look.

Lydia said: 'You must have him released immediately.'

'They are torturing him, at the moment.'

'No,' Lydia whispered. 'Oh, no.'

'They are flogging the soles of his feet – '

Lydia screamed.

Father raised his voice. ' – with thin, flexible, canes – '

There was a paper-knife on the writing-table.

' – which quickly cut the soft skin – '

I will kill him—

' – until there is so much blood—'

Lydia went berserk.

She picked up the paper-knife and rushed at her father. She lifted the knife high in the air and brought it down with all her might, aiming at his skinny neck, screaming all the while: 'I hate you, I hate you, I hate you—'

He moved aside, caught her wrist, forced her to drop the knife, and pushed her into a chair.

She burst into hysterical tears.

After a few minutes her father began to speak again, calmly, as if nothing had happened. 'I could have it stopped immediately,' he said. 'I can have the boy released whenever I choose.'

'Oh, please,' Lydia sobbed. 'I'll do anything you say.'

'Will you?' he said.

She looked up at him through her tears. An access of hope calmed her. Did he mean it? Would he release Feliks? 'Anything,' she said, 'anything.'

'I had a visitor while you were out,' he said conversationally. 'The Earl of Walden. He asked permission to call on you.'

'Who?'

'The Earl of Walden. He was Lord Highcombe when you met him last evening, but his father died in the night so now he's the Earl. "Earl" is the English for "Count".'

Lydia stared at her father uncomprehendingly. She remembered meeting the Englishman, but she could not understand why her father was suddenly rambling on about him. She said: 'Don't torture me. Tell me what I must do to make you release Feliks.'

'Marry the Earl of Walden,' her father said abruptly.

Lydia stopped crying. She stared at him, struck dumb. Was he really saying this? It sounded insane.

He continued: 'Walden will want to marry quickly. You would leave Russia and go to England with him. This appalling affair could be forgotten and nobody need know. It's the ideal solution.'

'And Feliks?' Lydia breathed.

'The torture would stop today. The boy would be released the moment you leave for England. You would never see him again as long as you live.'

'No,' Lydia whispered. 'In God's name, no.'

They were married eight weeks later.

'You really tried to stab your father?' Feliks said with a mixture of awe and amusement.

Lydia nodded. She thought: Thank God, he had not guessed the rest of it.

Feliks said: 'I'm proud of you.'

'It was a terrible thing to do.'

'He was a terrible man.'

'I don't think so any more.'

There was a pause. Feliks said softly: 'So, you never betrayed me, after all.'

The urge to take him into her arms was almost irresistible. She made herself sit frozen still. The moment passed.

'Your father kept his word,' he mused. 'The torture stopped that day. They let me out the day after you left for England.'

'How did you know where I had gone?'

'I got a message from the maid. She left it at the bookshop. Of course she didn't know of the bargain you had made.'

The things they had to say were so many and so weighty that they sat in silence. Lydia was still afraid to move. She noticed that he kept his right hand in his coat pocket all the time. She did not remember his having that habit before.

'Can you whistle yet?' he said suddenly.

She could not help laughing. 'I never got the knack.'

They lapsed into quiet again. Lydia wanted him to leave, and with equal desperation she wanted him to stay. Eventually she said: 'What have you been doing since then?'

Feliks shrugged. 'A good deal of travelling. You?'

'Bringing up my daughter.'

The years in between seemed to be an uncomfortable topic for both of them.

Lydia said: 'What made you come here?'

'Oh . . .' Feliks seemed momentarily confused by the question. 'I need to see Orlov.'

'Aleks? Why?'

'There's an anarchist sailor in jail – I have to persuade Orlov to release him . . . You know how things are in Russia, there's no justice, only influence.'

'Aleks isn't here any more. Someone tried to rob us in our carriage, and he got frightened.'

'Where can I find him?' Feliks said. He seemed suddenly tense.

'The Savoy Hotel – but I doubt if he'll see you.'

'I can try.'

'This is important to you, isn't it?'

'Yes.'

'You're still . . . political?'

'It's my life.'

'Most young men lose interest as they grow older.'

He smiled ruefully. 'Most young men get married and have a family.'

Lydia was full of pity. 'Feliks, I'm so sorry.'

He reached out and took her hand.

She snatched it back and stood up. 'Don't touch me,' she said.

He looked at her in surprise.

'I've learned my lesson, even if you haven't,' she said. 'I was brought up to believe that lust is evil, and destroys. For a while, when we were . . . together . . . I stopped believing that, or at least I pretended to stop. And look what happened – I ruined myself and I ruined you. My father was right – lust does destroy. I've never forgotten that, and I never will.'

He looked at her sadly. 'Is that what you tell yourself?'

'It's true.'

'The morality of Tolstoy. Doing good may not make you happy, but doing wrong will certainly make you unhappy.'

She took a deep breath. 'I want you to go away now, and never come back.'

He looked at her in silence for a long moment, then he stood up. 'Very well,' he said.

Lydia thought her heart would break.

He took a step toward her. She stood still, knowing she should move away from him, unable to do so. He put his hands on her shoulders and looked into her eyes, and then it was too late. She remembered how it used to be when they looked into each other's eyes, and she was lost. He drew her to him and kissed her, folding her into his arms. It was just as always, his restless mouth on her soft lips, busy, loving, gentle; she was melting. She pushed her body against his. There was a fire in her loins. She shuddered with pleasure. She searched for his hands and held them in her own, just to have something to hold, a part of his body to grip, to squeeze with all her might—

He gave a shout of pain.

They broke apart. She stared at him, nonplussed.

He held his right hand to his mouth. She saw that he had a nasty wound, and in squeezing his hand she had made it bleed. She moved to take his hand, to say sorry, but he stepped back. A change had come over him, the spell was broken. He turned and strode to the door. Horrified, she watched him go out. The door slammed. Lydia gave a cry of loss.

She stood for a moment gazing at the place where he had been. She felt as if she had been ravaged. She fell into a chair. She began to shake uncontrollably.

Her emotions whirled and boiled for minutes, and she could not think straight. Eventually they settled, leaving one predominant feeling: relief that she had not yielded to the temptation to tell him the last chapter of the story. That was a secret lodged deep within her, like a piece of shrapnel in a healed-over wound; and there it would stay until the day she died, when it would be buried with her.

Feliks stopped in the hall to put on his hat. He looked at himself in the mirror, and his face twisted into a grin of savage triumph. He composed his features and went out into the midday sunshine.

She was so gullible. She had believed his half-baked story about an anarchist sailor, and she had told him, without a second's hesitation, where to find Orlov. He was exultant that she was still so much in his power. She married Walden for my sake, he thought, and now I have made her betray her husband.

Nevertheless, the interview had had its dangerous moments for him. As she was telling her story he had watched her face, and a dreadful grief had welled up within him, a peculiar sadness that made him want to cry; but it had been so long since he shed tears that his body seemed to have forgotten how, and those dangerous moments had passed. I'm not really vulnerable to sentiment, he told himself: I lied to her, betrayed her trust in me, kissed her and ran away; I *used* her.

Fate is on my side today. It's a good day for a dangerous task.

He had dropped his gun in the park, so he needed a new weapon. For an assassination in an hotel room a bomb would be best. It did not have to be aimed accurately, for wherever it landed it would kill everyone in the room. If Walden should happen to be there with Orlov at the time, so much the better, Feliks thought.

It occurred to him that then Lydia would have helped him kill her husband.

So?

He put her out of his mind and began to think about chemistry.

He went to a chemist's shop in Camden Town and bought four pints of a common acid in concentrated form. The acid came in two two-pint bottles, and cost four shillings and fivepence including the price of the bottles, which was returnable.

He took the bottles home and put them on the floor of the basement room.

He went out again, and bought another four pints of the same acid in a different shop. The chemist asked him what he was going to use it for. 'Cleaning,' he said, and the man seemed satisfied.

In a third chemist's he bought four pints of a different acid. Finally he bought a pint of pure glycerine and a glass rod a foot long.

He had spent sixteen shillings and eightpence, but he would get four shillings and threepence back for the bottles when they were empty. That would leave him with just under three pounds.

Because he had bought the ingredients in different shops, none of the chemists had any reason to suspect that he was going to make explosives.

He went up to Bridget's kitchen and borrowed her largest mixing bowl.

'Would you be baking a cake?' she asked him.

He said: 'Yes.'

'Don't blow us all up, then.'

'I won't.'

Nevertheless, she took the precaution of spending the afternoon with a neighbour.

Feliks went back downstairs, took off his jacket, rolled up his sleeves, and washed his hands.

He put the mixing bowl in the washbasin.

He looked at the thirteen large brown bottles, with their ground-glass stoppers, lined up on the floor.

The first part of the job was not very dangerous.

He mixed the two kinds of acid together in Bridget's kitchen bowl, waited for the bowl to cool, then re-bottled the two-to-one mixture.

He washed the bowl, dried it, put it back into the sink, and poured the glycerine into it.

The sink was fitted with a rubber plug on a chain. He wedged the plug into the drain-hole sideways, so that it was partly blocked. He turned on the tap. When the water level reached almost to the rim of the kitchen bowl he turned the tap partly but not completely off, so that the water was flowing out as fast as it was flowing in and the level in the sink stayed constant without overflowing into the kitchen bowl.

The next part had killed more anarchists than the Ochrana.

Gingerly, he began to add the mixed acids to the glycerine, stirring gently but constantly with the glass rod.

The basement room was very warm.

Occasionally a wisp of reddish-brown smoke came off the bowl, a sign that the chemical reaction was beginning to get out of control; then Feliks would stop adding acid, but carry on stirring, until the flow of water through the washbasin cooled the bowl and moderated the reaction. When the fumes were gone he waited a minute or two then carried on mixing.

This is how Ilya died, he recalled; standing over a sink in a basement room, mixing acids and glycerine: perhaps he was impatient. When they finally cleared the rubble, there was nothing left of Ilya to bury.

Afternoon turned into evening. The air became cooler but Feliks perspired all the same. His hand was as steady as a rock. He could hear children in the street outside, playing a game and chanting a rhyme: 'Salt, mustard, vinegar *pepper*, salt, mustard, vinegar *pepper*.' He wished he had ice. He wished he had electric light. The room filled with acid fumes. His throat was raw. The mixture in the bowl stayed clear.

He found himself daydreaming about Lydia. In the daydream she came into the basement room, stark naked, smiling, and he told her to go because he was busy.

'Salt, mustard, vinegar *pepper*.'

He poured the last bottle of acid as slowly and gently as the first.

Still stirring, he increased the stream of water from the tap so that it overflowed into the bowl, then he meticulously washed away the surplus acids.

When he had finished he had a bowl of nitroglycerine.

It was an explosive liquid twenty times as powerful as gunpowder. It could be detonated by a blasting cap, but such a detonator was not essential, for it could also be set off by a lighted match or even the warmth from a nearby fire. Feliks had known a foolish man who carried a bottle of nitroglycerine in the breast pocket of his coat until the heat of his body detonated it and killed him and three other people and a horse in a St Petersburg street. A bottle of nitroglycerine would explode if smashed, or just dropped on the floor, or shaken or even jerked hard.

With the utmost care, Feliks dipped a clean bottle into the bowl and let it fill slowly with the explosive. When it was full he closed the bottle, making sure that there was no nitroglycerine caught between the neck of the bottle and the ground-glass stopper.

There was some liquid left in the bowl. Of course it could not be poured down the sink.

Feliks went over to his bed and picked up the pillow. The stuffing seemed to be cotton waste. He tore a small hole in the pillow and pulled out some of the stuff. It was chopped rag mixed with a few feathers. He poured some of it into the nitroglycerine remaining in the bowl. The stuffing absorbed the liquid quite well. Feliks added more stuffing until all the liquid was soaked up then he rolled it into a ball and wrapped it in newspaper. It was now much more stable, like dynamite – in fact dynamite was what it was. It would detonate much less readily than the pure liquid. Lighting the newspaper might do it, and it might not: what was really required was a paper drinking-straw packed with gunpowder. But Feliks did not plan to use the dynamite, for he needed something reliable and immediate.

He washed and dried the mixing bowl again. He

plugged the sink, filled it with water, then gently placed the bottle of nitroglycerine in the water, to keep cool.

He went upstairs and returned Bridget's kitchen bowl.

He came back down and looked at the bomb in the sink. He thought: I wasn't afraid. All afternoon, I was never frightened of dying. I still have no fear.

That made him glad.

He went off to reconnoitre the Savoy Hotel.

CHAPTER SEVEN

WALDEN OBSERVED that both Lydia and Charlotte were subdued at tea. He, too, was thoughtful. The conversation was desultory.

After he had changed for dinner, Walden sat in the drawing-room sipping sherry, waiting for his wife and his daughter to come down. They were to dine out, at the Pontadarvies'. It was another warm evening. So far it had been a fine summer for weather, if for nothing else.

Shutting Aleks up in the Savoy Hotel had not done anything to hasten the slow pace of negotiating with the Russians. Aleks inspired affection like a kitten, and had the kitten's surprisingly sharp teeth. Walden had put to him the counter-proposal, an international waterway from the Black Sea to the Mediterranean. Aleks had said flatly that this was not good enough, for in wartime – when the strait would become vital – neither Britain nor Russia, with the best will in the world, could prevent the Turks closing the channel. Russia wanted not only the right of passage but also the power to enforce that right.

While Walden and Aleks argued about how Russia might be given that power, the Germans had completed the widening of the Kiel Canal, a strategically crucial project which would enable their Dreadnoughts to pass from the North Sea battleground to the safety of the Baltic. In addition, Germany's gold reserves were at a record high, as a result of the financial manoeuvres which had prompted Churchill's visit to Walden Hall in May. Germany would never be better prepared for war: every day which passed made an Anglo-Russian alliance more indispensable. But Aleks had true nerve – he would make no concessions in haste.

And, as Walden learned more about Germany – its industry, its government, its army, its natural resources – he realized that it had every chance of replacing Britain as the most powerful nation in the world. Personally he did not much mind whether Britain was first, second or ninth, so long as she was free. He loved England. He was proud of his country. Her industry provided work for millions, and her democracy was a model for the rest of the world. Her population was becoming more educated, and following that process more of her people had the vote. Even the women would get it sooner or later, especially if they stopped breaking windows. He loved the fields and the hills, the opera and the music-hall, the frenetic glitter of the metropolis and the slow, reassuring rhythms of country life. He was proud of her inventors, her playwrights, her businessmen and her craftsmen. England was a damn good place, and it was not going to be spoiled by squareheaded Prussian invaders, not if Walden could help it.

He was worried because he was not sure he *could*

help it. He wondered just how far he really understood modern England, with its anarchists and suffragettes, ruled by young firebrands like Churchill and Lloyd George, swayed by even more disruptive forces such as the burgeoning Labour Party and the ever-more-powerful trade unions. Walden's kind of people still ruled – the wives were Good Society and the husbands were the Establishment – but the country was not as governable as it had used to be. Sometimes he had a terribly depressing feeling that it was all slipping out of control.

Charlotte came in, reminding him that politics was not the only area of life in which he seemed to be losing his grip. She was still wearing her tea-gown. Walden said: 'We must go soon.'

'I'll stay at home, if I may,' she said. 'I've a slight headache.'

'There'll be no hot dinner, unless you warn Cook quickly.'

'I shan't want it. I'll have a tray in my room.'

'You look a little pale. Have a small glass of sherry, it'll give you an appetite.'

'All right.'

She sat down and he poured the drink for her. As he gave it to her he said: 'Annie has a job and a home, now.'

'I'm glad,' she replied coldly.

He took a deep breath. 'It must be said that I was at fault in that affair.'

'Oh!' Charlotte said, astonished.

Is it so rare for me to admit that I'm in the wrong?

he wondered. He went on: 'Of course, I didn't know that her . . . young man . . . had run off and she was ashamed to go to her mother. But I should have inquired. As you quite rightly said, the girl was my responsibility.'

Charlotte said nothing, but sat beside him on the sofa and took his hand. He was touched.

He said: 'You have a kind heart, and I hope you'll always stay that way. Might I also be permitted to hope that you will learn to express your generous feelings with a little more . . . equanimity?'

She looked up at him. 'I'll do my best, Papa.'

'I often wonder whether we've protected you too much. Of course, it was your Mama who decided how you should be brought up, but I must say I agreed with her nearly all the time. There are people who say that children ought not to be protected from, well, what might be called the facts of life; but those people are very few, and they tend to be an awfully coarse type.'

They were quiet for a while. As usual, Lydia was taking for ever to dress for dinner. There was more that Walden wanted to say to Charlotte, but he was not sure he had the courage. In his mind he rehearsed various openings, none of which was less than acutely embarrassing. She sat with him in contented silence, and he wondered whether she had some idea of what was going on in his mind.

Lydia would be ready in a moment. It was now or never. He cleared his throat. 'You'll marry a good man, and together with him you'll learn about all sorts of things that are mysterious and perhaps a little worrying to you now.' That might be enough, he thought; this was the moment to back down, to duck the issue. Courage! 'But there is one thing you need to know in advance. Your mother should tell you, really, but somehow I think she may not, so I shall.'

He lit a cigar, just to have something to do with his hands. He was past the point of no return. He rather hoped Lydia would come in now to put a stop to the conversation; but she did not.

'You said you know what Annie and the gardener did. Well, they aren't married, so it was wrong. But when you are married, it's a very fine thing to do indeed.' He felt his face redden and hoped she would not look up just now. 'It's very good just physically, you know,' he plunged on. 'Impossible to describe, perhaps a bit like feeling the heat from a coal fire . . . However, the main thing is, the thing I'm sure you don't realize, is how wonderful the whole thing is spiritually. Somehow it seems to express all the affection and tenderness and respect and . . . well, just the love there is between a man and his wife. You don't necessarily understand that when you're young. Girls especially tend to see only the, well, coarse aspect; and some unfortunate people never discover the good side of it at all. But if you're expecting it, and you choose a good, kind, sensible man for your husband, it's sure to happen. So that's why I've told you. Have I embarrassed you terribly?'

To his surprise she turned her head and kissed his cheek. 'Yes, but not as much as you've embarrassed yourself,' she said.

That made him laugh.

Pritchard came in. 'The carriage is ready, my lord, and her ladyship is waiting in the hall.'

Walden stood up. 'Not a word to Mama, now,' he murmured to Charlotte.

'I'm beginning to see why everybody says you're such a good man,' Charlotte said. 'Enjoy your evening.'

'Goodbye,' he said. As he went out to join his wife he thought: Sometimes I get it right, anyway.

After that, Charlotte almost changed her mind about going to the suffragette meeting.

She had been in a rebellious mood, following the Annie incident, when she saw the poster stuck to the window of a jeweller's shop in Bond Street. The headline VOTES FOR WOMEN had caught her eye, then she had noticed that the hall in which the meeting was to be held was not far from her house. The notice did not name the speakers, but Charlotte had read in the newspapers that the notorious Mrs Pankhurst often appeared at such meetings without prior warning. Charlotte had stopped to read the poster, pretending (for the benefit of Marya, who was chaperoning her) to be looking at a tray of bracelets. As she was reading a boy came out of the shop and began to scrape the poster off the window. There and then Charlotte decided to go to the meeting.

Now Papa had shaken her resolution. It was a shock to see that he could be fallible, vulnerable, even humble; and even more of a revelation to hear him talk of sexual intercourse as if it were something beautiful.

She realized that she was no longer raging inwardly at him for allowing her to grow up in ignorance. Suddenly she saw his point of view.

But none of that altered the fact that she was still horribly ignorant, and she could not trust Mama and Papa to tell her the whole truth about things, especially about things like suffragism. I *will* go, she decided.

She rang the bell for Pritchard, and asked for a salad to be brought up to her room, then she went upstairs. One of the advantages of being a woman was that no one ever cross-questioned you if you said you had a headache: women were *supposed* to have headaches every now and then.

When the tray came she picked at the food for a while, until the time came when the servants would be having their supper, then she put on a hat and coat and went out.

It was a warm evening. She walked quickly toward Knightsbridge. She felt a peculiar sense of freedom, and realized that she had never before walked the streets of a city unaccompanied. I could do anything, she thought. I have no appointments and no chaperone. Nobody knows where I am. I could have dinner in a restaurant. I could catch a train to Scotland. I could take a room in an hotel. I could ride on an omnibus. I could eat an apple in the street, and drop the core in the gutter.

She felt conspicuous but nobody looked at her. She had always had the vague impression that if she went out alone strange men would embarrass her in unspecified ways. In reality they did not seem to see her.

The men were not lurking, they were all going somewhere, wearing their evening clothes or their worsted suits or their frock coats. How could there be any danger? she thought. Then she remembered the madman in the park, and she began to hurry.

As she approached the hall she noticed more and more women heading the same way. Some were in pairs or in groups, but many were alone like Charlotte. She felt safer.

Outside the hall was a crowd of hundreds of women. Many wore the suffragette colours of purple, green and white. Some were handing out leaflets or selling a newspaper called *Votes For Women.* There were several policemen about, wearing rather strained expressions of amused contempt. Charlotte joined the queue to get in.

When she reached the door a woman wearing a steward's armband asked her for sixpence. Charlotte turned, automatically, then realized she did not have Marya, or a footman, or a maid, to pay for things. She was alone, and she had no money. She had not anticipated that she would have to pay to get into the hall. She was not quite sure where she would have got sixpence even if she had foreseen the need.

'I'm sorry,' she said. 'I haven't any money . . . I didn't know . . .' She turned to leave.

The steward reached out to stop her. 'It's all right,' the woman said. 'If you've no money you get in free.' She had a middle-class accent, and although she spoke kindly Charlotte imagined that she was thinking: Such fine clothes, and no money!

Charlotte said: 'Thank you ... I'll send you a cheque ...' Then she went in, blushing furiously. Thank Heaven I didn't try to have dinner in a restaurant or catch a train, she thought. She had never needed to worry about carrying money around with her. Her chaperone always had petty cash, Papa kept accounts with all the shops in Bond Street, and if she wanted to have lunch at Claridge's or morning coffee in the Café Royal she would simply leave her card on the table and the bill would be sent to Papa. But this was one bill he would not pay.

She took her seat in the hall quite close to the front: she did not want to miss anything, after all this trouble. If I'm going to do this kind of thing often, she thought, I'll have to think of a way to get my hands on proper money, grubby pennies and gold sovereigns and crumpled banknotes.

She looked around her. The place was almost full of women, with just a scattering of men. The women were mostly middle-class, wearing serge and cotton rather than cashmere and silk. There were a few who looked distinctly more well-bred than the average – they talked more quietly and wore less jewellery – and those women seemed – like Charlotte – to be wearing last year's coats and rather undistinguished hats, as if to disguise themselves. As far as Charlotte could see there were no working-class women in the audience.

Up on the platform was a table draped with a purple, green and white 'Votes for Women' banner. A small lectern stood on the table. Behind it was a row of six chairs.

Charlotte thought: All these women – rebelling against men! She did not know whether to be thrilled or ashamed.

The audience applauded as five women walked on to the stage. They were all impeccably dressed in rather less-than-fashionable clothes – not a hobble skirt or a cloche hat among them. Were these really the people who broke windows, slashed paintings and threw bombs? They looked too respectable.

The speeches began. They meant little to Charlotte. They were about organization, finance, petitions, amendments, divisions and by-elections. She was disappointed: she was learning nothing. Ought she to read books about this before going to a meeting, in order to understand the proceedings? After almost an hour she was ready to leave. Then the current speaker was interrupted.

Two women appeared at the side of the stage. One was an athletic-looking girl in a motoring coat. Walking with her, and leaning on her for support, was a small, slight woman in a pale green spring coat and a large hat. The audience began to applaud. The women on the platform stood up. The applause grew louder, with shouts and cheers. Someone near Charlotte stood up, and in seconds a thousand women were on their feet.

Mrs Pankhurst walked slowly to the lectern.

Charlotte could see her quite clearly. She was what people called a handsome woman. She had dark, deep-set eyes, a wide, straight mouth, and a strong chin. She would have been beautiful but for a rather fat, flat nose. The effects of her repeated imprisonments and hunger strikes showed in the fleshlessness of her face and hands and the yellow colour of her skin. She seemed weak, thin and feeble.

She raised her hands, and the cheering and applause died down almost instantly.

She began to speak. Her voice was strong and clear, although she did not seem to shout. Charlotte was surprised to notice that she had a Lancashire accent.

She said: 'In 1894 I was elected to the Manchester Board of Guardians, in charge of the workhouse. The first time I went into that place I was horrified to see little girls seven and eight years old on their knees scrubbing the cold stones of the long corridors. These little girls were clad, summer and winter, in thin cotton frocks, low in the neck and short-sleeved. At night they wore nothing at all, nightdresses being considered too good for paupers. The fact that bronchitis was epidemic among them most of the time had not suggested to the Guardians any change in the fashion of the clothes. I need hardly add that, until I arrived, all the Guardians were men.

'I found that there were pregnant women in that workhouse, scrubbing floors, doing the hardest kind of work, almost until their babies came into the world. Many of them were unmarried women; very, very young, mere girls. These poor mothers were allowed to stay in the hospital after confinement for a short two weeks. Then they had to make a choice of staying in the workhouse and earning their living by scrubbing and other work, in which case they were separated from their babies; or of taking their discharges. They could stay and be paupers, or they could leave – leave with a two-week-old baby in their arms, without hope, without home, without money, without anywhere to go. What became of those girls, and what became of their hapless infants?'

Charlotte was stunned by the public discussion of such delicate matters. Unmarried mothers . . . mere girls . . . without home, without money . . . And why should they be separated from their babies in the workhouse? Could this be true?

There was worse to come.

Mrs Pankhurst's voice rose a fraction. 'Under the law, if a man who ruins a girl pays down a lump sum of twenty pounds, the boarding home is immune from inspection. As long as a baby-farmer takes only one child at a time, the twenty pounds being paid, the inspectors cannot inspect the house.'

Baby-farmers . . . a man who ruins a girl . . . the terms were unfamiliar to Charlotte, but they were dreadfully self-explanatory.

'Of course the babies die with hideous promptness, and then the baby-farmers are free to solicit another victim. For years women have tried to get the Poor Law changed, to protect all illegitimate children, and to make it impossible for any rich scoundrel to escape liability for his child. Over and over again it has been tried, but it has always failed – ' Here her voice became a passionate cry. ' – because the ones who really care about the thing are mere women!'

The audience burst into applause, and a woman next to Charlotte cried: 'Hear, hear!'

Charlotte turned to the woman and grabbed her arm. 'Is this true?' she said. 'Is this *true*?'

But Mrs Pankhurst was speaking again.

'I wish I had time, and strength, to tell you of all the tragedies I witnessed while I was on that board. In our out-relief department I was brought into contact with widows who were struggling desperately to keep their homes and families together. The law allowed these women relief of a certain very inadequate kind, but for herself and one child it offered no relief except the workhouse. Even if the woman had a baby at her breast she was regarded, under the law, as an able-bodied man. Women, we are told, should stay at home and take care of their children. I used to astound my men colleagues by saying to them: "When women have the vote they will see that mothers *can* stay at home and care for their children!"

'In 1899 I was appointed to the office of Registrar of Births and Deaths in Manchester. Even after my experience on the Board of Guardians I was shocked to be reminded over and over again of what little respect there was in the world for women and children. I have had little girls of thirteen come to my office to register the births of their babies, illegitimate, of course. There was nothing that could be done in most cases. The age of consent is sixteen years, but a man can usually claim that he thought the girl was over sixteen. During my term of office a very young mother of an illegitimate child exposed her baby, and it died. The girl was tried for murder and sentenced to death. The man who was, from the point of view of justice, the real murderer of the baby, received no punishment at all.

'Many times in those days I asked myself what was to be done. I had joined the Labour Party, thinking that through its councils something vital might come, some demand for the women's enfranchisement that the politicians could not possibly ignore. Nothing came.

'All these years my daughters had been growing up. One day Christabel startled me with the remark: "How long you women have been trying for the vote. For my part, I mean to get it." Since that day I have had two mottoes. One has been: "Votes for women." The other: "For my part, I mean to get it!"'

Someone shouted: 'So do I!' and there was another outburst of cheering and clapping. Charlotte was feeling dazed. It was as if she, like Alice in the story, had walked through the looking-glass and found herself in a world where nothing was what it seemed. When she had read in the newspapers about suffragettes, no mention had been made of the Poor Law, of thirteen-year-old mothers (was it *possible*?) or of little girls catching bronchitis in the workhouse. Charlotte would have believed none of it had she not seen with her own eyes Annie, a decent ordinary maid from Norfolk, sleeping on a London pavement after being 'ruined' by a man. What did a few broken windows matter while this sort of thing was going on?

'It was many years before we lighted the torch of militancy. We had tried every other measure, and our years of work and suffering and sacrifice had taught us that the Government would not yield to right and justice, but it would yield to expediency. We had to make England and every department of English life insecure and unsafe. We had to make English law a failure and the courts theatres of farce; we had to discredit the Government and Parliament in the eyes of the world; we had to spoil English sports, hurt business, destroy valuable property, demoralize the world of Society, shame the churches, upset the whole orderly conduct of life! We had to do as much of this guerrilla warfare as the people of England would tolerate. When they came to the point of saying to the Government: "Stop this, in the only way it can be stopped, by giving the women of England representation," then we should extinguish our torch.

'The great American statesman Patrick Henry summed up the causes that led to the American revolution like this: "We have petitioned, we have remonstrated, we have supplicated, we have prostrated ourselves at the foot of the throne, and it has all been in vain. We must fight – I repeat it, sir, we must fight." Patrick Henry was advocating killing people as the proper means of securing the political freedom of *men.* The suffragettes have not done that and never will. In fact, the moving spirit of militancy is a deep and abiding reverence for human life.

'It was in this spirit that our women went forth to war. On January 31st a number of putting greens were burned with acids. On February 7th and 8th telegraph and telephone wires were cut in several places and for some hours all communication between London and

Glasgow was suspended. A few days later windows in various of London's smartest clubs were broken, and the orchid houses at Kew were wrecked and many valuable blooms destroyed by cold. The jewel room at the Tower of London was invaded and a showcase broken. On February 18th a country house which was being built at Walton-on-the-Hill for Mr Lloyd George was partially destroyed, a bomb having been exploded in the early morning before the arrival of the workmen.

'Over one thousand women have gone to prison in the course of this agitation, have suffered their imprisonment, have come out of prison injured in health, weakened in body, but not in spirit. Not one of those women would, if women were free, be law-breakers. They are women who seriously believe that the welfare of humanity demands this sacrifice; they believe that the horrible evils which are ravaging our civilization will never be removed until women get the vote. There is only one way to put a stop to this agitation; there is only one way to break down this agitation. It is not by deporting us!'

'No!' someone shouted.

'It is not by locking us up in jail!'

The whole crowd shouted: 'No!'

'It is by doing us justice!'

'Yes!'

Charlotte found herself shouting with the rest. The little woman on the platform seemed to radiate righteous indignation. Her eyes blazed, she clenched her fists, she tilted up her chin, and her voice rose and fell with emotion.

'The fire of suffering whose flame is upon our sisters in prison is burning us also. For we suffer with them, we partake of their affliction, and we shall share their victory by-and-by. This fire will breathe into the ear of many a sleeper the one word "Awake", and she will arise to slumber no more. It will descend with the gift of tongues upon many who have hitherto been dumb, and they will go forth to preach the news of deliverance. Its light will be seen afar off by many who suffer and are sorrowful and oppressed, and will irradiate their lives with a new hope. For the spirit which is in women today cannot be quenched; it is stronger than all tyranny, cruelty and oppression; it is stronger – even – than – death – itself!'

During the day a dreadful suspicion had dawned on Lydia.

After lunch she had gone to her room to lie down. She had been unable to think about anything but Feliks. She was still vulnerable to his magnetism: it was foolish to pretend otherwise. But she was no longer a helpless girl. She had resources of her own. And she was determined that she would not lose control, would not let Feliks wreck the placid life she had so carefully made for herself.

She thought of all the questions she had not asked him. What was he doing in London? How did he earn his living? How had he known where to find her?

He had given Pritchard a false name. Clearly he had been afraid that she would not let him in. She realized why 'Constantine Dmitrich Levin' had seemed familiar: it was the name of a character in *Anna Karenina*, the book she had been buying when she first met Feliks. It was an alias with a double meaning, a sly mnemonic which lit up a host of dim memories, like a taste recalled from childhood. They had argued about the novel. It was brilliantly real, Lydia had said, for she knew what it was like when passion was released in the soul of a respectable woman; Anna *was* Lydia. But the book was not about Anna, said Feliks; it was about Levin and his search for the answer to the question: 'How should I live?' Tolstoy's answer was: 'In your heart you know what is right.' Feliks argued that it was this kind of empty-headed morality – deliberately ignorant of history, economics and psychology – which had led to the utter incompetence and degeneracy of the Russian ruling class. That was the night they ate pickled mushrooms and she tasted vodka for the first time. She had been wearing a turquoise dress which turned her grey eyes blue. Feliks had kissed her toes, and then—

Yes, he was sly, to remind her of all that.

Had he been in London a long time, she wondered, or had he come just to see Aleks? There was presumably a reason for approaching an admiral in London about the release of a sailor imprisoned in Russia. For the first time it occurred to Lydia that Feliks might not have told her the truth about that. After all, he was still an anarchist. In 1895 he had been determinedly non-violent, but he might have changed.

If Stephen knew that I had told an anarchist where to find Aleks . . .

She had worried about it through tea. She had worried about it while the maid was putting up her hair, with the result that the job was not properly done and she looked a fright. She had worried about it through dinner, with the result that she had been less than vivacious with the Marchioness of Quort, Mr Chamberlain, and a young man called Freddie who kept hoping aloud that there was nothing seriously wrong with Charlotte.

She recalled Feliks' cut hand, which had caused him to give such a shout when she squeezed it. She had only glimpsed the wound but it looked as if it had been bad enough to need stitches.

Nevertheless, it was not until the end of the evening, when she sat in her bedroom at home brushing her hair, that it occurred to her to connect Feliks with the madman in the park.

The thought was so frightening that she dropped a gold-backed hair-brush on to the dressing-table and broke a glass vial of perfume.

What if Feliks had come to London to kill Aleks?

Suppose it were Feliks who had attacked the coach in the park, not to rob them but to get at Aleks? Had the man with the gun been Feliks' height and build? Yes, roughly. And Stephen had wounded him with his sword . . .

Then Aleks had left the house because he was frightened (or perhaps, she now realized, because he *knew* the 'robbery' had been an assassination attempt) and Feliks had not known where to find him, so he had asked Lydia . . .

She stared at herself in the mirror. The woman she saw there had grey eyes, fair eyebrows, blonde hair, a pretty face, and the brain of a sparrow.

Could it be true? Could Feliks have deceived her so? Yes – because he had spent nineteen years imagining that she had betrayed him.

She picked up the pieces of broken glass from the vial and put them in a handkerchief, then she mopped up the spilled perfume. She did not know what to do now. She had to warn Stephen, but how? 'By the way, an anarchist called this morning and asked me where Aleks had gone; and because he used to be my lover I told him . . .' She would have to make up a story. She thought for a while. Once upon a time she had been an expert barefaced liar, but she was out of practice. Eventually she decided she could get away with a combination of the lies Feliks had told to her and to Pritchard.

She put on a cashmere robe over the silk nightgown and went through to Stephen's bedroom.

He was sitting at the window, in pyjamas and a dressing-gown, with a small glass of brandy in one hand and a cigar in the other, looking out over the moonlit park. He was surprised to see her come in, for it was always he who went to her room in the night. He stood up with a welcoming smile and embraced her. She realized that he misunderstood her visit: he thought she had come to make love.

She said: 'I want to talk to you.'

He released her. He looked disappointed. 'At this time of night?'

'I think I may have done something awfully silly.'

'You'd better tell me about it.'

They sat down on opposite sides of the cold fireplace. Suddenly Lydia wished she *had* come to make love. She said: 'A man called this morning. He said he had known me in St Petersburg. Well, the name was familiar and I thought I vaguely recalled him ... You know how it is, sometimes—'

'What was his name?'

'Levin.'

'Go on.'

'He said he wanted to see Prince Orlov.'

Stephen was suddenly very attentive. 'Why?'

'Something to do with a sailor who had been unjustly imprisoned. This ... Levin ... wanted to make a personal plea for the man's release.'

'What did you say?'

'I told him the Savoy Hotel.'

'Damn,' Stephen cursed, then apologized: 'Forgive me.'

'Afterwards it occurred to me that Levin might have been up to no good. He had a cut hand – and I remembered that you had cut the madman in the park ... so, you see, it dawned on me gradually ... I've done something dreadful, haven't I?'

'It's not your fault. In fact it's mine. I should have told you the truth about the man in the park, but I thought it better not to frighten you. I was wrong.'

'Poor Aleks,' Lydia said. 'To think that someone would want to kill him. He's so sweet.'

'What was Levin like?'

The question unsettled Lydia. For a moment she had been thinking of 'Levin' as an unknown assassin; now she was forced to describe Feliks. 'Oh . . . tall, thin, with dark hair, about my age, obviously Russian; a nice face, rather lined . . .' She tailed off. *And I yearn for him.*

Stephen stood up. 'I'll go and rouse Pritchard. He can drive me to the hotel.'

Lydia wanted to say: No, don't, take me to bed instead, I need your warmth and tenderness. She said: 'I'm so sorry.'

'It may be for the best,' Stephen said.

She looked at him in surprise. 'Why?'

'Because, when he comes to the Savoy Hotel to assassinate Aleks, I shall catch him.'

And then Lydia knew that before this was over one of the two men she loved would surely kill the other.

Feliks gently lifted the bottle of nitroglycerine out of the sink. He crossed the room as if he were walking on eggshells. His pillow was on the mattress. He had enlarged the rip until it was about six inches long, and now he put the bottle through the hole and into the pillow. He arranged the stuffing all around the bottle so that the bomb lay cocooned in shock-absorbing material. He picked up the pillow and, cradling it like a baby, placed it in his open suitcase. He closed the case and breathed more easily.

He put on his coat, his scarf, and his respectable hat. Carefully, he turned the cardboard suitcase on to its edge, then picked it up.

He went out.

The journey into the West End was a nightmare.

Of course he could not use the bicycle, but even walking was nerve-racking. Every second he visualized that green glass bottle in its pillow; every time his foot hit the pavement he imagined the little shock wave which must travel up his body and down his arm to the case; in his mind he saw the molecules of nitroglycerine vibrating faster and faster under his hand.

He passed a woman washing the pavement in front of her house. He went by on the road, in case he should slip on the wet flagstones, and she jeered: 'A-scared of getting yer feet wet, toff?'

Outside a factory in Euston a crowd of apprentices poured through the gates chasing a football. Feliks stood stock still as they rushed all around him, jostling and fighting for the ball. Then someone kicked it clear and they were gone as quickly as they had arrived.

Crossing the Euston Road was a dance with death. He stood at the kerb for five minutes, waiting for a good-sized gap in the stream of traffic; and then he had to walk across so fast he was almost running.

In Tottenham Court Road he went into a high-class stationer's. It was calm and hushed in the shop. He set the suitcase down gently on the counter. An assistant in a morning-coat said: 'Can I help you, sir?'

'I need an envelope, please.'

The assistant raised his eyebrows. 'Just the one, sir?'

'Yes.'

'Any particular kind, sir?'

'Just plain, but good quality.'

'We have blue, ivory, eau-de-nil, cream, beige—'

'White.'

'Very good, sir.'

'And a sheet of paper.'

'One sheet of paper, sir.'

They charged him threepence. On principle he would have preferred to run off without paying, but he could not run with the bomb in his case.

Charing Cross Road teemed with people on their way to work in shops and offices. It was impossible to walk at all without getting buffeted. Feliks stood in a doorway for a while, wondering what to do. Finally he decided to carry the case in his arms to protect it from the scurrying hordes.

In Leicester Square he took refuge in a bank. He sat at one of the writing-tables where the customers made out their cheques. There were a tray of pens and an inkwell. He put the case on the floor between his feet. He relaxed for a moment. Frock-coated bank clerks padded softly by with papers in their hands. Feliks took a pen and wrote on the front of his envelope:

Prince A. A. Orlov
The Savoy Hotel
Strand, London W.

He folded the blank sheet of paper and slipped it inside the envelope, just for the sake of its weight: he did not want the envelope to seem empty. He licked the gummed flap and sealed it shut. Then he reluctantly picked up the suitcase and left the bank.

In Trafalgar Square he dipped his handkerchief in the fountain and cooled his face with it.

He passed Charing Cross Station and walked east along the embankment. Near Waterloo Bridge a small group of urchins lounged against the parapet, throwing stones at the seagulls on the river. Feliks spoke to the most intelligent-looking boy.

'Do you want a penny?'

'Yes, guv!'

'Are your hands clean?'

'Yes, guv!' The boy showed a pair of filthy hands.

They would have to do, Feliks thought. 'Do you know where the Savoy Hotel is?'

'Too right!'

Feliks assumed this meant the same as 'Yes, guv.' He handed the boy the envelope and a penny. 'Count to a hundred slowly, then take this letter to the hotel. Do you understand?'

'Yes, guv!'

Feliks mounted the steps to the bridge. It was thronged with men in bowler hats coming across the river from the Waterloo side. Feliks joined the procession.

He went into a newsagent's and bought *The Times.* As he was leaving a young man rushed in through the door. Feliks stuck out his arm and stopped the man, shouting: 'Look where you're going!'

The man stared at him in surprise. As Feliks went out he heard the man say to the shopkeeper: 'Nervous type, is he?'

'Foreigner,' said the shopkeeper, and then Feliks was outside.

He turned off the Strand and went into the hotel. In the lobby he sat down and placed the suitcase on the floor between his feet. Not much farther now, he thought.

From his seat he could see both doors and the hall porter's desk. He put his hand inside his coat and consulted an imaginary fob watch, then opened his newspaper and settled down to wait, as if he were early for an appointment.

He pulled the suitcase closer to his seat and stretched out his legs either side of it, to protect it against an accidental kick from a careless passer-by. The lobby was crowded: it was just before ten o'clock. This is when the ruling class has breakfast, Feliks thought. He had not eaten: he had no appetite today.

He examined the other people in the lobby over the top of *The Times*. There were two men who might be detectives. Feliks wondered whether they might impede his escape. But even if they hear the explosion, he thought, how will they know which of the dozens of people walking through this lobby was responsible for it? Nobody knows what I look like. Only if I were being chased would they know. I'll have to make sure I'm not chased.

He wondered whether the urchin would come. After all, the boy had his penny already. Perhaps by now he had thrown the envelope into the river and gone off to the sweet shop. If so, Feliks would simply have to go through the whole rigmarole again until he found an honest urchin.

Looking up every few seconds, he read an article in the newspaper. The Government wanted to make those who gave money to the Women's Social and Political Union liable to pay for damage done by suffragettes. They planned to bring in special legislation to make this possible. How foolish governments are when they become intransigent, Feliks thought; everyone will just give money anonymously.

Where was that urchin?

He wondered what Orlov was doing right now. In all probability he was in one of the rooms of the hotel, a matter of yards above Feliks' head, eating breakfast, or shaving, or writing a letter, or having a discussion with Walden. I'd like to kill Walden too, Feliks thought.

It was not impossible that the two of them should walk through the lobby at any minute. That was too much to hope for. What would I do if it happened? thought Feliks.

I would throw the bomb, and die happy.

Through the glass door he saw the urchin.

The boy came along the narrow road which led to the hotel entrance. Feliks could see the envelope in his hand: he held it by one corner, almost distastefully, as if it were dirty and he were clean instead of the reverse. He approached the door but was stopped by a commissionaire in a top hat. There was some discussion, inaudible from inside, then the boy went away. The commissionaire came into the lobby with the envelope in his hand.

Feliks tensed. Would it work?

The commissionaire handed in the envelope at the hall porter's desk.

The hall porter looked at it, picked up a pencil, scribbled something in the top right-hand corner – a room number? – and summoned a pageboy.

It was working!

Feliks stood up, gently lifted his case, and headed for the stairs.

The pageboy passed him on the first floor and went on up.

Feliks followed.

It was almost too easy.

He allowed the pageboy to get one flight of stairs ahead, then he quickened his step to keep him in view.

On the fifth floor the boy walked along the corridor.

Feliks stopped and watched.

The boy knocked on a door. It was opened. A hand came out and took the envelope.

Got you, Orlov.

The pageboy made a pantomime of going away and was called back. Feliks could not hear the words. The boy received a tip. He said: 'Thank you very much indeed, sir, very kind of you.' The door closed.

Feliks started to walk along the corridor.

The boy saw his case and reached for it, saying: 'Can I help you with that, sir?'

'No!' Feliks said sharply.

'Very good, sir,' said the boy, and he passed on.

Feliks walked to the door of Orlov's room. Were there no more security precautions? Walden might imagine that a killer could not get into a London hotel room, but Orlov would know better. For a moment Feliks was tempted to go away and do some more thinking, or perhaps more reconnaissance; but he was too close to Orlov now.

He put the suitcase down on the carpet outside the door.

He opened the case, reached inside the pillow, and carefully withdrew the green bottle.

He straightened up slowly.

He knocked on the door.

CHAPTER EIGHT

WALDEN LOOKED at the envelope. It was addressed in a neat, characterless hand. It had been written by a foreigner, for an Englishman would have put *Prince Orlov* or *Prince Aleksei* but not *Prince A. A. Orlov.* Walden would have liked to know what was inside, but Aleks had moved out of the hotel in the middle of the night, and Walden could not open it in his absence – it was, after all, another gentleman's mail.

He handed it back to Basil Thomson, who had no such scruples.

Thomson ripped it open and took out a single sheet of paper. 'Blank!' he said.

There was a knock at the door.

They all moved quickly. Walden went over to the windows, away from the door and out of the line of fire, and stood behind a sofa, ready to duck. The two detectives moved to either side of the room and drew their guns. Thomson stood in the middle of the room behind a large overstuffed easy chair.

The knock came again.

Thomson called: 'Come in – it's open.'

The door opened, and there he stood.

Walden clutched at the back of the sofa. He *looked* frightening.

He was a tall man in a bowler hat and a black coat buttoned to the neck. He had a long, gaunt, white face. In his left hand he held a large green bottle. His eyes swept the room, and he understood in a flash that this was a trap.

He lifted the bottle and said: 'Nitro!'

'Don't shoot!' Thomson barked at the detectives.

Walden was sick with fear. He knew what nitroglycerine was: if the bottle fell they would all die. He wanted to live; he did not want to die in an instant of burning agony.

There was a long moment of silence. Nobody moved. Walden stared at the face of the killer. It was a shrewd, hard, determined face. Every detail was imprinted on Walden's mind in that short, terrible pause: the curved nose, the wide mouth, the sad eyes, the thick black hair showing beneath the brim of the hat. Is he mad? Walden wondered. Bitter? Heartless? Sadistic? The face showed only that he was fearless.

Thomson broke the silence. 'Give yourself up,' he said. 'Put the bottle on the floor. Stop being a fool.'

Walden was thinking: If the detectives shoot, and the man falls, could I get to him in time to catch the bottle before it crashes on to the floor—

No.

The killer stood motionless, bottle raised high. He's looking at me, not Thomson, Walden realized; he's studying me, as if he finds me fascinating; taking in the details, wondering what makes me tick. It's a personal look. He's as interested in me as I am in him.

He has realized Aleks isn't here – what will he do now?

The killer spoke to Walden in Russian: 'You're not as stupid as you look.'

Walden thought: Is he suicidal? Will he kill us all and himself too? Better keep him talking—

Then the man was gone.

Walden heard his footsteps running down the corridor.

Walden made for the door. The other three were ahead of him.

Out in the corridor, the detectives knelt on the floor, aiming their guns. Walden saw the killer running away with a queer fluid step, his left arm hanging straight down by his side, holding the bottle as steady as possible while he ran.

If it goes off now, Walden thought, will it kill us at this distance? Probably not.

Thomson was thinking the same. He said: 'Shoot!'

Two guns crashed.

The killer stopped and turned.

Was he hit?

He swung back his arm and hurled the bottle at them.

Thomson and the two detectives threw themselves flat. Walden realized in a flash that if the nitroglycerine exploded anywhere near them it would be no use to be lying flat.

The bottle turned over and over in the air as it flew at them. It was going to hit the floor five feet away from Walden. If it landed it would surely explode.

Walden ran *toward* the flying bottle.

It descended in a flat arc. He reached for it with both hands. He caught it. His fingers seemed to slip on the glass. He fumbled it, panicking; he almost lost it; then he grasped it again –

Don't slip Christ Jesus don't slip—

– and like a goalkeeper catching a football he drew it to his body, cushioning it against his chest, and spun around in the direction the bottle was travelling; then he lost his balance, and fell to his knees, and steadied himself, still holding the bottle, and thinking: I'm going to die.

Nothing happened.

The others stared at him, on his knees, cradling the bottle in his arms like a new-born baby.

One of the detectives fainted.

Feliks stared in amazement at Walden for a split second longer, then he turned and raced down the stairs.

Walden was amazing. What a nerve, to catch that bottle!

He heard a distant shout: 'Go after him!'

It's happening again, he thought; I'm running away again. What is the matter with me?

The stairs were endless. He heard running footsteps behind him. A shot rang out.

On the next landing he crashed into a waiter with a tray. The waiter fell, and crockery and food flew everywhere.

The pursuer was one or two flights behind him. He reached the foot of the staircase. He composed himself and walked into the lobby.

It was still crowded.

He felt as if he were walking a tightrope.

Out of the corner of his eye he spotted the two men he had identified as possibly detectives. They were deep in conversation, looking worried: they must have heard distant gunfire.

He walked slowly across the lobby, fiercely resisting the urge to break into a run. He had the illusion that everyone was staring at him. He looked ahead fixedly.

He reached the door and went out.

'Cab, sir?' said the doorman.

Feliks jumped into a waiting cab and it pulled away.

As it turned into the Strand he looked back at the hotel. One of the detectives from upstairs burst out of the door, followed by the two from the lobby. They spoke to the doorman. He pointed at Feliks' cab. The detectives drew their guns and ran after the cab.

The traffic was heavy. The cab stopped in the Strand.

Feliks jumped out.

The cabbie shouted: 'Oi! What's on, John?'

Feliks dodged through the traffic to the far side of the road and ran north.

He looked back over his shoulder. They were still after him.

He had to stay ahead until he could lose himself somewhere, in a maze of back alleys, or a railway station.

A uniformed policeman saw him running and watched suspiciously from the other side of the street. A minute later the detectives saw the policeman and yelled at him. He joined the chase.

Feliks ran faster. His heart pounded and his breath came in ragged gasps.

He turned a corner and found himself in the fruit and vegetable market of Covent Garden.

The cobbled streets were jammed with motor lorries and horsedrawn wagons. Everywhere there were market porters carrying wooden trays on their heads or pushing handcarts. Barrels of apples were being manhandled off wagons by heavily muscled men in undershirts. Boxes of lettuce and tomatoes and strawberries were bought and sold by men in bowler hats, and fetched and carried by men in caps. The noise was terrific.

Feliks plunged into the heart of the market.

He hid behind a stack of empty crates and peered through the slats. After a moment he saw his pursuers. They stood still, looking around. There was some conversation, then the four of them split up to search.

So Lydia betrayed me, Feliks thought as he caught his breath. Did she know in advance that I was after Orlov to kill him? No, she can't have. She wasn't acting a part that morning; she wasn't dissembling when she kissed me. But if she believed the story about getting a sailor out of jail, surely she would never have said anything to Walden. Well, perhaps later she realized that I had lied to her, so then she warned her husband, because she didn't want to have any part in the killing of Orlov. She didn't exactly betray me.

She won't kiss me next time.

There won't be a next time.

The uniformed policeman was coming his way.

He moved around the stack of crates and found himself alone in a little backwater, concealed by the boxes all around him.

Anyway, he thought, I escaped their trap. Thank God for nitroglycerine.

But *they* are supposed to be afraid of *me*.

I am the hunter; I am the one who sets traps.

It's Walden, he's the danger. Twice now he has got in the way. Who would have thought an aristocrat with grey hair would have had so much spunk?

He wondered where the policeman was. He peeped out.

He came face to face with the man.

The policeman's face was forming into an expression of astonishment when Feliks grabbed him by the coat and jerked him into the little enclosure.

The policeman stumbled.

Feliks tripped him. He fell on the floor. Feliks dropped on top of him and got him by the throat. He began to squeeze.

Feliks hated policemen.

He remembered Bialystock, when the strike-breakers – thugs with iron bars – had beaten up the workers outside the mill, while the police looked on unmoving. He remembered the pogrom, when the hooligans ran wild in the Jewish quarter, setting fire to houses and kicking old men and raping the young girls, while the police watched, laughing. He recalled Bloody Sunday, when the troops fired round after round into the peaceful crowd in front of the Winter Palace, and the police watched, cheering. He saw in his mind the police who had taken him to the Fortress of St Peter and St Paul to be tortured, and those who escorted him to Siberia and stole his coat, and those who had burst into the strike meeting in St Petersburg with their truncheons waving, hitting the women's heads, they always hit the women.

A policeman was a worker who had sold his soul.

Feliks tightened his grip.

The man's eyes closed, and he stopped struggling.

Feliks squeezed harder.

He heard a sound.

His head whipped around.

A small child of two or three years stood there, eating an apple, watching him strangle the policeman.

Feliks thought: What am I waiting for?

He let the policeman go.

The child walked over and looked down at the unconscious man.

Feliks looked out. He could not see any of the detectives.

The child said: 'Is he sleepy?'

Feliks walked away.

He got out of the market without seeing any of his pursuers.

He made his way to the Strand.

He began to feel safe.

In Trafalgar Square he caught an omnibus.

I almost died, Walden kept thinking; I almost died.

He sat in the hotel suite while Thomson gathered his team of detectives. Somebody gave him a glass of brandy-and-soda, and that was when he noticed that his hands were shaking. He could not put from his mind the image of that bottle of nitroglycerine in his hands.

He tried to concentrate on Thomson. The policeman changed visibly as he spoke to his men: he took his hands out of his pockets, he sat on the edge of his chair, and his voice altered from a drawl to a crisp snap.

Walden began to calm down as Thomson was talking. 'This man has slipped through our fingers,' Thomson said. 'It is not going to happen a second time. We know something about him now, and we're going to find out a great deal more. We know he was in St Petersburg during or before 1895, because Lady Walden remembers him. We know he's been to Switzerland, because the suitcase in which he carried the bomb was Swiss. And we know what he looks like.'

That face, Walden thought; and he clenched his fists.

Thomson went on: 'Watts, I want you and your lads

to spend a little money in the East End. The man is almost certainly Russian, so he's probably an anarchist and Jewish, but don't count on it. Let's see if we can put a name to him. If we can, cable Zurich and St Petersburg and ask for information.

'Richards, you start with the envelope. It was probably bought singly, so a shop assistant might remember the sale.

'Woods, you work on the bottle. It's a Winchester bottle with a ground-glass stopper. The name of the manufacturer is stamped on the bottom. Find out who in London they supply it to. Send your team around all the shops and see whether any chemists remember a customer answering to the description of our man. He will have bought the ingredients for nitroglycerine in several different shops, of course; and if we can find those shops we will know where in London to look for him.'

Walden was impressed. He had not realized that the killer had left behind so many clues. He began to feel better.

Thomson addressed a young man in a felt hat and a soft collar. 'Taylor, yours is the most important job. Lord Walden and I have seen the killer briefly, but Lady Walden has had a good long look at him. You'll come with us to see her ladyship, and with her help and ours you'll draw a picture of this fellow. I want the picture printed tonight and distributed to every police station in London by midday tomorrow.'

Surely, Walden thought, the man cannot escape us now. Then he remembered that he had thought the same when they set the trap here in the hotel room; and he began to tremble again.

Feliks looked in the mirror. He had had his hair cut very short, like a Prussian, and he had plucked his eyebrows until they were thin lines. He would stop shaving immediately, so that in a day he would look scruffy and in a week his beard and moustache would cover his distinctive mouth and chin. Unfortunately there was nothing he could do about his nose. He had bought a pair of second-hand spectacles with wire rims. The lenses were small so he could look over the top of them. He had changed his bowler hat and black coat for a blue sailor's pea-jacket and a tweed cap with a peak.

A close look would still reveal him as the same man, but to a casual glance he was completely different.

He knew he had to leave Bridget's house. He had bought all his chemicals within a mile or two of here, and when the police learned that they would begin a house-to-house search. Sooner or later they would end up in this street, and one of the neighbours would say: 'I know him, he stops in Bridget's basement.'

He was on the run. It was humiliating and depressing. He had been on the run at other times, but always after killing someone, never before.

He gathered up his razor, his spare underwear, his home-made dynamite, and his book of Pushkin stories, and tied them all up in his clean shirt. Then he went to Bridget's parlour.

'Jesus, Mary and Joseph, what have you done to your eyebrows?' she said. 'You used to be a handsome man.'

'I must leave,' he said.

She looked at his bundle. 'I can see your luggage.'

'If the police come, you don't have to lie to them.'

'I'll say I threw you out because I suspected you were an anarchist.'

'Goodbye, Bridget.'

'Take off those daft glasses and kiss me.'

Feliks kissed her cheek and went out.

'Good luck, boy,' she called after him.

He took the bicycle and, for the third time since he had arrived in London he went looking for lodgings.

He rode slowly. He was no longer weak from the sword wounds, but his spirit was sapped by his sense of failure. He went through North London and the City, then crossed the river at London Bridge. On the far side he headed south-east, passing a pub called The Elephant and Castle.

In the region of the Old Kent Road he found the kind of slum where he could get cheap accommodation and no questions asked. He took a room on the fourth floor of a tenement building owned, the caretaker told him lugubriously, by the Church of England. He would not be able to make nitroglycerine here: there was no water in the room, nor indeed in the building – just a stand-pipe and a privy in the courtyard.

The room was grim. There was a tell-tale mousetrap in the corner, and the one window was covered with a sheet of newspaper. The paint was peeling and the mattress stank. The caretaker, a stooped, fat man shuffling in carpet-slippers and coughing, said: 'If you want to mend the window, I can get glass cheap.'

Feliks said: 'Where can I keep my bicycle?'

'I should bring it up here if I were you, it'll get nicked anywhere else.'

With the bicycle in the room there would be just enough space to get from the door to the bed.

'I'll take the room,' Feliks said.

'That'll be twelve shillings, then.'

'You said three shillings a week.'

'Four weeks in advance.'

Feliks paid him. After buying the spectacles and trading in the clothes, he now had one pound and nineteen shillings.

The caretaker said: 'If you want to decorate, I can get you half-price paint.'

'I'll let you know,' said Feliks. The room was filthy but that was the least of his problems.

Tomorrow he had to start looking for Orlov again.

'Stephen! Thank Heaven you're all right!' said Lydia.

He put his arm around her.

'Of course I'm all right.'

'What happened?'

'I'm afraid we didn't catch our man.'

Lydia almost fainted with relief. Ever since Stephen had said, 'I shall catch the man,' she had been terrified twice over: terrified that Feliks would kill Stephen, and terrified that if not, she would be responsible for putting Feliks in jail for the second time in her life. She knew what he had gone through the first time, and the thought sickened her.

'You know Mr Basil Thomson, I think,' Stephen said, 'and this is Mr Taylor, the police artist. We're all going to help him draw the face of the killer.'

Lydia's heart sank. She would have to spend hours visualizing her lover in the presence of her husband. When will this end? she thought.

Stephen said: 'By the way, where is Charlotte?'

'Shopping,' Lydia told him.

'Good. I don't want her to know anything about this. In particular I don't want her to know where Aleks has gone.'

'Don't tell me, either,' Lydia said. 'I'd rather not know. That way I shan't be able to make the same mistake again.'

They sat down, and the artist got out his sketchbook.

Over and over again he drew that face. Lydia could have drawn it herself in five minutes. At first she tried to make the artist get it wrong, by saying 'Not quite' when something was exactly right and 'That's it' when something was crucially awry; but Stephen and Thomson had both seen Feliks clearly, if briefly, and they corrected her. In the end, fearful of being found out, she co-operated properly, knowing all the time that she might still be helping them to put Feliks in prison again. They ended up with a very good likeness of the face Lydia loved.

After that her nerves were so bad that she took a dose of laudanum and went to sleep. She dreamed that she was going to St Petersburg to meet Feliks. With the devastating logic of dreams, it seemed that she drove to catch the ship in a carriage with two duchesses who, in real life, would have expelled her from polite society had they known of her past. However, they made a mistake and went to Bournemouth instead of Southampton. There they stopped for a rest, although it was five o'clock and the ship sailed at seven. The duchesses told Lydia that they slept together at night and caressed each other in a perverted way. Somehow this came as no surprise at all, although they were both extremely old. Lydia kept saying, 'We must go, now,' but they took no notice. A man came with a message for Lydia. It was signed 'Your anarchist lover'. Lydia said to the messenger: 'Tell my anarchist lover that I'm *trying* to get the seven o'clock boat.' There: the cat was out of the bag. The duchesses exchanged knowing winks. At twenty minutes to seven, still in Bournemouth, Lydia realized that she had not yet packed her luggage. She raced around throwing things into cases but she could never find anything and the seconds ticked by and she was already too late and somehow her case *would not* fill up, and she panicked and went without her luggage and climbed on the carriage and drove herself, and lost her way on the sea front at Bournemouth and could not get out of town and woke up without getting anywhere near Southampton.

Then she lay in bed with her heart beating fast, her eyes wide open and staring at the ceiling, and she thought: It was only a dream. Thank God. Thank God!

*

Feliks went to bed miserable and woke up angry.

He was angry with himself. The killing of Orlov was not a superhuman task. The man might be guarded, but he could not be locked away in an underground vault like money in a bank; besides, even bank vaults could be robbed. Feliks was intelligent and determined. With patience and persistence he would find a way around all the obstacles they would put in his path.

He was being hunted. Well, he would not be caught. He would travel by the back streets, avoid his neighbours, and keep a constant look-out for blue police uniforms. Since he began his career of violence he had been hunted many times, but he had never been caught.

So he got up, washed at the stand-pipe in the courtyard, remembered not to shave, put on his tweed cap, his pea-jacket and his spectacles, had breakfast at a tea-stall, and cycled, avoiding the main roads, to St James's Park.

The first thing he saw was a uniformed policeman pacing up and down outside the Walden house.

That meant he could not take up his usual position for observing the house. He had to retreat much farther into the park and watch from a distance. He could not stay in the same place for too long, either, in case the policeman was alert and keen-eyed enough to notice.

At about midday a motor car emerged from the house. Feliks ran for his bicycle.

He had not seen the car go in, so presumably it was Walden's. Previously the family had always travelled in a coach, but there was no reason why they should not have both horse-drawn and motor vehicles. Feliks was too far away to be able to guess who was inside the car. He hoped it was Walden.

The car headed for Trafalgar Square. Feliks cut across the grass to intercept it.

The car was a few yards ahead of him when he reached the road. He kept up with it easily around Trafalgar Square, then it drew ahead of him as it headed north on Charing Cross Road.

He pedalled fast, but not desperately so. For one thing he did not want to draw attention to himself, and for another he wanted to conserve his strength. But he was too cautious, for when he reached Oxford Street the car was out of sight. He cursed himself for a fool. Which direction had it taken? There were four possibilities: left, straight on, right or sharp right.

He guessed, and went straight on.

In the traffic jam at the north end of Tottenham Court Road he saw the car again, and breathed a sigh of relief. He caught up with it as it turned east. He risked going close enough to see inside. In the front was a man in a chauffeur's cap. In the back was someone with grey hair and a beard: Walden!

I'll kill him too, Feliks thought; by Christ, I'll kill him.

In the traffic jam outside Euston Station he passed the car and got ahead, taking the chance that Walden might look at him when the car caught up again. He stayed ahead all down Euston Road, looking back over his shoulder continually to check that the car was still following him. He waited at the junction by King's

Cross, breathing hard, until the car passed him. It turned north. He averted his face as it went by, then followed.

The traffic was fairly heavy, and he was able to keep pace, although he was tiring. He began to hope that Walden was going to see Orlov. A house in North London, discreet and suburban, might be a good hiding-place. His excitement mounted. He might be able to kill them both.

After half a mile or so the traffic began to thin out. The car was large and powerful. Feliks had to pedal faster and faster. He was sweating heavily. He thought: How much farther?

Heavy traffic at Holloway Road gave him a brief rest, then the car picked up speed along Seven Sisters Road. He went as fast as he could. Any minute now the car might turn off the main road; it might be only minutes from its destination. All I want is some luck! he thought. He summoned up his last reserves of strength. His legs hurt now, and his breath came in ragged gasps. The car pulled remorselessly away from him. When it was a hundred yards ahead and still accelerating, he gave up.

He coasted to a halt and sat on the bicycle at the side of the road, bent over the handlebars, waiting to recover. He felt faint.

It was always the way, he thought bitterly: the ruling class fought in comfort. There was Walden, sitting comfortably in a big smooth car, smoking a cigar, not even having to drive.

Walden was plainly going out of town. Orlov could be anywhere north of London within half a day's journey by fast motor car. Feliks was utterly defeated – again.

For want of a better idea, he turned around and headed back toward St James's Park.

Charlotte was still tingling from Mrs Pankhurst's speech.

Of course there would be misery and suffering while all power was in the hands of one half of the world, and that half had no understanding of the problems of the other half. Men accepted a brutish and unjust world because it was brutish and unjust not to them but to women. If women had power, there would be nobody left to oppress.

The day after the suffragette meeting her mind teemed with speculations of this kind. She saw all the women around her – servants, shop assistants, nurses in the park, even Mama – in a new light. She felt she was beginning to understand how the world worked. She no longer resented Mama and Papa for lying to her. They had not really lied to her, except by omission; besides, insofar as deceit was involved, they deceived themselves almost as much as they had deceived her. And Papa had spoken frankly to her, against his evident inclinations. Still she wanted to find out things for herself, so that she could be sure of the truth.

In the morning she got hold of some money by the simple expedient of going shopping with a footman and saying to him: 'Give me a shilling.' Later, while he waited with the carriage at the main entrance to

Liberty's in Regent Street, she slipped out of a side entrance and walked to Oxford Street where she found a woman selling the suffragette newspaper *Votes For Women.* The paper cost a penny. Charlotte went back to Liberty's and, in the ladies' cloakroom, hid the newspaper under her dress. Then she returned to the carriage.

She read the paper in her room after lunch. She learned that the incident at the palace during her debut had not been the first time that the plight of women had been brought to the attention of the King and Queen. Last December three suffragettes in beautiful evening gowns had barricaded themselves inside a box at Covent Garden. The occasion was a gala performance of *Jeanne d'Arc* by Raymond Roze, attended by the King and Queen with a large entourage. At the end of the first act one of the suffragettes stood up and began to harangue the King through a megaphone. It took them half an hour to break down the door and get the women out of the box. Then forty more suffragettes in the front rows of the gallery stood up, threw showers of pamphlets down into the stalls, and walked out en masse.

Before and after this incident the King had refused to give an audience to Mrs Pankhurst. Arguing that all subjects had an ancient right to petition the King about their grievances, the suffragettes announced that a deputation would march to the palace, accompanied by thousands of women.

Charlotte realized that the march was to take place today – this afternoon – now.

She wanted to be there.

It was no good understanding what was wrong, she told herself, if one did nothing about it. And Mrs Pankhurst's speech was still ringing in her ears: 'The spirit which is in women today cannot be quenched . . .'

Papa had gone off with Pritchard in the motor car. Mama was lying down after lunch, as usual. There was nobody to stop her.

She put on a dowdy dress and her most unprepossessing hat and coat, then she went quietly down the stairs and out of the house.

Feliks walked about the park, keeping the house always in view, racking his brains.

Somehow he had to find out where Walden was going in the motor car. How might that be achieved? Could he try Lydia again? He might, at some risk, get past the policeman and into the house, but would he get out again? Would Lydia not raise the alarm? Even if she let him go, she would hardly tell him the secret of Orlov's hiding-place, now that she knew why he wanted to know. Perhaps he could seduce her – but where and when?

He could not follow Walden's car on a bicycle. Could he follow in another car? He could steal one, but he did not know how to drive them. Could he learn? Even then, would Walden's chauffeur not notice that he was being followed?

If he could hide in Walden's motor car . . . That meant getting inside the garage, opening the boot, spending several hours inside – all in the hope that nothing would be put inside the boot before the journey. The odds against success were too high for him to risk everything on that gamble.

The chauffeur must know, of course. Could he be bribed? Made drunk? Kidnapped? Feliks' mind was elaborating these possibilities when he saw the girl come out of the house.

He wondered who she was. She might be a servant, for the family always came and went in coaches; but she had left by the main entrance, and Feliks had never seen servants do that. She might be Lydia's daughter. She might know where Orlov was.

Feliks decided to follow her.

She walked toward Trafalgar Square. Leaving his bicycle in the bushes, Feliks went after her and got a closer look. Her clothes did not look like those of a servant. He recalled that there had been a girl in the coach on the night he had first tried to kill Orlov. He had not taken a good look at her, because all his attention had been – disastrously – riveted to Lydia. During his many days observing the house he had glimpsed a girl in the carriage from time to time. This was probably the girl, Feliks decided. She was sneaking out on a clandestine errand while her father was away and her mother was busy.

There was something vaguely familiar about her, he thought, as he tailed her across Trafalgar Square. He was quite sure he had never looked closely at her, yet he had a strong sense of *déjà vu* as he watched her trim figure walk, straight-backed and with a determined quick pace, through the streets. Occasionally he saw her face in profile when she turned to cross a road, and the tilt of her chin, or perhaps something about her eyes, seemed to strike a chord deep in his memory. Did she remind him of the young Lydia? Not at all, he realized: Lydia had always looked small and frail, and her features were all delicate. This girl had a strong-looking, angular face. It reminded Feliks of a painting by an Italian artist which he had seen in a gallery in Geneva. After a moment the name of the painter came back to him: Modigliani.

He got closer still to her, and a minute or two later he saw her full-face. His heart skipped a beat, and he thought: she's just beautiful.

Where was she going? To meet a boyfriend, perhaps? To buy something forbidden? To do something of which her parents would disapprove, such as go to a moving-picture show or a music-hall?

The boyfriend theory was the likeliest. It was also the most promising possibility from Feliks' point of view. He could find out who the boyfriend was, and threaten to give away the girl's secret unless she would tell him where Orlov was. She would not do it readily, of course, especially if she had been told that an assassin was after Orlov; but, given the choice between the love of a young man and the safety of a Russian cousin, Feliks reckoned that a young girl would choose romance.

He heard a distant noise. He followed the girl around a corner. Suddenly he was in a street full of marching women. Many of them wore the suffragette colours of green, white and purple. Many carried banners. There were *thousands* of them. Somewhere a band played marching tunes.

The girl joined the demonstration and began to march.

Feliks thought: Wonderful!

The route was lined with policemen, but they mostly faced inward, toward the women, so Feliks could dodge along the pavement behind their backs. He went with the march, keeping the girl in sight. He had been in need of a piece of luck, and he had been given one. She was a secret suffragette! She was vulnerable to blackmail, but there might be more subtle ways of manipulating her.

One way or another, Feliks thought, I'll get what I want from her.

Charlotte was thrilled. The march was orderly, with female stewards keeping the women in line. Most of the marchers were well-dressed, respectable-looking types. The band played a jaunty two-step. There were even a few men, carrying a banner which read: 'Fight the Government that Refuses to give Women the Parliamentary Vote'. Charlotte no longer felt like a misfit with heretical views. Why, she thought, all these thousands of women think and feel as I do! At times in the last twenty-four hours she had wondered whether men were right in saying that women were weak, stupid and ignorant, for she sometimes *felt* weak and stupid and she really was ignorant. Now she thought: If we educate ourselves we won't be ignorant; if we think for ourselves we won't be stupid; and if we struggle together we won't be weak.

The band began to play the hymn *Jerusalem*, and the women sang the words. Charlotte joined in lustily:

I will not cease from mental fight
Nor shall my sword sleep in my hand

I don't care if anybody sees me, she thought defiantly – not even the duchesses!

Till we have built Jerusalem
In England's green and pleasant land.

The march crossed Trafalgar Square and entered The Mall. Suddenly there were many more policemen, watching the women intently. There were also many spectators, mostly male, along either side of the road. They shouted and whistled derisively. Charlotte heard one of them say: 'All you need is a good swiving!' and she blushed crimson.

She noticed that many women carried a staff with a silver arrow fixed to its top. She asked the woman nearest her what that symbolized.

'The arrows on prison clothing,' the woman replied. 'All the women who carry that have been to jail.'

'To jail!' Charlotte was taken aback. She had known that a few suffragettes had been imprisoned, but as she looked around she saw hundreds of silver arrows. For the first time it occurred to her that she might end the day in prison. The thought made her feel weak. I won't go on, she thought. My house is just there, across the park; I can be there in five minutes. Prison! I would die! She looked back. Then she thought: I've done nothing wrong! Why am I afraid that I shall go to prison? Why should I not petition the King? Unless we do this women will always be weak, ignorant and stupid. Then the band began again, and she squared her shoulders and marched in time.

The facade of Buckingham Palace loomed up at the end of The Mall. A line of policemen, many on horseback, stretched across the front of the building. Charlotte was near the head of the procession: she wondered what the leaders intended to happen when they reached the gates.

She remembered once coming out of Derry & Toms and seeing an afternoon drunk lurching at her across the pavement. A gentleman in a top hat had pushed the drunk aside with his walking-cane, and the footman had quickly helped Charlotte up into the carriage which was waiting at the kerb.

Nobody would rush to protect her from a jostling today.

They were at the palace gates.

Last time I was here, Charlotte thought, I had an invitation.

The head of the procession came up against the line of policemen. For a moment there was deadlock. The people behind pressed forward. Suddenly Charlotte saw Mrs Pankhurst. She wore a jacket and skirt of purple velvet, a high-necked white blouse, and a green waistcoat. Her hat was purple with a huge white ostrich feather and a veil. She had detached herself from the body of the march and somehow had managed, unnoticed, to reach the far gate of the palace courtyard. She was such a brave little figure, marching with her head held high to the King's gate!

She was stopped by a police inspector in a flat hat. He was a huge, burly man, and looked at least a foot taller than she. There was a brief exchange of words. Mrs Pankhurst stepped forward. The inspector barred her way. She tried to push past him. Then, to Charlotte's horror, the policeman grabbed Mrs Pankhurst in a bear-hug, lifted her off her feet, and carried her away.

Charlotte was enraged – and so was every other woman in sight. The marchers pressed fiercely against the police line. Charlotte saw one or two break through and run toward the palace, chased by constables. The horses shifted, their iron hooves clattering threateningly on the pavement. The line began to break up. Several women struggled with policemen and were thrown to the ground. Charlotte was terrified of being manhandled. Some of the male bystanders rushed to the aid of the police, and then jostling turned into fighting. A middle-aged woman close to Charlotte was grabbed by the thighs. 'Unhand me, sir!' she said indignantly. The policeman said: 'My old dear, I can grip you where I like today!' A group of men in straw boaters waded into the crowd, pushing and punching the women, and Charlotte screamed. Suddenly a team of suffragettes wielding Indian clubs counter-attacked, and straw boaters flew everywhere. There were no longer any spectators: everyone was in the mêlée. Charlotte wanted to run away but every way she turned she saw violence. A fellow in a bowler picked up a young woman by getting one arm across her breasts and one hand in the fork of her thighs, and Charlotte heard him say: 'You've been wanting this for a long time, haven't you?' The bestiality of it all horrified Charlotte: it was like one of those medieval paintings of Purgatory in which everyone is suffering unspeakable tortures; but it was real and she was in the middle of it. She was pushed from behind and fell down, grazing her hands and bruising her knees. Someone trod on her hand. She tried to get up and was knocked down again. She realized she might be trampled by a horse and die. Desperately, she grabbed the skirts of a woman's coat and hauled herself to her feet.

Some of the women were throwing pepper into the eyes of the men, but it was impossible to throw accurately and they succeeded in incapacitating as many women as men. The fighting became vicious. Charlotte saw a woman lying on the ground with blood streaming from her nose. She wanted to help the woman but she could not move – it was as much as she could do to stay upright. She began to feel angry as well as scared. The men, police and civilians alike, punched and kicked women with relish. Charlotte thought hysterically: Why do they *grin* so? To her horror she felt a large hand grasp her breast. The hand squeezed and twisted. She turned, clumsily shoving the arm away from her. She was confronted by a man in his middle twenties, well-dressed in a tweed suit. He put out his hands and grabbed both her breasts, digging his fingers in hard. Nobody had *ever* touched her there. She struggled with the man, seeing on his face a wild look of mingled hatred and desire. He yelled: 'This is what you need, ain't it?' then he punched her in the stomach with his fist. The blow seemed to sink into her belly. The shock was bad and the pain was worse, but what made her panic was that she could not breathe. She stood, bending forward, with her mouth open. She wanted to gasp, she wanted to scream, but she could do neither. She felt sure she was going to die. She was vaguely aware of a very tall man pushing past her, dividing the crowd as if it were a field of corn. The tall man grabbed the lapel of the man in the tweed suit and hit him on the chin. The blow seemed to knock the young man off his feet and lift him into the air. The look of surprise on his face was almost comical. At last Charlotte was able to breathe, and she sucked in air with a great heave. The tall man put his arm firmly around her shoulders and said in her ear: 'This way.' She realized she was being rescued, and the sense of being in the hands of someone strong and protective was such a relief that she almost fainted.

The tall man propelled her toward the edge of the crowd. A police sergeant struck at her with a truncheon. Charlotte's protector raised his arm to ward off the blow, then gave a shout of pain as the wooden club landed on his forearm. He let go of Charlotte. There was a brief flurry of blows, then the sergeant was lying on the ground, bleeding, and the tall man was once again leading Charlotte through the crush.

Suddenly they were out of it. When Charlotte realized she was safe she began to cry, sobbing softly as tears ran down her cheeks. The man made her keep walking. 'Let's get right away,' he said. He spoke with a foreign accent. Charlotte had no will of her own: she went where he led her.

After a while she began to recover her composure. She realized they were in the Victoria area. The man stopped outside a Lyons Corner House and said: 'Would you like a cup of tea''

She nodded, and they went in.

He led her to a chair, then sat opposite her. She looked at him for the first time. For an instant she was frightened again. He had a long face with a curved nose. His hair was very short but his cheeks were unshaven. He looked somehow rapacious. But then she saw that there was nothing but compassion in his eyes.

She took a deep breath and said: 'How can I ever thank you?'

He ignored the question. 'Would you like something to eat?'

'Just tea.' She recognized his accent, and she began to speak Russian. 'Where are you from?'

He looked pleased that she could speak his language. 'I was born in Tambov province. You speak Russian very well.'

'My mother is Russian, and my governess.'

A waitress came, and he said: 'Two teas, please, love.'

Charlotte thought: He is learning English from Cockneys. She said in Russian: 'I don't even know your name. I'm Charlotte Walden.'

'Feliks Kschessinsky. You were brave, to join that march.'

She shook her head. 'Bravery had nothing to do with it. I simply didn't know it would be like that.' She was thinking: Who and what is this man? Where did he come from? He *looks* fascinating. But he's guarded. I'd like to know more about him.

He said: 'What did you expect?'

'On the march? I don't know . . . Why do those men *enjoy* attacking women?'

'This is an interesting question.' He was suddenly animated, and Charlotte saw that he had an attractive, expressive face. 'You see, we put women on a pedestal and pretend they are pure in mind and helpless in body. So, in polite society at least, men must tell themselves that they feel no hostility toward women, ever; nor do they feel lust for women's bodies. Now, here come some women – the suffragettes – who plainly are not helpless and need not be worshipped. What is more, they break the law. They deny the myths that men have made themselves believe, and they can be assaulted with impunity. The men feel cheated, and they give expression to all the lust and anger which they have been pretending not to feel. This is a great release to tension, and they enjoy it.'

Charlotte looked at him in amazement. It was fantastic – a complete explanation, just like that, off the top of his head! I like this man, she thought. She said: 'What do you do for a living?'

He became guarded again. 'Unemployed philosopher.'

The tea came. It was strong and very sweet, and it

restored Charlotte somewhat. She was intrigued by the weird Russian, and she wanted to draw him out. She said: 'You seem to think that all this – the position of women in society and so on – is just as bad for men as it is for women.'

'I'm sure of it.'

'Why?'

He hesitated. 'Men and women are happy when they love.' A shadow passed briefly across his face and was gone. 'The relation of love is not the same as the relation of worship. One worships a god. Only human beings can be loved. When we worship a woman we cannot love her. Then, when we discover she is not a god, we hate her. This is sad.'

'I never thought of that,' Charlotte said wonderingly.

'Also, every religion has good gods and bad gods. The Lord and the Devil. So, we have good women and bad women; and you can do anything you like to the bad women, for example suffragettes and prostitutes.'

'What are prostitutes?'

He looked surprised. 'Women who sell themselves for—' He used a Russian word that Charlotte did not know.

'Can you translate that?'

'Swiving,' he said in English.

Charlotte flushed and looked away.

He said: 'Is this an impolite word? I'm sorry, I know no other.'

Charlotte screwed up her courage and said in a low voice: 'Sexual intercourse.'

He reverted to Russian. 'I think *you* have been put on a pedestal.'

'You can't imagine how awful it is,' she said fiercely. 'To be so ignorant! Do women really sell themselves that way?'

'Oh, yes. Respectable married women must pretend not to like sexual intercourse. This sometimes spoils it for the men, so they go to the prostitutes. The prostitutes pretend to like it very much, although since they do it so often with so many different people they don't really enjoy it. Everyone ends up pretending.'

These things are *just* what I need to know! thought Charlotte. She wanted to take him home and chain him up in her room, so that he could explain things to her day and night. She said: 'How did we get like this – all this pretending?'

'The answer is a lifetime study. At least. However, I'm sure it has to do with power. Men have power over women, and rich men have power over poor men. A great many fantasies are required to legitimize this system – fantasies about monarchy, capitalism, breeding, and sex. These fantasies make us unhappy, but without them someone would lose his power. And men will not give up power, even if it makes them miserable.'

'But what is to be done?'

'A famous question. Men who will not give up power must have it taken from them. A transfer of power from one faction to another faction *within the same class* is called a coup and this changes nothing. A transfer of power from one *class* to another is called a revolution, and this does change things.' He hesitated. 'Although the changes are not necessarily the ones the revolutionaries sought.' He went on: 'Revolutions occur only when the people rise up en masse against their oppressors – as the suffragettes seem to be doing. Revolutions are always violent, for people will always kill to retain power. Nevertheless, they happen, for people will always give their lives in the cause of freedom.'

'Are you a revolutionary?'

He said in English: 'I'll give you three guesses.'

Charlotte laughed.

It was the laugh that did it.

While he spoke, a part of Feliks' mind had been watching her face, gauging her reactions. He warmed to her, and the affection he felt was somehow familiar. He thought: I am supposed to bewitch her, but she is bewitching me.

And then she laughed.

She smiled widely; crinkles appeared in the corners of her brown eyes; she tipped back her head so that her chin pointed forward; she held up her hands, palms forward, in a gesture that was almost defensive; and she chuckled richly, deep in her throat.

Feliks was transported back in time twenty-five years. He saw a three-roomed hut leaning against the side of a wooden church. Inside the hut a boy and a girl sat opposite one another at a crude table made of planks. On the fire was a cast-iron pot containing a cabbage, a small piece of bacon fat and a great deal of water. It was almost dark outside and soon the father would be home for his supper. Fifteen-year-old Feliks had just told his eighteen-year-old sister Natasha the joke about the traveller and the farmer's daughter. She threw back her head and laughed.

Feliks stared at Charlotte. She looked exactly like Natasha. He said: 'How old are you?'

'Eighteen.'

There occurred to Feliks a thought so astonishing, so incredible and so devastating that his heart stood still.

He swallowed, and said: 'When is your birthday?'

'The second of January.'

He gasped. She had been born exactly seven months after the wedding of Lydia and Walden; nine months after the last occasion on which Feliks had made love to Lydia.

And Charlotte looked exactly like Feliks' sister Natasha.

And now Feliks knew the truth.

Charlotte was his daughter.

CHAPTER NINE

'WHAT IS IT?' Charlotte said.

'What?'

'You look as if you'd seen a ghost.'

'You reminded me of someone. Tell me all about yourself.'

She frowned at him. He seemed to have a lump in his throat, she thought. She said: 'You've got a cold coming.'

'I never catch colds. What's your earliest memory?'

She thought for a moment. 'I was brought up in a country house called Walden Hall, in Norfolk. It's a beautiful grey stone building with a very lovely garden. In summer we had tea outdoors, under the chestnut tree. I must have been about four years old when I was first allowed to have tea with Mama and Papa. It was very dull. There was nothing to investigate on the lawn. I always wanted to go around to the back of the house, to the stables. One day they saddled a donkey and let me ride it. I had seen people ride, of course, and I thought I knew how to do it. They told me to sit still or I would fall off, but I didn't believe them. First somebody took the bridle and walked me up and down. Then I was allowed to take the reins myself. It all seemed so easy that I gave him a kick, as I had seen people do to horses, and made him trot. Next thing I knew, I was on the ground in tears. I just couldn't *believe* I had really fallen!' She laughed at the memory.

'It sounds like a happy childhood,' Feliks said.

'You wouldn't say that if you knew my governess. Her name is Marya and she's a Russian dragon. "Little ladies *always* have clean hands." She's still around – she's my chaperone now.'

'Still – you had good food, and clothes, and you were never cold, and there was a doctor when you were sick.'

'Is that supposed to make you happy?'

'I would have settled for it. What's your *best* memory?'

'When Papa gave me my own pony,' she said immediately. 'I had wanted one so badly, it was like a dream come true. I shall never forget that day.'

'What's he like?'

'Who?'

Feliks hesitated. 'Lord Walden.'

'Papa? Well . . .' It was a good question, Charlotte thought. For a complete stranger, Feliks was remarkably interested in her. But she was even more interested in him. There seemed to be some deep melancholy beneath his questions: it had not been there a few minutes ago. Perhaps that was because he had had an unhappy childhood and hers seemed so much better. 'I think Papa is probably a terribly *good* man . . .'

'But?'

'He will treat me as a child. I know I'm probably frightfully naive, but I'll never be anything else unless I learn. He won't explain things to me the way – well, the way you do. He gets very embarrassed if he talks about . . . men and women, you know . . . and when he speaks of politics his views seem a bit, I don't know, smug.'

'That's completely natural. All his life he's got everything he wanted, and got it easily. Of course he thinks the world is wonderful just as it is, except for a few small problems which will get ironed out in time. Do you love him?'

'Yes, except for the moments when I hate him.' The intensity of Feliks' gaze was beginning to make her uncomfortable. He seemed to be drinking in her words and memorizing her facial expressions. 'Papa is a very lovable man. Why are you so interested?'

He gave a peculiar, twisted smile. 'I've been fighting the ruling class all my life but I rarely get the chance to talk to one of them.'

Charlotte could tell that this was not the real reason, and she wondered vaguely why he should lie to her. Perhaps he was embarrassed about something – that was usually the reason why people were less than honest with her. She said: 'I'm not a member of the ruling class, any more than one of my father's dogs is.'

He smiled. 'Tell me about your mother.'

'She has bad nerves. Sometimes she has to take laudanum.'

'What's laudanum?'

'Medicine with opium in it.'

He raised his eyebrows. 'That sounds ominous.'

'Why?'

'I thought the taking of opium was considered degenerate.'

'Not if it's for medical reasons.'

'Ah.'

'You're sceptical.'

'Always.'

'Come, now, tell me what you mean.'

'If your mother needs opium, I suspect it is because she is unhappy, rather than because she is ill.'

'Why should she be unhappy?'

'You tell me, she's your mother.'

Charlotte considered. Was Mama unhappy? She certainly was not *content* in the way Papa seemed to be. She worried too much, and she would fly off the handle without much provocation. 'She's not relaxed,' she said. 'But I can't think of any reason why she should be unhappy. I wonder if it has to do with leaving your native country?'

'That's possible,' Feliks said, but he did not sound convinced. 'Have you any brothers and sisters?'

'No. My best friend is my cousin Belinda, she's the same age as me.'

'What other friends have you got?'

'No other friends, just acquaintances.'

'Other cousins?'

'Twin boys, six years old. Of course I've loads of cousins in Russia but I've never seen any of them, except Aleks, who's much older than me.'

'And what are you going to do with your life?'

'What a question!'

'Don't you know?'

'I haven't made up my mind.'

'What are the alternatives?'

'That's the big question, really. I mean, I'm expected to marry a young man of my own class and raise children. I suppose I shall have to marry.'

'Why?'

'Well, Walden Hall won't come to me when Papa dies, you know.'

'Why not?'

'It goes with the title – and I can't be the Earl of Walden. So the house will be left to Peter, the elder of the twins.'

'I see.'

'And I couldn't make my own living.'

'Of course you could.'

'I've been trained for nothing.'

'Train yourself.'

'What would I do?'

Feliks shrugged. 'Raise horses. Be a shopkeeper. Join the civil service. Become a professor of mathematics. Write a play.'

'You talk as if I might do anything I put my mind to.'

'I believe you could. But I have one quite serious idea. Your Russian is perfect – you could translate novels into English.'

'Do you really think I could?'

'I've no doubt whatsoever.'

Charlotte bit her lip. 'Why is it that you have such faith in me and my parents don't?'

He thought for a minute, then smiled. 'If I had

brought you up, you would complain that you were forced to do serious work all the time and never allowed to go dancing.'

'You've no children?'

He looked away. 'I never married.'

Charlotte was fascinated. 'Did you want to?'

'Yes.'

She knew she ought not to go on, but she could not resist it: she wanted to know what this strange man had been like when he was in love. 'What happened?'

'The girl married someone else.'

'What was her name?'

'Lydia.'

'That's my mother's name.'

'Is it?'

'Lydia Shatova, she was. You must have heard of Count Shatov, if you ever spent any time in St Petersburg.'

'Yes, I did. Do you carry a watch?'

'What? No.'

'Nor do I.' He looked around and saw a clock on the wall.

Charlotte followed his glance. 'Heavens, it's five o'clock! I intended to get home before Mother came down for tea.' She stood up.

'Will you be in trouble?' he said, getting up.

'I expect so.' She turned to leave the café.

He said: 'Oh, Charlotte . . .'

'What is it?'

'I don't suppose you could pay for the tea? I'm a very poor man.'

'Oh! I wonder whether I've any money. Yes! Look, elevenpence. Is that enough?'

'Of course.' He took sixpence from the palm of her hand and went to the counter to pay. It's funny, Charlotte thought, the things you have to remember when you're not in Society. What would Marya think of me, buying a cup of tea for a strange man? She would have apoplexy.

He gave her the change and held the door for her. 'I'll walk part of the way with you.'

'Thank you.'

Feliks took her arm as they walked along the street. The sun was still strong. A policeman came toward them, and Feliks made her stop and look in a shop window while he passed. She said: 'Why don't you want him to see us?'

'They may be looking for people who were seen on the march.'

Charlotte frowned. That seemed a bit unlikely, but he would know better than she.

They walked on. Charlotte said: 'I love June.'

'The weather in England is wonderful.'

'Do you think so? You've never been to the South of France, then.'

'You have, obviously.'

'We go every winter. We've a villa in Monte Carlo.' She was struck by a thought. 'I hope you don't think I'm boasting.'

'Certainly not.' He smiled. 'You must have realized by now that I think great wealth is something to be ashamed of, not proud of.'

'I suppose I should have realized, but I hadn't. Do you despise me, then?'

'No, but the wealth isn't yours.'

'You're the most interesting person I've ever met,' Charlotte said. 'May I see you again?'

'Yes,' he said. 'Have you got a handkerchief?'

She took one from her coat pocket and gave it to him. He blew his nose. 'You *are* catching a cold,' she said. 'Your eyes are streaming.'

'You must be right.' He wiped his eyes. 'Shall we meet at that café?'

'It's not a frightfully attractive place, is it?' she said. 'Let's think of somewhere else. I know! We'll go to the National Gallery. Then, if I see somebody I know, we can pretend we aren't together.'

'All right.'

'Do you like paintings?'

'I'd like you to educate me.'

'Then it's settled. How about the day after tomorrow, at three o'clock?'

'Fine.'

It occurred to her that she might not be able to get away. 'If something goes wrong, and I have to cancel, can I send you a note?'

'Well . . . er . . . I move about a lot . . .' He was struck by a thought. 'But you can always leave a message with Mrs Bridget Callahan at number nineteen, Cork Street, in Camden Town.'

She repeated the address. 'I'll write that down as soon as I get home. My house is just a few hundred yards away.' She hesitated. 'You must leave me here. I hope you won't be offended, but it really would be best if no one saw me with you.'

'Offended?' he said with his funny, twisted smile. 'No, not at all.'

She held out her hand. 'Goodbye.'

'Goodbye.' He shook her hand firmly.

She turned around and walked away. There will be trouble when I get home, she thought. They will have found out that I'm not in my room, and there will be an inquisition. I'll say I went for a walk in the park. They won't like it.

Somehow she did not care what they thought. She had found a true friend. She was very happy.

When she reached the gate she turned and looked back. He stood where she had left him, watching her. She gave a discreet wave. He waved back. For some reason he looked vulnerable and sad, standing there alone. That was silly, she realized as she remembered how he had rescued her from the riot: he was very tough indeed.

She went into the courtyard and up the steps to the front door.

Walden arrived at Walden Hall suffering from nervous indigestion. He had rushed away from London before lunch, as soon as the police artist had finished drawing the face of the assassin, and he had eaten a picnic and drunk a bottle of Chablis on the way down, without stopping the car. As well as that he was nervous.

Today he was due for another session with Aleks. He guessed that Aleks had a counter-proposal and expected the Czar's approval of it by cable today. He hoped the Russian Embassy had had the sense to forward cables to Aleks at Walden Hall. He hoped the counter-proposal was something reasonable, something he could present to Churchill as a triumph.

He was fiercely impatient to get down to business with Aleks, but he knew that in reality a few minutes made no difference, and it was always a mistake to appear eager during a negotiation; so he paused in the hall and composed himself before walking into the Octagon.

Aleks sat at the window, brooding, with a great tray of tea and cakes untouched beside him. He looked up eagerly and said: 'What happened?'

'The man came, but I'm afraid we failed to catch him,' Walden said.

Aleks looked away. 'He came to kill me . . .'

Walden felt a surge of pity for him. He was young, he had a huge responsibility, he was in a foreign country and a killer was stalking him. But there was no point in letting him brood. Walden put on a breezy tone of voice. 'We have the man's description now – in fact the police artist has made a drawing of him. Thomson will catch him in a day or so. And you're safe here – he can't possibly find out where you are.'

'We thought I was safe at the hotel – but he found out I was there.'

'That can't happen again.' This was a bad start to a

negotiating session, Walden reflected. He had to find a way to turn Aleks' mind to more cheerful subjects. 'Have you had tea?'

'I'm not hungry.'

'Let's go for a walk – it will give you an appetite for dinner.'

'All right.' Aleks stood up.

Walden got a gun – for rabbits, he told Aleks – and they walked down to the Home Farm. One of the two bodyguards provided by Basil Thomson followed ten yards behind them.

Walden showed Aleks his champion sow, the Princess of Walden. 'She's won first prize in the East Anglian Agricultural Show for the last two years.' Aleks admired the sturdy brick cottages of the tenants, the tall white-painted barns, and the magnificent shire horses.

'I don't make any money out of it, of course,' Walden said. 'All the profit is spent on new stock, or drainage, or buildings, or fencing . . . but it sets a standard for the tenanted farms; and the Home Farm will be worth a lot more when I die than it was when I inherited it.'

'We can't farm like this in Russia,' Aleks said. Good, thought Walden; he's thinking of something else. Aleks went on: 'Our peasants won't use new methods, won't touch machinery, won't take care of new buildings or good tools. They are still serfs, psychologically if not legally. When there is a bad harvest and they are starving, do you know what they do? They burn the empty barns.'

The men were mowing hay in the South Acre.

Twelve labourers made a ragged line across the field, stooped over their scythes, and there was a steady swish, swish as the tall stalks fell like dominoes.

Samuel Jones, the oldest of the labourers, finished his row first. He came over, scythe in hand, and touched his cap to Walden. Walden shook his calloused hand. It was like grasping a rock.

'Did your lordship find time to go to that there exhibition in Lunnun?' Samuel said.

'Yes, I did,' Walden replied.

'Did you see that mowing machine you are talking about?'

Walden put on a dubious face. 'It's a beautiful piece of engineering, Sam – but I don't know . . .'

Sam nodded. 'Machinery never does the job as well as a labourer.'

'On the other hand, we could cut the hay in three days instead of a fortnight – and by getting it in that much faster we run less risk of rain. Then we could rent the machine to the tenanted farms.'

'You'd need fewer labourers, too,' Sam said.

Walden pretended to be disappointed. 'No,' he said, 'I couldn't let anyone go. It would just mean we need not take on gypsies to help around harvest-time.'

'It wouldn't make that much difference, then.'

'Not really. And I'm a bit concerned about how the men would take to it – you know young Peter Dawkins will find any excuse to make trouble.'

Sam made a non-committal sound.

'Anyway,' Walden continued, 'Mr Samson is going to take a look at the machine next week.' Samson was the bailiff. 'I say!' Walden said as if he had been struck by an idea. 'I don't suppose you'd want to go with him, Sam?'

Sam pretended not to care much for the idea. 'To Lunnun?' he said. 'I went there in 1888. Didn't like it.'

'You could go up on the train with Mr Samson – perhaps take young Dawkins with you – see the machine, have your dinner in London, and come back in the afternoon.'

'I dunno what my missus would say.'

'I'd be glad to have your opinion of the machine, though.'

'Well, I should be interested.'

'That's settled, then. I'll tell Samson to make the arrangements.' Walden smiled conspiratorially. 'You can give Mrs Jones to understand I practically forced you to go.'

Sam grinned. 'I'll do that, m'lord.'

The mowing was almost done. The men stopped work. Any rabbits would be hidden within the last few yards of hay. Walden called Dawkins over and gave him the gun. 'You're a good shot, Peter. See if you can get one for yourself and one for the Hall.'

They all stood on the edge of the field, out of the line of fire, then cut the last of the hay from the side, to drive the rabbits into the open field. Four came out, and Dawkins got two with his first round and one with his second. The gunfire made Aleks wince.

Walden took the gun and one of the rabbits, then he and Aleks walked back toward the Hall. Aleks shook his head in admiration. 'You have a wonderful way with the men,' he said. 'I never seem to be able to strike the right balance between discipline and generosity.'

'It takes practice,' Walden said. He held up the rabbit. 'We don't really need this at the Hall – but I took it to remind them that the rabbits are mine, and that any they have are a gift from me, not theirs by right.' If I had a son, Walden thought, this is how I would explain things to him.

'One proceeds by discussion and consent,' Aleks said.

'It's the best method – even if you have to give something away.'

Aleks smiled. 'Which brings us back to the Balkans.'

Thank Heaven – at last, Walden thought.

'Shall I sum up?' Aleks went on. 'We are willing to fight on your side against Germany, and you are willing to recognize our right to pass through the Bosphorus and the Dardanelles. However, we want not just the right but the power. Our suggestion, that you should recognize the whole of the Balkan Peninsula from Rumania to Crete as a Russian sphere of influence did not meet with your approval: no doubt you felt it was giving us too much. My task, then, was to formulate a lesser demand: one which would secure our sea passage without committing Britain to an unreservedly pro-Russian Balkan policy.'

'Yes.' Walden thought: He has a mind like a surgeon's knife. A few minutes ago I was giving him fatherly advice, and now, suddenly, he seems my equal – at the least. I suppose this is how it is when your son becomes a man.

'I'm sorry it has taken so long,' Aleks said. 'I have to send coded cables via the Russian Embassy to St Petersburg, and discussion at this distance just can't be as quick as I should like.'

'I understand,' said Walden, thinking: Come on – out with it!

'There is an area of about ten thousand square miles, from Constantinople to Adrianople – it amounts to half of Thrace – which is at present part of Turkey. Its coastline begins in the Black Sea, borders the Bosphorus, the Sea of Marmara, and the Dardanelles, and finishes in the Aegean Sea. In other words it guards the whole of the passage between the Black Sea and the Mediterranean.' He paused. 'Give us that, and we're on your side.'

Walden concealed his excitement. Here was a real basis for bargaining. He said: 'The problem remains, that it isn't ours to give away.'

'Consider the possibilities if war breaks out,' Aleks said. 'One: If Turkey is on our side we will have the right of passage anyway. However, this is unlikely. Two: If Turkey is neutral, we would expect Britain to insist on our right of passage as a sign that Turkey's neutrality was genuine; and, failing that, to support our invasion of Thrace. Three: If Turkey is on the German side – which is the likeliest of the three possibilities – then Britain would concede that Thrace is ours as soon as we can conquer it.'

Walden said dubiously: 'I wonder how the Thracians would feel about all this.'

'They would rather belong to Russia than to Turkey.'

'I expect they'd like to be independent.'

Aleks gave a boyish smile. 'Neither you nor I – nor, indeed, either of our governments – is in the least concerned about what the inhabitants of Thrace might prefer.'

'Quite,' Walden said. He was forced to agree. It was Aleks' combination of boyish charm and thoroughly grown-up brains which kept putting Walden off balance. He always thought he had the discussion firmly under control, until Aleks came out with a punch line which showed that *he* had been controlling it all along.

They walked up the hill that led to the back of Walden Hall. Walden noticed the bodyguard scanning the woods on either side. Dust puffed around his heavy brown brogues. The ground was dry: it had hardly rained for three months. Walden was excited about Aleks' counter-proposal. What would Churchill say? Surely the Russians could be given part of Thrace – who cared about Thrace?

They crossed the kitchen garden. An under-gardener was watering lettuces. He touched his cap to them. Walden searched for the man's name, but Aleks beat him to it. 'A fine evening, Stanley,' said Aleks.

'We could do with a shower, your highness.'

'But not too much, eh?'

'Quite so, your highness.'

Aleks is learning, Walden thought.

They went into the house. Walden rang for a footman. 'I'll send a telegram to Churchill making an appointment for tomorrow morning. I'll motor to London first thing.'

'Good,' Aleks said. 'Time is running short.'

Charlotte got a big reaction from the footman who opened the door to her.

'Oh! Thank goodness you're home, Lady Charlotte!' he said.

Charlotte gave him her coat. 'I don't know why you should thank goodness, William.'

'Lady Walden has been worried about you,' he said. 'She asked that you should be sent to her as soon as you arrived.'

'I'll just go and tidy myself up,' Charlotte said.

'Lady Walden did say "immediately"—'

'And I said I'll go and tidy myself.' Charlotte went up to her room.

She washed her face and unpinned her hair. There was a dull, muscular ache in her stomach, from the punch she had received, and her hands were grazed, but not badly. Her knees were sure to be bruised, but no one ever saw them. She went behind the screen and took off her dress. It seemed undamaged. I don't *look* as if I've been in a riot, she thought. She heard her bedroom door open.

'Charlotte!' It was Mama's voice.

Charlotte slipped into a robe, thinking: Oh, dear, she's going to be hysterical. She came from behind the screen.

'We've been frantic with worry!' Mama said.

Marya came into the room behind her, looking self-righteous and steely-eyed.

Charlotte said: 'Well, here I am, safe and sound, so you can stop worrying now.'

Mama reddened. 'You impudent child!' she shrilled. She stepped forward and slapped Charlotte's face.

Charlotte fell back and sat down heavily on the bed. She was stunned, not by the blow but by the idea of it. Mama had never struck her before. Somehow it seemed to hurt more than all the blows she had received during the riot. She caught Marya's eye and saw a peculiar look of satisfaction on her face.

Charlotte recovered her composure and said: 'I shall never forgive you for that.'

'That you should speak of forgiving me!' In her rage Mama was speaking Russian. 'And how soon should I forgive you for joining a mob outside Buckingham Palace?'

Charlotte gasped. 'How did you know?'

'Marya saw you marching along The Mall with those . . . those suffragettes. I feel so *ashamed.* God knows who else saw you. If the King ever finds out we shall be banished from the court.'

'I see.' Charlotte was still smarting from the slap. She said nastily: 'So you weren't worried about my safety, just the family reputation.'

Mama looked hurt. Marya butted in: 'We were worried about both.'

'Keep quiet, Marya,' said Charlotte. 'You've done enough damage with your tongue.'

'Marya did the right thing!' Mama said. 'How could she *not* tell me?'

Charlotte said: 'Don't you think women should have the vote?'

'Certainly not – and you shouldn't think so, either.'

'But I do,' Charlotte said. 'There it is.'

'You know nothing – you're still a child.'

'We always come back to that, don't we? I'm a child, and I know nothing. Who is responsible for my ignorance? Marya has been in charge of my education for fifteen years. As for being a child, you know perfectly well that I'm nothing of the kind. You would be quite happy to see me married by Christmas. And some girls are mothers by the age of thirteen, married or not.'

Mama was shocked. 'Who tells you such things?'

'Certainly not Marya. She never told me anything important. Nor did you.'

Mama's voice became almost pleading. 'You have no need of such knowledge – you're a lady.'

'You see what I mean? You want me to be ignorant. Well, I don't intend to be.'

Mama said plaintively: 'I only want you to be happy!'

'No, you don't,' Charlotte said stubbornly. 'You want me to be like you.'

'No, no, no!' Mama cried. 'I don't want you to be like me! I don't!' She burst into tears, and ran from the room.

Charlotte stared after her, mystified and ashamed.

Marya said: 'You see what you've done.'

Charlotte looked her up and down: grey dress, grey hair, ugly face, smug expression. 'Go away, Marya.'

'You've no conception of the trouble and heartache you've caused this afternoon.'

Charlotte was tempted to say: If you had kept your mouth shut there would have been no heartache. Instead she said: 'Get out.'

'You listen to me, little Charlotte—'

'I'm *Lady* Charlotte to you.'

'You're little Charlotte, and—'

Charlotte picked up a hand mirror and hurled it at Marya. Marya squealed. The missile was badly aimed, and smashed against the wall. Marya scuttled out of the room.

Now I know how to deal with *her*, Charlotte thought.

It occurred to her that she had won something of a victory. She had reduced Mama to tears and chased Marya out of her room. That's something, she thought; I may be stronger than they after all. They deserved rough treatment: Marya went to Mama behind my back, and Mama slapped me. But I didn't grovel and apologize and promise to be good in future. I gave as good as I got. I should be proud.

So why do I feel so ashamed?

I hate myself, Lydia thought.

I know how Charlotte feels, but I can't *tell* her that I understand. I always lose control. I never used to be like this. I was always calm and dignified. When she was a little girl I could laugh at her peccadilloes. Now she's a woman. Dear God, what have I done? She's tainted with the blood of her father, of Feliks, I'm sure of it.

What am I going to do? I thought if I pretended she were Stephen's daughter she might actually become like a daughter of Stephen – innocent, ladylike, English. It was no good. All those years the bad blood was in her, dormant, and now it's coming out; now the amoral Russian peasant in her ancestry is taking her over. When I see those signs I panic, I can't help it. I'm cursed, we're all cursed, the sins of the fathers are visited upon the children, even unto the third and fourth generation, when will I be forgiven? Feliks is an anarchist and Charlotte is a suffragette, Feliks is a fornicator and Charlotte talks about thirteen-year-old mothers; she has no idea how awful it is to be possessed by passion; my life was ruined, hers will be too, that's what I'm afraid of, that's what makes me shout and cry and get hysterical and smack her, but, sweet Jesus, don't let her ruin herself, she's all I've lived for. I shall lock her away. If only she would marry a nice boy, soon, before she has time to go right off the rails, before everybody realizes there is something wrong with her breeding. I wonder if Freddie will propose to her before the end of the season – that would be the answer – I must make sure he does, I *must* have her married, quickly! Then it will be too late for her to ruin herself; besides, with a baby or two she won't have time. I must make sure she meets Freddie more often. She's quite pretty, she'll be a good enough wife to a strong man who can keep her under control, a decent man who will love her without unleashing her dark desires, a man who will sleep in an adjoining room and share her bed once a week with the light out, Freddie is just right for her, then she'll never have to go through what I've been through, she'll never have to learn the hard way that lust is wicked and destroys, the sin won't be passed down yet another generation, she won't be wicked like me. She thinks I want her to be like me. If only she knew. If only she knew!

Feliks could not stop crying.

People stared at him as he walked through the park to retrieve his bicycle. He shook with uncontrollable sobs and the tears poured down his face. This had never happened to him before and he could not understand it. He was helpless with grief.

He found the bicycle where he had left it, beneath a bush, and the familiar sight calmed him a little. What is happening to me? he thought. Lots of people have children. Now I know that I have too. So what? And he burst into tears again.

He sat down on the dry grass beside the bicycle. She's so beautiful, he thought. But he was not weeping for what he had found, he was weeping for what he had lost. For eighteen years he had been a father without knowing it. While he was wandering from one grim village to another, while he was in jail, and in the gold mine, and walking across Siberia, and making bombs in Bialystock, she had been growing up. She had learned to walk, and to talk, and to feed herself and tie her bootlaces. She had played on a green lawn under a chestnut tree in summer, and had fallen off a donkey and cried. Her 'father' had given her a pony while

Feliks had been working on the chain gang. She had worn white frocks in summer and woollen stockings in winter. She had always been bilingual in Russian and English. Someone else had read story-books to her; someone else had said 'I'll catch you!' and chased her, screaming with delight, up the stairs; someone else had taught her to shake hands and say 'How do you do?'; someone else had bathed her and brushed her hair and made her finish up her cabbage. Many times Feliks had watched Russian peasants with their children and had wondered how, in their lives of misery and grinding poverty, they managed to summon up affection and tenderness for the infants who took the bread from their mouths. Now he knew: the love just came, whether you wanted it or not. From his recollections of other people's children he could visualize Charlotte at different stages of development: as a toddler with a protruding belly and no hips to hold up her skirt; as a boisterous seven-year-old, tearing her frock and grazing her knees; as a lanky, awkward girl of ten with ink on her fingers and clothes always a little too small; as a shy adolescent, giggling at boys, secretly trying her mother's perfume, passionate about horses, and then—

And then this beautiful, brave, alert, inquisitive, admirable young woman.

And I'm her father, he thought.

Her *father.*

What was it she had said? *You're the most interesting person I've ever met – may I see you again?* He had been preparing to say goodbye to her for ever. When he knew that he would not have to, his self-control had begun to disintegrate. She thought he had a cold. Ah, she was young still, to make such bright, cheerful remarks to a man whose heart was breaking.

I'm becoming maudlin, he thought; I must pull myself together.

He stood up and picked up the bicycle. He mopped his face with the handkerchief she had given him. It had a bluebell embroidered in one corner, and he wondered whether she had done that herself. He mounted the bicycle and headed for the Old Kent Road.

It was supper time but he knew he would not be able to eat. That was just as well, for his money was running low and tonight he did not have the spirit to steal. He looked forward now to the darkness of his tenement room, where he could spend the night alone with his thoughts. He would go over every minute of this encounter, from the moment she emerged from the house to that last goodbye wave.

He would have liked a bottle of vodka for company, but he could not afford it.

He wondered whether anyone had ever given Charlotte a red ball.

The evening was mild but the city air was stale. The pubs of the Old Kent Road were already filling up with brightly dressed working-class women and their husbands, boyfriends or fathers. On impulse, Feliks stopped outside one. The sound of an elderly piano wafted through the open door. Feliks thought: I'd like someone to smile at me, even if it's only a barmaid. I could afford half a pint of ale. He tied his bicycle to a railing and went in.

The place was stifling, full of smoke and the unique beery smell of an English pub. It was early, but already there was a good deal of loud laughter and feminine squeals. Everyone seemed enormously cheerful. Feliks thought: Nobody knows how to spend money better than the poor. He joined the crush at the bar. The piano began a new tune, and everyone sang.

Once a young maiden climbed an old man's knee
Begged for a story, 'Do, uncle, please,
Why are you single, why live alone?
Have you no babies, have you no home?'
'I had a sweetheart, years, years ago;
Where is she now, pet, you will soon know
List to my story, I'll tell it all
I believed her faithless, after the ball.'

The stupid, sentimental, empty-headed damn song brought tears to Feliks' eyes and he left the pub without ordering his beer.

He cycled away, leaving the laughter and music behind. That kind of jollity was not for him, it never had been and never would be. He made his way back to the tenement and carried the bicycle up the stairs to his room on the top floor. He took off his hat and coat and lay on the bed. He would see her again in two days. They would look at paintings together. He would go to the municipal bath house before meeting her, he decided. He rubbed his chin: there was nothing he could do to make the beard grow decently in two days. He cast his mind back to the moment when she came out of the house. He had seen her from a distance, never dreaming . . .

What was I thinking of at that moment? he wondered.

And then he remembered.

I was asking myself whether she might know where Orlov is.

I haven't thought about Orlov all afternoon.

In all probability she *does* know where he is; if not she could find out.

I might use her to help me kill him.

Am I capable of that?

No, I am not. I will not do it. No, no, no!

What is happening to me?

Walden saw Churchill at the Admiralty at twelve noon. The First Lord was impressed. 'Thrace,' he said. 'Surely we can give them half of Thrace. Who the devil cares if they have the whole of it!'

'That's what I thought,' Walden said. He was pleased with Churchill's reaction. 'Now, will your colleagues agree?'

'I believe they will,' Churchill said thoughtfully. 'I'll see Grey after lunch and Asquith this evening.'

'And the Cabinet?' Walden did not want to do a deal with Aleks only to have it vetoed by the Cabinet.

'Tomorrow morning.'

Walden stood up. 'So I can plan to go back to Norfolk late tomorrow.'

'Splendid. Have they caught that damned anarchist yet?'

'I'm having lunch with Basil Thomson of the Special Branch – I'll find out then.'

'Keep me informed.'

'Naturally.'

'And thank you. For this proposal, I mean.' Churchill looked out of the window dreamily. 'Thrace!' he murmured to himself. 'Who has ever even heard of it?'

Walden left him to his reverie.

He was in a buoyant mood as he walked from the Admiralty to his club in Pall Mall. He usually ate lunch at home, but he did not want to trouble Lydia with policemen, especially as she was in a rather strange mood at the moment. No doubt she was worried about Aleks, as Walden was. The boy was the nearest thing to a son that they had: if anything should happen to him—

He went up the steps of his club and, just inside the door, handed his hat and gloves to a flunkey. 'What a lovely summer we're having, my lord,' the man said.

The weather had been remarkably fine for months, Walden reflected as he went up to the dining-room. When it broke there would probably be storms. We shall have thunder in August, he thought.

Thomson was waiting. He looked rather pleased with himself. What a relief it will be if he's caught the assassin, Walden thought. They shook hands, and Walden sat down. A waiter brought the menu.

'Well?' said Walden. 'Have you caught him?'

'All but,' Thomson said.

That meant No, Walden thought. His heart sank. 'Oh, *damn,*' he said.

The wine waiter came. Walden asked Thomson: 'Do you want a cocktail?'

'No, thank you.'

Walden approved. Cocktails were a nasty American habit. 'Perhaps a glass of sherry?'

'Yes, please.'

'Two,' Walden said to the waiter.

They ordered Brown Windsor soup and poached salmon, and Walden chose a bottle of hock to wash it down.

Walden said: 'I wonder if you realize quite how important this is? My negotiations with Prince Orlov are almost complete. If he were to be assassinated now the whole thing would fall through – with serious consequences for the security of this country.'

'I do realize, my lord,' Thomson said. 'Let me tell you what progress we've made. Our man is Feliks Kschessinsky. That's so hard to say that I propose we call him Feliks. He is forty, the son of a country priest, and he comes from Tambov province. My opposite number in St Petersburg has a very thick file on him. He has been arrested three times and is wanted in connection with half a dozen murders.'

'Dear God,' Walden muttered.

'My friend in St Petersburg adds that he is an expert bomb-maker and an extremely vicious fighter.' Thomson paused. 'You were terribly brave, to catch that bottle.'

Walden gave a thin smile: he preferred not to be reminded.

The soup came and the two men ate in silence for a while. Thomson sipped his hock frugally. Walden liked this club. The food was not as good as he got at home, but there was a relaxed atmosphere. The chairs in the smoking-room were old and comfortable, the waiters were old and slow, the wallpaper was faded and the paintwork was dull. They still had gas lighting. Men such as Walden came here because their homes were spick and span and feminine.

'I thought you said you had all but caught him,' Walden said as the poached salmon arrived.

'I haven't told you the half of it yet.'

'Ah.'

'At the end of May he arrived at the Jubilee Street anarchist club in Stepney. They didn't know who he was, and he told them lies. He's a cautious man – quite rightly so, from his point of view, for one or two of those anarchists are working for me. My spies reported his presence, but the information didn't come to my notice at that stage because he appeared to be harmless. Said he was writing a book. Then he stole a gun and moved on.'

'Without telling anyone where he was going, of course.'

'That's right.'

'Slippery fellow.'

A waiter collected their plates and said: 'Will you have a slice off the joint, gentlemen? It's mutton today.'

They both had mutton with redcurrant jelly, roast potatoes and asparagus.

Thomson said: 'He bought the ingredients for his nitroglycerine in four different shops in Camden Town. We made house-to-house inquiries there.' Thomson took a mouthful of mutton.

'And?' Walden asked impatiently.

'He's been living at nineteen Cork Street, Camden, in a house owned by a widow called Bridget Callahan.'

'But he's moved on.'

'Yes.'

'Damn it, Thomson, can't you see the fellow's cleverer than you?'

Thomson looked at him coolly and made no comment.

Walden said: 'I beg your pardon, that was discourteous of me, the fellow's got me rattled.'

Thomson went on: 'Mrs Callahan says she threw Feliks out because she thought he was a suspicious character.'

'Why didn't she report him to the police?'

Thomson finished his mutton and put down his knife and fork. 'She says she had no real reason to. I found that suspicious, so I checked up on her. Her husband was an Irish rebel. If she knew what our friend Feliks was up to, she might well have been sympathetic.'

Walden wished Thomson would not call Feliks 'our friend'. He said: 'Do you think she knows where the man went?'

'If she does, she won't say. But I can't think why he should tell her. The point is, he may come back.'

'Are you having the place watched?'

'Surreptitiously. One of my men has already moved into the basement room as a tenant. Incidentally, he found a glass rod of the kind used in chemistry laboratories. Evidently Feliks made up his nitroglycerine right there in the sink.'

It was chilling to Walden to think that in the heart of London anyone could buy a few chemicals, mix them together in a washhand-basin, and make a bottle of dreadfully explosive liquid – then walk with it into a suite in a West End hotel.

The mutton was followed by a savoury of foie gras. Walden said: 'What's your next move?'

'The picture of Feliks is hanging up in every police station in the County of London. Unless he locks himself indoors all day, he's bound to be spotted by an observant bobby sooner or later. But just in case that should be later rather than sooner, my men are visiting cheap hotels and lodging-houses, showing the picture.'

'Suppose he changes his appearance?'

'It's a bit difficult in his case.'

Thomson was interrupted by the waiter. Both men refused the Black Forest gateau and chose ices instead. Walden ordered half a bottle of champagne.

Thomson went on: 'He can't hide his height, nor his Russian accent. And he has distinctive features. He hasn't had time to grow a beard. He may wear different clothes, shave himself bald, or wear a wig. If I were he I should go about in a uniform of some kind – as a sailor, or a footman, or a priest. But policemen are alert to that sort of thing.'

After their ices they had Stilton cheese and sweet biscuits with some of the club's vintage port.

It was all too vague, Walden felt. Feliks was *loose*, and Walden would not feel safe until the fellow was locked up and chained to the wall.

Thomson said: 'Feliks is clearly one of the top killers of the international revolutionist conspiracy. He is very well informed: for example, he knew that Prince Orlov was going to be here in England. He is also clever, and formidably determined. However, we have hidden Orlov away.'

Walden wondered what Thomson was getting at.

'By contrast,' Thomson went on, 'you are still walking about the streets of London as large as life.'

'Why should I not?'

'If I were Feliks, I would now concentrate on you. I would follow you in the hope that you might lead me to Orlov; or I would kidnap you and torture you until you told me where he was.'

Walden lowered his eyes to hide his fear.

'How could he do that alone?'

'He may have help. I want you to have a bodyguard.'

Walden shook his head. 'I've got my man Pritchard. He would risk his life for me – he has done, in the past.'

'Is he armed?'

'No.'

'Can he shoot?'

'Very well. He used to come with me to Africa in my

big-game hunting days. That's when he risked his life for me.'

'Then let him carry a pistol.'

'All right,' Walden assented. 'I'll be going to the country tomorrow. I've got a revolver there which he can have.'

To finish the meal Walden had a peach and Thomson took a melba pear. Afterwards they went into the smoking-room for coffee and biscuits. Walden lit a cigar. 'I think I shall walk home, for my digestion's sake.' He tried to say it calmly, but his voice sounded oddly high-pitched.

'I'd rather you didn't,' Thomson said. 'Haven't you brought your carriage?'

'No—'

'I should be happier about your safety if you were to go everywhere in your own vehicles from now on.'

'Very well,' Walden sighed. 'I shall have to eat less.'

'For today, take a cab. Perhaps I'll accompany you.'

'Do you really think that's necessary?'

'He might be waiting for you outside this club.'

'How would he find out which club I belong to?'

'By looking you up in *Who's Who*.'

'Yes, of course.' Walden shook his head. 'One just doesn't think of these things.'

Thomson looked at his watch. 'I should get back to the Yard . . . if you're ready.'

'Certainly.'

They left the club. Feliks was not lying in wait outside. They took a cab to Walden's house, then Thomson took the cab on to Scotland Yard. Walden went into the house. It felt empty. He decided to go to his room. He sat at the window and finished his cigar.

He felt the need to talk to someone. He looked at his watch: Lydia would have had her siesta, and would now be putting on a gown ready to have tea and receive callers. He went through to her room.

She was sitting at her mirror in a robe. She looks strained, he thought; it's all this trouble. He put his hands on her shoulders, looking at her reflection in the mirror, then bent to kiss the top of her head. 'Feliks Kschessinsky.'

'*What?*' She seemed frightened.

'That's the name of our assassin. Does it mean something to you?'

'No.'

'I thought you seemed to recognize it.'

'It . . . it rings a bell.'

'Basil Thomson has found out all about the fellow. He's a killer, a thoroughly evil type. It's not impossible that you might have come across him in St Petersburg – that would explain why he seemed vaguely familiar when he called here, and why his name rings a bell.'

'Yes – that must be it.'

Walden went to the window and looked out over the park. It was the time of day when nannies took their charges for a walk. The paths were crowded with perambulators, and every bench was occupied by gossiping women in unfashionable clothes. It occurred to Walden that Lydia might have had some connection with Feliks, back in St Petersburg – some connection which she did not want to admit. The thought was shaming, and he pushed it out of his mind. He said: 'Thomson believes that, when Feliks realizes Aleks is hidden away, he will try to kidnap me.'

Lydia got up from her chair and came to him. She put her arms around his waist and laid her head on his chest. She did not speak.

Walden stroked her hair. 'I must go everywhere in my own coach, and Pritchard must carry a pistol.'

She looked up at him, and to his surprise he saw that her grey eyes were full of tears. She said: 'Why is this happening to us? First Charlotte gets involved in a riot, then you're threatened – it seems we're all in jeopardy.'

'Nonsense. You're in no danger, and Charlotte is only being a silly girl. And I'll be well protected.' He stroked her sides. He could feel the warmth of her body through the thin robe – she was not wearing her corset. He wanted to make love to her, right now. They had never done it in daylight.

He kissed her mouth. She pressed her body against his, and he realized that she, too, wanted to make love. He could not remember her being like this ever before. He glanced toward the door, thinking to lock it. He looked at her, and she gave a barely perceptible nod. A tear rolled down her nose. Walden went to the door.

Someone knocked.

'Damn!' Walden said quietly.

Lydia turned her face away from the door and dabbed at her eyes with a handkerchief.

Pritchard came in. 'Excuse me, my lord. An urgent telephone communication from Mr Basil Thomson.

They have tracked the man Feliks to his lodging. If you want to be in at the kill, Mr Thomson will pick you up here in three minutes.'

'Get my hat and coat,' Walden told him.

CHAPTER TEN

When Feliks went out to get the morning paper he seemed to see children every way he turned. In the courtyard a group of girls played a game involving dancing and chanting. The boys were playing cricket with a wicket chalked on the wall and a piece of rotten planking for a bat. In the street, older boys were pushing handcarts. He bought his newspaper from an adolescent girl. Coming back to his room, his way was blocked by a naked baby crawling up the stairs. As he looked at the child – it was a girl – she stood up unsteadily and slowly toppled backwards. Feliks caught her and put her down on the landing. Her mother came out of an open door. She was a pale young woman with greasy hair, already very pregnant with another child. She scooped the baby girl up off the floor and disappeared back into her room with a suspicious look at Feliks.

Every time he considered exactly how he would trick Charlotte into telling him the whereabouts of Orlov, he seemed to run up against a brick wall in his mind. He visualized getting the information out of her sneakily, without her knowing she was telling him; or by giving her a cock-and-bull story like the one he had given Lydia; or by telling her straight out that he wanted to kill Orlov; and his imagination recoiled at each scene.

When he thought about what was at stake he found his feelings ridiculous. He had a chance to save millions of lives and possibly spark the Russian Revolution – and he was worried about lying to an upper-class girl! It was not as if he intended to do her any harm – just use her, deceive her, and betray her trust, his own daughter, whom he had only just met . . .

To occupy his hands he began to fashion his home-made dynamite into a primitive bomb. He packed the nitroglycerine-soaked cotton waste into a cracked china vase. He considered the problem of detonation. Burning paper alone might not be sufficient. He stuffed half a dozen matches into the cotton so that only their bright red heads showed. It was difficult to get the matches to stand upright because his hands were unsteady.

My hands *never* shake.

What is happening to me?

He twisted a piece of newspaper into a taper and stuck one end into the middle of the match heads, then tied the heads together with a length of cotton. He found it very difficult to tie the knot.

He read all the international news in *The Times*, ploughing doggedly through the turgid English sentences. He was more or less sure that there would be a war, but more or less sure no longer seemed enough. He would have been happy to kill a useless idler like Orlov then find out that it had been to no purpose. But to destroy his relationship with Charlotte to no purpose . . .

Relationship? What relationship?

You know what relationship.

Reading *The Times* made his head ache. The print was too small and his room was dark. It was a wretchedly conservative newspaper. It ought to be blown up.

He longed to see Charlotte again.

He heard shuffling footsteps on the landing outside, then there was a knock at the door.

'Come in,' he called carelessly.

The caretaker came in, coughing. 'Morning.'

'Good morning, Mr Price.' What did the old fool want now?

'What's that?' said Price, nodding at the bomb on the table.

'Home-made candle,' Feliks said. 'Lasts months. What do you want?'

'I wondered if you needed a spare pair of sheets. I can get them at a very low price—'

'No, thank you,' Feliks said. 'Goodbye.'

'Goodbye, then.' Price went out.

I should have hidden that bomb, Feliks thought.

What is happening to me?

'Yes, he's in there,' Price said to Basil Thomson.

Tension knotted in Walden's stomach.

They sat in the back of a police car parked around the corner from Canada Buildings, where Feliks was. With them was an inspector from the Special Branch and a uniformed superintendent from Southwark police station.

If they could catch Feliks now, then Aleks would be safe: what a relief that will be, Walden thought.

Thomson said: 'Mr Price went to the police station to report that he had rented a room to a suspicious character with a foreign accent who had very little money and was growing a beard as if to change his appearance. He identified Feliks from our artist's drawing. Well done, Price.'

'Thank you, sir.'

The uniformed superintendent unfolded a large-scale map. He was maddeningly slow and deliberate. 'Canada Buildings consists of three five-storey tenements around a courtyard. Each building has three stairwells. As you stand at the entrance to the courtyard, Toronto House is on your right. Feliks is on the middle staircase and the top floor. Behind Toronto House is the yard of a builder's merchant.'

Walden contained his impatience.

'On your left is Vancouver House, and behind Vancouver House is another street. The third building, straight ahead of you as you stand at the courtyard entrance, is Montreal House, which backs on to the railway line.'

Thomson pointed to the map. 'What's that, in the middle of the courtyard?'

'The privy,' replied the superintendent. 'And a real stinker, too, with all those people using it.'

Walden thought: Get on with it!

Thomson said: 'It seems to me that Feliks has three

ways out of the courtyard. First, the entrance: obviously we'll block that. Second, at the opposite end of the courtyard on the left, the alley between Vancouver House and Montreal House. It leads to the next street. Put three men in the alley, superintendent.'

'Very good, sir.'

'Third, the alley between Montreal House and Toronto House. This alley leads to the builder's yard. Another three men in there.'

The superintendent nodded.

'Now, do these tenements have back windows?'

'Yes, sir.'

'So Feliks has a fourth escape route from Toronto House: out of the back window and across the builder's yard. Better put six men in the builder's yard. Finally, let's have a nice show of strength right here in the middle of the courtyard, to encourage him to come along quietly. Does all that meet with your approval, Superintendent?'

'More than adequate, I'd say, sir.'

He doesn't know what kind of man we're dealing with, Walden thought.

Thomson said: 'You and Inspector Sutton here can make the arrest. Got your gun, Sutton?'

Sutton pulled aside his coat to show a small revolver strapped under his arm. Walden was surprised: he had thought that no British policeman ever carried a firearm. Obviously the Special Branch was different. He was glad.

Thomson said to Sutton: 'Take my advice – have it in your hand when you knock on his door.' He turned to the uniformed superintendent. 'You'd better take my gun.'

The superintendent was mildly offended. 'I've been twenty-five years in the force and never felt the lack of a firearm, sir, so if it's all the same to you I shan't begin now.'

'Policemen have died trying to arrest this man.'

'I'm afraid I've never been taught to shoot, sir.'

Good God, Walden thought despairingly, how can people like us deal with people like Feliks?

Thomson said: 'Lord Walden and I will be at the courtyard entrance.'

'You'll stay in the car, sir?'

'We'll stay in the car.'

Let's *go*, thought Walden.

'Let's go,' said Thomson.

Feliks realized he was hungry. He had not eaten for more than twenty-four hours. He wondered what to do. Now that he had stubble on his chin and working-class clothes he would be watched by shopkeepers so it would be more difficult for him to steal.

He pulled himself up at that thought. It's *never* difficult to steal, he told himself. Let's see: I could go to a suburban house – the kind where they are likely to have only one or two servants – and walk in at the tradesman's entrance. There would be a maid in the kitchen, or perhaps a cook. 'I am a madman,' I would say with a smile, 'but if you make me a sandwich I won't rape you.' I would move toward the door to block her escape. She might scream, in which case I should go away and try another house. But, most likely, she would give me the food. 'Thank you,' I would say. 'You are kind.' Then I would walk away. It is never difficult to steal.

Money was a problem. Feliks thought: As if I could afford a pair of sheets! The caretaker was an optimist. Surely he knew that Feliks had no money . . .

Surely he knows I've no money.

On reflection, Price's reason for coming to Feliks' room was suspicious. Was he just optimistic? Or was he *checking*? I seem to be slowing down, Feliks thought. He stood up and went to the window.

Jesus *Christ*.

The courtyard was alive with blue-uniformed policemen.

Feliks stared down at them in horror.

The sight made him think of a nest of worms, wriggling and crawling over one another in a hole in the ground.

His instincts screamed: Run! Run! Run!

Where?

They had blocked all exits from the courtyard.

Feliks remembered the back windows.

He ran from his room and along the landing to the back of the tenement. There a window looked out on to the builder's yard behind. He peered down into the yard and saw five or six policemen taking up positions among the piles of bricks and stacks of planking. There was no escape that way.

That left only the roof.

He ran back to his room and looked out. The policemen were still, all but two men – one in uniform and one in plain clothes – who were walking purposefully across the courtyard toward Feliks' stair.

He picked up his bomb and the box of matches and ran down to the landing below. A small door with a latch gave access to a cupboard beneath the stairs. Feliks opened the door and placed the bomb inside. He lit the paper fuse and closed the cupboard door. He turned around. He had time to run up the stairs before the fuse burned down—

The baby girl was crawling up the stairs.

Shit.

He picked her up and dashed through the door into her room. Her mother sat on the dirty bed, staring vacantly at the wall. Feliks thrust the baby into her arms and yelled: 'Stay here! Don't move!' The woman looked scared.

He ran out. The two men were one floor down. Feliks raced up the stairs –

Don't blow now don't blow now don't—

– to his landing. They heard him, and one shouted: 'Hey, you!' They broke into a run.

Feliks dashed into his room, picked up the cheap straight-backed chair, carried it out to the landing and positioned it directly under the trapdoor leading to the loft.

The bomb had not exploded.

Perhaps it would not work.

Feliks stood on the chair.

The two men hit the stairs.

Feliks pushed open the trapdoor.

The uniformed policeman shouted: 'You're under arrest!'

The plain-clothes man raised a gun and pointed it at Feliks.

The bomb went off.

There was a big dull thud like something very heavy falling and the staircase broke up into matchwood which flew everywhere and the two men were flung backward and the debris burst into flames and Feliks hauled himself up into the loft.

'Damn, he's exploded a damn bomb!' Thomson shouted.

Walden thought: It's going wrong – again.

There was a crash as shards of glass from a third-floor window hit the ground.

Walden and Thomson jumped out of the car and ran across the courtyard.

Thomson picked two uniformed policemen at random. 'You and you – come inside with me.' He turned to Walden. 'You stay here.' They ran inside.

Walden backed across the courtyard, looking up at the windows of Toronto House.

Where is Feliks?

He heard a policeman say: 'He've gorn out the back, you mark my words.'

Four or five slates fell off the roof and shattered in the courtyard – loosened, Walden assumed, by the explosion.

Walden kept feeling the urge to look back over his shoulder, as if Feliks might suddenly appear behind him, from nowhere.

The residents of the tenements were coming to their doors and windows to see what was going on, and the courtyard began to fill with people. Some of the policemen made half-hearted attempts to send them back inside. A woman ran out of Toronto House screaming: 'Fire!'

Where is Feliks?

Thomson and a policeman came out carrying Sutton. He was unconscious, or dead. Walden looked more closely. No, he was not dead: his pistol was gripped in his hand.

More slates fell off the roof.

The policeman with Thomson said: 'It's a bloody mess in there.'

Walden said: 'Did you see where Feliks is?'

'Couldn't see anything.'

Thomson and the policeman went back inside.

More slates fell—

Walden was struck by a thought. He looked up.

There was a hole in the roof, and Feliks was climbing up through it.

'There he is!' Walden yelled.

They all watched, helpless, as Feliks crawled out of the loft and scrambled up the roof to the ridge.

If I had a gun—

Walden knelt over the unconscious body of Sutton and prised the pistol from his fingers.

He looked up. Feliks was kneeling on the peak of

the roof. I wish it was a rifle, Walden thought as he lifted the gun. He sighted along the barrel. Feliks looked at him. Their eyes met.

Feliks moved.

A shot rang out.

He felt nothing.

He began to run.

It was like running along a tightrope. He had to hold out his arms for balance, he had to place his feet squarely on the narrow ridge, and he had to avoid thinking about the fifty-foot drop to the courtyard.

There was another shot.

Feliks panicked.

He ran at top speed. The end of the roof loomed up. He could see the down-sloping roof of Montreal House ahead. He had no idea how wide was the gap between the two buildings. He slowed down, hesitating; then Walden fired again.

Feliks ran full-tilt at the end of the ridge.

He jumped.

He flew through the air. He heard his own voice, as if distantly, screaming.

He caught a momentary glimpse of three policemen, in the alley fifty feet below him, staring up at him open-mouthed.

Then he hit the roof of Montreal House, landing hard on his hands and knees.

The impact winded him. He slid backwards down

the roof. His feet hit the gutter. It seemed to give under the strain, and he thought he was going to slide right off the edge of the roof and fall, fall, endlessly – but the gutter held and he stopped sliding.

He was frightened.

A distant corner of his mind protested: But I'm never frightened!

He scrambled up the roof to the peak and then down the other side.

Montreal House backed on to the railway. There were no policemen on the lines or the embankment. They didn't anticipate this, Feliks thought exultantly; they thought I was trapped in the courtyard, it never occurred to them I might escape over the rooftops.

Now all I have to do is get down.

He peered over the gutter at the wall of the building beneath him. There were no drainpipes – the gutters emptied through spouts which jutted out from the edge of the roof, like gargoyles. But the top-floor windows were close to the eaves and had wide ledges.

With his right hand Feliks grasped the gutter and pulled it, testing its strength.

Since when have I cared whether I live or die?

(You know since when.)

He positioned himself over a window, gripped the gutter with both hands, and slowly eased himself over the edge.

For a moment he hung free.

His feet found the window-ledge. He took his right hand from the gutter and felt the brickwork around the window for a handhold. He got his fingers into a shallow groove, then let go of the gutter with his other hand.

He looked through the window. Inside, a man saw him and shouted in fright.

Feliks kicked the window in and dropped into the room. He pushed the frightened occupant aside and rushed out through the doorway.

He ran down the stairs four at a time. If he could reach the ground floor he could get out through the back windows and on to the railway line.

He reached the last landing and stopped at the top of the last flight of stairs, breathing hard. A blue uniform appeared at the front entrance. Feliks spun around and raced to the back of the landing. He lifted the window. It stuck. He gave a mighty heave and threw it open. He heard boots running up the stairs. He clambered over the windowsill, eased himself out, hung by his hands for a moment, pushed himself away from the wall and dropped.

He landed in the long grass of the railway embankment. To his right, two men were jumping over the fence of the builders' yard. A shot came from his far left. A policeman came to the window from which Feliks had jumped.

He ran up the embankment to the railway.

There were four or five pairs of lines. In the distance a train was approaching fast. It seemed to be on the farthermost track. He suffered a moment of cowardice, frightened to cross in front of the train; then he broke into a run.

The two policemen from the builders' yard and the one from Montreal House chased him across the tracks. From the far left a voice shouted: 'Clear the field of fire!' The three pursuers were making it difficult for Walden to get a shot.

Feliks glanced over his shoulder. They had fallen back. A shot rang out. He began to duck and zig-zag. The train sounded very loud. He heard its whistle. There was another shot. He turned aside suddenly, then stumbled and fell on to the last pair of railway lines. There was a terrific thunder in his ears. He saw the locomotive bearing down on him. He jerked convulsively, catapulting himself off the track on to the gravel on the far side. The train roared past his head. He caught a split-second glimpse of the engineman's face, white and scared.

He stood up and ran down the embankment.

Walden stood at the fence watching the train. Basil Thomson came up beside him.

Those policemen who had got on to the railway line ran across to the last track then stood there, helpless, waiting for the train to pass. It seemed to take for ever.

When it had gone, there was no sign of Feliks.

'The bugger's got away,' a policeman said.

Basil Thomson said: 'God damn it all to hell.'

Walden turned away and walked back to the car.

*

Feliks dropped down on the far side of a wall and found himself in a poor street of small row houses. He was also in the goalmouth of an improvised soccer pitch. A group of small boys in large caps stopped playing and stared at him in surprise. He ran on.

It would take them a few minutes to redeploy the police on the far side of the railway line. They would come looking for him, but they would be too late: by the time they got a search under way he would be half a mile from the railway and still moving.

He kept running until he reached a busy shopping street. There, on impulse, he jumped on an omnibus.

He had escaped, but he was terribly worried. This kind of thing had happened to him before, but previously he had never been scared, he had never panicked. He remembered the thought that had gone through his mind as he slid down the roof: I don't want to die.

In Siberia he had lost the ability to feel fear. Now it had come back. For the first time in years, he wanted to stay alive. I have become human again, he thought.

He looked out of the window at the mean streets of south-east London, wondering whether the dirty children and the white-faced women could look at him and see a reborn man.

It was a disaster. It would slow him down, cramp his style, interfere with his work.

I'm afraid, he thought.

I want to live.

I want to see Charlotte again.

CHAPTER ELEVEN

THE FIRST tram of the day woke Feliks with its noise. He opened his eyes and watched it go by, striking bright blue sparks from the overhead cable. Dull-eyed men in working clothes sat at its windows, smoking and yawning, on their way to jobs as street cleaners and market porters and road menders.

The sun was low and bright, but Feliks was in the shade of Waterloo Bridge. He lay on the pavement with his head to the wall, wrapped in a blanket of newspapers. On one side of him was a stinking old woman with the red face of a drunkard. She looked fat, but now Feliks could see, between the hem of her dress and the tops of her man's boots, a few inches of dirty white legs like sticks; and he concluded that her apparent obesity must be due to several layers of clothing. Feliks liked her: last night she had amused all the vagrants by teaching him the vulgar English words for various parts of the body. Feliks had repeated them after her and everyone had laughed.

On his other side was a red-haired boy from Scotland. For him, sleeping in the open was an adventure. He was tough and wiry and cheerful. Looking now at his sleeping face, Feliks saw that he had no morning beard: he was terribly young. What would happen to him when winter came?

There were about thirty of them in a line along the pavement, all lying with their heads to the wall and their feet toward the road, covered with coats or sacks or newspapers. Feliks was the first to stir. He wondered whether any of them had died in the night.

He got up. He ached after a night on the cold street. He walked out from under the bridge into the sunshine. Today he was to meet Charlotte. No doubt he looked and smelled like a tramp. He contemplated washing himself in the Thames, but the river appeared to be dirtier than he was. He went looking for a municipal bath-house.

He found one on the south side of the river. A notice on the door announced that it would open at nine o'clock. Feliks thought that characteristic of social-democratic government: they would build a bath-house so that working men could keep clean, then open it only when everyone was at work. No doubt they complained that the masses failed to take advantage of the facilities so generously provided.

He found a tea-stall near Waterloo Station and had breakfast. He was severely tempted by the fried-egg sandwiches but he could not afford one. He had his usual bread and tea and saved the money for a newspaper.

He felt contaminated by his night with the deadbeats. That was ironic, he thought, for in Siberia he had been glad to sleep with pigs for warmth. It was not difficult to understand why he felt differently now: he was to meet his daughter, and she would be fresh and clean, smelling of perfume and dressed in silk, with gloves and a hat and perhaps a parasol to shade her from the sun.

He went into the railway station and bought *The Times*, then sat on a stone bench outside the bath-house and read the paper while he waited for the place to open.

The news shocked him to the core.

AUSTRIAN HEIR AND HIS WIFE MURDERED
SHOT IN BOSNIAN TOWN
A STUDENT'S POLITICAL CRIME
BOMB THROWN EARLIER IN THE DAY
THE EMPEROR'S GRIEF

The Austro-Hungarian Heir-Presumptive, the Archduke Francis Ferdinand, and his wife, the Duchess of Hohenberg, were assassinated yesterday morning at Sarajevo, the capital of Bosnia. The actual assassin is described as a high school student, who fired bullets at his victims with fatal effect from an automatic pistol as they were returning from a reception at the Town Hall.

The outrage was evidently the fruit of a carefully laid plot. On their way to the Town Hall the Archduke and his Consort had narrowly escaped death. An individual, described as a compositor from Trebinje, a garrison town in the extreme south of Herzegovina, had thrown a bomb at their motor car. Few details of this first outrage have been received. It is stated that the Archduke warded off the bomb with his arm, and that it exploded behind the car, injuring the occupants of the second carriage.

The author of the second outrage is stated to be a native of Grahovo, in Bosnia. No information as to his race or creed is yet forthcoming. It is presumed that he belongs to the Serb or Orthodox section of the Bosnian population.

Both criminals were immediately arrested, and were with difficulty saved from being lynched.

While this tragedy was being enacted in the Bosnian capital, the aged Emperor Francis Joseph was on his way from Vienna to his summer residence at Ischl. He had an enthusiastic send-off from his subjects in Vienna and an even more enthusiastic reception on reaching Ischl.

Feliks was stunned. He was delighted that another useless aristocratic parasite had been destroyed, another blow struck against tyranny; and he felt ashamed that a schoolboy had been able to kill the heir to the Austrian throne while he, Feliks, had failed repeatedly to kill a Russian prince. But what occupied his mind most was the change in the world political picture that must surely follow. The Austrians, with the Germans backing them, would take their revenge on Serbia. The Russians would protest. Would the Russians mobilize their army? If they were confident of British support, they probably would. Russian mobilization would mean German mobilization; and once the Germans had mobilized no one could stop their generals going to war.

Feliks painstakingly deciphered the tortured English of the other reports, on the same page, to do with the assassination. There were stories headlined OFFICIAL REPORT OF THE CRIME, AUSTRIAN EMPEROR AND THE NEWS, TRAGEDY OF A ROYAL HOUSE, and SCENE OF THE MURDER (From Our Special Correspondent). There was a good deal of nonsense about how shocked and horrified and grieved everyone was; plus repeated assertions that there was no cause for undue alarm, and that tragic though it was the murder would make no real difference to Europe – sentiments which Feliks had already come to recognize as being characteristic of *The Times*, which would have described the Four Horsemen of the Apocalypse as strong rulers who could do nothing but good for the stability of the international situation.

So far there was no talk of Austrian reprisals, but it would come, Feliks was sure. And then—

Then there would be war.

There was no real reason for Russia to go to war, Feliks thought angrily. The same applied to England. It was France and Germany that were belligerent: the French had been wanting since 1871 to win back their lost territories of Alsace and Lorraine, and the German generals felt that Germany would be a second-class power until she began to throw her weight about.

What might stop Russia going to war? A quarrel with her allies. What would cause a quarrel between Russia and England? The killing of Orlov.

If the assassination in Sarajevo could start a war, another assassination in London could stop a war.

And Charlotte could find Orlov.

Wearily, Feliks contemplated afresh the dilemma that had haunted him for the last forty-eight hours. Was anything changed by the murder of the Archduke? Did that give him the right to take advantage of a young girl?

It was almost time for the bath-house to open. A small crowd of women carrying bundles of washing gathered around the door. Feliks folded his newspaper and stood up.

He knew that he *would* use her. He had not resolved the dilemma – he had simply decided what to do. His whole life seemed to lead up to the murder of Orlov. There was a momentum in his progress toward that goal, and he could not be deflected, even by the knowledge that his life had been founded on a mistake.

Poor Charlotte.

The doors opened, and Feliks went into the bath-house to wash.

Charlotte had it all planned. Lunch was at one o'clock when the Waldens had no guests. By two-thirty Mama would be in her room, lying down. Charlotte would be able to sneak out of the house in time to meet Feliks at three. She would spend an hour with him. By four-thirty she would be at home in the morning-room, washed and changed and demurely ready to pour tea and receive callers with Mama.

It was not to be. At midday Mama ruined the whole plan by saying: 'Oh, I forgot to tell you – we're lunching with the Duchess of Middlesex at her house in Grosvenor Square.'

'Oh, dear,' Charlotte said. 'I really don't feel like a luncheon party.'

'Don't be silly, you'll have a lovely time.'

I said the wrong thing, Charlotte thought immediately. I should have said I've got a splitting headache and I can't possibly go. I was too half-hearted. I could have lied if I'd known in advance but I can't do it on the spur of the moment. She tried again. 'I'm sorry, Mama, I don't want to go.'

'You're coming, and no nonsense,' Mama said. 'I want the Duchess to get to know you – she really is most useful. And the Marquess of Chalfont will be there.'

Lunch parties generally started at one-thirty and went on past three. I might be home by three-thirty, so I could get to the National Gallery by four, Charlotte thought; but by then he will have given up and gone away, and besides, even if he is still waiting, I would have to leave him almost immediately in order to be home for tea. She wanted to talk to him about the assassination: she was eager to hear his views. She did not want to have lunch with the old Duchess and—

'Who is the Marquess of Chalfont?'

'You know, Freddie. He's charming, don't you think?'

'Oh, him. Charming? I haven't noticed.' I could write a note, address it to that place in Camden Town, and leave it on the hall table on my way out for the footman to post; but Feliks doesn't actually live at that address, and anyway he wouldn't get the note before three o'clock.

Mama said: 'Well, notice him today. I fancy you may have bewitched him.'

'Who?'

'*Freddie.* Charlotte, you really must pay a little attention to a young man when he pays attention to you.'

So that was why she was so keen on this lunch party. 'Oh, Mama, don't be silly—'

'What's silly about it?' Mama said in an exasperated voice.

'I've hardly spoken three sentences to him.'

'Then it's not your conversation that has bewitched him.'

'Please!'

'All right, I won't tease. Go and change. Put on that cream dress with the brown lace – it suits your colouring.'

Charlotte gave in, and went up to her room. I suppose I should be flattered about Freddie, she thought, as she took off her dress. Why can't I get interested in any of these young men? Maybe I'm just not ready for all that yet. At the moment there's too much else to occupy my mind. At breakfast Papa said there would be a war, because of the shooting of the Archduke. But girls aren't supposed to be too interested in that sort of thing. The summit of my ambition should be to get engaged before the end of my first season – that's what Belinda is thinking about.

But not all girls are like Belinda – remember the suffragettes.

She got dressed and went downstairs. She sat and made idle conversation while Mama drank a glass of sherry, then they went to Grosvenor Square.

The Duchess was an overweight woman in her sixties: she made Charlotte think of an old wooden ship rotting beneath a new coat of paint. The lunch was a real hen-party. If this were a play, Charlotte thought, there would be a wild-eyed poet, a discreet Cabinet Minister, a cultured Jewish banker, a Crown Prince, and at least one remarkably beautiful woman. In fact the only men present, apart from Freddie, were a nephew of the Duchess and a Conservative M.P. Each of the women was introduced as the wife of so-and-so. If I ever get married, Charlotte thought, I shall insist on being introduced as myself, not as somebody's wife.

Of course it was difficult for the Duchess to have interesting parties because so many people were banned from her table: all Liberals, all Jews, anybody in trade, anybody who was on the stage, all divorcees, and all of the many people who had at one time or another offended against the Duchess's idea of what was the done thing. It made for a dull circle of friends.

The Duchess's favourite topic of conversation was the question of what was ruining the country. The main candidates were subversion (by Lloyd George and Churchill), vulgarity (Diaghilev and the post-impressionists), and supertax (one shilling and threepence in the pound).

Today, however, the ruin of England took second place to the death of the Archduke. The Conservative M.P. explained at somewhat tedious length why there would be no war. The wife of a South American ambassador said in a little-girlish tone which infuriated Charlotte: 'What I don't understand is why these nihilists want to throw bombs and shoot people.'

The Duchess had the answer to that. Her doctor had explained to her that all suffragettes had a nervous ailment known to medical science as hysteria; and in her view the revolutionists suffered from the male equivalent of this disease.

Charlotte, who had read *The Times* from cover to cover that morning, said: 'On the other hand, perhaps the Serbs simply don't want to be ruled by Austria.' Mama gave her a black look and everyone else glanced at her for a moment as if she were quite mad and then ignored what she had said.

Freddie was sitting next to her. His round face always seemed to gleam slightly. He spoke to her in a low voice. 'I say, you do say the most outrageous things.'

'What was outrageous about it?' Charlotte demanded.

'Well, I mean to say, anyone would think you approved of people shooting archdukes.'

'I think if the Austrians tried to take over England, you would shoot archdukes, wouldn't you?'

'You're priceless,' Freddie said.

Charlotte turned away from him. She was beginning to feel as if she had lost her voice: nobody seemed to hear anything she said. It made her very cross.

Meanwhile the Duchess was getting into her stride. The lower classes were idle, she said; and Charlotte thought: You who have never done a day's work in your life! Why, the Duchess said, she understood that nowadays each workman had a lad to carry his tools around: surely a man could carry his own tools, she said as a footman held out for her a silver salver of boiled potatoes. Beginning her third glass of sweet wine, she said that they drank so much beer in the middle of the day that they were incapable of working in the afternoon. People today wanted to be mollycoddled, she said as three footmen and two maids cleared away the third course and served the fourth; it was no business of the Government's to provide Poor Relief and medical insurance and pensions. Poverty would encourage the lower orders to be thrifty, and that was a virtue, she said, at the end of a meal which would have fed a working-class family of ten for a fortnight. People must be self-reliant, she said, as the butler helped her rise from the table and walk into the drawing-room.

By this time Charlotte was boiling with suppressed rage. Who could blame revolutionists for shooting people like the Duchess?

Freddie handed her a cup of coffee and said: 'She's a marvellous old warhorse, isn't she?'

Charlotte said: 'I think she's the nastiest old woman I've ever met.'

Freddie's round face became furtive and he said: 'Hush!'

At least, Charlotte thought, no one could say I'm encouraging him.

A carriage clock on the mantel struck three with a tinkling chime. Charlotte felt as if she were in jail. Feliks was now waiting for her on the steps of the National Gallery. She had to get out of the Duchess's house. She thought: What am I doing here when I could be with someone who talks sense?

The Conservative M.P. said: 'I must get back to the House.' His wife stood up to go with him. Charlotte saw her way out.

She approached the wife and spoke quietly. 'I have a slight headache,' she said. 'May I come with you? You must pass my house on the way to Westminster.'

'Certainly, Lady Charlotte,' said the wife.

Mama was talking to the Duchess. Charlotte interrupted them and repeated the headache story. 'I know Mama would like to stay a little longer, so I'm going with Mrs Shakespeare. Thank you for a lovely lunch, your grace.'

The Duchess nodded regally.

I managed that rather well, Charlotte thought, as she walked out into the hall and down the stairs.

She gave her address to the Shakespeares' coachman and added: 'There's no need to drive into the courtyard – just stop outside.'

On the way, Mrs Shakespeare advised her to take a spoonful of laudanum for the headache.

The coachman did as he had been told, and at three-twenty Charlotte was standing on the pavement outside her home, watching the coach drive off. Instead of going into the house she headed for Trafalgar Square.

She arrived just after three-thirty and ran up the

steps of the National Gallery. She could not see Feliks. He's gone, she thought; after all that. Then he emerged from behind one of the massive pillars, as if he had been lying in wait, and she was so pleased to see him she could have kissed him.

'I'm sorry to have made you wait about,' she said as she shook his hand. 'I got involved in a dreadful luncheon party.'

'It doesn't matter, now that you're here.' He was smiling, but uneasily, like – Charlotte thought – someone saying hello to a dentist before having a tooth pulled.

They went inside. Charlotte loved the cool, hushed museum, with its glass domes and marble pillars, grey floors and beige walls, and the paintings shouting out colour and beauty and passion. 'At least my parents taught me to look at pictures,' she said.

He turned his sad dark eyes on her. 'There's going to be a war.'

Of all people who had spoken of that possibility today, only Feliks and Papa had seemed to be *moved* by it. 'Papa said the same thing. But I don't understand why.'

'France and Germany both think they stand to gain a lot by war. Austria, Russia and England may get sucked in.'

They walked on. Feliks did not seem to be interested in the paintings. Charlotte said: 'Why are you so concerned? Shall you have to fight?'

'I'm too old. But I think of all the millions of innocent Russian boys, straight off the farm, who will be crippled or blinded or killed in a cause they don't understand and wouldn't care about if they did.'

Charlotte had always thought of war as a matter of men killing one another, but Feliks saw it as men being killed by war. As usual, he showed her things in a new light. She said: 'I never looked at it that way.'

'The Earl of Walden never looked at it that way either. That's why he will let it happen.'

'I'm sure Papa wouldn't let it happen if he could help—'

'You're wrong,' Feliks interrupted. 'He is making it happen.'

Charlotte frowned, puzzled. 'What do you mean?'

'That's why Prince Orlov is here.'

Her puzzlement deepened. 'How do you know about Aleks?'

'I know more about it than you do. The police have spies among the anarchists, but the anarchists have spies among the police spies. We find things out. Walden and Orlov are negotiating a treaty, the effect of which will be to drag Russia into the war on the British side.'

Charlotte was about to protest that Papa would not do such a thing, then she realized that Feliks was right. It explained some of the remarks passed between Papa and Aleks while Aleks was staying at the house, and it explained why Papa was shocking his friends by consorting with Liberals like Churchill.

She said: 'Why would he do that?'

'I'm afraid he doesn't care how many Russian peasants die so long as England dominates Europe.'

Yes, of course, Papa would see it in those terms, she thought. 'It's awful,' she said. 'Why don't you *tell* people? Expose the whole thing – shout it from the rooftops!'

'Who would listen?'

'Wouldn't they listen in Russia?'

'They will if we can find a dramatic way of bringing the thing to their notice.'

'Such as?'

Feliks looked at her. 'Such as kidnapping Prince Orlov.'

It was so outrageous that she laughed, then stopped abruptly. It crossed her mind that he might be playing a game, pretending in order to make a point; then she looked at his face and knew that he was deadly serious. For the first time she wondered whether he was perfectly sane. 'You don't mean that,' she said incredulously.

He smiled awkwardly. 'Do you think I'm crazy?'

She knew he was not. She shook her head. 'You're the sanest man I ever met.'

'Then sit down, and I'll explain it to you.'

She allowed herself to be led to a seat.

'The Czar already distrusts the English, because they let political refugees like me come to England. If one of us were to kidnap his favourite nephew there would be a real quarrel – then they could not be sure of each other's help in a war. And, when the Russian people learn what Orlov was trying to do to them, they will be so angry that the Czar will not be able to make them go to war anyway. Do you see?'

Charlotte watched his face as he talked. He was quiet, reasonable, and only a little tense. There was no mad light of fanaticism in his eye. Everything he said made sense, but it was like the logic of a fairy tale – one thing followed from another, but it seemed to be a story about a different world, not the world she lived in.

'I do see,' she said, 'but you can't kidnap Aleks, he's such a nice man.'

'That *nice man* will lead a million other nice men to their deaths if he's allowed to. This is *real*, Charlotte; not like the battles in these paintings of gods and horses. Walden and Orlov are discussing *war* – men cutting each other open with swords, boys getting their legs blown off by cannonballs, people bleeding and dying in muddy fields, screaming in pain with no one to help them. This is what Walden and Orlov are trying to arrange. Half the misery in the world is caused by nice young men like Orlov who think they have the right to organize wars between nations.'

She was struck by a frightening thought. 'You've already tried once to kidnap him.'

He nodded. 'In the park. You were in the carriage. It went wrong.'

'Oh, my word.' She felt sickened and depressed.

He took her hand. 'You know I'm right, don't you?'

It seemed to her that he *was* right. His world was the real world: she was the one who lived in a fairy tale. In fairyland the debutantes in white were presented to the King and Queen, and the Prince went to war, and the

Earl was kind to his servants who all loved him, and the Duchess was a dignified old lady, and there was no such thing as sexual intercourse. In the real world Annie's baby was born dead because Mama let Annie go without a reference, and a thirteen-year-old mother was condemned to death because she had let her baby die, and people slept on the streets because they had no homes, and there were baby farms, and the Duchess was a vicious old harridan, and a grinning man in a tweed suit punched Charlotte in the stomach outside Buckingham Palace.

'I know you're right,' she said to Feliks.

'That's very important,' he said. 'You hold the key to the whole thing.'

'Me? Oh, no!'

'I need your help.'

'No, please don't say that!'

'You see, I can't find Orlov.'

It's not fair, she thought; it has all happened too quickly. She felt miserable and trapped. She wanted to help Feliks, and she could see how important it was, but Aleks was her cousin, and he had been a guest in her house – how could she betray him?

'Will you help me?' Feliks said.

'I don't know where Aleks is,' she said evasively.

'But you could find out.'

'Yes.'

'Will you?'

She sighed. 'I don't know.'

'Charlotte, you must.'

'There's no *must* about it!' she flared. 'Everyone tells me what I *must* do – I thought you had more respect for me!'

He looked crestfallen. 'I wish I didn't have to ask you.'

She squeezed his hand. 'I'll think about it.'

He opened his mouth to protest, and she put a finger to his lips to silence him. 'You'll have to be satisfied with that,' she said.

At seven-thirty Walden went out in the Lanchester, wearing evening dress and a silk hat. He was using the motor car all the time, now: in an emergency it would be faster and more manoeuvrable than a carriage. Pritchard sat in the driving seat with a revolver holstered beneath his jacket. Civilized life seemed to have come to an end. They drove to the back entrance of Number Ten, Downing Street. The Cabinet had met that afternoon to discuss the deal Walden had worked out with Aleks. Now Walden was to hear whether or not they had approved it.

He was shown into the small dining-room. Churchill was already there with Asquith, the Prime Minister. They were leaning on the sideboard drinking sherry. Walden shook hands with Asquith.

'How do you do, Prime Minister.'

'Good of you to come, Lord Walden.'

Asquith had silver hair and a clean-shaven face. There were traces of humour in the wrinkles around his eyes, but his mouth was small, thin-lipped and stubborn-looking, and he had a broad, square chin. Walden thought there was in his voice a trace of a Yorkshire accent which had survived the City of London School and Balliol College, Oxford. He had an unusually large head which was said to contain a brain of machine-like precision; but then, Walden thought, people always credit Prime Ministers with more brains than they've got.

Asquith said: 'I'm afraid the Cabinet would not approve your proposal.'

Walden's heart sank. To conceal his disappointment he adopted a brisk manner. 'Why not?'

'The opposition came mainly from Lloyd George.'

Walden looked at Churchill and raised his eyebrows.

Churchill nodded. 'You probably thought, like everyone else, that L.G. and I vote alike on every issue. Now you know otherwise.'

'What's his objection?'

'Matter of principle,' Churchill answered. 'He says we're passing the Balkans around like a box of chocolates: help yourself, choose your favourite flavour, Thrace, Bosnia, Bulgaria, Serbia. Small countries have their rights, he says. That's what comes of having a Welshman in the Cabinet. A Welshman and a solicitor too, I don't know which is worse.'

His levity irritated Walden. This is his project as much as mine, he thought: why isn't the man as dismayed as I am?

They sat down to dinner. The meal was served by

the butler. Asquith ate sparingly. Churchill drank too much, Walden thought. Walden was gloomy, mentally damning Lloyd George with every mouthful.

At the end of the first course Asquith said: 'We must have this treaty, you know. 'There will be a war between France and Germany sooner or later; and, if the Russians stay out of it, Germany will conquer Europe. We can't have that.'

Walden asked: 'What must be done to change Lloyd George's mind?'

Asquith smiled thinly. 'If I had a pound note for every time that question has been asked I'd be a rich man.'

The butler served quail and poured claret. Churchill said: 'We must come up with a modified proposal which will meet L.G.'s objection.'

Churchill's casual tone infuriated Walden. 'You know perfectly well it's not that simple,' he snapped.

'No indeed,' Asquith said mildly. 'Still, we must try. Thrace to be an independent country under Russian protection, something like that.'

'I've spent the past month beating them down,' Walden said wearily.

'Still, the murder of poor old Francis Ferdinand changes the complexion of things,' Asquith said. 'Now that Austria is getting aggressive in the Balkans again, the Russians need more than ever that toehold in the area which, in principle, we're trying to give them.'

Walden set aside his disappointment and began to think constructively. After a moment he said: 'What about Constantinople?'

'What do you mean?'

'Suppose we offered Constantinople to the Russians – would Lloyd George object to that?'

'He might say it was like giving Cardiff to the Irish Republicans,' Churchill said.

Walden ignored him and looked at Asquith.

Asquith put down his knife and fork. 'Well. Now that he has made his principled stand, he may be keen to show how reasonable he can be when offered a compromise. I think he may agree to it. Will it be enough for the Russians?'

Walden was not sure, but he was buoyed up by his new idea. Impulsively he said: 'If you can sell it to Lloyd George, I can sell it to Orlov.'

'Splendid!' said Asquith. 'Now, then, what about this anarchist?'

Walden's optimism was punctured. 'They're doing everything possible to protect Aleks, but still it's damned worrying.'

'I thought Basil Thomson was a good man.'

'Excellent,' Walden said. 'But I'm afraid Feliks might be even better.'

Churchill said: 'I don't think we should let the fellow *frighten* us—'

'I am frightened, gentlemen,' Walden interrupted. 'Three times Feliks has slipped through our grasp: the last time we had thirty policemen to arrest him. I don't see how he can get at Aleks now, but the fact that I can't see a way doesn't mean that he can't see a way. And we know what will happen if Aleks is killed: our alliance with Russia will fall through. Feliks is the most dangerous man in England.'

Asquith nodded, his expression sombre. 'If you're less than perfectly satisfied with the protection Orlov is getting, please contact me directly.'

'Thank you.'

The butler offered Walden a cigar, but he sensed that he was finished here. 'Life must go on,' he said, 'and I must go to a crush at Mrs Glenville's. I'll smoke my cigar there.'

'Don't tell them where you had dinner,' Churchill said with a smile.

'I wouldn't dare – they'd never speak to me again.' Walden finished his port and stood up.

'When will you put the new proposal to Orlov?' Asquith asked.

'I'll motor to Norfolk first thing in the morning.'

'Splendid.'

The butler brought Walden's hat and gloves and he took his leave.

Pritchard was standing at the garden gate, chatting to the policeman on duty. 'Back to the house,' Walden told him.

He had been rather rash, he reflected as they drove. He had promised to secure Aleks' consent to the Constantinople plan, but he was not sure now. It was worrying. He began to rehearse the words he would use tomorrow.

He was home before he had made any progress. 'We'll need the car again in a few minutes, Pritchard.'

'Very good, my lord.'

Walden entered the house and went upstairs to wash

his hands. On the landing he met Charlotte. 'Is Mama getting ready?' he said.

'Yes, she'll be a few minutes. How goes your politicking?'

'Slowly.'

'Why have you suddenly got involved in all that sort of thing again?'

He smiled. 'In a nutshell: to stop Germany conquering Europe. But don't you worry your pretty little head—'

'I shan't worry. But where on earth have you hidden cousin Aleks?'

He hesitated. There was no harm in her knowing; yet, once she knew, she would be capable of accidentally letting the secret out. Better for her to be left in the dark. He said: 'If anyone asks you, say you don't know.' He smiled and went on up to his room.

There were times when the charm of English life wore thin for Lydia.

Usually she liked crushes. Several hundred people would gather at someone's home to do nothing whatsoever. There was no dancing, no formal meal, no cards. You shook hands with the hostess, took a glass of champagne, and wandered around some great house chatting to your friends and admiring people's clothes. Today she was struck by the pointlessness of the whole thing. Her discontent took the form of nostalgia for Russia. There, she felt, the beauties would surely be more ravishing, the intellectuals less polite, the conversations deeper, the evening air not so balmy and soporific. In truth she was too worried – about Stephen, about Feliks and about Charlotte – to enjoy socializing.

She ascended the broad staircase with Stephen on one side of her and Charlotte on the other. Her diamond necklace was admired by Mrs Glenville. They moved on. Stephen peeled off to talk to one of his cronies in the Lords: Lydia heard the words 'Amendment Bill' and listened no more. They moved through the crowd, smiling and saying hello. Lydia kept thinking: What am I doing here?

Charlotte said: 'By the way, Mama, where has Aleks gone?'

'I don't know, dear,' Lydia said absently. 'Ask your father. Good evening, Freddie.'

Freddie was interested in Charlotte, not Lydia. 'I've been thinking about what you said at lunch,' he said. 'I've decided that the difference is, we're English.'

Lydia left them to it. In my day, she thought, political discussions were decidedly *not* the way to win a man; but perhaps things have changed. It begins to look as if Freddie will be interested in whatever Charlotte wants to talk about. I wonder if he will propose to her. Oh Lord, what a relief that would be.

In the first of the reception-rooms, where a string quartet played inaudibly, she met her sister-in-law Clarissa. They talked about their daughters, and Lydia was secretly comforted to learn that Clarissa was terribly worried about Belinda.

'I don't mind her buying those ultra-fashionable

clothes and showing her ankles, and I shouldn't mind her smoking cigarettes if only she were a little more discreet about it,' Clarissa said. 'But she goes to the most dreadful places to listen to nigger bands playing jazz music, and last week she went to a boxing match!'

'What about her chaperone?'

Clarissa sighed. 'I've said she can go out without a chaperone if she's with girls we know. Now I realize that was a mistake. I suppose Charlotte is always chaperoned.'

'In theory, yes,' Lydia said. 'But she's frightfully disobedient. Once she sneaked out and went to a suffragette meeting.' Lydia was not prepared to tell Clarissa the whole disgraceful truth: 'a suffragette meeting' did not sound quite as bad as 'a demonstration'. She added: 'Charlotte is interested in the most unladylike things, such as politics. I don't know where she gets her ideas.'

'Oh, I feel the same,' Clarissa said. 'Belinda was always brought up with the very best of music, and good society, and wholesome books and a strict governess . . . so naturally one wonders where on earth she got her taste for vulgarity. The worst of it is, I can't make her realize that I am worried for her happiness, not my own.'

'Oh, I'm so glad to hear you say that!' Lydia said. 'It's *just* how I feel. Charlotte seems to think there's something false or silly about our protecting her.' She sighed. 'We must marry them off quickly, before they come to any harm.'

'Absolutely! Is anyone interested in Charlotte?'

'Freddie Chalfont.'

'Ah, yes, I'd heard that.'

'He even seems to be prepared to talk politics to her. But I'm afraid she's not awfully interested in him. What about Belinda?'

'The opposite problem. She likes them all.'

'Oh, dear!' Lydia laughed, and moved on, feeling better. In some ways Clarissa, as a stepmother, had a more difficult task than Lydia. I suppose I have much to be thankful for, she thought.

The Duchess of Middlesex was in the next room. Most people stayed on their feet at a crush, but the Duchess, characteristically, sat down and let people come to her. Lydia approached her just as Lady Gay-Stephens was moving away.

'I gather Charlotte is quite recovered from her headache,' the Duchess said.

'Yes, indeed; it's kind of you to inquire.'

'Oh, I wasn't inquiring,' the Duchess said. 'My nephew saw her in the National Gallery at four o'clock.'

The National Gallery! What in Heaven's name was she doing there? She had sneaked out again! But Lydia was not going to let the Duchess know that Charlotte had been misbehaving. 'She has always been fond of art,' she improvised.

'She was with a man,' the Duchess said. 'Freddie Chalfont must have a rival.'

The little minx! Lydia concealed her fury. 'Indeed,' she said, forcing a smile.

'Who is he?'

'Just one of their set,' Lydia said desperately.

'Oh, no,' said the Duchess with a malicious smile. 'He was about forty, and wearing a tweed cap.'

'A tweed cap!' Lydia was being humiliated, and she knew it, but she hardly cared. Who could the man be? What was Charlotte thinking of? Her reputation—

'They were holding hands,' the Duchess added, and she smiled broadly, showing rotten teeth.

Lydia could no longer pretend that everything was all right. 'Oh, my God,' she said. 'What has the child got into now?'

The Duchess said: 'In my day the chaperone system was found effective in preventing this sort of thing.'

Lydia was suddenly very angry at the pleasure the Duchess was taking in this catastrophe. 'That was a hundred years ago,' she snapped. She walked away. A tweed cap! Holding hands! Forty years old! It was too appalling to be contemplated. The cap meant he was working class, the age meant he was a lecher, and the hand-holding implied that matters had already gone far, perhaps too far. What can I do, she thought helplessly, if the child goes out of the house without my knowledge? Oh, Charlotte, Charlotte, you don't know what you're doing to yourself!

'What was the boxing match like?' Charlotte asked Belinda.

'In a horrid sort of way it was terribly exciting,' Belinda said. 'These two enormous men wearing nothing but their shorts, standing there trying to beat each other to death.'

Charlotte did not see how that could be exciting. 'It sounds dreadful.'

'I got so worked up – ' Belinda lowered her voice – 'that I almost let Peter Go Too Far.'

'What do you mean?'

'You know. Afterwards, in the cab on the way home. I let him . . . kiss me, and so on.'

'What's *and so on*?'

Belinda whispered: 'He kissed my bosom.'

'Oh!' Charlotte frowned. 'Was it nice?'

'Heavenly!'

'Well, well.' Charlotte tried to picture Freddie kissing her bosom, and somehow she knew it would not be heavenly.

Mama walked past and said: 'We're leaving, Charlotte.'

Belinda said: 'She looks cross.'

Charlotte shrugged. 'Nothing unusual in that.'

'We're going to a coon show afterwards – why don't you come with us?'

'What's a coon show?'

'Jazz. It's wonderful music.'

'Mama wouldn't let me.'

'Your Mama is so old-fashioned.'

'You're telling me! I'd better go.'

'Bye.'

Charlotte went down the stairs and got her wrap from the cloakroom. She felt as if two people were inhabiting her skin, like Dr Jekyll and Mr Hyde. One of them smiled and made polite conversation and talked to Belinda about girlish matters; the other thought about kidnapping and treachery, and asked sly questions in an innocent tone of voice.

Without waiting for her parents she went outside and said to the footman: 'The Earl of Walden's car.'

A couple of minutes later the Lanchester pulled up at the kerb. It was a warm evening, and Pritchard had the hood down. He got out of the car and held the door for Charlotte.

She said: 'Pritchard, where is Prince Orlov?'

'It's supposed to be a secret, m'lady.'

'You can tell me.'

'I'd rather you asked your Papa, m'lady.'

It was no good. She could not bully these servants who had known her as a baby. She gave up, and said: 'You'd better go into the hall and tell them I'm waiting in the car.'

'Very good, m'lady.'

Charlotte sat back on the leather seat. She had asked the three people who might have known where Aleks was, and none of them would tell her. They did not trust her to keep the secret, and the maddening thing was that they were of course quite right. She still had not decided whether to help Feliks, however. Now, if she could not get the information he wanted, perhaps she would not have to make the agonizing decision. What a relief that would be.

She had arranged to meet Feliks the day after tomorrow, same place, same time. What would he say when she turned up empty-handed? Would he despise her for failing? No, he was not like that. He would be terribly disappointed. Perhaps he would be able to think of another way to find out where Aleks was. She could not wait to see him again. He was so interesting, and she learned so much from him, that the rest of her life seemed unbearably dull without him. Even the anxiety of this great dilemma into which he had thrown her was better than the boredom of choosing dresses for yet another day of empty social routine.

Papa and Mama got into the car and Pritchard drove off. Papa said: 'What's the matter, Lydia? You look rather upset.'

Mama looked at Charlotte. 'What were you doing in the National Gallery this afternoon?'

Charlotte's heart missed a beat. She had been found out. Someone had spied on her. Now there would be trouble. Her hands started to shake and she held them together in her lap. 'I was looking at pictures.'

'You were with a man.'

Papa said: 'Oh, *no.* Charlotte, what *is* all this?'

'He's just somebody I met,' Charlotte said. 'You wouldn't approve of him.'

'Of course we wouldn't approve!' Mama said. 'He was wearing a tweed cap!'

Papa said: 'A tweed cap! Who the devil is he?'

'He's a terribly *interesting* man, and he understands things—'

'And he holds your hand!' Mama interrupted.

Papa said sadly: 'Charlotte, how vulgar! In the National Gallery!'

'There's no romance,' Charlotte said. 'You've nothing to fear.'

'Nothing to fear?' Mama said with a brittle laugh.

'That evil old Duchess knows all about it, and she'll tell everyone.'

Papa said: 'How could you do this to your Mama?'

Charlotte could not speak. She was close to tears. She thought: I did nothing wrong, just held a conversation with someone who talks sense! How can they be so – so brutish? I hate them!

Papa said: 'You'd better tell me who he is. I expect he can be paid off.'

Charlotte shouted: 'I should think he's one of the few people in the world who can't!'

'I suppose he's some Radical,' Mama said. 'No doubt it is he who has been filling your head with foolishness about suffragism. He probably wears sandals and eats potatoes with the skins on.' She lost her temper. 'He probably believes in Free Love! If you have—'

'No, I haven't,' Charlotte said. 'I told you, there's no romance.' A tear rolled down her nose. 'I'm not the romantic type.'

'I don't believe you for a minute,' Papa said disgustedly. 'Nor will anyone else. Whether you realize it or not, this episode is a social catastrophe for all of us.'

'We'd better put her in a convent!' Mama said hysterically, and she began to cry.

'I'm sure that won't be necessary,' Papa said.

Mama shook her head. 'I didn't mean it. I'm sorry to be so shrill, but I just get so *worried* . . .'

'However, she can't stay in London, after this.'

'Certainly not.'

The car pulled into the courtyard of their house. Mama dried her eyes so that the servants would not see her upset. Charlotte thought: And so they will stop me from seeing Feliks, and send me away, and lock me up. I wish now I had promised to help him, instead of hesitating and saying I would think about it. At least then he would know I'm on his side. Well, they won't win. I shan't live the life they have mapped out for me. I shan't marry Freddie and become Lady Chalfont and raise fat, complacent children. They can't keep me locked away for ever. As soon as I'm twenty-one I'll go and work for Mrs Pankhurst, and read books about anarchism, and start a rest home for unmarried mothers, and if I ever have children I will never, never tell them lies.

They went into the house. Papa said: 'Come into the drawing-room.'

Pritchard followed them in. 'Would you like some sandwiches, my lord?'

'Not just now. Leave us alone for a while, would you, Pritchard?'

Pritchard went out.

Papa made a brandy-and-soda and sipped it. 'Think again, Charlotte,' he said. 'Will you tell us who this man is?'

She wanted to say: He's an anarchist who is trying to prevent you starting a war! But she merely shook her head.

'Then you must see,' he said almost gently, 'that we can't possibly trust you.'

You could have, once, she thought bitterly; but not any more.

Papa spoke to Mama. 'She'll just have to go to the

country for a month, it's the only way to keep her out of trouble. Then, after the Cowes Regatta, she can come to Scotland for the shooting.' He sighed. 'Perhaps she'll be more manageable by next season.'

Mama said: 'We'll send her to Walden Hall, then.'

Charlotte thought: They're talking about me as if I weren't here.

Papa said: 'I'm driving down to Norfolk in the morning, to see Aleks again. I'll take her with me.'

Charlotte was stunned.

Aleks was at Walden Hall.

I never even thought of that!

Now I know!

'She'd better go up and pack,' Mama said.

Charlotte stood up and went out, keeping her face down so that they should not see the light of triumph in her eyes.

CHAPTER TWELVE

AT A QUARTER to three Feliks was in the lobby of the National Gallery. Charlotte would probably be late, like last time, but anyway he had nothing better to do.

He was nervy and restless, sick of waiting and sick of hiding. He had slept rough again the last two nights, once in Hyde Park and once under the arches of Charing Cross. During the day he had hidden in alleys and railway sidings and patches of waste ground, coming out only to get food. It reminded him of being on the run in Siberia, and the memory was unpleasant. Even now he kept moving, going from the lobby into the domed rooms, glancing at the pictures, and returning to the lobby to look for her. He watched the clock on the wall. At half past three she still had not come. She had got involved in another dreadful luncheon party.

She would surely be able to find out where Orlov was. She was an ingenious girl, he was certain. Even if her father would not tell her straightforwardly, she would think of a way to discover the secret. Whether she would pass the information on was another matter. She was strong-willed, too.

He wished . . .

He wished a lot of things. He wished he had not deceived her. He wished he could find Orlov without her help. He wished human beings did not make themselves into Princes and Earls and Kaisers and Czars. He wished he had married Lydia and known Charlotte as a baby. He wished she would come: it was four o'clock.

Most of the paintings meant nothing to him: the sentimental religious scenes, the portraits of smug Dutch merchants in their lifeless homes. He liked Bronzino's *Allegory*, but only because it was so sensual. Art was an area of human experience which he had passed by. Perhaps one day Charlotte would lead him into the forest and show him the flowers. But it was unlikely. First, he would have to live through the next few days, and escape after killing Orlov. Even that much was not certain. Then he would have to retain Charlotte's affection despite having used her, lied to her, and killed her cousin. That was close to impossible, but even if it happened he would have to find ways of seeing her while avoiding the police . . . No, there was not much chance he would know her after the assassination. He thought: Make the most of her now.

It was four-thirty.

She's not just late, he thought with a sinking heart: she is unable to come. I hope she's not in trouble with Walden. I hope she didn't take risks and get found out. I wish she would come running up the steps, out of breath and a little flushed, with her hat slightly awry and an anxious look on her pretty face, and say: 'I'm terribly sorry to have made you wait about, I got involved in . . .'

The building seemed to be emptying out. Feliks wondered what to do next. He went outside and down the steps to the pavement. There was no sign of her. He went back up the steps and was stopped at the door by an attendant. 'Too late, mate,' the man said. 'We're closing.' Feliks turned away.

He could not wait about on the steps, in the hope that she would come later, for he would be too conspicuous right here in Trafalgar Square. Anyway, she was now two hours late: she was not going to come.

She was not going to come.

Face it, he thought: she has decided to have nothing more to do with me, and quite sensibly. But would she not have come, if only to tell me that? She might have sent a note—

She might have sent a note.

She had Bridget's address. She *would* have sent a note.

Feliks headed north.

He walked through the alleys of Theatreland and the quiet squares of Bloomsbury. The weather was changing. All the time he had been in England it had been sunny and warm, and he had yet to see rain. But for the last day or so the atmosphere had seemed oppressive, as if a storm were slowly gathering.

He thought: I wonder what it is like to live in Bloomsbury, in this prosperous middle-class atmosphere, where there is always enough to eat and money left over for books. But after the revolution we will take down the railings around the parks.

He had a headache. He had not suffered headaches since childhood. He wondered whether it was caused by the stormy air. More likely it was worry. After the revolution, he thought, headaches will be prohibited.

Would there be a note from her waiting at Bridget's house? He imagined it. 'Dear Mr Kschessinsky, I regret I am unable to keep our appointment today. Yours truly, Lady Charlotte Walden.' No, it would surely not be like that. 'Dear Feliks, Prince Orlov is staying at the home of the Russian Naval Attaché, 25A Wilton Place, second floor, left front bedroom. Your affectionate friend, Charlotte.' That was more like it. 'Dear Father, Yes – I have learned the truth. But my "Papa" has locked me in my room. Please come and rescue me. Your loving daughter, Charlotte Kschessinsky.' Don't be a damned fool.

He reached Cork Street and looked along the road. There were no policemen guarding the house, no hefty characters in plain clothes reading newspapers outside the pub. It looked safe. His heart lifted. There's something marvellous about a warm welcome from a woman, he thought, whether she's a slip of a girl like Charlotte or a fat old witch like Bridget. I've spent too much of my life with men – or alone.

He knocked on Bridget's door. As he waited, he looked down at the window of his old basement room, and saw that there were new curtains. The door opened.

Bridget looked at him and smiled widely. 'It's my favourite international terrorist, begod,' she said. 'Come in, you darling man.'

He went into her parlour.

'Do you want some tea? It's hot.'

'Yes, please.' He sat down. 'Did the police trouble you?'

'I was interrogated by a superintendent. You must be a big cheese.'

'What did you tell him?'

She looked contemptuous. 'He'd left his truncheon at home – he got nothing out of me.'

Feliks smiled. 'Have you got a letter—'

But she was still talking. 'Did you want your room back? I've let it to another fellow, but I'll chuck him out – he's got side-whiskers, and I never could abide side-whiskers.'

'No, I don't want my room—'

'You've been sleeping rough, I can tell by the look on you.'

'That's right.'

'Whatever it was you came to London to do, you haven't done it yet.'

'No.'

'Something's happened – you've changed.'

'Yes.'

'What, then?'

He was suddenly grateful for someone to whom he could talk about it. 'Years ago I had a love affair. I didn't know it, but the woman had a baby. A few days ago . . . I met my daughter.'

'Ah.' She looked at him with pity in her eyes. 'You poor bugger. As if you didn't have enough on your mind already. Is she the one that wrote the letter?'

Feliks gave a grunt of satisfaction. 'There's a letter.'

'I supposed that's what you came for.' She went to the mantelpiece and reached behind the clock. 'And is the poor girl mixed up with oppressors and tyrants?'

'Yes.'

'I thought so from the crest. You don't get much luck, do you?' She handed him the letter.

Feliks saw the crest on the back of the envelope. He ripped it open. Inside were two pages covered with neat, stylish handwriting.

Walden Hall
July 1st, 1914

Dear Feliks,

By the time you get this you will have waited in vain for me at our rendezvous. I am most awfully sorry to let you down. Unfortunately I was seen with you on Monday and it is assumed I have a clandestine lover!!!

If she's in trouble she seems cheerful enough about it, Feliks thought.

I have been banished to the country for the rest of the season. However, it is a blessing in disguise. Nobody would tell me where Aleks was, but now I know because he is here!!!

Feliks was filled with savage triumph. 'So that's where the rats have their nest.'

Bridget said: 'Is this child helping you?'

'She was my only hope.'

'Then you deserve to look troubled.'
'I know.'

Take a train from Liverpool Street Station to Waldenhall Halt. This is our village. The house is three miles out of the village on the north road. However, don't come to the house of course!!! On the left-hand side of the road you will see a wood. I always ride through the wood, along the bridle path, before breakfast between 7 and 8 o'clock. I will look out for you each day until you come.

Once she decided whose side she was on, Feliks thought, there were no half measures.

I'm not sure when this will get sent. I will put it on the hall table as soon as I see some other letters for posting there: that way, nobody will see my handwriting on an envelope, and the footman will just pick it up along with all the rest when he goes to the post office.

'She's a brave girl,' Feliks said aloud.

I am doing this because you are the only person I ever met who talks sense to me.
Yours most affectionately,
Charlotte.

Feliks sat back in his seat and closed his eyes. He was so proud of her, and so ashamed of himself, that he felt close to tears.

Bridget took the letter from his unresisting fingers and began to read.

'So she doesn't know you're her father,' she said.

'No.'

'Why is she helping you, then?'

'She believes in what I'm doing.'

Bridget made a disgusted noise. 'Men like yourself always find women to help them. I should know, bechrist.' She read on. 'She writes like a schoolgirl.'

'Yes.'

'How old is she?'

'Eighteen.'

'Old enough to know her own mind. Aleks is the one you're after?'

Feliks nodded.

'What is he?'

'A Russian prince.'

'Then he deserves to die.'

'He's dragging Russia into war.'

Bridget nodded. 'And you're dragging Charlotte into it.'

'Do you think I'm doing wrong?'

She handed the letter back to him. She seemed angry. 'We'll never be sure, will we?'

'Politics is like that.'

'Life is like that.'

Feliks tore the envelope in half and dropped it in the waste-paper basket. He intended to rip up the letter but he could not bring himself to do it. When it's all over, he thought, this may be all I have to remember her by. He folded the two sheets of paper and put them in his coat pocket.

He stood up. 'I've got a train to catch.'

'Do you want me to make you a sandwich to take with you?'

He shook his head. 'Thank you, I'm not hungry.'

'Have you money for your fare?'

'I never pay train fares.'

She put her hand into the pocket of her apron and took out a sovereign. 'Here. You can buy a cup of tea as well.'

'It's a lot of money.'

'I can afford it this week. Away with you before I change my mind.'

Feliks took the coin and kissed her goodbye. 'You have been kind to me.'

'It's not for you, it's for my Sean, God rest his merry soul.'

'Goodbye.'

'Good luck to you, boy.'

Feliks went out.

Walden was in an optimistic mood as he entered the Admiralty building. He had done what he had promised: he had sold Constantinople to Aleks. The previous afternoon Aleks had sent a message to the Czar recommending acceptance of the British offer. Walden was confident that the Czar would follow the advice of his favourite nephew, especially after the assassination in Sarajevo. He was not so sure that Lloyd George would bend to the will of Asquith.

He was shown into the office of the First Lord of the Admiralty. Churchill bounced up out of his chair and came around his desk to shake hands. 'We sold it to Lloyd George,' he said triumphantly.

'That's marvellous!' Walden said. 'And I sold it to Orlov!'

'I knew you would. Sit down.'

I might have known better than to expect a thank you, Walden thought. But even Churchill could not damp his spirits today. He sat on a leather chair and glanced around the room, at the charts on the walls and the naval memorabilia on the desk. 'We should hear from St Petersburg at any time,' he said. 'The Russian Embassy will send a note directly to you.'

'The sooner the better,' Churchill said. 'Count Hoyos has been to Berlin. According to our intelligence, he took with him a letter asking the Kaiser whether Germany would support Austria in a war against Serbia. Our intelligence also says the answer was yes.'

'The Germans don't want to fight Serbia—'

'No,' Churchill interrupted, 'they want an excuse to fight France. Once Germany mobilizes, France will mobilize, and that will be Germany's pretext for invading France. There's no stopping it now.'

'Do the Russians know all this?'

'We've told 'em. I hope they believe us.'

'Can nothing be done to make peace?'

'Everything is being done,' Churchill said. 'Edward Grey is working night and day, as are our ambassadors in Berlin, Paris, Vienna and St Petersburg. Even the King is firing off telegrams to his cousins, Kaiser "Willy" and Czar "Nicky". It'll do no good.'

There was a knock at the door, and a young male secretary came in with a piece of paper. 'A message from the Russian Ambassador, sir,' he said.

Walden tensed.

Churchill glanced at the paper and looked up with triumph in his eyes. 'They've accepted.'

Walden beamed. 'Bloody good show!'

The secretary went out. Churchill stood up. 'This calls for a whisky-and-soda. Will you join me?'

'Certainly.'

Churchill opened a cupboard. 'I'll have the treaty drafted overnight and bring it down to Walden Hall tomorrow afternoon. We can have a little signing ceremony tomorrow night. It will have to be ratified by the Czar and Asquith, of course, but that's a formality – so long as Orlov and I sign as soon as possible.'

The secretary knocked and came in again. 'Mr Basil Thomson is here, sir.'

'Show him in.'

Thomson came in and spoke without preamble. 'We've picked up the trail of our anarchist again.'

'Good!' said Walden.

Thomson sat down. 'You'll remember that I put a man in his old basement room in Cork Street, just in case he should go back there.'

'I remember,' Walden said.

'He did go back there. When he left, my man followed him.'

'Where did he go?'

'To Liverpool Street Station.' Thomson paused. 'And he bought a ticket to Waldenhall Halt.'

CHAPTER THIRTEEN

WALDEN WENT cold.

His first thought was for Charlotte. She was vulnerable there: the bodyguards were concentrating on Aleks, and she had nobody to protect her but her servants. How could I have been so stupid? he thought.

He was nearly as worried for Aleks. The boy was almost like a son to Walden. He thought he was safe in Walden's home – and now Feliks was on his way there, with a gun or a bomb, to kill him, and perhaps Charlotte too, and sabotage the treaty—

Walden burst out: 'Why the devil haven't you stopped him?'

Thomson said mildly: 'I don't think it's a good idea for one man alone to go up against our friend Feliks, do you? We've seen what he can do against several men. He seems not to care about his own life. My chappie has instructions to follow him and report.'

'It's not enough—'

'I *know*, my lord,' Thomson interrupted.

Churchill said: 'Let us be calm, gentlemen. At least we know where the fellow is. With all the resources of His Majesty's Government at our disposal we shall catch him. What do you propose, Thomson?'

'As a matter of fact I've already done it, sir. I spoke by telephone with the chief constable of the county. He will have a large detachment of men waiting at Waldenhall Halt to arrest Feliks as he gets off the train. Meanwhile, in case anything should go wrong, my chappie will stick to him like glue.'

'That won't do,' Walden said. 'Stop the train and arrest him before he gets anywhere near my home.'

'I did consider that,' Thomson said. 'The dangers outweigh the advantages. Much better to let him go on thinking he's safe, then catch him unawares.'

Churchill said, 'I agree.'

'It's not your home!' Walden said.

'You're going to have to leave this to the professionals,' Churchill said.

Walden realized he could not overrule them. He stood up. 'I shall motor to Walden Hall immediately. Will you come, Thomson?'

'Not tonight. I'm going to arrest the Callahan woman. Once we've caught Feliks, we have to mount a prosecution, and she may be our chief witness. I'll come down tomorrow to interrogate Feliks.'

'I don't know how you can be so confident,' Walden said angrily.

'We'll catch him this time,' Thomson said.

'I hope to God you're right.'

The train steamed into the falling evening. Feliks watched the sun setting over the English cornfields. He was not young enough to take mechanical transport for granted: he still found travelling by train almost magical. The boy who had walked in clogs across the muddy Russian meadows could not have dreamed this.

He was alone in the carriage but for a young man who seemed intent on reading every line of that evening's *Pall Mall Gazette.* Feliks' mood was almost gay. Tomorrow morning he would see Charlotte. How fine she would look on a horse, with the wind streaming her hair. They would be working together. She would tell him where Orlov's room was, where he was to be found at different times of day. She would help him get hold of a weapon.

It was her letter that had made him so cheerful, he realized. She was on *his* side now, come what may. Except—

Except that he had told her he was going to kidnap Orlov. Each time he recalled this he wanted to squirm in his seat. He tried to put it out of his mind, but the thought was like an itch that could not be ignored and had to be scratched. Well, he thought, what is to be done? I must begin to prepare her for the news, at least. Perhaps I should tell her that I am her father. What a shock it will be!

For a moment he was tempted by the idea of going away, vanishing, and never seeing her again; leaving her in peace. No, he thought; that is not her destiny, nor is it mine.

I wonder what *is* my destiny, after the killing of Orlov? Shall I die? He shook his head, as if he could get rid of the thought like shaking off a fly. This was not time for gloom. He had plans to make.

How will I kill Orlov? There will be guns to steal in an earl's country house: Charlotte can tell me where they are, or bring me one. Failing that there will be knives in the kitchen. And I have my bare hands.

He flexed his fingers.

Will I have to go into the house, or will Orlov come out? Shall I do it by day or by night? Shall I kill Walden too? Politically the death of Walden would make no difference, but I should like to kill him anyway. So it's personal – so what?

He thought again of Walden catching the bottle. Don't underestimate that man, he told himself.

I must be careful that Charlotte has an alibi – no one must ever know she helped me.

The train slowed down and entered a little country station. Feliks tried to recall the map he had looked at in Liverpool Street Station. He seemed to remember that Waldenhall Halt was the fourth station after this one.

His travelling companion at last finished the *Pall Mall Gazette* and put it down on the seat beside him. Feliks decided that he could not plan the assassination until he had seen the lie of the land, so he said: 'May I read your newspaper?'

The man seemed startled. Englishmen did not speak to strangers on trains, Feliks recalled. 'By all means,' the man said.

Feliks had learned that this phrase meant yes. He picked up the paper. 'Thank you.'

He glanced at the headlines. His companion stared out of the window, as if embarrassed. He had the kind of facial hair that had been fashionable when Feliks was a boy. Feliks tried to remember the English word ... 'side-whiskers', that was it.

Side-whiskers.

Did you want your room back? I've let it to another fellow, but I'll chuck him out – he's got side-whiskers, and I never could abide side-whiskers.

And now Feliks recalled that this man had been behind him in the queue at the ticket office.

He felt a stab of fear.

He held the newspaper in front of his face in case his thoughts should show in his expression. He made himself think calmly and clearly. Something Bridget had said had made the police suspicious enough to place a watch on her house. They had done that by the simple means of having a detective live in the room Feliks had vacated. The detective had seen Feliks call, had recognized him, and had followed him to the station. Standing behind Feliks in the queue, he had heard him ask for Waldenhall Halt and bought himself a ticket to the same destination. Then he had boarded the train along with Feliks.

No, not quite. Feliks had sat in the train for ten minutes or so before it pulled out. The man with the side-whiskers had jumped aboard at the last minute. What had he been doing in those few missing minutes?

He had probably made a telephone call.

Feliks imagined the conversation as the detective sat in the stationmaster's office speaking into a telephone:

'The anarchist returned to the house in Cork Street, sir. I'm following him now.'

'Where are you?'

'At Liverpool Street Station. He bought a ticket to Waldenhall Halt. He's on the train now.'

'Has it left?'

'Not for another . . . seven minutes.'

'Are there any police in the station?'

'Just a couple of bobbies.'

'It's not enough . . . this man is dangerous.'

'I can have the train delayed while you get a team down here.'

'Our anarchist might get suspicious and bolt for it. No. You stay with him . . .'

And what, Feliks wondered, would they do then? They could either take him off the train somewhere along the route, or wait to catch him at Waldenhall Halt.

Either way he had to get off the train, fast.

What to do about the detective? He must be left behind, on the train, unable to give the alarm, so that Feliks would have time to get clear.

I could tie him up, if I had anything to tie him with, Feliks thought. I could knock him out if I had something heavy and hard to hit him with. I could strangle him, but that would take time, and someone might see. I could throw him off the train, but I want to leave him on the train . . .

The train began to slow down. They might be waiting for me at the next station, he thought. I wish I had a weapon. Does the detective have a gun? I doubt it. I could break the window and use a shard of glass to cut his throat – but that would surely draw a crowd.

I must get off the train.

A few houses could be seen alongside the railway track. They were coming into a village or a small town. The brakes of the train squealed, and a station slid into view. Feliks watched intently for signs of a police trap. The platform appeared empty. The locomotive shuddered to a halt with a hiss of steam.

People began to get off. A handful of passengers walked past Feliks' window, heading for the exit: a family with two small children, a woman with a hat-box, a tall man in tweeds.

I could hit the detective, he thought, but it's so hard to knock somebody unconscious just with your fists.

The police trap could be at the next station. I must get off now.

A whistle blew.

Feliks stood up.

The detective looked startled.

Feliks said: 'Is there a lavatory on the train?'

The detective was thrown by this. 'Er . . . sure to be,' he said.

'Thank you.' He doesn't know whether to believe me, Feliks thought.

He stepped out of the compartment and into the corridor.

He ran to the end of the carriage. The train chuffed and jerked forward. Feliks looked back. The detective poked his head out of the compartment. Feliks went into the lavatory, and came back out again. The detective was still watching. The train moved a little faster. Feliks went to the carriage door. The detective came running.

Feliks turned back and punched him full in the face. The blow stopped the detective in his tracks. Feliks hit him again, in the stomach. A woman screamed. Feliks got him by the coat and dragged him into the lavatory. The detective struggled and threw a wild punch which caught Feliks in the ribs and made him gasp. He got the detective's head in his hands and banged it against the edge of the washbasin. The train picked up speed. Feliks banged the detective's head again, and then again. The man went limp. Feliks dropped him and stepped out of the lavatory. He went to the door and opened it. The train was moving at running speed. A woman at the other end of the corridor watched him, white-faced. Feliks jumped. The door banged shut behind him. He landed running. He stumbled and regained his balance. The train moved on, faster and faster.

Feliks walked to the exit.

'You left it a bit late,' said the ticket man.

Feliks nodded and handed over his ticket.

'This ticket takes you three more stations,' the ticket man said.

'I changed my mind at the last minute.'

There was a squeal of brakes. They both looked along the track. The train was stopping: someone had pulled the emergency brake. The ticket man said: 'Here, what's going on?'

Feliks forced himself to shrug unconcernedly. 'Search me,' he said. He wanted to run, but that would be the worst thing he could do.

The ticket man hovered, torn between his suspicion of Feliks and his concern for the train. Finally he said: 'You wait here,' and ran along the platform. The train stopped a couple of hundred yards out of the station. Feliks watched the ticket man run to the end of the platform and down on to the embankment.

He looked around. He was alone. He walked briskly out of the station and into the town.

A few minutes later a car with three policemen in it went past him at top speed, heading for the station.

On the outskirts of the town Feliks climbed over a gate and went into a cornfield, where he lay down to wait for nightfall.

The big Lanchester roared up the drive to Walden Hall. All the lights were on in the house. A uniformed policeman stood at the door, and another was patrolling, sentry-fashion, along the terrace. Pritchard brought the car to a halt. The policeman at the entrance stood to attention and saluted. Pritchard opened the car door and Walden got out.

Mrs Braithwaite, the housekeeper, came out of the house to greet him. 'Good evening, my lord.'

'Hello, Mrs Braithwaite. Who's here?'

'Sir Arthur is in the drawing-room with Prince Orlov.'

Walden nodded and they entered the house

together. Sir Arthur Langley was the Chief Constable and an old school friend of Walden's.

'Have you dined, my lord?' said Mrs Braithwaite.

'No.'

'Perhaps a piece of game pie, and a bottle of burgundy?'

'I leave it to you.'

'Very good, my lord.'

Mrs Braithwaite went away and Walden entered the drawing-room. Aleks and Sir Arthur were leaning on the mantelpiece with brandy glasses in their hands. Both wore evening dress.

Sir Arthur said: 'Hello, Stephen. How are you?'

Walden shook his hand. 'Did you catch the anarchist?'

'I'm afraid he slipped through our fingers—'

'Damnation!' Walden exclaimed. 'I was afraid of that! No one would listen to me.' He remembered his manners, and shook hands with Aleks. 'I don't know what to say to you, dear boy – you must think we're a lot of fools.' He turned back to Sir Arthur. 'What the devil happened, anyway?'

'Feliks hopped off the train at Tingley.'

'Where was Thomson's precious detective?'

'In the lavatory with a broken head.'

'Marvellous,' Walden said bitterly. He slumped into a chair.

'By the time the town constabulary had been roused, Feliks had melted away.'

'He's on his way here, do you realize that?'

'Yes, of course,' said Sir Arthur in a soothing tone.

'Your men should be instructed that next time he is sighted he's to be shot.'

'Ideally, yes – but of course they don't have guns.'

'They damn well should have!'

'I think you're right, but public opinion—'

'Before we discuss that, tell me what is being done.'

'Very well. I've got five patrols covering the roads between here and Tingley.'

'They won't see him in the dark.'

'Perhaps not, but at least their presence will slow him down, if not stop him altogether.'

'I doubt it. What else?'

'I've brought a constable and a sergeant to guard the house.'

'I saw them outside.'

'They'll be relieved every eight hours, day and night. The Prince already has two bodyguards from the Special Branch, and Thomson is sending four more down here by car tonight. They'll take twelve-hour shifts, so he'll always have three men with him. My men aren't armed but Thomson's are – they have revolvers. My recommendation is that until Feliks is caught, Prince Orlov should remain in his room and be served his food and so on by the bodyguards.'

Aleks said: 'I will do that.'

Walden looked at him. He was pale but calm. He's very brave, Walden thought. If I were he, I should be raging about the incompetence of the British police. Walden said: 'I don't think a few bodyguards is enough. We need an army.'

'We'll have one by tomorrow morning,' Sir Arthur

replied. 'We're mounting a search, beginning at nine o'clock.'

'Why not at dawn?'

'Because the army has to be mustered. A hundred and fifty men will be coming here from all over the county. Most of them are now in bed – they have to be visited and given their instructions, and they have to make their ways here.'

Mrs Braithwaite came in with a tray. There was cold game pie, half a chicken, a bowl of potato salad, bread rolls, cold sausages, sliced tomatoes, a wedge of Cheddar cheese, several kinds of chutney and some fruit. A footman followed with a bottle of wine, a jug of milk, a pot of coffee, a dish of ice-cream, an apple tart and half of a large chocolate cake. The footman said: 'I'm afraid the burgundy hasn't had time to breathe, my lord – shall I decant it?'

'Yes, please.'

The footman fussed with a small table and a place setting. Walden was hungry but he felt too tense to eat. I don't suppose I shall be able to sleep, either, he thought.

Aleks helped himself to more brandy. He is drinking steadily, Walden realized. His movements were deliberate and machine-like, as if he had himself rigidly under control.

'Where is Charlotte?' Walden said suddenly.

Aleks answered: 'She went to bed.'

'She mustn't leave the house while all this is going on.'

Mrs Braithwaite said: 'Shall I tell her, my lord?'

'No don't wake her. I'll see her at breakfast.' Walden took a sip of wine, hoping it would relax him a little. 'We could move you again, Aleks, if it would make you feel better.'

Aleks gave a tight little smile. 'I don't think there's much point, do you? Feliks always manages to find me. The best plan is for me to hide in my room, sign the treaty as soon as possible, and then go home.'

Walden nodded. The servants went out. Sir Arthur said: 'Um, there is something else, Stephen.' He seemed embarrassed. 'I mean, the question of just what made Feliks suddenly catch a train to Waldenhall Halt.'

In all the panic Walden had not even considered that. 'Yes – how in Heaven's name did he find out?'

'As I understand it, only two groups of people knew where Prince Orlov had gone. One is the embassy staff, who of course have been passing telegrams and so on to and fro. The other group is your people here.'

'A traitor among my servants?' Walden said. The thought was chilling.

'Yes,' said Sir Arthur hesitantly. 'Or, of course, among the family.'

Lydia's dinner party was a disaster. With Stephen away, his brother George had to sit in as host, which made the numbers uneven. More seriously, Lydia was so distracted that her conversation was barely polite, let alone sparkling. All but the most kind-hearted guests asked after Charlotte, knowing full well that she was in disgrace. Lydia just said that she had gone to the country for a few days' rest. She spoke mechanically, hardly knowing what she was saying. Her mind was full of nightmares: Feliks being arrested, Stephen being shot, Feliks being beaten, Stephen bleeding, Feliks running, Stephen dying. She longed to tell someone how she felt, but with her guests she could talk only of last night's ball, the prospects for the Cowes Regatta, the Balkan situation and Lloyd George's budget.

Fortunately they did not linger after dinner: they were all going to a ball, or a crush, or a concert. As soon as the last one had left Lydia went into the hall and picked up the telephone. She could not speak to Stephen, for Walden Hall was not yet on the telephone, so she called Winston Churchill's home in Eccleston Square. He was out. She tried the Admiralty, Number Ten, and the National Liberal Club without success. She *had* to know what had happened. Finally she thought of Basil Thomson, and she telephoned Scotland Yard. Thomson was still at his desk, working late.

'Lady Walden, how are you?' he said.

Lydia thought: People *will* be polite! She said: 'What is the news?'

'Bad, I'm afraid. Our friend Feliks has slipped through our fingers again.'

Relief washed over Lydia in a tidal wave. 'Thank . . . thank you,' she said.

'I don't think you need to worry too much,' Thomson went on. 'Prince Orlov is well guarded, now.'

Lydia blushed with shame: she had been so pleased that Feliks was all right that she had momentarily forgotten to worry about Aleks and Stephen. 'I . . . I'll try not to worry,' she said. 'Good night.'

'Good night, Lady Walden.'

She put down the telephone.

She went upstairs and rang for her maid to come and unlace her. She felt distraught. Nothing was resolved, everyone she loved was still in danger. How long could it go on? Feliks would not give up, she was sure, unless he got caught.

The maid came and unbuttoned her gown and unlaced her corset. Some ladies confided in their maids, Lydia knew. She did not. She had once, in St Petersburg . . .

She decided to write to her sister, for it was too early to go to bed. She told the maid to bring writing paper from the morning-room. She put on a wrap and sat by the open window, staring into the darkness of the park. The evening was close. It had not rained for three months, but during the last few days the weather had become thundery, and soon there would surely be storms.

The maid brought paper, pens, ink and envelopes. Lydia took a sheet of paper and wrote: *Dear Tatyana—*

She did not know where to begin. How can I explain about Charlotte, she thought, when I don't understand her myself? And I daren't say anything about Feliks, for

Tatyana might tell the Czar, and if the Czar knew how close Aleks had come to being killed . . .

Feliks is so *clever.* How on earth did he find out where Aleks is hiding? We wouldn't even tell Charlotte!

Charlotte.

Lydia went cold.

Charlotte?

She stood upright and cried: 'Oh, no!'

He was about forty, and wearing a tweed cap.

A sense of inevitable horror possessed her. It was like one of those crucifying dreams in which you think of the worst thing that could possibly happen and that thing immediately begins to happen: the ladder falls, the child is run over, the loved one dies.

She buried her face in her hands. She felt dizzy.

I must think, I must try to *think.*

Please, God, help me think.

Charlotte met a man in the National Gallery. That evening, she asked me where Aleks was. I didn't tell her. Perhaps she asked Stephen, too: he wouldn't have told her. Then she was sent home, to Walden Hall, and of course she discovered that Aleks was there. Two days later Feliks went to Waldenhall Halt.

Make this be a dream, she prayed; make me wake up, now, please, and find myself in my own bed, make it be morning.

It was not a dream. Feliks was the man in the tweed cap. Charlotte had met her father. They had been holding hands.

It was horrible, horrible.

Had Feliks told Charlotte the truth, had he said: 'I

am your real father,' had he revealed the secret of nineteen years? Did he even know? Surely he must have. Why else would she be . . . collaborating with him?

My daughter, conspiring with an anarchist to commit murder.

She must be helping him still.

What can I do? I must warn Stephen – but how can I do that without telling him he's not Charlotte's father? I wish I could *think.*

She rang for her maid again. I must find a way to put an end to this, she thought. I don't know what I'm going to do but I must do something. When the maid came she said: 'Start packing. I shall leave first thing in the morning. I have to go to Walden Hall.'

After dark Feliks headed across the fields. It was a warm, humid night, and very dark: heavy cloud hid the stars and the moon. He had to walk slowly for he was almost blind. He found his way to the railway line and turned north.

Walking along the tracks he could go a little faster, for there was a faint shine on the steel lines, and he knew there would be no obstacles. He passed through dark stations, creeping along the deserted platforms. He heard rats in the empty waiting-rooms. He had no fear of rats: once upon a time he had killed them with his hands and eaten them. The names of the stations were stamped on sheet-metal signs, and he could read them by touch.

When he reached Waldenhall Halt he recalled Charlotte's directions: *The house is three miles out of the village on the north road.* The railway line was running roughly north-north-east. He followed it another mile or so, measuring the distance by counting his paces. He had reached one thousand six hundred when he bumped into someone.

The man gave a shout of surprise and then Feliks had him by the throat.

An overpowering smell of beer came from the man. Feliks realized he was just a drunk going home, and relaxed his grip.

'Don't be frightened,' the man said in a slurred voice.

'All right,' Feliks said. He let go.

'It's the only way I can get home see, without getting lost.'

'On your way, then.'

The man moved on. A moment later he said: 'Don't go to sleep on the line – the milk train comes at four o'clock.'

Feliks made no reply and the drunk shuffled off.

Feliks shook his head, disgusted with himself for being so jumpy: he might have killed the man. He was weak with relief. This would not do.

He decided to find the road. He moved off the railway line, stumbled across a short stretch of rough ground, then came up against a flimsy three-wire fence. He waited for a moment. What was in front of him? A field? Someone's back garden? The village green? There was no darkness like a dark night in the country, with the nearest street light a hundred miles away. He heard a sudden movement close to him, and out of the corner of his eye he saw something white. He bent down and fumbled on the ground until he found a small stone, then threw it in the direction of the white thing. There was a whinny, and a horse cantered away.

Feliks listened. If there were dogs near by the whinny ought to make them bark. He heard nothing.

He stooped and clambered through the fence. He walked slowly across the paddock. Once he stumbled into a bush. He heard another horse but did not see it.

He came up against another wire fence, climbed through it, and bumped into a wooden building. Immediately there was a tremendous noise of chickens clucking. A dog started to bark. A light came on in the window of a house. Feliks threw himself flat and lay still. The light showed him that he was in a small farmyard. He had bumped into the hen-house. Beyond the farmhouse he could see the road he was looking for. The chickens quieted, the dog gave a last disappointed howl, and the light went out. Feliks walked to the road.

It was a dirt road bordered by a dry ditch. Beyond the ditch there seemed to be woodland. Feliks remembered: *On the left hand side of the road you will see a wood.* He was almost there.

He walked north along the uneven road, his hearing strained for the sound of someone approaching. After more than a mile he sensed that there was a wall on his left. A little farther on, the wall was broken by a gate, and he saw a light.

He leaned on the iron bars of the gate and peered through. There seemed to be a long drive. At its far end he could see, dimly illuminated by a pair of flickering lamps, the pillared portico of a vast house. As he watched, a tall figure walked across the front of the house: a sentry.

In that house, he thought, is Prince Orlov. I wonder which is his bedroom window?

Suddenly he heard the sound of a car approaching very fast. He ran back ten paces and threw himself into the ditch. A moment later the car's headlights swept along the wall and it pulled up in front of the gate. Someone got out.

Feliks heard knocking. There must be a gatehouse, he realized: he had not seen it in the darkness. A window was opened and a voice shouted: 'Who's there?'

Another voice replied: 'Police, from the Special Branch of Scotland Yard.'

'Just a minute.'

Feliks lay perfectly still. He heard footsteps as the man who had got out of the car moved around restlessly. A door was opened. A dog barked, and a voice said: 'Quiet, Rex!'

Feliks stopped breathing. Was the dog on a lead? Would it smell Feliks? Would it come snuffling along the ditch and find him and start to bark?

The iron gates creaked open. The dog barked again. The voice said: 'Shut *up*, Rex!'

A car door slammed and the car moved off up the drive. The ditch was dark again. Now, Feliks thought, if the dog finds me I can kill it and the gatekeeper and run away . . .

He tensed, ready to jump up as soon as he heard a snuffling sound near to his ear.

The gates creaked shut.

A moment later the gatehouse door slammed.

Feliks breathed again.

CHAPTER FOURTEEN

CHARLOTTE WOKE at six o'clock. She had drawn back the curtains of her bedroom windows so that the first rays of the sun would shine on her face and rouse her from sleep: it was a trick she had used years ago, when Belinda was staying, and the two of them had liked to roam around the house while the grown-ups were still in bed and there was no one to tell them to behave like little ladies.

Her first thought was for Feliks. They had failed to catch him – he was so clever! Today he would surely be waiting for her in the wood. She jumped out of bed and looked outside. The weather had not yet broken: he would have been dry in the night, anyway.

She washed in cold water and dressed quickly in a long skirt, riding boots and a jacket. She never wore a hat for these morning rides.

She went downstairs. She saw nobody. There would be a maid or two in the kitchen, lighting fires and heating water, but otherwise the servants were still in bed. She went out of the south front door and almost bumped into a large uniformed policeman.

'Heavens!' she exclaimed. 'Who are you?'

'Constable Stevenson, Miss.'

He called her *Miss* because he did not know who she was. 'I'm Charlotte Walden,' she said.

'Pardon me, m'lady.'

'That's all right. What are you doing here?'

'Guarding the house, m'lady.'

'Oh, I see: guarding the Prince, you mean. How reassuring. How many of you are there?'

'Two outside and four inside. The inside men are armed. But there'll be a lot more later.'

'How so?'

'Big search party, m'lady. I hear there'll be a hundred and fifty men here by nine. We'll get this anarchist chappie – never you fear.'

'How splendid.'

'Was you thinking of going riding, m'lady? I shouldn't, if I was you. Not today.'

'No, I shan't,' Charlotte lied.

She walked away, around the east wing of the house to the back. The stables were deserted. She went inside and found her mare, Spats, so called because of the white patches on her forelegs. She talked to her for a minute, stroking her nose, and gave her an apple. Then she saddled her, led her out of the stable, and mounted her.

She rode away from the back of the house and around the park in a wide circle, staying out of sight and out of earshot of the policeman. She galloped across the west paddock and jumped the low fence into the wood. She walked Spats through the trees until she came to the bridle path, then let her trot.

It was cool in the wood. The oak and beech trees

were heavy with leaf, shading the path. In the patches where the sun came through, dew rose from the ground like wisps of steam. Charlotte felt the heat of those stray sunbeams as she rode through them. The birds were very loud.

She thought: What can he do against a hundred and fifty men? His plan was impossible, now: Aleks was too well guarded and the hunt for Feliks was too well organized. At least Charlotte could warn him off.

She reached the far end of the wood without seeing him. She was disappointed: she had been sure he would be here today. She began to worry, for if she did not see him she could not warn him, and then he would surely be caught. But it was not yet seven o'clock: perhaps he had not begun to watch out for her. She dismounted and walked back, leading Spats. Perhaps Feliks had seen her and was waiting to check whether she had been followed. She stopped in a glade to watch a squirrel. They did not mind people, although they would run away from dogs. Suddenly she felt she was being watched. She turned around, and there he was, looking at her with a peculiarly sad expression.

He said: 'Hello, Charlotte.'

She went to him and held both his hands. His beard was quite full, now. His clothes were covered with bits of greenery. 'You look dreadfully tired,' she said in Russian.

'I'm hungry. Did you bring food?'

'Oh, dear, no!' She had brought an apple for her horse and nothing for Feliks. 'I didn't think of it.'

'Never mind. I've been hungrier.'

'Listen,' she said. 'You must go away, immediately. If you leave now you can escape.'

'Why should I escape? I want to kidnap Orlov.'

She shook her head. 'It's impossible, now. He has armed bodyguards, the house is patrolled by policemen, and by nine o'clock there will be a hundred and fifty men searching for you.'

He smiled. 'And if I escape, what will I do with the rest of my life?'

'But I won't help you commit suicide!'

'Let's sit on the grass,' he said. 'I have something to explain to you.'

She sat with her back against a broad oak tree. Feliks sat in front of her and crossed his legs, like a Cossack. Dappled sunlight played across his weary face. He spoke rather formally, in complete sentences which sounded as if they might have been rehearsed. 'I told you I was in love, once, with a woman called Lydia; and you said: "That's my mother's name." Do you remember?'

'I remember everything you've ever said to me.' She wondered what this was all about.

'It *was* your mother.'

She stared at him. 'You were in love with Mama?'

'More than that. We were lovers. She used to come to my rooms, alone – do you understand what I mean?'

Charlotte blushed with confusion and embarrassment. 'Yes, I do.'

'Her father, your grandfather, found out. The old Count had me arrested, then he forced your mother to marry Walden.'

'Oh, how terrible,' Charlotte said softly. For some reason she was frightened of what he might say next.

'You were born seven months after the wedding.'

He seemed to think that was very significant. Charlotte frowned.

Feliks said: 'Do you know how long it takes for a baby to grow and be born?'

'No.'

'It takes nine months, normally, although it can take less.'

Charlotte's heart was pounding. 'What are you getting at?'

'You might have been conceived before the wedding.'

'Does that mean you might be my father?' she said incredulously.

'There's more. You look *exactly* like my sister Natasha.'

Charlotte's heart seemed to rise into her throat and she could hardly speak. 'You think you *are* my father?'

'I'm sure of it.'

'Oh, God.' Charlotte put her face in her hands and stared into space, seeing nothing. She felt as if she were waking from a dream and could not yet make out which aspects of the dream had been real. She thought of Papa, but he was not her Papa; she thought of Mama, having a lover; she thought of Feliks, her friend and suddenly her father . . .

She said: 'Did they lie to me even about this?'

She was so disoriented that she felt she would not be able to stand upright. It was as if someone had told her that all the maps she had ever seen were forgeries and she really lived in Brazil; or that the real owner of Walden Hall was Pritchard; or that horses could talk but merely kept silent by choice; but it was much worse than all those things. She said: 'If you were to tell me that I am a boy, but my mother always dressed me in girl's clothing . . . it would be like this.'

She thought: Mama . . . and Feliks? That made her blush again.

Feliks took her hand and stroked it. He said: 'I suppose all the love and concern that a man normally gives to his wife and children went, in my case, into politics. I have to try to get Orlov, even if it's impossible; the way a man would have to try to save his child from drowning, even if the man could not swim.'

Charlotte suddenly realized how confused Feliks must feel about *her*, the daughter he never really had. She understood, now, the odd, painful way he had looked at her sometimes.

'You poor man,' she said.

He bit his lip. 'You have such a generous heart.'

She did not know why he should say that. 'What are we going to do?'

He took a deep breath. 'Could you get me inside the house and hide me?'

She thought for a moment. 'Yes,' she said.

He mounted the horse behind her. The beast shook its head and snorted, as if offended that it should be expected to carry a double weight. Charlotte urged it into a trot. She followed the bridle path for a while, then turned off it at an angle and headed through the wood. They went through a gate, across a paddock, and into a little lane. Feliks did not yet see the house: he realized she was circling around it to approach from the north side.

She was an astonishing child. She had such strength of character. Had she inherited it from him? He wanted to think so. He was very happy to have told her the truth about her birth. He had the feeling she had not quite accepted it, but she would. She had listened to him turn her world upside down, and she had reacted with emotion but without hysteria – she did not get *that* kind of equanimity from her mother.

From the lane they turned into an orchard. Now, looking between the tops of the trees, Feliks could see the roofs of Walden Hall. The orchard ended in a wall. Charlotte stopped the horse and said: 'You'd better walk beside me from here. That way, if anyone should glance out of a window, they won't be able to see you very easily.'

Feliks jumped off. They walked alongside the wall and followed it around a corner. 'What's behind the wall?' Feliks asked.

'Kitchen garden. Better not talk, now.'

'You're marvellous,' Feliks whispered, but she did not hear.

They stopped at the next corner. Feliks could see some low buildings and a yard. 'The stables,' Charlotte murmured. 'Stay here for a moment. When I give you the signal, follow me as fast as you can.'

'Where are we going?'

'Over the roofs.'

She rode into the yard, dismounted, and looped the reins over a rail. Feliks watched her cross to the far side of the little yard, look both ways, then come back and look inside the stables.

He heard her say: 'Oh, hello, Peter.'

A boy of about twelve years came out, taking off his cap. 'Good morning, m'lady.'

Feliks thought: How will she get rid of him?

Charlotte said: 'Where's Daniel?'

'Having his breakfast, m'lady.'

'Go and fetch him, will you, and tell him to come and unsaddle Spats.'

'I can do it, m'lady.'

'No, I want Daniel,' Charlotte said imperiously. 'Off you go.'

Marvellous, Feliks thought.

The boy ran off. Charlotte turned toward Feliks and beckoned. He ran to her.

She jumped on to a low iron bunker, then climbed on to the corrugated tin roof of a lean-to shed, and from there got on to the slate roof of a one-storey stone building.

Felix followed.

They edged along the slate roof, moving sideways on all fours, until it ended up against a brick wall, then they crawled up the slope to the ridge of the roof.

Feliks felt dreadfully conspicuous and vulnerable.

Charlotte stood upright and peeped through a window in the brick wall.

Feliks whispered: 'What's in there?'

'Parlourmaids' bedroom. But they're downstairs by now, laying the breakfast table.'

She clambered on to the window-ledge and stood upright. The bedroom was an attic room and the window was in the gable end, so that the roof peaked just above the window and sloped down either side. Charlotte moved along the sill, then cocked her leg over the edge of the roof.

It looked dangerous. Feliks frowned, frightened that she would fall. But she hauled herself on to the roof with ease.

Feliks did the same.

'Now we're out of sight,' Charlotte said.

Feliks looked around. She was right: they could not be seen from the ground. He relaxed a fraction.

'There are four acres of roof,' Charlotte told him.

'Four acres! Most Russian peasants haven't got that much land.'

It was quite a sight. On all sides were roofs of every material, size and pitch. Ladders and strips of decking were provided so that people could move around without treading on the slates and tiles. The guttering was as complex as the piping in the oil refinery Feliks had seen at Batum. 'I've never seen such a big house,' he said.

Charlotte stood up. 'Come on, follow me.'

She led him up a ladder to the next roof, along a board footway, then up a short flight of wooden steps leading to a small, square door set in a wall. She said: 'At one time this must have been the way they got out on to the roofs for maintenance – but now everybody has forgotten about it.' She opened the door and crawled through.

Gratefully, Feliks followed her into the welcoming darkness.

Lydia borrowed a motor car and driver from her brother-in-law George and, having lain awake all night, left London very early. The car entered the drive at Walden Hall at nine o'clock, and she was astonished to see, in front of the house and spreading over the park, hundreds of policemen, dozens of vehicles, and scores of dogs. George's driver threaded the car through the crowd to the south front of the house. There was an enormous tea-urn on the lawn, and the policemen were queuing up with cups in their hands. Pritchard walked by carrying a mountain of sandwiches on a huge tray and looking harassed. He did not even notice that his mistress had arrived. A trestle table had been set up on the terrace, and behind it sat Stephen with Sir Arthur Langley, giving instructions to half a dozen police officers who stood in front of them in a semicircle. Lydia went over to them. Sir Arthur had a map in front of him. She heard him say: 'Each team will have a local man, to keep you on the correct route, and a motorcyclist to dash back here and report progress every hour.' Stephen looked up, saw Lydia, and left the group to speak to her.

'Good morning, my dear, this is a pleasant surprise, how did you get here?'

'I borrowed George's car. What is going on?'

'Search parties.'

'Oh.' With all these men looking for him, how could Feliks possibly escape?

Stephen said: 'Still, I wish you had stayed in Town. I should have been happier for your safety.'

'And I should have spent every minute wondering whether bad news was on its way.' And what would count as good news? she wondered. Perhaps if Feliks were simply to give up and go away. But he would not do that, she was sure. She studied her husband's face. Beneath his customary poise there were signs of tiredness and tension. Poor Stephen: first his wife, and now his daughter, deceiving him. A guilty impulse made her reach up and touch his cheek. 'Don't wear yourself out,' she said.

A whistle blew. The policemen hastily drained their teacups, stuffed the remains of sandwiches into their mouths, put on their helmets, and formed themselves into six groups, each around a leader. Lydia stood with Stephen, watching. There were a lot of shouted orders and a good deal more whistling. Finally they began to move out. The first group went south, fanning out across the park, and entered the wood. Two more headed west, into the paddock. The other three groups went down the drive toward the road.

Lydia regarded her lawn. It looked like the site of a Sunday-school outing when all the children have gone home. Mrs Braithwaite began to organize the clearing-up with a pained expression on her face. Lydia went into the house.

She met Charlotte in the hall. Charlotte was surprised to see her. 'Hello, Mama,' she said. 'I didn't know you were coming down.'

'One gets so bored in Town,' Lydia said automatically, then she thought: What rubbish we talk.

'How did you get here?'

'I borrowed Uncle George's car.' Lydia saw that Charlotte was making small talk, and thinking of something else.

'You must have started very early,' Charlotte said.

'Yes.' Lydia wanted to say: Stop it! Let's not pretend! Why don't we speak the truth? But she could not bring herself to do it.

'Have all those policemen gone yet?' Charlotte asked. She was looking at Lydia in a strange way, as if seeing her for the first time. It made Lydia uncomfortable. I wish I could read my daughter's mind, she thought.

She replied: 'Yes, they've all gone.'

'Splendid.'

That was one of Stephen's words – splendid. There was, after all, something of Stephen in Charlotte: the curiosity, the determination, the poise – since she had not inherited those things, she must have acquired them simply by imitating him . . .

Lydia said: 'I hope they catch this anarchist,' and watched Charlotte's reaction.

'I'm sure they will,' Charlotte said gaily.

She's very bright-eyed, Lydia thought. Why should she look that way, when hundreds of policemen are combing the county for Feliks? Why is she not depressed and anxious, as I am? It must be that she does *not* expect them to catch him. For some reason she thinks he is safe.

Charlotte said: 'Tell me something, Mama. How long does it take for a baby to grow and be born?'

Lydia's mouth fell open and the blood drained from her face. She stared at Charlotte, thinking: She knows! She knows!

Charlotte smiled and nodded, looking faintly sad. 'Never mind,' she said. 'You've answered my question.' She went on down the stairs.

Lydia held on to the banister, feeling faint. Feliks had told Charlotte. It was just too cruel, after all these years. She felt angry at Feliks: why had he ruined Charlotte's life this way? The hall spun around her head, and she heard a maid's voice say: 'Are you all right, my lady?'

Her head cleared. 'A little tired, after the journey,' she said. 'Take my arm.'

The maid took her arm and together they walked upstairs to Lydia's room. Another maid was already unpacking Lydia's cases. There was hot water ready for her in the dressing-room. Lydia sat down. 'Leave me now, you two,' she said. 'Unpack later.'

The maids went out. Lydia unbuttoned her coat but did not have the energy to take it off. She thought about Charlotte's mood. It had been almost vivacious, even though there was obviously a lot on her mind. Lydia understood that; she recognized it; she had sometimes felt that way. It was the mood you were in when you had spent time with Feliks. You felt that life was endlessly fascinating and surprising, that there were important things to be done, that the world was full of colour and passion and change. Charlotte had seen Feliks, and she believed him to be safe.

Lydia thought: What am I going to do?

Wearily, she took off her clothes. She spent time washing and dressing again, taking the opportunity to calm herself. She wondered how Charlotte felt about Feliks being her father. She obviously liked him very much. People do, Lydia thought; people love him. Where had Charlotte got the strength to hear such news without collapsing?

Lydia decided she had better take care of the housekeeping. She looked in the mirror and composed her face, then she went out. On the way downstairs she met a maid with a tray laden with sliced ham, scrambled eggs, fresh bread, milk, coffee and grapes. 'Who is that for?' she asked.

'For Lady Charlotte, m'lady,' said the maid.

Lydia passed on. Had Charlotte not even lost her appetite? She went into the morning-room and sent for Cook. Mrs Rowse was a thin, nervous woman who never ate the kind of rich food she prepared for her employers. She said: 'I understand Mr Thomson will be arriving for lunch, m'lady, and Mr Churchill also for dinner.' Lydia discussed the menus with her, then sent her away. Why on earth was Charlotte having such a massive breakfast in her room? she wondered. And so late! In the country Charlotte was normally up early, and had finished breakfast before Lydia surfaced.

She sent for Pritchard and made the table plan with

him. Pritchard told her that Aleks was having all his meals in his room until further notice. It made little difference to the table plan: they still had too many men, and in the present situation Lydia could hardly invite people to make up the right numbers. She did the best she could, then sent Pritchard away.

Where had Charlotte seen Feliks? And why was she confident that he would not be caught? Had she found him a hiding-place? Was he in some impenetrable disguise?

She moved around the room, looking at the pictures, the little bronzes, the glass ornaments, the writing-desk. She had a headache. She began to rearrange the flowers in a big vase by the window, and knocked over the vase. She rang for someone to clear up the mess, then left the room.

Her nerves were very bad. She contemplated taking some laudanum. These days it did not help her as much as it had used to.

What will Charlotte do now? Will she keep the secret? Why don't children talk to one?

She went along to the library with the vague idea of getting a book to take her mind off everything. When she walked in she gave a guilty start on seeing that Stephen was there, at his desk. He looked up at her as she entered, smiled in a welcoming way, and went on writing.

Lydia wandered along the bookshelves. She wondered whether to read the Bible. There had been a great deal of Bible-reading in her childhood, and family prayers and much church-going. She had had stern nurses who were keen on the horrors of hell and the penalties of uncleanliness, and a Lutheran German governess who talked a great deal about sin. But, since Lydia had committed fornication and brought retribution upon herself and her daughter, she had never been able to take any consolation from religion. I should have gone into that convent, she thought, and put myself right with God; my father's instinct was correct.

She took a book at random and sat down with it open on her lap. Stephen said: 'That's an unusual choice for you.' He could not read the title from where he was sitting, but he knew where all the authors were placed on the shelves. He read so many books, Lydia did not know how he found the time. She looked at the spine of the book she was holding. It was Thomas Hardy's *Wessex Poems.* She did not like Hardy: did not like those determined, passionate women nor the strong men whom they made helpless.

They had often sat like this, she and Stephen, especially when they first came to Walden Hall. She recalled nostalgically how she would sit and read while he worked. He had been less tranquil in those days, she remembered: he used to say that nobody could make money out of agriculture any more, and that if this family were to continue to be rich and powerful it would have to get ready for the twentieth century. He had sold off some farms at that time, many thousands of acres at very low prices, then he had put the money into railroads and banks and London property. The plan must have worked, for he soon stopped looking worried.

It was after the birth of Charlotte that everything seemed to settle down. The servants adored the baby and loved Lydia for producing her. Lydia got used to English ways and was well liked by London society. There had been eighteen years of tranquillity.

Lydia sighed. Those years were coming to an end. For a while she had buried the secrets so successfully that they tormented nobody but her, and even she had been able to forget them at times; but now they were coming out. She had thought that London was at a safe distance from St Petersburg, but perhaps California would have been a better choice; or it might be that nowhere was far enough. The time of peace was over. It was all falling apart. What would happen now?

She looked down at the open page, and read:

She would have given a world to breathe 'yes' truly,
So much his life seemed hanging on her mind,
And hence she lied, her heart persuaded thoroughly
'Twas worth her soul to be a moment kind.

Is that me? she wondered. Did I give my soul when I married Stephen in order to save Feliks from incarceration in the Fortress of St Peter and St Paul? Ever since then I've been playing a part, pretending I'm not a wanton, sinful, brazen whore. But I am! And I'm not the only one. Other women feel the same. Why else would the Viscountess and Charlie Stott want adjoining bedrooms? And why would Lady Girard tell me about them with a wink, if she did not understand how they felt? If I had been just a little wanton, perhaps Stephen would have come to my bed more often, and we might have had a son. She sighed again.

'Penny for 'em,' Stephen said.

'What?'

'A penny for your thoughts.'

Lydia smiled. 'Will I never stop learning English expressions? I've never heard that one.'

'Nobody ever stops learning. It means tell me what you're thinking.'

'I was thinking about Walden Hall going to George's son when you die.'

'Unless we have a son.'

She looked at his face: the bright blue eyes, the neat grey beard. He was wearing a blue tie with white spots.

He said: 'Is it too late?'

'I don't know,' she said, thinking: That depends on what Charlotte does next.

'Do let's keep trying,' he said.

This was an unusually frank conversation: Stephen had sensed that she was in a mood to be candid. She got up from her chair and went over to stand beside him. He had a bald spot on the back of his head, she noticed. How long had that been there? 'Yes,' she said, 'let's keep trying.' She bent down and kissed his forehead: then, on impulse, she kissed his lips. He closed his eyes.

After a moment she broke away. He looked a little embarrassed: they rarely did this sort of thing during the day, for there were always so many servants about. She thought: Why do we live the way we do, if it doesn't make us happy? She said: 'I *do* love you.'

He smiled. 'I know you do.'

Suddenly she could stand it no longer. She said: 'I must go and change for lunch before Basil Thomson arrives.'

He nodded.

She felt his eyes following her as she left the room. She went upstairs, wondering whether there might still be a chance that she and Stephen could be happy.

She went into her bedroom. She was still carrying the book of poems. She put it down. Charlotte held the key to all this. Lydia had to talk to her. One *could* say difficult things, after all, if one had the courage; and what now was left to lose? Without having a clear idea of what she would say, she headed for Charlotte's room on the next floor.

Her footsteps made no noise on the carpet. She reached the top of the staircase and looked along the corridor. She saw Charlotte disappearing into the old nursery. She was about to call out, then stopped herself. What had Charlotte been carrying? It had looked very like a plate of sandwiches and a glass of milk.

Puzzled, Lydia went along to Charlotte's bedroom. There on the table was the tray Lydia had seen the maid carrying. All the ham and all the bread had gone. Why would Charlotte order a tray of food, then make sandwiches of it and eat it in the nursery? There was nothing in the nursery, as far as Lydia knew, except furniture covered with dust-sheets. Was Charlotte so anxious that she needed to retreat into the cosy world of childhood?

Lydia decided to find out. She felt uneasy about interrupting Charlotte's private ritual, whatever it was; but then she thought: It's my house, she's my daughter, and perhaps I ought to know. And it might create a moment of intimacy, and help me say what I need to say. So she left Charlotte's bedroom and went along the corridor and into the nursery.

Charlotte was not there.

Lydia looked around. There was the old rocking-horse, his ears making twin peaks in the dust-sheet. Through an open door she could see the schoolroom, with maps and childish drawings on the wall. Another door led to the bedroom: that, too, was empty but for shrouds. Will all this ever be used again? Lydia wondered. Will we have nurses, and nappies, and tiny, tiny clothes; and a nanny, and toy soldiers, and exercise books filled with clumsy handwriting and ink blots?

But where was Charlotte?

The closet door was open. Suddenly Lydia remembered: of course! Charlotte's hideaway! The little room she thought no one else knew of, where she used to go when she had been naughty. She had furnished it herself, with bits and pieces from around the house, and everyone had pretended not to know how certain things had disappeared. One of the few indulgent decisions Lydia had made was to allow Charlotte her hideaway, and to forbid Marya to 'discover' it; for Lydia herself hid away sometimes, in the flower-room, and she knew how important it was to have a place of your own.

So Charlotte still used that little room! Lydia moved closer, more reluctant now to disturb Charlotte's privacy, but tempted all the same. No, she thought; I'll leave her be.

Then she heard voices.

Was Charlotte talking to herself?

Lydia listened carefully.

Talking to herself in Russian?

Then there was another voice, a man's voice, replying in Russian, in low tones; a voice like a caress, a voice which sent a sexual shudder through Lydia's body.

Feliks was in there.

Lydia thought she would faint. Feliks! Within touching distance! Hidden, in Walden Hall, while the police searched the county for him! Hidden by Charlotte.

I mustn't scream!

She put her fist to her mouth and bit herself. She was shaking.

I must get away. I can't think straight. I don't know what to do.

Her head ached horribly. I need a dose of laudanum, she thought. That prospect gave her strength. She controlled her trembling. After a moment she tip-toed out of the nursery.

She almost ran along the corridor and down the stairs to her room. The laudanum was in the dresser. She opened the bottle. She could not hold the spoon steady, so she took a gulp directly from the bottle. After a few moments she began to feel calmer. She put the bottle and the spoon away and closed the drawer. A feeling of mild contentment began to come over her as her nerves settled down. Her head ached less. Nothing would really matter now for a while. She went to her wardrobe and opened the door. She stood staring at the rows of dresses, totally unable to make up her mind what to wear for lunch.

Feliks paced the tiny room like a caged tiger, three steps each way, bending his head to avoid the ceiling, listening to Charlotte.

'Aleks' door is always locked,' she said. 'There are two armed guards inside and one outside. The inside ones won't unlock the door unless their colleague outside tells them to.'

'One outside, and two inside.' Feliks scratched his head and cursed in Russian. Difficulties, there are always difficulties, he thought. Here I am, right in the house, with an accomplice in the household, and still it isn't easy. Why shouldn't I have the luck of those boys in Sarajevo? Why did it have to turn out that I'm a part of this family? He looked at Charlotte and thought: Not that I regret it.

She caught his look, and said: 'What?'

'Nothing. Whatever happens, I'm glad I found you.'

'Me too. But what are you going to do about Aleks?'

'Could you draw a plan of the house?'

Charlotte made a face. 'I can try.'

'You must know it, you've lived here all your life.'

'Well, I know this part, of course – but there are bits of the house I've never been in. The butler's bedroom, the housekeeper's rooms, the cellars, the place over the kitchens where they store flour and things . . .'

'Do your best. One plan for each floor.'

She found a piece of paper and a pencil among her childish treasures and knelt at the little table.

Feliks ate another sandwich and drank the rest of the milk. She had taken a long time to bring him the food because the maids had been working in her corridor. As he ate he watched her draw, frowning and biting the end of her pencil. At one point she said: 'One doesn't realize how difficult this is until one tries it.' She found an eraser among her old crayons and used it frequently. Feliks noticed that she was able to draw perfectly straight lines without using a rule. He found the sight of her like this very touching. So she must have sat, he thought, for years in the schoolroom, drawing houses, then Mama and 'Papa', and later the map of Europe, the leaves of the English trees, the park in winter . . . Walden must have seen her like this many times.

'Why have you changed your clothes?' Feliks asked.

'Oh, everybody has to change all the time here. Every hour of the day has its appropriate clothes, you see. You must show your shoulders at dinner-time but not at lunch. You must wear a corset for dinner but not for tea. You can't wear an indoors gown outside. You can wear woollen stockings in the library but not in the morning-room. You can't imagine the rules I have to remember.'

He nodded. He was no longer capable of being surprised by the degeneracy of the ruling class.

She handed him her sketches, and he became businesslike again. He studied them. 'Where are the guns kept?' he said.

She touched his arm. 'Don't be so abrupt,' she said. 'I'm on your side – remember?'

Suddenly she was grown-up again. Feliks smiled ruefully. 'I had forgotten,' he said.

'The guns are kept in the gun-room.' She pointed it out on the plan. 'You really did have an affair with Mama.'

'Yes.'

'I find it so hard to believe that she would do such a thing.'

'She was very wild, then. She still is, but she pretends otherwise.'

'You really think she's still like that?'

'I know it.'

'Everything, *everything* turns out to be different from how I thought it was.'

'That's called growing up.'

She was pensive. 'What should I call you, I wonder?'

'What do you mean?'

'I should feel very strange, calling you Father.'

'Feliks will do for now. You need time to get used to the idea of me as your father.'

'Shall I have time?'

Her young face was so grave that he held her hand. 'Why not?'

'What will you do when you have Aleks?'

He looked away so that she should not see the guilt in his eyes. 'That depends just how and when I kidnap him, but most likely I'll keep him tied up right here. You'll have to bring us food, and you'll have to send a telegram to my friends in Geneva, in code, telling them what has happened. Then, when the news has achieved what we want it to achieve, we'll let Orlov go.'

'And then?'

'They will look for me in London, so I'll go north. There seem to be some big towns – Birmingham, Manchester, Hull – where I could lose myself. After a few weeks I'll make my way back to Switzerland, then eventually to St Petersburg – that's the place to be, that's where the revolution will start.'

'So I'll never see you again.'

You won't want to, he thought. He said: 'Why not? I may come back to London. You may go to St Petersburg. We might meet in Paris. Who can tell? If there is such a thing as Fate, it seems determined to bring us together.' I wish I could believe this, I wish I could.

'That's true,' she said with a brittle smile, and he saw that she did not believe it either. She got to her feet. 'Now I must get you some water to wash in.'

'Don't bother. I've been a good deal dirtier than this. I don't mind.'

'But I do. You smell awful. I'll be back in a minute.'

With that she went out.

It was the dreariest luncheon Walden could remember in years. Lydia was in some kind of daze. Charlotte was silent but uncharacteristically nervy, dropping her cutlery and knocking over a glass. Thomson was taciturn. Sir Arthur Langley attempted to be convivial but nobody responded. Walden himself was withdrawn, obsessed by the puzzle of how Feliks had found out that Aleks was at Walden Hall. He was tortured by the ugly suspicion that it had something to do with Lydia. After all, Lydia had told Feliks that Aleks was at the Savoy Hotel; and she had admitted that Feliks was 'vaguely familiar' from St Petersburg days. Could it be that Feliks had some kind of hold on her? She had been behaving oddly, as if distracted, all summer. And now, as he thought about Lydia in a detached way for the first time in nineteen years, he admitted to himself that she was sexually lukewarm. Of course, well-bred women were supposed to be like that; but he knew perfectly well that this was a polite fiction, and that women generally suffered the same longings as men. Was it that Lydia longed for someone else, someone from her past? That would explain all sorts of things which until now had not seemed to need explanation. It was perfectly horrible, he found, to look at his lifetime companion and see a stranger.

After lunch Sir Arthur went back to the Octagon, where he had set up his headquarters. Walden and Thomson put on their hats and took their cigars out on to the terrace. The park looked lovely in the sunshine, as always. From the distant drawing-room came the crashing opening chords of the Tchaikovsky piano concerto: Lydia was playing. Walden felt sad. Then the music was drowned by the roar of a motor-cycle as another messenger came to report the progress of the search to Sir Arthur. So far there had been no news.

A footman served coffee then left them alone. Thomson said: 'I didn't want to say this in front of Lady Walden, but I think we may have a clue to the identity of the traitor.'

Walden went cold.

Thomson said: 'Last night I interviewed Bridget Callahan, the Cork Street landlady. I'm afraid I got nothing out of her. However, I left my men to search her house. This morning they showed me what they had found.' He took from his pocket an envelope which had been torn in half, and handed the two pieces to Walden.

Walden saw with a shock that the envelope bore the Walden Hall crest.

Thomson said: 'Do you recognize the handwriting?'

Walden turned the pieces over. The envelope was addressed:

Mr F. Kschessinksy
c/o 19 Cork Street
London, N.

Walden said: 'Oh, dear God, not Charlotte.' He wanted to cry.

Thomson was silent.

'She led him here,' Walden said. 'My own daughter.' He stared at the envelope, willing it to disappear. The handwriting was quite unmistakable, like a juvenile version of his own script.

'Look at the postmark,' Thomson said. 'She wrote it as soon as she arrived here. It was mailed from the village.'

'How could this happen?' Walden said.

Thomson made no reply.

'Feliks was the man in the tweed cap,' Walden said. 'It all fits.' He felt hopelessly sad, almost bereaved, as if someone dear to him had died. He looked out over his park, at trees planted fifty years ago by his father, at a lawn that had been cared for by his family for a hundred years, and it all seemed worthless, worthless. He said quietly: 'You fight for your country, and you are betrayed from within by socialists and revolutionists; you fight for your class, and you're betrayed by Liberals; you fight for your family, and even they betray you. Charlotte! Why, Charlotte, why?' He felt a choking sensation. 'What a damnable life this is, Thomson. What a damnable life.'

'I'll have to interview her,' Thomson said.

'So will I.' Walden stood up. He looked at his cigar. It had gone out. He threw it away. 'Let's go in.'

They went in.

In the hall Walden stopped a maid. 'Do you know where Lady Charlotte is?'

'I believe she's in her room, my lord. Shall I go and see?'

'Yes. Tell her I wish to speak to her in her room immediately.'

'Very good, m'lord.'

Thomson and Walden waited in the hall. Walden looked around. The marble floor, the carved staircase, the stucco ceiling, the perfect proportions – worthless. A footman drifted by silently, eyes lowered. A motorcycle messenger came in and headed for the Octagon. Pritchard crossed the hall and picked up the letters for posting from the hall table, just as he must have the day Charlotte's treacherous letter to Feliks was written. The maid came down the stairs.

'Lady Charlotte is ready to see you, my lord.'

Walden and Thomson went up.

Charlotte's room was on the second floor at the front of the house, looking over the park. It was sunny and light, with pretty fabrics and modern furniture. It's a long time since I've been in here, Walden thought vaguely.

'You look rather fierce, Papa,' Charlotte said.

'I've reason to be,' Walden replied. 'Mr Thomson has just given me the most dreadful piece of news of my whole life.'

Charlotte frowned.

Thomson said: 'Lady Charlotte, where is Feliks?'

Charlotte turned white. 'I've no idea, of course.'

Walden said: 'Don't be so damned cool!'

'How dare you swear at me!'

'I beg your pardon.'

Thomson said: 'Perhaps if you'd leave it to me, my lord . . .'

'Very well.' Walden sat down in the window-seat, thinking: How did I find myself apologizing?

Thomson addressed Charlotte. 'Lady Charlotte, I'm a policeman, and I can prove that you have committed conspiracy to murder. Now my concern, and your father's, is to let this go no farther; and, in particular, to ensure that you will not have to go to jail for a period of many years.'

Walden stared at Thomson. Jail! Surely he's merely frightening her. But no, he realized with a sense of overwhelming dread; he's right, she's a criminal . . .

Thomson went on: 'As long as we can prevent the murder, we feel we can cover up your participation. But, if the assassin succeeds, I will have no option but to bring you to trial – and then the charge will not be conspiracy to murder, but accessory to murder. In theory you could be hanged.'

'No!' Walden shouted involuntarily.

'Yes,' Thomson said quietly.

Walden buried his face in his hands.

Thomson said: 'You must save yourself that agony – and not only yourself, but your Mama and Papa. You must do everything in your power to help us find Feliks and save Prince Orlov.'

It could not be, Walden thought desperately. He felt as if he was going insane. My daughter could not be hanged. But if Aleks is killed Charlotte will have been one of the murderers. But it would never come to trial. Who was Home Secretary? McKenna. Walden did not know him. But Asquith would intervene to prevent a prosecution . . . wouldn't he?

Thomson said: 'Tell me when you last saw Feliks.'

Walden watched Charlotte, waiting for her response. She stood behind a chair, gripping its back with both hands. Her knuckles showed white, but her face appeared calm. Finally she spoke. 'I have nothing to tell you.'

Walden groaned aloud. How could she continue to be like this now that she was found out? What was going on in her mind? She seemed a stranger. He thought: When did I lose her?

'Do you know where Feliks is now?' Thomson asked her.

She said nothing.

'Have you warned him of our security precautions here?'

She looked blank.

'How is he armed?'

Nothing.

'Each time you refuse to answer a question, you become a little more guilty, do you realize that?'

Walden noticed a change of tone in Thomson's voice, and looked at him. He seemed genuinely angry now.

'Let me explain something to you,' Thomson said. 'You may think that your Papa can save you from justice. He is perhaps thinking the same thing. But, if Orlov dies, I swear to you that I will bring you to trial for murder. Now think about that!'

Thomson left the room.

Charlotte was dismayed to see him go. With a stranger in the room she had just about managed to keep her composure. Alone with Papa she was afraid she would break down.

'I'll save you if I can,' Papa said sadly.

Charlotte swallowed thickly and looked away. I wish he'd be angry, she thought; I could cope with that.

He looked out of the window. 'I'm responsible, you see,' he said painfully. 'I chose your mother, I fathered you, and I brought you up. You're nothing but what I've made you. I can't understand how this has happened, I really can't.' He looked back at her. 'Can you explain it to me, please?'

'Yes, I can,' she said. She was eager to make him understand, and she was sure he would, if she could tell it right. 'I don't want you to succeed in making Russia go to war, because if you do, millions of innocent Russians will be killed or wounded to no purpose.'

He looked surprised. 'Is that it?' he said. 'Is *that* why you've done these awful things? Is that what Feliks is trying to achieve?'

Perhaps he *will* understand, she thought joyfully. 'Yes,' she said. She went on enthusiastically: 'Feliks also wants a revolution in Russia – even you might think that could be a good thing – and he believes it will begin when the people there find out that Aleks has been trying to drag them into war.'

'Do you think I want a war?' he said incredulously. 'Do you think I would like it? Do you think it would do me any good?'

'Of course not – but you'd let it happen, under certain circumstances.'

'Everyone would – even Feliks, who wants a revolution, you tell me. And if there's to be a war, we must win it. Is that an evil thing to say?' His tone was almost pleading.

She was desperate for him to understand. 'I don't know whether it's evil, but I do know it's wrong. The Russian peasants know nothing of European politics, and they care less. But they will be shot to pieces, and have their legs blown off, and all awful things like that because you made an agreement with Aleks!' She fought back tears. 'Papa, can't you see that's wrong?'

'But think of it from the British point of view – from your own personal point of view. Imagine that Freddie Chalfont and Peter and Jonathan go to war as officers, and their men are Daniel the groom, and Peter the stable-lad, and Jimmy the boot-boy, and Charles the footman, and Peter Dawkins from the Home Farm – wouldn't you want them to get some help? Wouldn't you be *glad* that the whole of the Russian nation was on their side?'

'Of course – especially if the Russian nation had chosen to help them. But they won't choose, will they, Papa? You and Aleks will choose. You should be working to prevent war, not to win it.'

'If Germany attacks France, we have to help our friends. And it would be a disaster for Britain if Germany conquered Europe.'

'How could there be a bigger disaster than a war?'

'Should we never fight, then?'

'Only if we're invaded.'

'If we don't fight the Germans in France, we'll have to fight them here.'

'Are you sure?'

'It's likely.'

'When it happens, then we should fight.'

'Listen. This country hasn't been invaded for eight hundred and fifty years. Why? Because we've fought other people on their territory, not ours. That is why you, Lady Charlotte Walden, grew up in a peaceful and prosperous country.'

'How many wars were fought to prevent war? If we had not fought on other people's territory, would they have fought at all?'

'Who knows?' he said wearily. 'I wish you had studied more history. I wish you and I had talked more about this sort of thing. With a son, I would have – but, Lord! I never dreamed my daughter would be interested in foreign policy! And now I'm paying the price of that mistake. What a price. Charlotte, I promise you that the arithmetic of human suffering is not as straightforward as this Feliks has led you to believe. Could you not believe me when I tell you that? Could you not trust me?'

'No,' she said stubbornly.

'Feliks wants to *kill* your cousin. Does that make no difference?'

'He is going to kidnap Aleks, not kill him.'

Papa shook his head. 'Charlotte, he's tried twice to kill Aleks and once to kill me. He has killed many people in Russia. He's not a kidnapper, Charlotte, he's a murderer.'

'I don't believe you.'

'But why?' he said plaintively.

'Did you tell me the truth about suffragism? Did you tell me the truth about Annie? Did you tell me that in democratic Britain most people still can't vote? Did you tell me the truth about sexual intercourse?'

'No, I didn't.' To her horror, Charlotte saw that his cheeks were wet with tears. 'It may be that everything I ever did, as a father, was mistaken. I didn't know the world would change the way it has. I had no idea of what a woman's role would be in the world of 1914. It begins to look as if I have been a terrible failure. But I did what I thought best for you, because I loved you, and I still do. It's not your politics that are making me cry. It's the betrayal, you see. I mean, I shall fight tooth and nail to keep you out of the courts, even if you do succeed in killing poor Aleks, because you're my daughter, the most important person in the world to me. For you I will let justice and reputation and England go to hell. I would do wrong for you, without a moment's hesitation. For me, you come above all principles, all politics, everything. That's how it is in families. What hurts me so much is that you will not do the same for me. Will you?'

She wanted desperately to say yes.

'Will you be loyal to me, for all that I may be in the wrong, just because I am your father?'

But you're not, she thought. She bowed her head: she could not look at him.

They sat in silence for a minute. Then Papa blew his nose. He got up and went to the door. He took the key out of the lock, and went outside. He closed the door behind him. Charlotte heard him turn the key, locking her in.

She burst into tears.

It was the second appalling dinner party Lydia had given in two days. She was the only woman at the table. Sir Arthur was glum because his vast search operation had utterly failed to turn up Feliks. Charlotte and Aleks were locked in their rooms. Basil Thomson and Stephen were being icily polite to each other, for Thomson had found out about Charlotte and Feliks, and had threatened to send Charlotte to jail. Winston Churchill was there. He had brought the treaty with him and he and Aleks had signed it, but there was no rejoicing on that account, for everyone knew that if Aleks were to be assassinated then the Czar would refuse to ratify the deal. Churchill said that the sooner Aleks was off English soil the better. Thomson said he would devise a secure route and arrange a formidable bodyguard, and Aleks could leave tomorrow. Everyone went to bed early, for there was nothing else to do.

Lydia knew she would not sleep. Everything was unresolved. She had spent the afternoon in an indecisive haze, drugged with laudanum, trying to forget that Feliks was there in her house. Aleks would leave tomorrow: if only he could be kept safe for a few more hours . . . She wondered whether there might be some way she could make Feliks lie low for another day. Could she go to him and tell him a lie, say that he would have his opportunity of killing Aleks tomorrow night? He would never believe her. The scheme was hopeless. But once she had conceived the idea of going to see Feliks she could not get it out of her mind. She thought: Out of this door, along the passage, up the stairs, along another passage, through the nursery, through the closet, and there . . .

She closed her eyes tightly and pulled the sheet up over her head. Everything was dangerous. It was best to do nothing at all, to be motionless, paralysed. Leave Charlotte alone, leave Feliks alone, forget Aleks, forget Churchill.

But she did not know what was going to *happen.* Charlotte might go to Stephen and say: 'You're not my father.' Stephen might kill Feliks. Feliks might kill Aleks. Charlotte might be accused of murder. Feliks might come here, to my room, and kiss me.

Her nerves were bad again and she felt another headache coming on. It was a very warm night. The laudanum had worn off, but she had drunk a lot of wine at dinner and she still felt woozy. For some reason her skin was tender tonight, and every time she moved, the silk of her nightdress seemed to scrape her breasts. She was irritable, both mentally and physically. She half-wished Stephen would come to her, then she thought: No, I couldn't bear it.

Feliks' presence in the nursery was like a bright light shining in her eyes, keeping her awake. She threw off the sheet, got up, and went to the window. She opened it wider. The breeze was hardly cooler than the air in the room. Leaning out and looking down, she could see the twin lamps burning at the portico, and the policeman walking along the front of the house, his boots crunching distantly on the gravel drive.

What was Feliks doing up there? Was he making a bomb? Loading a gun? Sharpening a knife? Or was he sleeping, content to wait for the right moment? Or wandering around the house, trying to find a way to get past Aleks' bodyguards?

There's nothing I can do, she thought; nothing.

She picked up her book. It was Hardy's *Wessex Poems.* Why did I choose this? she thought. It opened at the page she had looked at that morning. She turned up the night-light, sat down, and read the whole poem. It was called 'Her Dilemma'.

The two were silent in a sunless church,
Whose mildewed walls, uneven paving-stones,
And wasted carvings passed antique research;
And nothing broke the clock's dull monotones.

Leaning against a wormy poppy-head,
So wan and worn that he could scarcely stand,
– For he was soon to die, – he softly said,
'Tell me you love me!' – holding hard her hand.

She would have given a world to breathe 'yes' truly,
So much his life seemed hanging on her mind,
And hence she lied, her heart persuaded thoroughly
'Twas worth her soul to be a moment kind.

But the sad need thereof, his nearing death,
So mocked humanity that she shamed to prize
A world conditioned thus, or care for breath
Where Nature such dilemmas could devise.

That's right, she thought; when life is like this, who can do right?

Her headache was so bad she thought her skull would split. She went to the drawer and took a gulp from the bottle of laudanum. Then she took another gulp.

Then she went to the nursery.

CHAPTER FIFTEEN

Something had gone wrong. Feliks had not seen Charlotte since midday, when she had brought him a basin, a jug of water, a towel and a cake of soap. There must have been some kind of trouble to keep her away – perhaps she had been forced to leave the house, or perhaps she felt she might be under observation. But she had not given him away, evidently, for here he was.

Anyway, he did not need her any more.

He knew where Orlov was and he knew where the guns were. He was not able to get into Orlov's room, for the security seemed too good; so he would have to make Orlov come out. He knew how to do that.

He had not used the soap and water, because the little hideaway was too cramped to allow him to stand up straight and wash himself, and anyway he did not care much about cleanliness; but now he was very hot and sticky, and he wanted to feel fresh before going about his work, so he took the water out into the nursery.

It felt very strange, to be standing in the place where Charlotte had spent so many hours of her childhood. He put the thought out of his mind: this was no time for sentiment. He took off all his clothes and washed himself by the light of a single candle. A familiar, pleasant feeling of anticipation and excitement filled him, and he felt as if his skin were glowing. I shall win tonight, he thought savagely, no matter how many I have to kill. He rubbed himself all over roughly with the towel. His movements were jerky, and there was a tight sensation in the back of his throat which made him want to shout. This must be why warriors yell war-cries, he thought. He looked down at his body and saw that he had the beginnings of an erection.

Then he heard Lydia say: 'Why, you've grown a beard.'

He spun around and stared into the darkness, stupefied.

She came forward into the circle of candlelight. Her blonde hair was unpinned and hung around her shoulders. She wore a long, pale nightdress with a fitted bodice and a high waist. Her arms were bare and white. She was smiling.

They stood still, looking at one another. Several times she opened her mouth to speak, but no words came out. Feliks felt the blood rush to his loins. How long, he thought wildly, how long since I stood naked before a woman?

She moved, but it did not break the spell. She stepped forward and knelt at his feet. She closed her eyes and nuzzled his body. As Feliks looked down on her unseeing face, candlelight glinted off the tears on her cheeks.

*

Lydia was nineteen again, and her body was young and strong and tireless. The simple wedding was over, and she and her new husband were in the little cottage they had taken in the country. Outside, snow fell quietly in the garden. They made love by candlelight. She kissed him all over, and he said: 'I have always loved you, all these years,' although it was only weeks since they had met. His beard brushed her breasts, although she could not remember his growing a beard. She watched his hands, busy all over her body, in all the secret places, and she said: 'It's you, you're doing this to me, it's you, Feliks, Feliks,' as if there had ever been anyone else who did these things to her, who gave her this rolling, swelling pleasure. With her long fingernail she scratched his shoulder. She watched as the blood welled up, then leaned forward and licked it greedily. 'You're an animal,' he said. They touched each other busily, all the time; they were like children let loose in a sweet shop, moving restlessly from one thing to another, touching and looking and tasting, unable to believe in their astonishing good fortune. She said: 'I'm so glad we ran away together,' and for some reason that made him look sad, so she said: 'Stick your finger up me,' and the sad look went and desire masked his face, but she realized that she was crying, and she could not understand why. Suddenly she realized that this was a dream, and she was terrified of waking up, so she said: 'Let's do it now, quickly,' and they came together, and she smiled through her tears and said: 'We fit.' They seemed to move like dancers, or courting butterflies, and she said: 'This is so nice, dear Jesus this is so nice,' and then she said: 'I thought this would never happen to me again,' and her breath came in sobs. He buried his face in her neck, but she took his head in her hands and pushed it away so that she could see him. Now she knew that this was not a dream. She was awake. There was a taut string stretched between the back of her throat and the base of her spine, and every time it vibrated, her whole body sang a single note of pleasure which got louder and louder. 'Look at me!' she said as she lost control, and he said gently: 'I'm looking,' and the note got louder. 'I'm wicked!' she cried as the climax hit her, 'Look at me, I'm wicked!' and her body convulsed, and the string got tighter and tighter and the pleasure more piercing until she felt she was losing her mind, and then the last high note of joy broke the string and she slumped and fainted.

Feliks laid her gently on the floor. Her face in the candlelight was peaceful, all the tension gone; she looked like one who had died happy. She was pale, but breathing normally. She had been half asleep, probably drugged, Feliks knew, but he did not care. He felt drained and weak and helpless and grateful, and very much in love. We could start again, he thought: she's a free woman, she could leave her husband, we could live in Switzerland, Charlotte could join us—

This is not an opium dream, he told himself. He and Lydia had made such plans before, in St Petersburg, nineteen years ago; and they had been utterly impotent against the wishes of respectable people. It doesn't happen, not in real life, he thought; they would frustrate us all over again.

They will never let me have her.

But I shall have my revenge.

He got to his feet and quickly put on his clothes. He picked up the candle. He looked at her once more. Her eyes were still closed. He wanted to touch her once more, to kiss her soft mouth. He hardened his heart. Never again, he thought. He turned and went through the door.

He walked softly along the carpeted corridor and down the stairs. His candle made weird moving shadows in the doorways. I may die tonight, but not before I have killed Orlov and Walden, he thought. I have seen my daughter, I have lain with my wife; now I will kill my enemies, and then I can die.

On the first-floor landing he stepped on a hard floor and his boot made a loud noise. He froze and listened. He saw that there was no carpet here, but a marble floor. He waited. There was no noise from the rest of the house. He took off his boots and went on in his bare feet – he had no socks.

The lights were out all over the house. Would anyone be roaming around? Might someone come down to raid the larder, feeling hungry in the middle of the night? Might a butler dream he heard noises and make a tour of the house to check? Might Orlov's bodyguards need to go to the lavatory? Feliks strained his hearing, ready to snuff out the candle and hide at the slightest noise.

He stopped in the hall and took from his coat pocket

the plans of the house Charlotte had drawn for him. He consulted the ground-floor plan briefly, holding the candle close to the paper, then turned to his right and padded along the corridor.

He went through the library into the gun-room.

He closed the door softly behind him and looked around. A great hideous head seemed to leap at him from the wall, and he jumped, and grunted with fear. The candle went out. In the darkness he realized he had seen a tiger's head, stuffed and mounted on the wall. He lit the candle again. There were trophies all around the walls: a lion, a deer, and even a rhinoceros. Walden had done some big-game hunting in his time. There was also a big fish in a glass case.

Feliks put the candle down on the table. The guns were racked along one wall. There were three pairs of double-barrelled shotguns, a Winchester rifle and something that Feliks thought must be an elephant gun. He had never seen an elephant gun. He had never seen an elephant. The guns were secured by a chain through their trigger-guards. Feliks looked along the chain. It was fastened by a large padlock to a bracket screwed into the wooden end of the rack.

Feliks considered what to do. He had to have a gun. He thought he might be able to snap the padlock, given a tough piece of iron such as a screwdriver to use as a lever; but it seemed to him that it might be easier to unscrew the bracket from the wood of the rack and then pass chain, padlock and bracket through the trigger-guards to free the guns.

He looked again at Charlotte's plan. Next to the

gun-room was the flower-room. He picked up his candle and went through the communicating door. He found himself in a small, cold room with a marble table and a stone sink. He heard a footstep. He doused his candle and crouched down. The sound had come from outside, from the gravel path: it had to be one of the sentries. The light of a torch flickered outside. Feliks flattened himself against the door, beside the window. The light grew stronger and the footsteps became louder. They stopped right outside and the torch shone in through the window. By its light Feliks could see a rack over the sink and a few tools hanging by hooks: shears, secateurs, a small hoe and a knife. The sentry tried the door against which Feliks stood. It was locked. The footsteps moved away and the light went. Feliks waited a moment. What would the sentry do? Presumably he had seen the glimmer of Feliks' candle. But he might think it had been the reflection of his own torch. Or someone in the house might have had a perfectly legitimate reason to go into the flower-room. Or the sentry might be the ultra-cautious type, and come and check.

Leaving the doors open, Feliks went from the flower-room, through the gun-room, and into the library, feeling his way in the dark, holding his unlit candle in his hand. He sat on the floor in the library behind a big leather sofa and counted slowly to one thousand. Nobody came. The sentry was not the cautious type.

He went back into the gun-room and lit the candle. The windows were heavily curtained here – there had been no curtains in the flower-room. He went cautiously into the flower-room, took the knife he had seen over the sink, came back into the gun-room, and bent over the gun rack. He used the blade of the knife to undo the screws which held the bracket to the wood of the rack. The wood was old and hard, but eventually the screws came loose and he was able to unchain the guns.

There were three cupboards in the room. One held bottles of brandy and whisky together with glasses. Another held bound copies of a magazine called *Horse and Hound* and a huge leather-bound ledger marked 'Game Book'. The third was locked: that must be where the ammunition was kept.

Feliks broke the lock with the garden knife.

Of the three types of gun available – Winchester, shotgun or elephant gun – he preferred the Winchester. However, as he searched through the boxes of ammunition he realized there were no cartridges here either for the Winchester or for the elephant gun: those weapons must have been kept as souvenirs. He had to be content with a shotgun. All three pairs were twelve-bore, and all the ammunition consisted of cartridges of number six shot. To be sure of killing his man he would have to fire at close range – no more than twenty yards, to be absolutely certain. And he would have only two shots before reloading.

Still, he thought, I only want to kill two people.

The image of Lydia lying on the nursery floor kept coming back to him. When he thought of how they had made love, he felt exultant. He no longer felt the fatalism which had gripped him immediately afterwards. Why should I die? he thought. And when I have killed Walden, who knows what might happen then?

He loaded the gun.

And now, Lydia thought, I shall have to kill myself.

She saw no other possibility. She had descended to the depths of depravity for the second time in her life. All her years of self-discipline had come to nothing, just because Feliks had returned. She could not live with the knowledge of what she was. She wanted to die, now.

She considered how it might be done. What could she take that was poisonous? There must be rat poison somewhere on the premises, but of course she did not know where. An overdose of laudanum? She was not sure she had enough. You could kill yourself with gas, she recalled, but Stephen had converted the house to electric light. She wondered whether the top storeys were high enough for her to die by jumping from a window. She was afraid she might merely break her back and be paralysed for years. She did not think she had the courage to slash her wrists; and besides, it would take so long to bleed to death. The quickest way would be to shoot herself. She thought she could probably load a gun and fire it: she had seen it done innumerable times. But, she remembered, the guns were locked up.

Then she thought of the lake. Yes, that was the answer. She would go to her room and put on a robe, then she would leave the house by a side door, so that the policemen should not see her; and she would walk across the west side of the park, beside the rhododendrons, and through the woods until she came to the water's edge; then she would just keep walking, until the cool water closed over her head; then she would open her mouth, and a minute or so later it would be all over.

She left the nursery and walked along the corridor in the dark. She saw a light under Charlotte's door, and hesitated. She wanted to see her little girl one last time. The key was in the lock on the outside. She unlocked the door and went in.

Charlotte sat in a chair by the window, fully dressed but asleep. Her face was pale but for the redness around her eyes. She had unpinned her hair. Lydia closed the door and went over to her. Charlotte opened her eyes.

'What's happened?' she said.

'Nothing,' Lydia said. She sat down.

Charlotte said: 'Do you remember when Nannie went away?'

'Yes. You were old enough for a governess, and I didn't have another baby.'

'I had forgotten all about it for years. I've just remembered. You never knew, did you, that I thought Nannie was my mother?'

'I don't know . . . did you think so? You always called me Mama, and her Nannie . . .'

'Yes.' Charlotte spoke slowly, almost desultorily, as if she were lost in the fog of distant memory. 'You were Mama, and Nannie was Nannie, but everybody had a mother, you see, and when Nannie said you were my mother, I said don't be silly, Nannie, *you* are my mother.

And Nannie just laughed. Then you sent her away. I was broken-hearted.'

'I never realized . . .'

'Marya never told you, of course – what governess would?'

Charlotte was just repeating the memory, not accusing her mother, just explaining something. She went on: 'So you see, I have the wrong mother, and now I have the wrong father, too. The new thing made me remember the old, I suppose.'

Lydia said: 'You must hate me. I understand. I hate myself.'

'I don't hate you, Mama. I've been dreadfully angry toward you, but I've never hated you.'

'But you think I'm a hypocrite.'

'Not even that.'

A feeling of peace came over Lydia.

Charlotte said: 'I'm beginning to understand why you're so fiercely respectable, why you were so determined that I should never know anything of sex . . . you just wanted to save me from what happened to you. And I've found out that there are hard decisions, and that sometimes one can't tell what's good and right to do; and I think I've judged you harshly, when I had no right to judge you at all . . . and I'm not very proud of myself.'

'Do you know that I love you?'

'Yes . . . and I love you, Mama, and that's why I feel so wretched.'

Lydia was dazed. This was the last thing she had expected. After all that had happened – the lies, the treachery, the anger, the bitterness – Charlotte still loved her. She was suffused with a kind of tranquil joy. Kill myself? she thought. Why should I kill myself?

'We should have talked like this before,' Lydia said.

'Oh, you've no idea how much I wanted to,' Charlotte said. 'You were always so good at telling me how to curtsey, and carry my train, and sit down gracefully, and put up my hair . . . and I longed for you to explain important things to me in the same way – about falling in love and having babies – but you never did.'

'I never could,' Lydia said. 'I don't know why.'

Charlotte yawned. 'I think I'll sleep now.' She stood up.

Lydia kissed her cheek, then embraced her.

Charlotte said: 'I love Feliks, too, you know; that hasn't changed.'

'I understand,' said Lydia. 'I do, too.'

'Goodnight, Mama.'

'Goodnight.'

Lydia went out quickly and closed the door behind her. She hesitated outside. What would Charlotte do if the door were left unlocked? Lydia decided to save her the anxiety of the decision. She turned the key in the lock.

She went down the stairs, heading for her own room. She was so glad she had talked to Charlotte. Perhaps, she thought, this family could be mended, after all; I've no idea how, but surely it might be done. She went into her room.

'Where have you been?' said Stephen.

*

Now that Feliks had a weapon, all he had to do was get Orlov out of his room. He knew how to do that. He was going to burn the house down.

Carrying the gun in one hand and the candle in the other, he walked – still barefoot – through the west wing and across the hall into the drawing-room. Just a few more minutes, he thought; give me just a few more minutes and I will be done. He passed through two dining-rooms and a serving-room and entered the kitchens. Here Charlotte's plans became vague, and he had to search for the way out. He found a large rough-hewn door closed with a bar. He lifted the bar and quietly opened the door.

He put out his candle and waited in the doorway. After a minute or so he found he could just about make out the outlines of the buildings. That was a relief: he was afraid to use the candle outside because of the sentries.

In front of him was a small cobbled courtyard. On its far side, if the plan was right, there was a garage, a workshop, and – a petrol tank.

He crossed the yard. The building in front of him had once been a barn, he guessed. Part of it was enclosed – the workshop, perhaps – and the rest was open. He could vaguely make out the great round headlamps of two large cars. Where was the fuel tank? He looked up. The building was quite high. He stepped forward, and something hit his forehead. It was a length of flexible pipe with a nozzle at the end. It hung down from the upper part of the building.

It made sense: they put the cars in the barn and the

petrol tank in the hayloft. They simply drove the cars into the courtyard and filled them with fuel from the pipe.

Good! he thought.

Now he needed a container. A two-gallon can would be ideal. He entered the garage and walked around the cars, feeling with his feet, careful not to stumble over anything noisy.

There were no cans.

He recalled the plans again. He was close to the kitchen garden. There might be a watering-can in that region. He was about to go and look when he heard a sniff.

He froze.

The policeman went by.

Feliks could hear the beat of his own heart.

The light from the policeman's oil-lamp meandered around the courtyard. Did I shut the kitchen door? Feliks thought in a panic. The lamp shone on the door: it looked shut.

The policeman went on.

Feliks realized he had been holding his breath, and he let it out in a long sigh.

He gave the policeman a minute to get some distance away, then he went in the same direction, looking for the kitchen garden.

He found no cans there, but he stumbled over a coil of hose. He estimated its length at about a hundred feet. It gave him a wicked idea.

First he needed to know how frequently the policeman patrolled. He began to count. Still counting, he carried the garden hose back to the courtyard and concealed it and himself behind the motor cars.

He had reached nine hundred and two when the policeman came around again.

He had about fifteen minutes.

He attached one end of the hose to the nozzle of the petrol pipe, then walked across the courtyard, paying out the hose as he went. He paused in the kitchen to find a sharp meat skewer and to relight his candle. Then he retraced his steps through the house, laying the hose through the kitchen, the serving-room, the dining-rooms, the drawing-room, the hall and the passage, and into the library. The hose was heavy, and it was difficult to do the job silently. He listened all the while for footsteps, but all he heard was the noise of an old house settling down for the night. Everyone was in bed, he was sure: but would someone come down to get a book from the library, or a glass of brandy from the drawing-room, or a sandwich from the kitchen?

If that were to happen now, he thought, the game would be up.

Just a few more minutes – just a few more minutes!

He had been worried about whether the hose would be long enough, but it just reached through the library door. He walked back, following the hose, making holes in it every few yards with the sharp point of the meat skewer.

He went out through the kitchen door and stood in the garage. He held his shotgun two-handed, like a club.

He seemed to wait an age.

At last he heard footsteps. The policeman passed him and stopped, shining his torch on the hose, and gave a grunt of surprise.

Feliks hit him with the gun.

The policeman staggered.

Feliks hissed: 'Fall down, damn you!' and hit him again with all his might.

The policeman fell down, and Feliks hit him again with savage satisfaction.

The man was still.

Feliks turned to the petrol pipe and found the place where the hose was connected. There was a tap to stop and start the flow of petrol.

Feliks turned on the tap.

'Before we were married,' Lydia said impulsively, 'I had a lover.'

'Good lord!' said Stephen.

Why did I say that? she thought. Because lying about it has made everyone unhappy, and I'm finished with all that.

She said: 'My father found out about it. He had my lover jailed and tortured. He said that if I would agree to marry you, the torture would stop immediately; and that as soon as you and I had left for England, my lover would be released from jail.'

She watched his face. He was not hurt as she had expected, but he was horrified. He said: 'Your father was wicked.'

'I was wicked, to marry without love.'

'Oh . . .' Now Stephen looked pained. 'For that matter, I wasn't in love with you. I proposed to you because my father had died and I needed a wife to be Countess of Walden. It was later that I fell so desperately in love with you. I'd say I forgive you, but there's nothing to forgive.'

Could it be this easy? she thought. Might he forgive me everything and go on loving me? It seemed that, because death was in the air, anything was possible. She found herself plunging on. 'There's more to be told,' she said, 'and it's worse.'

His expression was painfully anxious. 'You'd better tell me.'

'I was . . . I was already with child when I married you.'

Stephen paled. 'Charlotte!'

Lydia nodded silently.

'She . . . she's not mine?'

'No.'

'Oh, God.'

Now I have hurt you, she thought; this you never dreamed. She said: 'Oh, Stephen, I am so dreadfully sorry.'

He stared at her. 'Not mine,' he said stupidly. 'Not mine.'

She thought of how much it meant to him: more than anyone else the English nobility talked about breeding and bloodlines. She remembered him looking at Charlotte and murmuring: 'Bone of my bones, and flesh of my flesh;' it was the only verse of the Bible she had ever heard him quote. She thought of her own feelings, of the mystery of the child starting life as part of oneself and then becoming a separate individual, but never completely separate: it must be the same for men, she thought; sometimes one thinks it isn't, but it must be.

His face was grey and drawn. He looked suddenly older. He said: 'Why are you telling me this now?'

I can't, she thought; I can't reveal any more, I've hurt him so much already. But it was as if she was on a downhill slope and could not stop. She blurted: 'Because Charlotte has met her real father, and she knows everything.'

'Oh, the poor child.' Stephen buried his face in his hands.

Lydia realized that his next question would be: Who is the father? She was overcome by panic. She could not tell him that. It would kill him. But she *needed* to tell him; she wanted the weight of these guilty secrets to be lifted for ever. Don't ask, she thought; not yet, it's too much.

He looked up at her. His face was frighteningly expressionless. He looked like a judge, she thought, impassively pronouncing sentence; and she was the guilty prisoner in the dock.

Don't ask.

He said: 'And the father is Feliks, of course.'

She gasped.

He nodded, as if her reaction was all the confirmation he needed.

What will he do? she thought fearfully. She watched

his face, but she could not read his expression: he was like a stranger to her.

He said: 'Oh, dear God in Heaven, what have we done.'

Lydia was suddenly garrulous. 'He came along just when she was beginning to see her parents as frail human beings, of course: and there he was, full of life and ideas and iconoclasm . . . just the kind of thing to enchant an independent-minded young girl . . . I know, something like that happened to me . . . and so she got to know him, and became fond of him, and helped him . . . but she loves you. Stephen, she's yours in that way. People can't help loving you . . . can't help it . . .'

His face was wooden. She wished he would curse, or cry, or abuse her, or even beat her, but he sat there looking at her with that judge's face, and said: 'And you? Did you help him?'

'Not intentionally, no . . . but I haven't helped you, either. I am such a hateful, evil woman.'

He stood up and held her shoulders. His hands were cold as the grave. He said: 'But are you mine?'

'I wanted to be, Stephen – I really did.'

He touched her cheek, but no love showed in his face. She shuddered. She said: 'I told you it was too much to forgive.'

He said: 'Do you know where Feliks is?'

She made no reply. If I tell, she thought, it will be like killing Feliks. If I don't tell, it will be like killing Stephen.

'You do know,' he said.

She nodded dumbly.

'Will you tell me?'

She looked into his eyes. If I tell him, she thought, will he forgive me?

Stephen said: 'Choose.'

She felt as if she were falling headlong into a pit.

Stephen raised his eyebrows expectantly.

Lydia said: 'He's in the house.'

'Good God! Where?'

Lydia's shoulders slumped. It was done. She had betrayed Feliks for the last time. 'He's been hiding in the nursery,' she said dejectedly.

His expression was no longer wooden. His cheeks coloured and his eyes blazed with fury.

Lydia said: 'Say you forgive me . . . please?'

He turned around and ran from the room.

Feliks ran through the kitchen and through the serving-room, carrying his candle, the shotgun and his matches. He could smell the sweet, slightly nauseating vapour of petrol. In the dining-room a thin, steady jet was spouting through a hole in the hosepipe. Feliks shifted the hose across the room, so that the fire would not destroy it too quickly, then struck a match and threw it on to a petrol-soaked patch of rug. The rug burst into flames.

Feliks grinned and ran on.

In the drawing-room he picked up a velvet cushion and held it to another hole in the hosepipe for a minute. He put the cushion down on a sofa, set fire to it, and threw some more cushions on to it. They blazed merrily.

He ran across the hall and along the passage to the library. Here the petrol was gushing out of the end of the pipe and running over the floor. Feliks pulled handfuls of books off the shelves and threw them on the floor into the spreading puddle. Then he crossed the room and opened the communicating door to the gun-room. He stood in the doorway for a moment, then threw his candle into the puddle.

There was a noise like a huge gust of wind and the library caught fire. Books and petrol burned fiercely. In a moment the curtains were ablaze, then the seats and the panelling caught. The petrol continued to pour out of the hosepipe, feeding the fire. Feliks laughed aloud.

He turned into the gun-room. He stuffed a handful of extra cartridges into the pocket of his coat. He went from the gun-room into the flower-room. He unbolted the door to the garden, opened it quietly, and stepped out.

He walked directly west, away from the house, for two hundred paces, containing his impatience. Then he turned south for the same distance, and finally he walked east until he was directly opposite the main entrance to the house, looking at it across the darkened lawn.

He could see the second police sentry standing in front of the portico, illuminated by the twin lamps, smoking a pipe. His colleague lay unconscious, perhaps dead, in the kitchen courtyard. Feliks could see the flames in the windows of the library, but the policeman was some distance away from there and he had not noticed them yet. He would see them at any moment.

Between Feliks and the house, about fifty yards from the portico, was a big old chestnut tree. Feliks walked toward it across the lawn. The policeman seemed to be looking more or less in Feliks' direction, but he did not see him. Feliks did not care: if he sees me, he thought, I'll shoot him dead. It doesn't matter now. No one could stop the fire. Everyone will have to leave the house. Any minute now, any minute now, I'll kill them both.

He came up behind the tree and leaned against it, with the shotgun in his hands.

Now he could see flames at the opposite end of the house, in the dining-room windows.

He thought: What are they doing in there?

Walden ran along the corridor to the bachelor wing and knocked on the door of the Blue Room, where Thomson was sleeping. He went in.

'What is it?' Thomson's voice said from the bed.

Walden turned on the light. 'Feliks is in the house.'

'Good God!' Thomson got out of bed. 'How?'

'Charlotte let him in,' Walden said bitterly.

Thomson was hastily putting on trousers and a jacket. 'Do we know where?'

'In the nursery. Have you got your revolver?'

'No, but I've got three men with Orlov, remember? I'll peel two of them off and then take Feliks.'

'I'm coming with you.'

'I'd rather—'

'Don't argue!' Walden shouted. 'I want to see him die.'

Thomson gave a queer, sympathetic look, then ran out of the room. Walden followed.

They went along the corridor to Aleks' room. The bodyguard outside the door stood up and saluted Thomson. Thomson said: 'It's Barrett, isn't it?'

'Yes, sir.'

'Who's inside?'

'Bishop and Anderson, sir.'

'Get them to open up.'

Barrett tapped on the door.

Immediately a voice said: 'Password?'

'Mississippi,' said Barrett.

The door opened. 'What's on, Charlie? Oh, it's you, sir.'

Thomson said: 'How is Orlov?'

'Sleeping like a baby, sir.'

Walden thought: Let's get on with it!

Thomson said: 'Feliks is in the house. Barrett and Anderson, come with me and his lordship. Bishop, stay inside the room. Check that your pistols are loaded, please, all of you.'

Walden led the way along the bachelor wing and up the back stairs to the nursery suite. His heart was pounding, and he felt the curious mixture of fear and eagerness which had always come over him when he got a big lion in the sights of his rifle.

He pointed at the nursery door.

Thomson whispered: 'Is there electric light in that room?'

'Yes,' Walden replied.

'Where's the switch?'

'Left-hand side of the door, at shoulder height.'

Barrett and Anderson drew their pistols.

Walden and Thomson stood either side of the door, out of the line of fire.

Barrett threw open the door, Anderson dashed in and stepped to one side, and Barrett threw the light switch.

Nothing happened.

Walden looked into the room.

Anderson and Barrett were checking the schoolroom and the bedroom. A moment later Barrett said: 'No one here, sir.'

The nursery was bare and bright with light. There was a bowl of dirty water on the floor, and next to it a crumpled towel.

Walden pointed to the closet door. 'Through there is a little attic.'

Barrett opened the closet door. They all tensed. Barrett went through with his gun in his hand.

He came back a moment later. 'He *was* there.'

Thomson scratched his head.

Walden said: 'We must search the house.'

Thomson said: 'I wish we had more men.'

'We'll start with the west wing,' Walden said. 'Come *on*.'

They followed him out of the nursery and along the

corridor to the staircase. As they went down the stairs Walden smelled smoke. 'What's that?' he said.

Thomson sniffed.

Walden looked at Barrett and Anderson: neither of them was smoking.

The smell became more powerful, and now Walden could hear noise like wind in the trees.

Suddenly he was filled with fear. 'My house is on fire!' he shouted. He raced down the stairs.

The hall was full of smoke.

Walden ran across the hall and pushed open the door of the drawing-room. Heat hit him like a blow and he staggered back. The room was an inferno. He despaired: it could never be put out. He looked along to the west wing, and saw that the library was afire too. He turned. Thomson was right behind him. Walden shouted: 'My house is burning down!'

Thomson took his arm and pulled him back to the staircase. Anderson and Barrett stood there. Walden found he could breathe and hear more easily in the centre of the hall. Thomson was very cool and collected. He began to give orders.

'Anderson, go and wake up those two bobbies outside. Send one to find a garden hose and a tap. Send the other running to the village to telephone for a fire engine. Then run up the back stairs and through the servants' quarters, waking everyone. Tell them to get out the quickest way they can then gather on the front lawn to be counted. Barrett, go and wake up Mr Churchill and make sure he gets out. I'll fetch Orlov. Walden, you get your wife and daughter. Move!'

Walden ran up the stairs and into Lydia's room. She was sitting on the chaise-longue in her nightdress, and her eyes were red with weeping. 'The house is on fire,' Walden said breathlessly. 'Go out quickly on to the front lawn. I'll get Charlotte.' Then he thought of something: the dinner bell. 'No,' he said. 'You get Charlotte. I'll ring the bell.'

He raced down the stairs again, thinking: Why didn't I think of this before? In the hall was a long silk rope which would ring bells all over the house to warn guests and servants that a meal was about to be served. Walden pulled on the rope, and heard faintly the response of the bells from various parts of the house. He noticed a garden hose trailing through the hall. Was somebody fighting the fire already? He could not think who. He kept on pulling the rope.

Feliks watched anxiously. The blaze was spreading too quickly. Already large areas of the first floor were burning – he could see the glow in the windows. He thought: Come out, you fools. What were they doing? He did not want to burn everyone in the house – he wanted them to come out. The policeman in the portico seemed to be asleep. I'll give the alarm myself, Feliks thought desperately; I don't want the wrong people to die—

Suddenly the policeman looked around. His pipe fell out of his mouth. He dashed into the porch and began to hammer on the door. At last! thought Feliks. Now raise the alarm, you fool! The policeman ran around to a window and broke it.

Just then the door opened and someone rushed out in a cloud of smoke. It's happening, Feliks thought. He raised the shotgun and peered through the darkness. He could not see the face of the newcomer. The man shouted something, and the policeman ran off. I've got to be able to see their faces, Feliks thought; but if I go too close I'll be seen too soon. The newcomer rushed back into the house before Feliks could recognize him. I'll have to get nearer, Feliks thought, and take the chance. He moved across the lawn. Within the house, bells began to ring.

Now they will come, thought Feliks.

Lydia ran along the smoke-filled corridor. How could this happen so *quickly*? In her room she had smelled nothing, but now there were flames flickering underneath the doors of the bedrooms she passed. The whole house must be blazing. The air was too hot to breathe. She reached Charlotte's room and turned the handle of the door. Of course, it was locked. She turned the key. She tried again to open the door. It would not move. She turned the handle and threw her weight against the door. Something was wrong, the door was jammed, Lydia began to scream and scream—

'Mama!' Charlotte's voice came from within the room.

Lydia bit her lip hard and stopped screaming. 'Charlotte!'

'Open the door!'

'I can't I can't I can't—'

'It's locked!'

'I've unlocked it and it won't open and the house is on fire oh dear Jesus help me help—'

The door shook and the handle rattled as Charlotte tried to open it from the inside.

'Mama!'

'Yes!'

'Mama, stop screaming and listen carefully to me – the floor has shifted and the door is wedged in its frame – it will have to be broken down – go and fetch help!'

'I can't leave you—'

'MAMA! GO AND GET HELP OR I'LL BURN TO DEATH!'

'Oh, God – all right!' Lydia turned and ran, choking, toward the staircase.

Walden was still ringing the bell. Through the smoke he saw Aleks, flanked by Thomson and the third detective, Bishop, coming down the stairs. Lydia and Churchill and Charlotte should be here too, he thought, then he realized that they might come down any one of several staircases: the only place to check was out on the front lawn where everyone had been told to gather.

'Bishop!' shouted Walden. 'Come here!'

The detective ran across.

'Ring this. Keep going as long as you can.'

Bishop took the rope and Walden followed Aleks out of the house.

*

It was a very sweet moment for Feliks.

He lifted the gun and walked toward the house.

Orlov and another man walked toward him. They had not yet seen him. As they came closer Walden appeared behind them.

Like rats in a trap, Feliks thought triumphantly.

The man Feliks did not know looked back over his shoulder and spoke to Walden.

Orlov was twenty yards away.

This is it, Feliks thought.

He put the stock of the gun to his shoulder, aimed carefully at Orlov's chest, and – just as Orlov opened his mouth to speak – pulled the trigger.

A large black hole appeared in Orlov's nightshirt as an ounce of number six shot, about four hundred pellets, tore into his body. The other two men heard the bang and stared at Feliks in astonishment. Blood gushed from Orlov's chest, and he fell backward.

I did it, Feliks thought exultantly; I killed him.

Now for the other tyrant.

He pointed the gun at Walden. 'Don't move!' he yelled.

Walden and the other man stood motionless.

They all heard a scream.

Feliks looked in the direction from which the sound came.

Lydia was running out of the house with her hair on fire.

Feliks hesitated for a split second, then he dashed toward her.

Walden did the same.

As he ran, Feliks dropped the gun and tore off his coat. He reached Lydia a moment before Walden. He wrapped the coat around her head, smothering the flames.

She pulled the coat off her head and yelled at them: 'Charlotte is trapped in her room!'

Walden turned and ran toward the house.

Feliks ran with him.

Lydia, sobbing with fright, saw Thomson dart forward and pick up the shotgun Feliks had dropped.

She watched in horror as Thomson raised it and took aim at Feliks' back.

'No!' she screamed. She threw herself at Thomson, knocking him off balance.

The gun discharged into the ground.

Thomson stared at her in bewilderment.

'Don't you know?' she shouted hysterically. 'He's suffered enough!'

Charlotte's carpet was smouldering.

She put her fist to her mouth and bit her knuckles to stop herself screaming.

She ran to her washstand, picked up the jug of water, and threw it into the middle of the room. It made more smoke, not less.

She went to the window, opened it, and looked out. Smoke and flames poured out of the windows below her. The wall of the house was faced with smooth stone:

there was no way to climb down. If I have to I'll jump; it will be better than burning, she thought. The idea terrified her and she bit her knuckles again.

She ran to the door and shook the handle impotently.

'Somebody, help, quickly!' she screamed.

Flames rose from the carpet, and a hole appeared in the centre of the floor.

She ran around the edge of the room to be near the window, ready to jump.

She heard someone sobbing and realized it was her.

The hall was full of smoke. Feliks could hardly see. He stayed close behind Walden, thinking: Not Charlotte, I won't let Charlotte die, not Charlotte.

They ran up the staircase. The whole first floor was ablaze. The heat was terrific. Walden dashed through a wall of flame and Feliks followed him.

Walden stopped outside a door and was seized by a fit of coughing. Helpless, he pointed at the door. Feliks rattled the handle and pushed the door with his shoulder. It would not move. He shook Walden and shouted: 'Run at the door!' He and Walden – still coughing – stood on the other side of the corridor, facing the door.

Feliks said: 'Now!'

They threw themselves at the door together.

The wood split but the door stayed shut.

Walden stopped coughing. His face showed sheer terror. 'Again!' he shouted at Feliks.

They stood against the opposite wall.

'Now!'

They threw themselves at the door.

It cracked a little more.

From the other side of the door, they heard Charlotte scream.

Walden gave a roar of anger. He looked about him desperately. He picked up a heavy oak chair. Feliks thought it was too heavy for Walden to lift but Walden raised it above his head and smashed it against the door. The wood began to splinter.

In a frenzy of impatience Feliks put his hands into the crack and began to tear at the splintered wood. His fingers became slippery with blood.

He stood back and Walden swung with the chair again. Again Feliks pulled out the shards. His hands were full of splinters. He heard Walden muttering something and realized it was a prayer. Walden swung the chair a third time. The chair broke, its seat and legs coming away from its back; but there was a hole in the door big enough for Feliks – but not for Walden – to crawl through.

Feliks dragged himself through the hole and fell into the bedroom.

The floor was on fire, and he could not see Charlotte.

'Charlotte!' he shouted at the top of his voice.

'Here!' Her voice came from the far side of the room.

Feliks ran around the outside of the room where the fire was less. She was sitting on the sill of the open window, breathing in ragged gulps. He picked her up by the waist and threw her over his shoulder. He ran back around the edge of the room to the door.

Walden reached through the door to take her.

Walden put his head and one shoulder through the hole to take Charlotte from Feliks. He could see that Feliks' face and hands were burned black and his trousers were on fire. Charlotte's eyes were open and wide with terror. Behind Feliks, the floor began to collapse. Walden got one arm beneath Charlotte's body. Feliks seemed to stagger. Walden withdrew his head, put his other arm through the hole, and got his hand under Charlotte's armpit. Flames licked around her nightdress and she screamed. Walden said: 'All right, Papa's got you.' Suddenly he was taking her entire weight. He drew her through the hole. She fainted and went limp. As he pulled her out the bedroom floor fell in, and Walden saw Feliks' face as Feliks dropped into the inferno.

Walden whispered: 'May God have mercy on your soul.'

Then he ran downstairs.

Lydia was held in an iron grip by Thomson, who would not let her go into the blazing house. She stood, staring at the door, willing the two men to appear with Charlotte.

A figure appeared. Who was it?

It came closer. It was Stephen. He was carrying Charlotte.

Thomson let Lydia go. She ran to them. Stephen laid Charlotte gently on the grass. Lydia stared at him in a panic. She said: 'What – what—'

'She's not dead,' Stephen said. 'Just fainted.'

Lydia got down on the grass, cradled Charlotte's head in her lap, and felt her chest beneath her left breast. There was a strong heartbeat.

'Oh, my baby,' Lydia said.

Stephen sat beside her. She looked at him. His trousers had burned and his skin was black and blistered. But he was alive.

She looked toward the door.

Stephen saw her glance.

Lydia became aware that Churchill and Thomson were standing near, listening.

Stephen took Lydia's hand. 'He saved her,' he said. 'Then he passed her to me. Then the floor fell in. He's dead.'

Lydia's eyes filled with tears. Stephen saw, and squeezed her hand. He said: 'I saw his face as he fell. I don't think I'll ever forget it, as long as I live. You see, his eyes were open, and he was conscious, but – he wasn't frightened. In fact he looked . . . satisfied.'

The tears streamed down Lydia's face.

Churchill spoke to Thomson. 'Get rid of the body of Orlov.'

Poor Aleks, Lydia thought, and she cried for him too.

Thomson said incredulously: 'What?'

Churchill said: 'Hide it, bury it, throw it into the fire,

I don't care how you do it, I just want you to get rid of that body.'

Lydia stared at him aghast, and through a film of tears she saw him take a sheaf of papers from the pocket of his dressing-gown.

'The agreement is signed,' Churchill said. 'The Czar will be told that Orlov died by accident, in the fire that burned down Walden Hall. Orlov was not murdered, do you understand? There was no assassin.' He looked around at each of them with his aggressive, pudgy face set in a fierce scowl. 'There was never anybody called Feliks.'

Stephen stood up and went over to where Aleks' body lay. Someone had covered his face. Lydia heard Stephen say: 'Aleks, my boy . . . what am I going to say to your mother?' He bent down and folded the hands over the hole in the chest.

Lydia looked at the fire, burning down all those years of history, consuming the past.

Stephen came over and stood beside her. He whispered: 'There was never anybody called Feliks.'

She looked up at him. Behind him, the sky in the east was pearly grey. Soon the sun would rise, and it would be a new day.

EPILOGUE

On 2 August 1914 Germany invaded Belgium. Within days the German army was sweeping through France. Toward the end of August, when it seemed that Paris might fall, vital German troops were withdrawn from France to defend Germany against a Russian invasion from the east; and Paris did not fall.

In 1915 the Russians were officially given control of Constantinople and the Bosphorus.

Many of the young men Charlotte had danced with at Belinda's ball were killed in France. Freddie Chalfont died at Ypres. Peter came home shell-shocked. Charlotte trained as a nurse and went to the front.

In 1916 Lydia gave birth to a boy. The delivery was expected to be difficult because of her age, but in the event there were no problems. They called the boy Aleks.

Charlotte caught pneumonia in 1917 and was sent home. During her convalescence she translated *The Captain's Daughter* by Pushkin into English.

After the war, women got the vote. Lloyd George became Prime Minister. Basil Thomson got a knighthood.

Charlotte married a young officer she had nursed in France. The war had made him a pacifist and a socialist, and he was one of the first Labour Members of Parliament. Charlotte became the leading English translator of nineteenth-century Russian fiction. In 1931 the two of them went to Moscow and came home declaring that the U.S.S.R. was a workers' paradise. They changed their minds at the time of the Nazi–Soviet pact. Charlotte's husband was a Junior Minister in the Labour government of 1945.

Charlotte is still alive. She lives in a cottage on what used to be the Home Farm. The cottage was built by her father for his bailiff, and it is a spacious, sturdy house full of comfortable furniture and bright fabrics. The Home Farm is now a housing estate but Charlotte likes to be surrounded by people. Walden Hall was rebuilt by Lutyens and is now owned by the son of Aleks Walden.

Charlotte is sometimes a little confused about the recent past but she remembers the summer of 1914 as if it were yesterday. A rather distant look comes into those sad brown eyes, and she's off on one of her hair-raising stories.

She's not all memories, though. She denounces the Communist Party of the Soviet Union for giving socialism a bad name and Margaret Thatcher for giving feminism a bad name. If you tell her that Mrs Thatcher is no feminist she will say that Brezhnev is no socialist.

She doesn't translate any more, of course, but she is reading *The Gulag Archipelago* in the original Russian. She says Solzhenitsyn is self-righteous but she's determined to finish the book. As she can read only for half an hour in the morning and half an hour in the afternoon, she calculates that she will be ninety-nine by the time she gets to the end.

Somehow I think she'll make it.